Praise for M...

'A pacy read about the strong bonds between three sisters...A great book to take to the beach!'   *Daily Mail*

...otionally-charged new novel'   *Take a Break*

...: for sisters everywhere, it's both heartbreaking and
...g'   *My Weekly*

...ctive novel that gets under your skin'   *Gill Paul*

...'s *Secret* is a compelling page turning read about secrets
...ies and the unwitting consequences thereof. I was
...ly hooked on this story of love, sacrifice and the things
...ill do to keep the truth from coming out. A sad, powerful
...rbing story'   *Julia Williams*

...n a compelling and emotional read that pulled me in from
...y first page – full of intrigue and secrets, a riveting story
...hat I know will stay with me for a very long time'
                    Alexandra Brown

Praise for *The Atlas of Us*:

'An ambitious and deeply poignant story that will take you into another world'   *Heat*

'I was left absolutely traumatised in a totally brilliant way…
Beautiful, heartbreaking, uplifting…Really worth a read' *Hello!*

'I could see it playing out like a movie as I was reading…I
loved it' *Novelkicks*

no
turning
back

tracy buchanan

avon

AVON

A division of HarperCollins*Publishers*
1 London Bridge Street,
London SE1 9GF

www.harpercollins.co.uk

A Paperback Original 2016

1

Copyright © Tracy Buchanan 2016

Tracy Buchanan asserts the moral right to
be identified as the author of this work

A catalogue record for this book is
available from the British Library

ISBN 978-0-00-817513-9

Set in Minion by Palimpsest Book Production Limited,
Falkirk, Stirlingshire

Printed and bound in Great Britain by Clays Ltd, St Ives plc

ABOUT THE AUTHOR

Tracy Buchanan lives in Buckinghamshire with her husband, their little girl and their one-eyed Jack Russell. Tracy travelled extensively while working as a travel magazine editor, and has always been drawn to the sea after spending her childhood holidays on the south coast visiting family, a fascination that inspires her writing. She now dedicates her time to writing and procrastinating on Twitter.

To find out more about Tracy follow her on Twitter @TracyBuchanan or visit her website and blog www.tracybuchanan.co.uk.

By the same author:

THE ATLAS OF US
MY SISTER'S SECRET

For my wonderful mum

Prologue

The First One

I shift my legs so I can peer up at the light. It sends shivers of pain along the tendons in my neck, down my calves and along my shoulder. But it's worth it, a brief respite from the darkness.

The light is like nectar: soft yellow, swirling with dust particles. I open my mouth, imagine drinking it, almost feel it slipping down my parched throat and filling me with a luminosity that might heal my bruises.

There's a faint glow of light and a shadow moves above. I think about the moment I crossed paths with him.

Oh God, is this really happening? I shake my head to somehow control my thoughts and my cheek scrapes against the brick, skin tearing, pain burning.

The sound of my voice echoes up the narrow space, bouncing off the walls then back again, seeming to wrap tight around me, stifling me.

Then there. The shadow again. A slight pause.

He's standing above, his dark form blocking some of the glow.

1

My heart pounds, a bird trying to flutter its way out of a cage. I'm breathing fast and heavy, my bare shoulders scraping the brick with each movement.

But I keep looking up, not caring about the pain. He hunches down, his pale fingers curling around the wooden slats above me. I hear his breath, deep and low.

My own breath quickens in response, rasping, heart flapping flapping flapping.

Then he lies on his belly to look through the slats. I crunch against the wall, curl myself inwards, my fringe falling over my forehead.

One eye, blue and heavily lashed, blinks down at me.

'I can see you!' he says, voice echoing towards me. Panic flutters inside. 'Can you hear me?' he asks.

I clamp my hand over my mouth.

'Please,' he says again, voice weaker with each word he utters. 'I'm hurt, it's really bad. Please help me.'

I quickly shove my hand down the slim gap at my side, fumbling for the door handle. The door clicks, air rushing in and I stride out, his cries echoing after me as I lock the door then double check it.

I have to be careful, the boy might find a way to get down here, even escape.

And that just won't do, it won't do at all.

Chapter One

1 July 2015

Coast to Coast. Your Say Question of the Day: Has the war on drugs failed?

Caller A: 'Yes, it bloody has! I was mugged last week by a druggie, the government's too lenient.' (Fiona, 47)

Caller B: 'No. I'm a recovering addict now working in rehabilitation. I've really noticed a change actually, especially over how drug addiction is now seen as a health issue.' (Ryan, 27)

Caller C: 'It's out of our control with all these immigrants flooding into the country!' (Dawn, 37)

The screen blurred in front of Anna's eyes. She put her hands to her face briefly, the smell of her little girl still on her palms: the sweet scent of baby lotion and that indescribable Joni smell. It brought with it the sight of her baby's smile, flowering first in her brown eyes before spreading to those cherub cheeks and pink lips. Anna felt her whole being ache to be with her. She was only two hours into her first day back at work after eight months of maternity leave and she was already desperate to be back with her daughter.

'Thoughts, Anna?' She looked up to see Heather, her new producer, giving her a stern look through the glass window dividing them. Anna quickly took a gulp of her coffee, caffeine's magic taking effect. The memory of Joni's smile faded away, her scent replaced by the tart smell of coffee beans.

She leaned forward and pressed one of the buttons on her microphone. 'Let's take caller C out,' she said.

Heather frowned. 'I'm not sure that's wise. In the months you've been away we've found immigration calls go down well with the public, really puts fire into their bellies.'

'I've found in the past *seven years* I've been presenting the show, it's best to keep the focus tight. This phone-in isn't about immigration, it's about the success or failure of the government's fight against drug abuse.'

'I understand what you're saying,' Heather said, tucking a wisp of black hair behind her ear that had dared escape her trademark tight bun. 'But I'd like to keep it in. I was a senior news reporter at Radio 4, remember, Anna? An investigation I did on this very subject won me an award. I have an *instinct* about these things.'

Anna suppressed her irritation. Every opportunity Heather could get, she'd bring up her investigative reporter days. The two women held each other's gazes. Heather had been appointed as

Anna's new producer after the station's much-loved producer had retired a few months before Anna went on maternity leave. From the moment she'd started, Heather had got people's backs up, challenging everything Anna said, making it clear to everyone she wouldn't pander to the presenters. Some of the admin girls had told Anna they thought it was because Heather believed that as a woman, she wouldn't get the respect she deserved unless she played up her aggressive side. Anna wasn't so sure. To her, Heather was simply what her gran called a 'real-life dementer', somebody who sucked the happiness and light out of any encounter.

'Look, Heather,' Anna said, unable to stop herself yawning. She'd never felt quite so exhausted. After a spate of sleeping well, Joni had chosen the night before Anna returned to work to wake every hour. Maybe it was the heat, or maybe she was just going through a bad patch. Either way, the timing couldn't be worse. 'Things might have been a certain way while I was on maternity leave. But there's a reason Coast to Coast's listening figures doubled after I joined.' Anna cringed inside at the boastful remark. But she had to stand her ground, show Heather she too had made a success of things. She'd watched Coast to Coast grow from a barely known regional station covering just one small area while working out of a debilitated warehouse on the Docks, to a popular south-coast station attracting enough listeners and ad revenue to rent a glossy studio by the sea.

Anna peered out of the large window lining the corridor outside. The studio occupied a sought-after spot next to the village's seafront shops and cafes, its cocoon-shaped glass-fronted building reflecting the waves in its shiny windows. *She'd* played a role in securing enough money to pay for this building.

She looked Heather in the eye. 'The fact is, I'm back now so let's find a way to get those listening figures back up again.'

Heather bristled. 'I wouldn't quite say you're *back*, Anna.'

'What do you mean?'

Heather's black eyes glistened with spite. 'You know what I mean, you're clearly not with it today. Having a baby can take its toll.'

Anna looked at her in shock. 'What does having a baby have to do with all this?'

'What I'm trying to say is…well, look at you,' Heather said, flinging her hand towards Anna. 'You're exhausted.'

'Everyone's exhausted, Heather! We get here for five in the morning, for God's sake.'

Anna tried to keep the tremble out of her voice. She didn't want to give Heather the satisfaction of seeing she'd got to her. But the truth was, she *was* exhausted and she *was* worried it would affect her performance. Juggling work and looking after Joni plus everything else that had happened the past few weeks had been difficult.

Her mobile phone buzzed. She took the chance to break Heather's gaze and look down at her phone. She'd been like this since arriving that morning, any little beep from her phone making her wonder if it was the nursery calling. Even the fact her mother-in-law owned the nursery didn't stop Anna worrying. To make matters worse, she'd have to turn the phone off when the show went on air. What if there was an emergency? Sure, the nursery had the main switchboard number but it didn't feel the same.

Anna spent an unhealthy amount of time thinking of

emergencies when it came to Joni. Falls, cuts, choking, even accidental strangulation. Her friend Suzanne reassured her that everyone had them. But Anna couldn't help but wonder if *everyone* imagined the horrors in quite as much detail as she did.

Anna quickly clicked into her phone, relieved to see it was a text message from her gran.

Knock them dead, darling, you can do it. And remember, drink lots of coffee…and ignore the dementer! x

She smiled to herself, remembering the first time she'd got her gran a mobile phone, five Christmases ago. She'd looked at it in disgust, told Anna if she needed someone she'd walk to their house and talk to them. But now it never left her side and she seemed to have an uncanny knack of messaging Anna just when she needed her most.

Anna quickly typed back a message: *Two cups consumed already. See you later. x*

Anna looked back up at Heather. 'I've just had a brilliant idea for our next phone-in.'

Heather raised an eyebrow. 'Yes?'

'We can ask the question: do new mothers get discriminated against at work?'

Heather's face flushed and the assistant producer behind Heather suppressed a smirk.

'I'd take caller C out,' a voice said from the doorway. Anna peered up to see her co-presenter Nathan. 'We have a replacement for caller C, right?' he asked Heather.

Anna smiled to herself as she noticed the brief look of irritation on Heather's face.

'I'm not sure we need one, Nathan,' Heather said. 'We—'

'This is about drug legislation, remember, not immigration,' Nathan said. 'Keep the focus tight.'

Heather blinked rapidly as Anna's smile deepened. Nathan gave Anna a quick wink and strode in.

'Maybe we can replace it with this one?' Anna said, tapping her keyboard until one of the rejected callers lit up on their screens. 'Sanjeet talking about how the younger generation pop pills like they're sweets?'

'Perfect,' Nathan said, green eyes smiling as he sat down across from her. 'Bloody new mums, full of good ideas.'

Anna did a faux eye roll. 'Sexist bastard.'

Heather turned away from them both, crossing her arms. She didn't argue with him. *Nobody* agued with housewives' favourite, Nathan Wheeler. He'd once worked for a big national radio station but couldn't bear the commute any more. So three years ago he joined Coast to Coast as it gained in popularity and his presence further cemented the station's success. Anna and Nathan were the ideal co-presenters.

He was dressed casually today in a white polo t-shirt and blue jeans, his fair hair sticking up at the back from the way he criss-crossed his hands behind his head while on air. He liked to lean back in his chair, long legs stretched out on the table, a look of concentration on his face as he listened to someone moaning about something or another. That was Nathan's skill, the fact he *really* listened. That and his boyish good looks which helped when the station's publicity team pushed him as the 'poster boy' of the station.

As for Anna, she was the rough to his smooth with her gravelly voice and quick-witted responses to difficult, sometimes abusive, listeners and guests. She might not be pushed as the face of the station like Nathan was, but she'd grown a reputation for perfectly reflecting the public's mood with her own opinions. It wasn't intentional. She just had what her dad used to call the 'crowd's gut': a natural instinct to know what the zeitgeist was at any given time.

Nathan leaned towards Anna. 'So good to have you back.'

She smiled. 'Thanks, Nathan, it's good to be back.'

And the fact was, despite missing Joni, the exhaustion and contending with Heather, it *did* feel good to be back doing what she knew best: radio.

Nathan switched off the speaker system so only Anna could hear him. 'So you accepted an offer on the house then?'

'Yep,' Anna said, trying to hide the jolt of pain she felt when she thought of it. 'We'll be out in a month.'

'That's it? It's definitely over between you and Guy?'

Anna took a sip of coffee, clutching the handle of the mug tight to stop Nathan seeing the way her hand trembled. 'I think selling the house is pretty final, don't you?'

'I'm so sorry, Anna.'

'It's fine,' she said, shrugging, trying to pretend it really was fine when it was so far from that. 'It's for the best. I didn't think that at the start but now I see it really is.'

'Still hurts like a bugger though, doesn't it?'

She felt her sinuses sting at the threat of tears. She saw it all over again in her mind, Guy softly pressing his lips against Joni's head three months before, whispering he'd see her very soon. Anna had begged him to stay then instantly felt foolish, desperate, *weak*. She hated appearing weak. But the fact was, Joni was too young to watch her father walk away, just five months old at the time. And Anna had never dreamed of being a single mother, a *divorcee*, it just wasn't how she'd envisaged her life unfolding. Yes, their marriage had been having difficulties for a while. But why wouldn't he fight for it like she was willing to?

She surprised herself now as a sob escaped her. She quickly clamped her hand over her mouth.

'Come here,' Nathan said, putting his arms out to her. She hesitated a moment, peering through the glass divider at the production studio. But Heather and the assistant producer had their backs to them, peering at the computer screens. So Anna sank into Nathan's arms, taking comfort from the familiar musky smell of his aftershave. 'Cry all you want,' he said into her ear. 'I might even have some mascara in my drawer from that photoshoot I did with the *Ridgmont Waters Chronicle* a while back.'

She laughed into his polo shirt. 'I'm just tired, that's all.'

'Are you sure you need to be here?' he asked, looking down at her. 'Might be better you get yourself home, pick up that gorgeous baby of yours and have a duvet day in your new home. I can do the show alone.'

Anna pulled away and shook her head, the ends of her long brown hair skimming her arms. 'Absolutely not, I've only been back a couple of hours. I'm fine, really. Just first-day-back jitters, that's all.'

Nathan tilted his head as he examined Anna's face.

'What?' Anna frowned, putting her hand to her cheek. Were there still flakes on her face from the stale blueberry muffin she'd gulped down for breakfast that morning?

'You're a tough cookie, always have been,' he said.

Tough cookie.

That's what everyone said when they discovered what had happened to her when she was a kid. You go through all the stuff she had, you survive it and what are you left with? Comparisons to a biscuit. Thing is, she wasn't feeling so tough at the moment. Did that mean she could crumble any minute?

'I'm not the only working mother in the world, Nathan.'

'I know. But with everything going on at home too…'

'It's hard,' Anna said, making her voice strong. 'But I'll get through it. As long as Joni is okay, that's all that matters.' She looked at the photo she had of Joni. She'd taken it during one of their regular afternoon walks along the beach. She was sitting on the pebbles, her yellow sundress grubby, her dark hair a tangled mess around her red cheeks, brown eyes sparkling.

Nathan followed Anna's gaze. 'She's adorable.'

Anna's face softened. 'She's everything.'

He nodded as he turned the speaker system back on. 'Keep that strong in your mind, all right? That's all that matters.'

Anna looked at the photo on Nathan's desk of his twin boys: one fair like Nathan, the other dark like Val, his wife.

'One minute to airtime,' Heather's uptight voice blurted into their ears.

Nathan smiled. 'Here we go.'

'Here we go.' Anna took a long deep breath as Heather started counting down. 'Five…four…three…'

The show's intro tune pounded in Anna's ears, giving her strength.

'Two…one…'

Anna opened her eyes, a smile set on her face. 'Morning,

11

morning, morning!' she said. 'This is Anna Graves, welcome to "Your Say" on the south coast's most popular regional radio show, Coast to Coast.'

'And this is Nathan Wheeler. It's seven a.m. and everything is right with the world because we have our wonderful Anna Graves back this week.'

'Oh, isn't he a charmer,' Anna said into her microphone, smiling at Nathan. 'Yes, I *am* back and I'd like to say I'm raring to go. But any of you *exhausted* parents out there will know that's not a phrase we use at this time of the morning.' She narrowed her eyes at Heather as Nathan tried to suppress a smile.

'You have coffee though,' he said.

'Yes, plenty of coffee,' Anna replied, lifting her mug to the webcam in the corner. 'My saviour.'

'So what have we got in store for our listeners today, Anna?'

'In our "Your Say" phone-in this morning, we're asking: has the war on drugs failed? We're also sharing tips on how to keep cool in a month where we're told temperatures may reach record highs.' She fanned her face with an envelope as she raised her eyebrow at the webcam.

'And twenty years from when the last victim of the Ophelia Killer was discovered,' Nathan said, 'we have a special report asking the question: will the families of those seven young boys murdered that summer ever get justice?'

Anna felt herself tense slightly at the mention of the Ophelia Killings, just as she had when she'd seen them on the running order that morning. But as Nathan reeled off the rest of the show's itinerary, Anna felt the anxiety dissipate, replaced by that familiar thrill that came with doing her job.

Soon, it was like she'd never been gone.

Anna pushed Joni's pushchair down the small path that lined the pebbly beach, pointing out the seagulls jutting their beaks at the remains of someone's ice-cream cone. Ridgmont Waters, the seaside village where she'd grown up, spread out behind them, a thin strip of pretty houses, shops and cafes overlooking the sea. People stretched out on the beach, soaking up the sun's rays, children screaming in delight as they ran in and out of the shallow waves. In the distance, the old lighthouse her family owned lorded over the sea, tall and white atop craggy grey rocks.

Anna squinted up at the sun, letting out a contented sigh. It was good to finally be out of the studio and with her daughter, the more bearable warmth of the late afternoon sun on her skin, the smell of salt and seaweed blowing the cobwebs away. The small house she was currently renting in the town's new estate might not be as pretty or as full of character as the Victorian terrace she'd renovated with Guy, but it was closer to the sea, just a two-minute walk.

That was something, wasn't it?

'Love you, baby,' Anna said, peering down at Joni's soft brown hair.

Joni peered up at her mother and smiled, making Anna's heart swell. She looked just like Anna with her brown eyes and oval cheeks.

'Mama,' she gurgled.

Anna paused. 'Did you just say mama?'

Joni gave her a sweet smile and Anna leaned down in front of the pushchair. 'You said mama. Oh darling, you said mama!'

'Mama!' Joni said again, giggling in delight.

Anna thought about how Guy would react when she told him later. Then she remembered: he was gone and soon the house they'd worked so hard to make their own would belong to someone else. She felt the tears come again and squeezed her face into Joni's chubby neck. This wasn't how she'd envisaged things panning out, a single mum living in a downsized property, ruled over by some upstart at work. But she was managing, wasn't she? And Joni was happy. That was what was most important.

'Right, we better go say goodnight to your granddad before you start wanting your dinner.'

She headed towards the small patch of beach that lay in the lighthouse's shadow, leaving the chatter from the busier part of the beach behind. It was empty here, apart from the odd seagull or two, due to the lack of sunlight. She used the large wheels on Joni's buggy to negotiate the pebbles before stopping right at the sea's edge, the soft waves lapping at the pram's wheels, making Joni giggle. Anna sat on one of the steps leading to the concrete platform where the lighthouse stood, the craggy rocks behind it. She could smell the new varnish from the lighthouse's glossy red door at its front. Her gran must have got someone to repaint it. A crab skittered out of view at the sight of Anna, and a seagull landed on one of the lighthouse's windows above.

Joni clapped her hands as she looked up at the lighthouse. Anna smiled and quietly sang the song her gran said her father used to sing to Anna when he'd brought her here as a baby:

Goodnight to the sea, goodnight goodnight
Let it tickle our toes all mermaid-like,
Goodnight to the sea, goodnight goodnight
Seaweed and cockles to tuck us up tight

'I did okay today, Dad,' she whispered as she looked up at the lighthouse's highest window. 'It was tough going back, leaving your granddaughter behind. But I did it.' She took a deep breath, trying not to look at the hint of the rocks behind the lighthouse. 'Night night, Dad,' she whispered.

She'd been doing this ever since her father died when she was eleven, walking along the beach and wrapping his old blanket around her shoulders as she stared up at the lighthouse, yearning to turn back time. Her mother never asked where she'd been when she slipped back home after dark, just continued staring out into the distance, her brother barely looking up from his homework.

A cloud crept across the sun, the air cooling slightly. For the first time, Anna noticed black clouds hovering out to sea. Looked like a storm was coming. Time to head home for a seafood pasta before wrapping herself up in Joni's bedtime routine. It could be a chore sometimes, especially today, when she would be exhausted from work, desperate to put her feet up instead of being soaked by bath bubbles and protests when Joni didn't want to get out of her bath. But ever since splitting up from Guy, her time with Joni felt even more precious. They tried to split the days they each had their daughter evenly, but Anna missed her desperately when she didn't have her. She liked knowing Joni was upstairs asleep when the night drew in.

That night, she'd have to do some prep work for the show the next day, feet curled under her on her Chesterfield sofa, maybe some Joni Mitchell, Joni's namesake, playing from the old record player her dad had left her. If she had time, she could prepare dinner for the next day. She liked to cook the food she foraged from the sea: cockles and limpets, bladderwrack and sweetoar weed. She'd immerse herself in the routine of twisting and prying the meat from the shells, cleaning the seaweed then adding it all to stews or imbuing them in all sorts of delicious flavours. She'd become famous for her foraged meals among the village community, the regular dinner parties she threw with Guy were a popular feature among their friends.

What now? Would she continue with those dinner parties, all alone?

'Oh pull yourself together, Anna,' she said to herself.

She stood and went to push the buggy back up towards the path but noticed there were now three teenagers sitting on it cross-legged a few metres up, passing a cigarette between them.

Or maybe it was a joint?

Anna thought of the radio show that morning, and one particular caller who spoke about how her once mild-mannered son had turned into a violent thug after years of drug abuse.

She paused a moment. The teenagers looked scruffy, different from the kids she usually saw around the village. They looked more like the kids who haunted the rundown dockyard area of Ridgmont Waters just beyond the lighthouse, known by locals as The Docks. She helped her gran with some community work there sometimes. Generally, the kids were decent enough, troubled backgrounds but just kids at the end of the day. But there had been some trouble lately with a particular gang of teenagers – robberies mainly, one or two that had even turned ugly. It had been all Anna's friends had been able to talk about at their last get-together a couple of weeks before. Usually it was easy to forget about The Docks, which was separated from the village by the lighthouse and a large expanse of green. But the fact was, The Docks was just a five-minute walk from the heart of the village, the recent thefts ramming that home for villagers.

One of the teenagers looked up, a kid of about sixteen or seventeen with lank black hair and an ill-fitting leather jacket on, despite the heat. His eyes fell to Joni, and Anna felt a quiver of fear.

Before she'd had Joni, she'd think 'screw them' and bowl past. Not now though.

'Let's go another way,' Anna said, pushing Joni's buggy up the pebbles towards the field that divided the village and The Docks. There was a path that led from it right into the heart of the village and its cobbled streets. She could walk through the village then back down to her new estate. It might add another five minutes onto her journey but she didn't want to risk it.

The teenagers stood up and started heading towards her.

Anna quickened her step towards the field, heart ricocheting against her chest. Joni squirmed to get out of her pushchair, something she'd taken to doing lately.

Anna peered over her shoulder, saw the teenagers were getting closer.

All the scenarios she'd imagined of Joni being hurt seemed to cram inside her mind. She started jogging, the pushchair juddering over the pebbles as she dashed towards the green.

Suddenly, another teenager appeared over a brow in the green, this one dressed in a school uniform.

He looked frantic, eyes wild…and he was running towards her.

Anna stopped, glancing back at the teenagers. She was trapped between them. Was this some kind of set-up, a chance to rob her?

She reached into her bag, wrapping her fingers around her red long-tooth comb.

The schoolboy drew closer, his pale face slick with sweat, his blue eyes confused.

He slowed down and blinked as he looked at Anna, body swaying slightly as he shook his head. He was clearly out of it. 'I won't let you hurt me,' he hissed. Then he started striding towards her again.

Anna backed away, confused. 'I don't know you.'

'Hey, lady!' one of the teenagers behind Anna shouted.

She swivelled around, frantically looking between the three teenagers and the schoolboy.

What were they going to do?

When she turned back, the schoolboy was running at her, nearly within reach of Joni! Anna scrambled around in her bag for her purse and held it out to him. 'Just take it!' she said, shoving it into his chest.

'Leave me alone!' he screamed. He pulled out a small knife.

Anna's senses immediately heightened, honing in on the knife, the glint of its silver blade filling her sight; the screech of the nearby seagulls invading her ears like metal scraping against bone. She imagined she could smell the rusty stench of it, its acrid taste on the tip of her tongue.

Anna pulled her comb out of her bag and yanked the pushchair so Joni was behind her, protected.

'Get away!' Anna screamed, jutting the end of the comb at the schoolboy, the handles of Joni's pram digging into her back.

The schoolboy lifted his arm, the knife poised in his hand.

Adrenalin rushed through Anna. She lunged at him, trying to grab the knife off him. He swiped it towards her, and Anna felt a searing pain in her cheek as the blade sliced through her skin like butter. She put her fingers to her skin, felt warm blood spill over them.

It shocked her into submission. She staggered backwards but he followed her, swiping the knife at her again.

Joni screamed out and the pushchair toppled over.

The schoolboy darted towards it.

Horror filled Anna to the brim, made her head buzz, made her whole body tingle. She ran towards the schoolboy and raised the sharp end of the comb.

He twisted around to look at her then suddenly lost his footing, falling against her.

Against the comb.

She felt blood slick against her hand, heard a gurgling sound.

The schoolboy fell to the ground, knees thudding onto the pebbles as he clutched at the comb protruding from his neck.

Anna stared at him, eyes blinking. Then she heard Joni cry.

She ran to her daughter, yanking the pushchair up so she could release Joni from it with trembling fingers. Joni reached out for her mother and Anna could see she was fine, she was okay.

'Oh man, he's gonna die,' the lank-haired teenager said, dropping a teddy from his hands – Joni's favourite teddy, a tiny blue bear. Anna realised then she must have dropped it. That's why the three teenagers had followed her, to return it.

Anna turned back to the schoolboy. He was lying on the pebbles now, clawing at the comb in his neck.

'No, no he won't die,' Anna said, running to him and kneeling beside him.

The boy looked at her, eyes wide with fear. He looked so young.

He suddenly yanked the comb out of his neck.

Blood spurted over Anna's face.

'Oh God, oh Jesus,' Anna said, using her free hand to press it against the blood. But it wouldn't stop, it was going everywhere, the pebbles turning red with it, the warmth of it seeping under Anna's nails.

'Call an ambulance,' she screamed at the teenage boys behind her, yanking off her thin yellow cardigan and pressing it against the wound as the boy choked on his own blood.

The cardigan turned instantly red, everything was red, it was even getting into Anna's eyes, Joni's hair as it spurted out from the boy's neck. 'Oh God, don't die, don't die,' she screamed.

The boy suddenly went still. He looked up towards the gathering clouds, eyes softening.

Then he was gone.

Chapter Two

Anna woke with a gasp. She checked for Joni, felt her small warm body against her. Then she looked at her own hands in the darkness. Only moments before, they'd been covered with the boy's blood.

But that had just been a dream.

The day before hadn't been a dream though. The day before, it had been real. She knew because she could still smell his blood, the sickly metallic tang of it. Still see the way his eyes had looked into nothingness as he took his last shuddering breath. It wasn't as bad as when she'd seen her father dead, his long body twisted on the rocks, the sea a violent thunder of grey behind. But it came close. The schoolboy was sprawled on the ground, blue eyes staring up, comb glistening with his blood as it lay by his side.

Anna hardly remembered what happened after that, it came in a flash of images, sounds and tastes. Shrill sirens getting closer and closer. People appearing on the beach like ants from the village and The Docks, news already spreading so fast. Then police officers running along the pebbles from all directions, the whine of a distant helicopter. Anna's own desperate screams when a female police officer tried to take Joni away. The feel of the handcuffs against her wrists, a police officer softly grasping her elbow. She found comfort in that, the gentle way he'd handled her. Did that mean they understood she had only been protecting herself, most of all her daughter?

They weren't so gentle when she was questioned in the stiflingly hot police station later, the storm that had been threatening earlier was now in full force outside, thunder and lightning making Anna jump. Anna could even hear the sea, the waves were so ferocious, despite the police station being one of the most inland buildings of the village.

Detective Morgan, a middle-aged man with a bulbous red nose and piercing blue eyes, was assigned to her case. He sat with his arms crossed, eyes hard, skin glistening with sweat from the unbearable heat. Next to Anna was the only solicitor she knew, a small bald man called Jeremy from the firm of local solicitors in the village she'd been using for the house move.

Did she know the boy, the detective asked? Did she carry the comb in self-defence? Had she *intended* to kill him?

No, no, no, she answered before asking over and over when she could see her daughter. The detective had reassured her she was in the safe hands of Anna's gran now, that she'd had a check-up and was fine. But that didn't stop Anna needing to see Joni.

Then she was left alone in the room with her solicitor for what seemed like an eternity. She remembered putting her hand to her own cheek, feeling the large gauze over it and not even remembering how the gauze had got there, how the stitches in her cheek had been etched into her skin either.

After a while, the detective returned.

'I'm sorry I was hard on you, Anna,' he said, sitting across from her, face softer now, eyes kinder. 'But you need to understand the position we're in.'

'I just want to see my daughter,' she said.

'What's the charge, Detective Morgan?' her solicitor asked him, the only fan in the room lifting the few strands of hair he had.

The detective looked Anna in the eye. 'No charge. We'll be releasing you pending further investigation, Anna.'

'But I was arrested.'

'Yes, but we have decided not to charge you. It was clear self-defence, Anna. You said yourself the boy fell against your comb and we have three witnesses to back that up.'

The relief had been immense. 'So I can leave?' she'd asked, incredulous.

'Yes, everything you've said matches up with witness statements. But Anna,' the detective said, looking her in the eye, 'tensions are high out there. I recommend you leave via the back entrance.'

'What do you mean?'

'The boy's family. Your name isn't out there yet but people saw you at the scene, someone may recognise you and...' His voice trailed off.

'But I didn't mean to kill him,' Anna said.

'We know that. But right now, his family will be wanting a target for their grief, especially the brother.'

The brother.

'We understand,' her solicitor, Jeremy, said, nodding. He turned to Anna. 'Maybe you should stay at Florence's this evening?' he said, referring to Anna's gran. 'Just to be on the safe side.'

Panic fluttered inside Anna's chest. 'But no one knows where I live, do they?'

'Someone may have recognised you from your estate,' the detective said. 'You're a radio presenter, after all.'

Anna shook her head. 'Nathan's the public face of the station, people only know my voice.'

'I still think Jeremy's right. Your daughter's with your grand-mother anyway, it would certainly be worth you staying there tonight.'

A few moments later, Jeremy drove Anna away from the station to her gran's house. As they passed the front, she looked out to see a group of people gathered on the marble steps. A thin dark-haired woman was being comforted by a red-haired man. A red-haired woman was leaning against a pillar, smoking as she scowled up at the station. Two other women, one with a child in a pushchair, were sobbing as they clutched onto each other.

Standing apart from them all was a man with tattooed arms, looking out towards the sea, his back to Anna.

Anna looked at the dark-haired woman again. Was that the boy's mother? The large red-haired man next to her turned towards Anna, his blue eyes – blue eyes just like the boy's – sinking into hers.

They were filled with fury.

She quickly looked away.

She'd caused that grief, that anger.

'Oh Christ,' Anna said, the memories crashing over her now.

The floorboards creaked and her gran Florence appeared at the door.

'You look predictably exhausted, poppet,' Florence said,

wrapping her soft fleece dressing gown around her plump frame as she sat on the bed, the early morning sun highlighting the creases around her blue eyes.

Anna blinked in disbelief. 'It really happened, didn't it?'

'I'm afraid it did, Anna.'

Anna peered out at the sea through a gap in the curtains. A fisherman wandered down the shore, his nets trailing out behind him, a boat bobbing up and down nearby. Seagulls squawked, a child shrieking in happiness as his mother chased him in and out of the tide, probably one of the many tourists that visited at this time of year. The pebbles were still wet from the storm the day before but the sky was bright blue, promising yet another blisteringly hot day.

Florence followed Anna's gaze as she watched the mother and son outside. 'You did what any mother would do,' she said gently.

Anna looked down at Joni. 'Like the boy's mother? Does she want to kill me like I killed her son?'

'Don't let guilt eat you up. If you hadn't done what you did…' Florence shuddered. 'I can't even contemplate it.'

Joni stirred, stretching her tiny arms above her head and yawning. Anna gently lifted Joni, placing her against her shoulder. Anna didn't usually let Joni sleep in bed with her unless she was ill, she'd not wanted to get into the habit. But she hadn't been able to bear having Joni out of sight the night before. She wondered if she'd ever let Joni sleep alone after what happened.

Then she thought of the boy again. He'd been a baby once. Had his mother slept with him beside her when he was ill, stroked his head and dreamed of his future like Anna did with Joni?

Anna felt nausea work its way up her body. She quickly handed

Joni over to Florence and ran to the bathroom, retching into the toilet.

'Anna?' she heard Florence say.

'I'm fine,' she choked back. She pulled the toilet lid down and leaned on it, trying to compose herself as she looked at the montage of family photos hanging on the wall: Anna and Joni by the beach a few months ago; an old one of her father smoking a cigarette as he looked out to sea from the lighthouse; another of her mother, her long dark hair clouding around her head as she drew on her easel.

Anna and Florence had agreed not to disturb Anna's mother. No news had been leaked yet linking Anna to the murder, and the last thing Anna needed right now was to be worrying about her mother's fragile state. So they'd agreed they'd go over later to tell her face-to-face then Florence would call Anna's brother, Leo, to tell him. She knew how her brother would react and didn't need it that day.

As for Guy, luckily he was on a business trip in New York, one of the many places his job as an architect took him. She'd called him not long after arriving at her gran's the night before. They'd barely spoken on the phone since he'd left, mainly communicating over text to arrange drop-offs and pick-ups for Joni. So it had been strange to hear his voice over the phone line. After the initial relief that Joni was safe, Guy couldn't seem to wrap his head around the fact the schoolboy had died…and Anna had killed him.

It had made her feel even worse.

And that was just Guy's reaction. She dreaded to think about how her mother would react.

She stared at the photo of her father and imagined him peering up from the Dictaphone he used for all his news interviews, a sad smile on his handsome face. 'You did what you had to do, my beautiful girl,' she imagined him saying.

She had, hadn't she? It was like Florence had said to her the night before, it was an instinctive reaction, a reflex, like the way a leg flings up when knocked on the knee. And anyway, what was the alternative? Anna dead right now? Or worse, Anna lying in an empty bed, grieving the loss of her precious child?

She wrapped her arms around herself. The fact was, no matter how much she tried to dress things up, she had taken a life.

She was a killer.

Anna moved the rake through the sand, slowly surely, until she heard the clink of metal on shell. She knelt down, wet sand on her knees, and plucked the cockle from the sand, rubbing the grains off its ribbed back with her thumb. It was clamped shut, its fleshy insides protected by the white-brown shell. Anna imagined herself curled up in that shell, Joni against her belly, safe.

She reached up to the gauze on her cheek and suddenly saw the boy's eyes again, felt his blood on her hands.

She grabbed her rake and stood again, searching the sand for the tell-tale circular impressions the cockles left.

Above her, the sun shone bright. The sea was calm after its outburst the night before. Anna noticed Florence watching from her garden, Joni napping on a blanket beside her in the shade. She lifted her gloved hand to wave at Anna, and Anna smiled, waving back. She was grateful to be here, at her gran's, on a secluded part of the sandiest bit of Ridgmont Waters' beach.

She'd always loved this place. It was one of three houses built by a local architect in the twenties to replicate an American-style white beach hut with solid enough materials to withstand the regular battering of the British sea. Anna still remembered the first time she visited it when she was a child. They rarely visited their gran's house despite the fact Florence was desperate to see her grandchildren. Anna's mother had always had a strained relationship with her mother and if they did meet up, it would usually be for a quick tense coffee in town or during brief visits from Florence for birthdays and at Christmas. Anna quickly gave up asking why they couldn't see her gran more when her mother always replied with a terse 'you wouldn't understand' each time.

The spring just before Anna's father died, her mother had surprised her by taking her and her brother to visit their gran. Florence had met someone new after spending years alone since Anna's grandfather had passed away, and she'd invited them all over for lunch to meet him. It was the first time Anna had visited her gran's house. Anna remembered feeling completely at home as soon as she'd got there, its big comfy sofas and thick woollen rugs, reclaimed wooden shelves littered with family photos, the smell of baking bread and lavender making Anna yearn for that in her own home. The apartment she'd grown up in with her parents wasn't small; it adorned the top floor of a block of apartments and overlooked the sea. But it had never felt homely with its dark walls and modern furniture. Florence's house felt like a proper home with two large windows looking right out onto a wooden veranda leading down to the sea. Her gran had seemed so happy, her new partner a tall, handsome older man called Alistair with sparking green eyes who made Anna giggle by pretending to pull magic shells from behind her ears.

Her parents had sat tense and quiet throughout the lunch, and had made excuses to leave not long after, despite protests from their children. Anna still remembered how sad Florence had looked as she'd watched them all walk from the house and Anna had promised herself she'd see more of her gran, even if it meant sneaking out of the apartment to see her.

It wasn't until Anna's father died a few months later that she did just that, finding herself walking towards Florence's house one day. Her gran hadn't been there, so Anna had curled up on her veranda and fallen asleep. She'd woken to the sound of Florence's gasp and seen her and Alistair looking down at her.

'Oh, poppet,' Florence had said. 'Come in before you catch your death.' Anna was there every day from then on, her mother barely noticing, so wrapped up in her grief and depression. Anna grew close to her gran, and Alistair too. He'd never had children and Anna found herself becoming something of a surrogate daughter for him. She was devastated when he too passed away a few months later after a short battle with cancer. It made Anna and Florence even closer, joined in their grief over his death.

Florence had been a godsend for Anna, bringing her out of her shell, even funding her journalism course. There had been no turning back after that. Anna blossomed from an introverted quiet girl into a talented student with an army of local friends she still met with almost every week.

And it had all started in this house. Anna ought to feel a sense of comfort there now, especially as she searched for cockles, something that usually brought her a measure of calm. But as she dragged her rake back and forth through the sand, she felt anything but comforted.

Joni let out a cry. Anna looked up, heart pounding. But she was fine, Florence was lifting her from her blanket, rocking her. Anna picked the bucket up and put the rake over her shoulder, carrying her findings towards her gran.

'I think she's getting too hot,' Florence said when Anna got to them. 'Not known morning heat like this for a long time. Good haul?' she asked Anna, looking at the bucket.

'Not bad,' Anna said as Florence took her rake from her. 'Enough to go with the sole you got. I'll put some aside for Mum too. I'll prepare them while Joni naps.'

'Lovely. I'll just finish here then come help you,' she said, gesturing to the garden. 'Got to get my daily exercise.'

Anna picked Joni up and walked into the house, the sound of the waves disappearing as she closed the door. She placed Joni on Florence's comfy blue sofa, bunched up by several colourful scatter cushions so she didn't fall off, her blue teddy clutched close to her. The sun peeked through the vast windows making light bounce off her gran's TV screen. Anna had purposely avoided the News. She knew her name hadn't got out yet, otherwise she'd be getting calls. It would happen eventually though, she ought to ready herself. That's what Florence had told her over breakfast that morning.

'Game face,' she'd said. 'Better get it ready.'

What would the headlines be when her name was leaked?

Radio presenter kills schoolboy

Schoolboy tries to murder radio presenter's baby daughter

Before she knew what she was doing, she was reaching for the remote controls and switching on the TV. She'd usually go for the radio first, but she needed to *see* the boy again. She switched the channel from CBeebies, which Joni had been watching that morning, to BBC News 24, and there the boy was right away, eyes staring out at Anna from the screen.

Her legs seemed to crumble beneath her and she sank onto the sofa.

He looked so young. That neat dark hair of his, rosy cheeks, distinctive blue eyes. And in his school uniform too.

She caught sight of the words racing along the bottom of the screen.

'…notorious family.'

'…deprived docklands area…'

'…known to police…'

'…mother released with no charge…'

So it was '*Schoolboy tries to murder mother and baby*'. Not just schoolboy but *poor* schoolboy, *criminal* schoolboy, schoolboy from *troubled* family.

And then there, his name: Elliot Nunn.

Elliot. A child's name. An innocent name.

The screen cut to a live feed, a young male reporter standing in front of a line of tired-looking flowers. Anna turned the sound up.

'…from the estate reserved for dock workers at the once-famous Ridgmont HM Dockyards. Here we are before the building Elliot Nunn lived in with his mother, father and two of his sisters. Mourners have been leaving flowers outside all day.' The camera zoomed out to reveal a graffitied brick wall lined with flowers and teddies, and beyond, an untidy garden littered by rubbish. The faded flowery curtains of the family's flat were closed, a small child's bike discarded at the doorstep. Behind it all was the debilitated dockyard, hints of the skeletal remains of ships long abandoned since The Docks closed in the eighties. It had swallowed up a huge 300-acre site in its heyday, churning out hundreds of navy ships and employing thousands of people. When it closed, most of it was taken over by private investors and eventually turned into a smart new estate where Anna was now living. But the former housing put aside for dock workers remained – now known as The Docks – two rusting cranes and the huge tower block Elliot Nunn had lived in standing garish and tall over them. Either side of them were crumbling brick buildings, graffitied and vandalised. There had been promises to demolish the site, but that would cost money, money the local council would rather plough into the new builds dotting up around the area.

In the middle of it was a school, an ugly sixties building with a faded brick exterior. Elliot must have been a pupil there. Had he walked straight from school to the beachfront where Anna was walking with Joni, one goal in mind: to kill someone?

I won't let you hurt me.

Why had he said that?

'I'm joined by Dawn Williams,' the reporter said now, interrupting Anna's thoughts. 'Dawn, you're Elliot Nunn's aunt.'

Anna felt her heart gallop and she moved closer to the TV. She ought to turn it off, but she just couldn't. The camera focused on a large woman with frizzy red hair to her shoulders, the same woman who'd been outside the police station smoking.

The woman's blue eyes looked like steel but her bottom lip

quivered slightly, her smudged eyeliner hinting at a sleepless night and many tears.

Anna put her hand to her mouth.

'Thank you for joining us,' the new reporter said softly. 'We understand what a difficult time this must be for you and your family.'

The woman nodded, jaw clenching. 'They asked me to represent.'

'Of course. How *are* Elliot's parents coping?'

'Gutted. Absolutely gutted. He was a gorgeous boy, so kind and gentle, wouldn't hurt a fly.' She wiped her nose and looked into the distance.

Kind and gentle? Anna saw Elliot's hand raising, the glint of silver. She shook her head, eyes brimming with tears. How could a kind and gentle boy do such a thing?

'It must be a comfort to see so many well-wishers?' the reporter asked, gesturing towards the flowers.

'Yeah, my brother and sister-in-law want to say thanks.' Two young boys pedalled past on their bikes, waving at the camera. In the distance, a seagull landed on a bin overspilling with rubbish, making it shudder.

Anna looked at the floral tributes. It was as though a child had been killed by a heartless killer.

Maybe Anna was a heartless killer. She'd raised the comb in the air. What had she been planning to do before he fell against it? Would she have jutted it into his skin anyway to protect Joni?

Anna wrapped her arms around her belly, feeling like she might get sick again. She looked at Joni. She was alive. Safe. Wasn't that all that mattered?

The reporter tilted his head. 'You say your nephew wouldn't hurt a fly but he did hurt a mother, attempt to harm her child too. What were your—'

'Piss off!' a man's voice shouted off camera. The camera wobbled as a hand covered it. There was the sound of a scuffle then the hand was removed and the reporter appeared on camera again, rearranging his tie, a look of panic in his eyes. Behind him, the aunt was being marched away by a man with short fair hair, muscular arms.

The reporter seemed to compose himself and followed them down the drive, shiny grey trousers catching in the light. 'Jamie? Are you Jamie Nunn?' The reporter looked over his shoulder at the camera, eyes sparking with excitement. 'Elliot Nunn's older brother,' he explained to viewers.

Anna thought of what Detective Morgan had said about Elliot's brother.

'Leave us alone,' Elliot's brother hissed without turning. 'My little brother's dead, just leave us the fuck alone or you'll end up like him.' He continued with his aunt down the path, the grief and anger throbbing off them both.

Anna put her head in her hands. *She'd* caused that grief.

'Oh, Anna.' She looked up to see Nathan standing in the doorway, Florence behind him.

'He guessed you'd come here,' she said apologetically. 'He knows.'

'How?' Anna asked Nathan.

He sighed. 'Sources.'

'So my name will be out soon?'

'Eventually. I wish you'd just told me the truth instead of calling in sick.'

34

'I'll leave you to it,' Florence said softly, putting her hand on Nathan's shoulder. 'Good to see you again, Nathan.'

When Florence walked out, Nathan peered towards Joni. 'She's okay?'

'Yes, physically, anyway,' Anna said, trying to keep her voice strong. 'But she witnessed what happened which can't be good for her…' Her voice trailed off and she turned away, trying desperately not to cry.

Game face.

Nathan walked across the room and pulled her into a hug. 'I'm so sorry, Anna. Of all the people for this to happen to.'

She looked up at him. 'I killed a boy, Nathan.'

'You had to and I'm not the only one who thinks it,' he said fiercely. 'The Coast to Coast "Your Say" lines were jammed this morning with—'

She pulled away from him. 'You did a *phone-in* on it?'

'Before we knew it was you, Anna! Don't tell me you wouldn't have?'

She sighed. 'I suppose not.'

'Everyone's on your side, bar the usual devil's advocate, of course. You have nothing to worry about.'

'I still killed him.'

Nathan shook his head. 'Self-defence. You weren't charged, were you? It'll be fine. You're a bloody hero.'

'It doesn't feel like it.' She sank onto a sofa, raking her hands through her long hair. She'd washed it, over and over, when she'd got in the night before. But she could swear she could still feel and smell the boy's blood in it.

Nathan sat next to her and they both watched the TV. The

newsreader was now discussing whether it was right that Anna – or the 'unnamed mother' as they referred to her – hadn't been charged. It was clear the newsreader thought it was right.

And then there it was again, that photo of Elliot stretched across the news studio behind them.

'I don't understand why he did it,' Anna said.

'We have our fair share of nutters and stalkers.'

'No, he wasn't a stalker. He seemed to recognise me but he was surprised to see me. If he'd been stalking me, surely he'd know I'd be there? I do that walk every evening.' She thought of the look in Elliot's eyes before he ran at her. 'He seemed *scared* of me too.'

'Scared? Why on earth would he be scared of you?'

'I don't know,' Anna said with a sigh. 'But something's not adding up, I can *feel* it.'

'*Feel?*' Nathan said with a raised eyebrow. 'So your gut's telling you that, is it? We'll make an investigative reporter out of you yet, Anna Graves. Just like your father.'

Anna shook her head vehemently. 'I'll never be an investigative reporter, not after what it did to him. Does everyone at work know?' Anna thought of Heather's smug face. *I always knew there was something a bit odd about Anna Graves,* she'd probably say.

'Just a couple of the senior reporters,' Nathan said. 'I've bribed them to keep quiet for now, amazing the blackmail material you get at Christmas dos.'

He smiled but Anna didn't smile back. Instead, she scratched at her arms. What would it be like when her name got out?

Another photo of Elliot appeared again on TV, this time with his parents at a wedding, according to the caption. The mother's black greasy hair piled on top of her head, a pink dress hanging off her thin frame. The father looked angry, his russet hair long and messy, eyes hard as he looked into the camera. Elliot stood between them, his hands thrust into the pockets of black trousers that were too short for him, dark hair smartly combed. He looked sullen, eyes away from the camera.

Anna looked at his mother again. Her life was etched into the lines in her face, the dark circles under her eyes. She'd be crippled with grief right now.

But then so might Anna if she hadn't protected herself and Joni like she did.

She put her face in her hands and let the tears come, praying she'd wake up from this horrible nightmare.

Anna walked down the path towards her mother's bungalow. The grass was overgrown, the roses Florence had so carefully planted the month before already neglected and dying. Anna remembered how she'd felt the first time she saw the bungalow, two months after her father had died, one in a row of many. It had seemed so tiny, so claustrophobic compared to the large apartment that had been their family home. It was too far away from the cobbled touristy centre of the village where their apartment had been… and where Anna had lived with Guy until recently.

'I think Daddy would have liked this,' she remembered saying to her mother, lying to make her feel better. The truth was, the bungalow was too far away from the sea for Anna's liking. Still just a ten-minute walk, but that was enough to make Anna feel land-locked and trapped.

'Rubbish,' her brother Leo had hissed. 'He hated the bungalows here, said they smelled of decay, didn't he, Mother?'

But their mother had just stared into the distance, eyes blank, already lost to the anti-anxiety pills her doctor had prescribed her.

'The curtains are closed,' Florence said now as she peered at the bungalow.

Anna sighed. That was usually a sign her mother was going through one of her more reclusive periods. The last time Anna had seen her was two weeks ago. Her mother had been okay then; even sat on the floor and played with Joni. Anna had tried to enjoy the brief respite from her usual indifference. But she couldn't help but think it meant her mother was due a down episode. That's the way it was with her mother, a rollercoaster of ups and downs since she'd lost her husband.

Anna walked up the concrete path, Joni sucking her thumb as she looked around her. She always seemed nervous when they visited her 'nanny's', sensing Anna's nerves no doubt. Florence put a protective arm around them both.

As they approached the bungalow, the curtains were flung open and Anna's brother, Leo, appeared at the window, his dark hair slicked back, his brown suit too small. His nostrils flared as he saw his sister and gran approaching. One less opportunity to gloat to Anna about being the 'only person to see Mother this weekend'. He enjoyed putting guilt trips on Anna, mostly about her needing to spend more time with their mother, or more recently about the fact she'd returned to work after having Joni, something his timid wife Trudy 'wouldn't dream of doing' after having their twins.

'Great,' Anna muttered. 'Leo's here. I was hoping I could get away with a phone call to tell him.'

'At least you can kill two birds with one stone.' Anna flinched and Florence sighed. 'Sorry, poppet, wrong choice of words.'

'What a surprise,' her brother said as he opened the door. His eyes paused on the gauze over Anna's cheek. 'What happened to you?'

Anna put her hand to her cheek.

'Hello, Leo,' Florence said, stepping inside and giving him a kiss on his pale cheek. 'Trudy not here with the kids?'

Anna admired how her gran could still show Leo affection, despite how cold he was with her. Anna tried, but gave up most of the time when it came to her brother.

'Trudy's taken them swimming,' Leo replied. 'Thought I'd take the chance to see Mother without the children, you know how she can get with the noise they make,' he added, looking pointedly at Joni.

Anna repressed her anger. This wasn't the time to argue with her brother. 'How is Mum today?' she asked instead.

'Talkative.'

Anna and Florence exchanged a look. Maybe she wasn't having one of her down days then. But the 'up' manic days weren't so great either. Her mother generally had two moods: quiet and detached, or talkative and angry. Anna wasn't sure which one she preferred.

They walked through to the small living room with its faded red sofas and patterned carpet. The shelves either side of the small fireplace were cluttered with books and ornaments, no family photos like at Florence's.

Anna's mother was leaning over, tickling the chin of her black and white cat, Korky, her long grey hair grazing her plump knees.

She peered up, a look of surprise on her face when she saw Anna and Florence walk in.

'Hello, Beatrice,' Florence said, sweeping into the room and leaning down to kiss her daughter on the cheek. Anna's mother flinched. She didn't like affection.

'How are you, Mum?' Anna asked.

'Too hot. And tired,' her mother replied. 'The sirens kept me awake.'

Anna avoided her gaze, focusing on placing Joni on the floor with the toys she'd brought with her.

Her mother scrutinised Anna's face. 'What happened to your face?'

Leo frowned. 'Anna's just visiting, Mother. I know it's a rare occurrence but—'

'Honestly, Leo, Anna comes every week, that's hardly rare,' Florence snapped.

Leo bristled. Florence may be the most loving person Anna knew, but she also knew when to put people in their place.

'Anna?' her mother pushed.

'I have something to tell you, Mum,' Anna said, looking her mother in the eye.

Her brother frowned. The last time they'd had a conversation like this was when Anna told them her and Guy were splitting up. It had triggered one of her mother's episodes, meaning she'd refused to see anyone for two weeks.

'Someone tried to hurt me and Joni yesterday,' Anna said, trying to keep her voice calm.

Her mother's eyes widened.

'As you can see, we're fine, I just got a bit of a cut to my cheek,' Anna added quickly as Joni tried to reach for the cat. 'But I had to—' Anna swallowed. 'I had to protect Joni and – and I...'

'Spit it out, Anna,' her brother snapped.

She couldn't say the words, which was totally unlike her. She looked at her gran beseechingly.

Florence put her hand on Beatrice's arm. 'Anna and Joni were attacked on the beach yesterday, Beatrice. Anna had to defend herself, defend Joni. The boy died.'

'Died?' Beatrice asked incredulously.

'My God,' Leo said as he stared at Anna. '*You're* the one they're talking about on the news, the mother who killed the boy from The Docks?'

'She had to protect Joni,' Florence said.

'By killing a schoolboy?' Leo asked.

Anna ignored him, looking at her mother who started scratching her arms, something she did when she was nervous.

'I didn't mean to,' Anna said to Beatrice. 'It was an accident. I had a comb, a long-toothed one. It was the only thing I could grab, the boy had a knife, and – and the comb went into his neck...'

'How old was the boy?' Beatrice asked Anna.

Anna swallowed, tears brimming at her eyes. 'Fourteen.'

'Just a boy,' Beatrice said. She turned away to look out of the window, face drawn.

'Couldn't you have bloody stabbed him in the leg or something?' Leo said.

Anna closed her eyes, saw the comb's end slipping into the soft skin of the boy's neck, smelt his blood, felt it on her hands again.

'I didn't…he – he struck out with his knife, and I had – had to do something. Then he fell…'

'You'd do the same to protect one of the twins,' Florence said gently.

'I wouldn't be that bloody stupid,' Leo retorted. 'There are ways of protecting one's children without resorting to *murder*.'

Anna kept her eyes on her mother. All she wanted, all she'd ever wanted, was for Beatrice to look at her, really look at her and hold her and tell her it was okay. Like the time her father died, the ambulance sirens disappearing into the distance, leaving her with her mother and her brother. She'd grasped at Beatrice's cold hand, desperate for comfort. But Beatrice had just walked away, disappearing into her own private grief, not offering any word of comfort to her children.

It was no different now, Anna *needed* her mother.

But instead, all she got was a cold gaze. 'Leo's right,' Beatrice said. 'You shouldn't have gone for his neck.' Leo stood next to his mother, putting his hand on her shoulder. They both stared at Anna and Anna felt as she always had with them: ostracised, alone, *judged*.

A sob escaped her mouth.

'Right then,' Florence said, scooping Joni and her toys up as she tried to contain her anger. 'We've done what we came to do, Anna. Shall we go?'

Anna nodded, suppressing her disappointment. 'Let's go.'

That evening, Anna tried to drive thoughts of her encounter with her mother and brother away. She ought to be used to it. She'd felt increasingly isolated from them after her father died. They'd sit quietly in the bungalow, reading and wallowing, refusing to talk about Anna's father. Anna had wanted to talk about him, think about him, *remember* him. She didn't want him to fade away. So she'd retreat to the lighthouse or to visit her gran, the only person she felt able to share memories of her father with. It was no different now.

No, she mustn't dwell on the past. She had to focus on the now, on Joni. Guy would be looking after her that weekend, he was coming to collect her straight from the airport. As much as it pained Anna to be apart from Joni, she had to stick to their agreement, especially seeing as social services would be visiting, 'just standard procedure after an incident like this,' according to her solicitor. She couldn't be seen to be breaking her agreement with Guy. And anyway, despite the problems between her and Guy, she knew he would keep Joni safe.

Anna focused on playing with Joni that evening, bathing her and forcing herself to remember over and over, 'Look, you saved your daughter's life. She's here!' But she still saw Elliot's face, the awkward angle of the comb jutting from his neck, the blood and the gurgles, guilt piled upon guilt thanks to her mother and brother's reactions.

As she read Joni's bedtime story to her, she wondered if Elliot's mother used to do the same for him. Did she brush her nose against his soft hair like Anna did with Joni? Hold his warmth close, marvel at how lucky she was to have him?

'Mama.' Anna looked up to see Joni peering at her, her little brow creased.

Anna forced a smile, kissing her forehead. 'Okay, darling, bedtime.' She lifted her into the travel cot that Florence had bought so Joni could stay there every now and again when Anna and Guy needed a break. Anna was still staying with her gran, not quite ready to return home yet. And Joni was still in with Anna, Anna not quite ready for her to be in a separate room.

She flicked on her video monitor then stepped out of the room. Joni cried, lifting her arms out to her. She did this sometimes. Just when Anna thought she'd slipped into a good sleeping phase, Joni would throw a curveball and refuse to sleep. Anna hoped this was just one of her fussy sleeping phases, not a result of what she'd witnessed. Anna stroked her head, shushed her, watching as her eyes grew heavy again. Then she tiptoed downstairs.

'Joni okay?' Florence asked, delicious smells wafting in from her kitchen as she cooked the cockles Anna had collected that morning. Anna had learnt all she knew about cooking seafood from Florence, a skill passed down the generations.

'Just a bit unsettled,' Anna said.

Florence tilted her head, examining her granddaughter's face. 'Are *you* okay?'

'I keep thinking about something Elliot Nunn said before he tried to hurt us.'

'What was that?'

'"I won't let you hurt me". He was *scared* of me.'

'Maybe you misheard him?'

Anna shook her head. 'No. He definitely said it and it's important, I just don't know how. I can feel it in my gut.'

Florence raised an eyebrow. 'Your father used to say that when he was doing one of his investigations. Let the police do their job, darling, you've been through enough.' Florence gestured towards the living room. 'There's a glass of wine waiting for you. Dinner will be ready in twenty minutes.'

Anna squeezed her gran's hand. 'I'm so lucky to have you.'

Florence's face softened. 'I'm always here for you, you know that.' She gave Anna a big hug then went into the kitchen.

Anna walked into the living room and sank onto the sofa, directing the fan towards her face as she stared out to sea. The sofa was positioned right next to the large folding doors that opened onto the veranda, offering a perfect view of the setting sun. The storm had held off and now the evening was warm, the sun a bright orange glow, reflected like fire in the sea. A couple strolled by hand in hand and Anna thought of how she used to walk along the beach with Guy on summer evenings. They even had picnics out there, Anna giddy from wine as she lay back, not caring about the sand in her hair as she stared up at the orange sky.

As she thought that, an image of Elliot Nunn suddenly came to her, his dark hair filthy with sand, his eyes wide open as he stared oblivious towards a sky he'd never see again.

Anna turned away from the sea and pulled her laptop out, resisting the temptation to open a browser and google herself. She'd know if her name was out by the calls and texts. She quickly clicked into her emails, saw one from the station's PR manager about an interview request with the local newspaper. The radio station was going to try to push the 'working mother' angle to the media to raise Anna's profile now she was back from maternity leave. Anna hadn't been so keen. Her father had started to get a little publicity before he died because of his news reports and look what that had done to him. Better to just get on with the job, head down. That would all change once her name got out though. The station would be inundated with a new angle: child-killing local radio presenter.

Anna looked at the name of the journalist who was requesting the interview. Yvonne Fry, a woman Anna had gone to school with, even been friends with until Yvonne had left to work for the local paper at just sixteen and they lost contact. Imagine what she would think when she found out Anna was the mother all over the news? Anna sighed and clicked into her emails. There was one from her friend Maxine inviting her and some other friends over for dinner the week after to discuss their plans for the village's annual fireworks display in November. It seemed a long way off but Maxine liked to be organised. Anna stared at the email. It was so jolly, so innocent, talk of 'wine on tap' and 'chocolate cake and chatter…unless the kids wake up, of course!' Usually Anna would smile and reply with an instant 'yes'. But what would life hold for her when her name got out? Could her friends forgive her for killing a local schoolboy?

She ignored Maxine's email, going to another one. The production assistant had forwarded on some listeners' emails from the day before. They were all good, praising Anna for her return. There was even one from another mother who'd just returned from maternity leave herself and had found courage listening to Anna on the way into work.

Anna felt a sense of grief for her life before all this. If this were a normal day, this email would have given *her* strength, made her feel it was all worth it. But now all it did was make her realise just how much everything would change. Could she still be an inspiration to women like this one with the death of a boy over her head?

She clicked out of the email then she froze.

There was an email in her inbox with the subject line 'Elliot Nunn'.

Impossible! Her name hadn't been publicly connected to the case yet.

Then she noticed the 'from' field: *Ophelia Killer*. A shudder of fear ran through her body.

She quickly opened the email, fingers trembling.

From: The Ophelia Killer
To: Anna Graves
Subject: Elliot Nunn

Yes, I thought the subject line would catch your eye, Anna. Tell me, did he look beautiful when he died? Those blue eyes staring up into sheer nothingness, the pallor of his skin, that special silver veil that only comes with death.

The blood, I wouldn't have liked the blood. But still, one can't be fussy. Maybe you took a photo? If so, please do send! I'm finding myself rather fascinated with this one, the boy's potential for murder was rather appealing, wasn't it? He was a bit naughty for targeting you while you had that pretty daughter of yours with you though…

Take care now. TOK

Anna barely breathed for a few seconds as she stared at the email. The Ophelia Killer had terrorised The Docks over one hot summer, killing seven teenage boys. But then the killings had abruptly stopped. Her father had investigated the murders, spending every spare minute he could looking into them. Then he'd killed himself, throwing himself from the lighthouse. Anna had always blamed his obsession with the killings for that.

Was someone *pretending* to be the notorious Ophelia Killer? It couldn't be the real one, surely. Whoever it was, how did they know about Elliot? Was Anna's name out? She quickly googled her name with trembling fingers. But the same old results came up: her website, her profile page on the Coast to Coast website, her Twitter profile, various articles. Nothing connecting her to Elliot Nunn's death.

Her eyes slipped to the last line of the email.

...that pretty daughter of yours...

She shoved the laptop off her knees and ran upstairs, relieved to see Joni sleeping soundly.

'You okay, Anna?' Florence called up to her.

'Not really.' Anna went back downstairs and showed Florence the email.

A frown creased Florence's head. 'The Ophelia Killer? I don't understand.'

'Me neither. I ought to call the police.'

Anna called the number Detective Morgan had given her. He answered on the first ring.

'Your name must be getting out,' he said straight after she told him about the email. 'It'll be a nutter.'

'No, I googled myself, no one's connecting me to the death yet.'

'Forward the email to me,' he said. 'I'll get someone to look at it.'

'Is there any chance we can we get some protection, maybe one officer? When I send the email, you'll notice the last line mentions Joni, it made me feel uncomfortable.'

'Of course, we'll get a car to sit outside. You're still at your grandmother's?'

'Yes. Thank you so much, Detective Morgan.'

'No problem, Anna. Anything else I can help you with?'

She peered out towards the angry sea. 'Do you know yet why Elliot might have tried to hurt me and Joni?'

'All we have at the moment is maybe he heard you on the radio and grew obsessed with you.'

Anna shook her head. 'No, that just doesn't add up. I just can't shake the feeling it was more than that.'

He was quiet and Anna sensed something in the silence. Was he thinking the same as her? 'Detective Morgan?' she asked.

'Try not to worry about it, Anna. We'll do everything we can to find out why Elliot Nunn did what he did. Do send me that email, won't you?' Then he was gone.

Anna sank back in her chair, peering up at the ceiling. Even if it was someone trying to get her attention, as Detective Morgan suggested, is this how it was going to be from now on, emails from people pretending to be serial killers? Would she *ever* be able to feel secure in Joni's safety again?

'Are they sending someone over?' Florence asked, wrapping her arms around herself as she peered out into the darkness.

Anna felt a stab of guilt. Florence was nearly seventy. Despite how robust she was, she didn't need to be feeling scared in her own home. She put her hand on her gran's arm. 'I'm so sorry, Gran, this is your house. I don't want you to be scared here.'

'Oh, poppet, we'll be fine,' Florence said, squeezing her grand-daughter's hand. 'This place is like Fort Knox the amount of locks that double glazing man put in, we'll be safe here.' She sighed. 'I hate you having to go through this though.'

'Me too.'

They both looked out to sea, watching as the waves clashed into each other beneath darkening skies.

The next evening, Anna saw Guy for the first time since Elliot's death. He stood on the doorstep of Florence's house wearing crisp jeans and a casual white shirt, his dark hair and beard longer than they had been the last time she'd seen him, the week before. Her heart lurched at the sight of him. She missed him so much, especially now. How could everything have fallen to pieces in just a matter of weeks? His brown eyes held Anna's for a moment then he noticed Joni crawling down the hallway towards him. He grabbed her into a hug and swirled her around as she giggled.

'My gorgeous little girl,' he said as he cuddled her. Then he held her out in front of him, examining her all over with his eyes.

'She's fine,' Anna said.

He looked at Anna. 'How are you?'

'Still trying to wrap my head around what happened.'

'Yeah, me too,' he said, jaw flexing. 'It's all over the news.'

'My name isn't though.'

'Not yet. I just can't—' He stopped talking.

'What?'

'I didn't think you'd be capable of killing someone.'

'Wouldn't you, for Joni?'

He thought about it. 'Before all this, I'd have said hell yeah. But now the reality is in front of me, I don't know.'

Anna crossed her arms, tears brimming. 'Well I did and your daughter is alive in your arms right now because of that.'

His face softened. 'I know, Anna, I'm sorry. It's just a lot to take in. Do they know why the kid tried to hurt you both?'

'I have no idea.'

Guy frowned as Joni played with his necklace. 'Could he have been a stalker? What if there are others out there like him?'

'No, he wasn't a stalker, Guy. This is a one-off freak occurrence.'

'Maybe I should take Joni for a few weeks, until this settles down?'

Panic flooded Anna's chest. 'No! She'll be safe with me, I promise.'

'Then why are you here at your gran's?' he said, looking around him.

'It's just a precaution.'

'I'm not very comfortable with all this.'

'Guy, please don't do this. You know I'd never risk Joni's safety.'

He held her gaze. 'Really? She nearly got stabbed, Anna.'

'For God's sake! I was walking along the beach just like I do every day with her, with you too when we were together. I'm already struggling enough with the guilt.'

He sighed. 'I know, sorry. I'm tired, I've been cooped up in a plane then a car the past few hours and it's bloody hot out there. And I'm worried, that's all.'

She tried to calm herself down. 'I understand. But our daughter is safe, okay? I promise.'

As she said that, she thought of the email she'd got from the person claiming to be the Ophelia Killer. A trickle of fear ran through her.

She handed Joni's changing bag to Guy. 'Remember she's dropped her midday feed like we discussed.'

'Yep. Say goodbye to Mummy,' he said, handing Joni over to Anna.

She kissed her daughter's cheek. 'Be a good girl for Daddy, darling,' she said, breathing in her scent. 'You'll see Mummy in three days. I love you so much.'

Joni wrapped her arms around her mother's neck and pressed her nose against her cheek. 'Mama.'

'Mama?' Guy asked, tilting his head.

'Yes, she said it for the first time the other day.' She didn't want to say *what* day.

'What a clever girl!'

'I know, isn't she?'

They smiled at each other and her heart ached for all that was lost between them. Then Guy broke her gaze.

She handed Joni back to him, trying to stop herself crying. This was unbearable, she didn't want to lose sight of her daughter for one moment and yet here she was, handing her over for three whole days.

It's for the best, she reasoned with herself. *Joni will be safe with her father.*

'We have lots of plans, little girl,' he said to Joni. 'Your Uncle James and Auntie Liz are coming over with Isobel and Anya tomorrow.'

Joni smiled, recognising her little cousins' names.

'Then I'm thinking a day at the beach is in order if it's not too hot.'

'Sounds fun,' Anna said, forcing a smile for the sake of her daughter.

Guy looked at Anna. 'It'll all work out, Anna.'

Joni reached her chubby hand out for her mother. Anna grasped it.

It *had* to work out.

The rest of the evening, Anna tried to relax, picking up one of Florence's magazines and flicking through it. Then she paused. There was an article about the community centre in The Docks that her gran sometimes helped out at, Anna too, on occasion.

Could she have met Elliot Nunn at one of those events? She remembered meeting a few of the kids at some event a few months ago. But there had been so many of them, their faces blurring into one. Except one kid, Ben Miller. His father worked as a caretaker for the building where Guy's architect company was based. His mother had died when he was just eleven, just as Anna's father had died when she was eleven.

He worked at the newsagents down the road.

Before she knew what she was doing, she jumped up, grabbing her cardigan and pulling its hood over her head, putting some sunglasses on.

'Just popping out,' she shouted up to Florence.

Florence appeared at the landing, a look of alarm on her face. 'Out? Anna, is that a good idea?'

'Look at me,' she said, gesturing to her sunglasses. 'If I see someone who saw me that day, they won't recognise me.'

'I don't know, poppet…'

'I need the fresh air. I'll be fine. I'll be back in fifteen minutes.'

She blew her gran a kiss then let herself out. As the door shut behind her, she paused a few moments, blinking up at the setting sun. She hadn't walked outside alone since what happened and her heart hammered at the thought.

She put her hand back on the door handle. Maybe Florence was right? Anyway, what exactly did she think she'd achieve going to see Ben Miller?

But then her fingers slipped from the handle and she found herself walking to the newsagents. It was just a couple of minutes away, right next to the greengrocers and facing the sea. She saw the headline scream out at her from the placard outside: 'Dead boy's father is known criminal.' Anna shuddered and lowered her head, quickly walking into the newsagents.

She was relieved to see it was empty inside apart from Ben Miller who was bopping along to some music as he filled up the shelves, his dark fringe bouncing in his eyes, the smart red shirt he wore for work creased. A fan behind him lifted the edges of the newspapers nearby, Elliot's face on every one of them.

Anna took her sunglasses off. 'Hi, Ben,' she said, trying to keep her voice normal.

He peered up and smiled. 'Oh, hello, Mrs Graves. How's Joni?'

She smiled. 'Joni's good.'

He'd always been so polite, so sweet. His father was a good man, trying his best for his two sons by working hard. His eldest son had been in trouble with the police. But Ben had kept on the straight and narrow, working at the shop, keeping his head down with his studies, even helping the community centre out every now and again. He'd once confided in Anna during one of those events that he wanted to leave Ridgmont Waters. That was the way it was with the kids who lived on the coast. While 'inlanders', as the villagers referred to people inland, were desperate to flock to the sea in the summer, if you'd lived there all your life, you were desperate to get away. All you saw was the way the salt air rotted the houses, how the harsh winters gobbled up any free time, how if the wind was in the wrong direction, the village could stink of dead fish and seaweed.

Anna hadn't been like most kids though. Her father used to say the sea ran through her veins. She loved it there and couldn't imagine leaving.

Until now. Maybe she'd have no choice when her name got out?

'How are you?' Anna asked Ben now, grabbing some milk.

His face flickered with sadness. 'All right, I suppose,' he said as he walked around the counter

'Did you know Elliot Nunn?' she asked softly, her heart thudding in her ears. She knew how strange and maybe *wrong* this conversation would seem to Ben once news of Anna got out. But this might be her only chance to talk to him.

Ben flinched. 'Yeah, he was my mate.'

'I'm really sorry, Ben.'

He shrugged. 'That's okay.'

'Do you think Elliot meant to hurt the woman and her baby?' Anna asked, trying to be casual as she dug around in her purse for some money.

Ben frowned. 'No, Elliot wasn't like that.'

She peered up at Ben. 'Not violent?'

'No way! Not until the other day anyway. I mean his family…'

He peered over Anna's shoulder then lowered his voice. 'They're a bit dodgy, everyone's scared of his brother. But not Elliot.'

'That event I went to in the spring, the Easter digathon? Was Elliot there?'

'Yeah, I think he was actually.'

Anna handed her money over. 'So he did go to some of the community centre events then?'

'Sometimes, if his dad let him.'

'Why wouldn't his dad let him?'

'Says it's for Nancy boys.'

Anna couldn't help rolling her eyes. 'That's silly.'

'Yeah, he's an idiot, Mr Nunn is.' His eyes widened, fear filling them. 'But don't tell him I said that!'

'I won't, don't worry. Thanks, Ben. Take care, okay?' She looked him in the eyes and smiled, trying to somehow show him she was a good person, that she didn't mean to kill his friend even though he didn't yet know she had. Then she left the newsagents, the door swinging shut behind her.

'You got milk?' Florence asked with a frown when Anna stepped inside a couple of minutes later.

'Yes.'

'We don't need milk.'

Anna popped it in the fridge. 'You can never have too much milk.'

Florence crossed her arms. 'Anna, what's going on?'

Anna sighed. Her gran knew her so well. 'I went to talk to Ben Miller.'

Florence's eyes widened. 'Why on earth would you do that?'

'I just don't think Elliot trying to hurt me and Joni was random.'

'Well no, poppet, he was probably stalking you like Inspector Morgan said.'

'He wasn't, I just know he wasn't. But I think I know why he recognised me. He went to some of the community centre events, he must have seen me there.'

Florence shook her head. 'Do you realise how risky it was to talk to Ben Miller like that?'

'Why? He doesn't know it's me.'

'But he might put two and two together, tell someone you're staying here.'

'He won't, trust me.' Anna walked up to Florence, holding her hands. 'I'm fine, Gran. It was just a quick chat.'

Florence sighed. 'I'm just so worried.'

Anna looked into her eyes. She hadn't considered the strain this would put her gran under too.

'I'm sorry,' she said softly. 'I don't like worrying you.'

Florence stroked her cheek. 'Please let the police do their job, poppet. I don't want any more harm coming to my two girls.'

'Okay,' Anna said. 'I promise.'

But as she did the washing up later, staring out towards the dark sea while Florence put the rubbish out, she felt a stirring in her tummy. Is this how her father had felt before he started investigating the Ophelia Killings?

Anna thought back to that summer. It had been hot just like this one. Anna remembered how excited she and Leo had been when their parents had dragged a blow-up pool into the apartment-block gardens for them to cool down in. They'd spent days splashing about and giggling. But then suddenly it all stopped, they weren't allowed outside.

As the summer wore on and police sirens became a familiar background noise to her life, Anna began to understand why. She started to glean more about what was going on in her town: teenage boys from The Docks were being killed, all found drowned in their garden ponds surrounded by beautiful flowers, just like Ophelia from *Hamlet*. When Leo grew scared, Anna played the adult despite being two years younger than him, telling him they'd be safe, that the killer wouldn't get them because they lived in the 'good bit of town'. He would have nightmares about the murders though, waking in the night screaming. But Anna grew fascinated, following her father around whenever he was home, asking questions about the case, which he refused to answer.

'You're too young, darling,' he'd say, brushing her cheek with his finger as he smiled at her. 'Now go play with your Barbies, isn't that what little girls like you are supposed to do?'

But that wasn't what Anna wanted at all. She wanted to be like her father. So one night, four months after the first victim was found, as summer began to fade, Anna got into her father's study while he slept and found a photo of one of the victims on his desk, an image that still haunted her: a boy with pale skin lying in a pond, blank blue eyes wide open, dirty ripples of water below him, hints of bright soaked flowers around his head. And then, dotted over his torso, five round bloody marks, skin removed by the Ophelia Killer as trophies, as Anna later learnt.

That was the penultimate victim. A couple of weeks later, her father killed himself on the same day the last victim was found, jumping from the top floor of the lighthouse to the rocks below, the horror of the case finally getting to him.

Anna felt tears spring to her eyes and scrubbed at a plate to force the memories away. Florence was right, she'd been silly to question Ben Miller like that. She needed to leave the investigations to the police. If her dad had, maybe he'd still be alive, not driven to depression by the horror and stress of it all.

She removed the plug, watching as the bubbles spun down the sink. Then the sound of something smashing outside pierced the silence. Florence was out there! She quickly dried her hands and ran out of the open back door, calling her gran's name.

Then she froze.

Standing on the beach outside was a crowd of people, candles flickering in the darkness. 'Child killer,' someone hissed.

It was Elliot's father, his blue eyes fierce with anger.

Chapter Three

The Second One

You're staring out towards the dockyards, brow creased. You will not look at me. I want you to look at me.

'Look,' I say, pointing out of the other window facing towards the beach. 'It's starting.'

You turn and narrow your eyes.

'There, see,' I say, pointing towards the family spilling out of a car, their bright towels flapping in the wind. There's a mum and dad, a boy and two girls. The pebbles of the beach shine under the sun, small boats shimmying over the waves in the distance. They're from The Docks, I can tell from their decrepit old car.

Something changes in you as you look out of the window, eyes alighting on the sullen boy who helps his father get out a tatty-looking picnic hamper. At least this family are trying, taking their kids out for a Sunday afternoon on the beach.

'Shall we go to the beach?' you say, smiling now.

'Really?'

'Why not? We can get lunch at the cafe.'

'Oh!'

You laugh. 'Come on.'

As we walk to the beach together, I feel free like that seagull over there, soaring above the lighthouse and craggy rocks. It doesn't matter that the sandwiches are a bit dry when we get to the cafe, the fizzy drink too warm. I start to feel like this is the best day of my life, being here with you.

I watch you bite into your sandwich. Your eyes are on the boy again. He's fourteen or fifteen. He has headphones on, head hunched over a comic book. His dark hair is too long, and he's wearing cut-off jeans and a grey t-shirt with a growling dog on the front.

The boy looks up, catches me watching him.

I turn away.

'Don't be shy,' you say in a quiet voice. 'You should go talk to the boy. That way he won't bat an eyelid when you see him next. He'll be relaxed.'

I think of the last boy, the first one, and a tremor of fear rushes through me. 'I don't know.'

'Look, this is the perfect opportunity.'

The mum gets up and takes the girls to the water's edge as the dad strolls to the cafe.

The boy's alone now.

You jog your arm into mine. 'Go. Practise on him.' You stand up, stretching. 'I'm getting another drink.'

You give me a look – the look – then stride off.

I stay where I am for a few moments, fear battling curiosity. Can I really do this? Do I want to do this? You think I can but I'm not so sure.

I take a deep breath then walk along the beach to the boy, weaving between all the people who are cluttering the beach now. The boy doesn't notice me for a bit as I stand over him. Then he looks up, scowling.

'Looks interesting,' I say, gesturing to the comic book.

The boy takes his headphones off. 'What?' He looks angry. It's clear he doesn't want to talk to me.

I think about heading back, then peer at the cafe. You nod at me, encouraging. I don't want to disappoint you.

I kneel down beside the boy. 'I've met the man who illustrates those,' I lie.

'Oh yeah?' the boy says, feigning disinterest but I see his eyes light up.

'Yep. My friend's brother knew him.'

He looks me up and down. 'I've seen you at school.'

'That's right. You like it there?'

He laughs. 'Does anyone?'

I laugh back and we start to talk.

After a while, I sneak a peek back at the cafe to see you watching us, this strange intense look in your eyes. I look back at the boy and know things aren't going to end well for him.

Chapter Four

'Get back inside,' Anna's gran called over her shoulder. 'Lock the door, call the police.'

'No,' Anna said, striding down the path towards Florence as the angry-looking crowd throbbed in front of them.

'You're Anna Graves?' Elliot's father shouted at her, his red hair like blood under the moonlight.

'No, she isn't,' Florence said, shaking her head. 'You've got the wrong person.'

'Liar,' Elliot's father hissed at her.

He strode towards Anna. Florence tried to get in the way but he pushed her aside.

'Gran!' Anna went to help her but Elliot's father grabbed her with one hand, using his free one to look at his phone as Anna struggled against him.

She caught sight of the screen. It was a tweet featuring the publicity shot the station always used of her – one eyebrow wryly raised, arms crossed, long brown hair smooth and shiny. Below it were the words: 'BREAKING NEWS: Mother who killed Elliot Nunn is named as local radio presenter, Anna Graves.'

She looked out at the crowd. There were about twenty people on the beach, jeering at her, glaring at her, hatred in their eyes.

She saw her gran try to pull herself up, wincing slightly.

Anna fumbled in the pocket of her cardigan, finding the door keys. She pulled them out, jutting one between her two fingers and pointing it at Elliot's father's face.

'Let go of me,' she hissed.

'What you going to do, *knife* me?' the man spat. 'Not young enough though, am I? You only kill innocent school kids, right?' He dragged her towards the crowd, her bare feet scraping against the pebbles. 'Elliot's murdering bitch is here!' he shouted to everyone.

More people started jogging over from the direction of The Docks. Anna stumbled backwards but the man grabbed her wrist, twisting it painfully. 'You're not going anywhere, child killer.'

'Please, I didn't mean it, please,' she said, the reality dawning on her that she might get hurt, that her gran already was.

People drew closer, gathering around her. Someone flicked her face, another kicking the back of her legs and making her buckle. One man with tattoos on his folded arms watched with hatred in his eyes.

She heard Florence cry out her name and Anna struggled desperately to get to her but couldn't match Elliot's father's strength.

'Wait!' a woman shouted. Anna looked up to see a woman walking through the crowds towards her.

Elliot's mother.

Part of Anna felt relief. Was his mother going to stop them? But then Anna saw the look in her eyes.

'Is it true?' Elliot's mother said, grabbing Anna's chin and looking her in the eye, her breath stinking of cigarettes.

'He tried to kill my baby,' Anna said. 'I had no choice.'

'You killed *my* baby,' she said. 'So now *I* don't have any choice, do I?'

People laughed, even cheered. The man with the tattoos just continued glaring at her. It was even more chilling than the laughter.

The two mothers stared at each other. Beneath the rage, Anna saw the gaping hole of loss and desperation in the woman's eyes. She wanted to hold her, so foolish, she knew. But maybe, more than anyone here, Anna had got the closest to experiencing how she felt, the hint of that acidic loss she'd have felt if Joni had been killed. It occurred to her in that moment how ironic that was, to be the one who might understand…and yet to also be the one to have taken her son from her.

'Please,' Anna pleaded. 'You must understand why I had to try to protect myself.'

His mother's face softened for a moment. Then her husband whispered something in her ear. She looked down and Anna followed her gaze.

Elliot's father had slipped a small knife into his wife's hand.

Anna closed her eyes, thought of Joni. If this was the sacrifice she needed to make to have saved Joni, so be it.

'Open your eyes,' Elliot's father shouted in her face.

But Anna kept her eyes squeezed shut, felt the crowd close in. Someone yanked off the gauze on her cheek and she felt the cool breeze slice over her wound.

Then her foot was swiped from beneath her and she fell to the ground, darkness descending.

A man pulled her up, the man with tattooed arms. He was in his late twenties, fair hair, stubbled cheeks, fierce blue eyes blinking down at her in the semi-darkness. His fingers sank painfully into her arm.

'Please don't hurt me,' she whispered.

His eyes ran over her scar, brow creasing.

'Go!' he suddenly hissed, shoving her away. 'Get inside, lock the doors, both of you.'

'What are you talking about?' Elliot's father shouted at him. 'The child killer's staying and she's getting what she deserves.'

Elliot's father tried to shove Anna's rescuer out of the way but the young man stayed rock still. 'Just. Fucking. Go. Run!' he shouted into Anna's face.

Anna looked into his blue eyes for a moment then she grabbed her gran and stumbled into the house.

Anna sat in the kitchen nursing a cup of tea as Florence talked to a police officer. Her gran was fine, just a bruised leg. She'd been more intent on tending to Anna's wounded cheek when they got in, placing a new gauze over it.

Anna's phone rang and rang, no doubt friends and colleagues discovering *she* was the mother who killed Elliot Nunn. But she ignored it, instead focusing on the sound of the waves sloshing against the pebbles outside, her eyes straying towards the light-house in the distance and the pile of rocks…the same rocks her father had died on.

She thought of the rage in Elliot's father's eyes, the grief in his mother's. She thought of the man who'd helped her, felt his fingertips on her wrists still. He'd been among the crowd. Why had he decided to help her? What would have happened if he hadn't?

She closed her eyes, taking a deep breath.

'Right, I think that's everything,' the police officer said, closing his notepad. 'Can you stay anywhere else, Mrs Graves? Maybe somewhere a bit more out of the way? What about your mother's house, isn't that on the edge of town?'

Anna exchanged a look with Florence.

'I can't,' Anna said.

'Maybe you should?' Florence said. 'I know it's not ideal. But your safety is important.'

Anna looked into her gran's eyes. She felt as though she were going back in time, being forced to live at that bungalow after a terrible tragedy. But what choice did she have?

'What about you?' she asked Florence. 'Will you be safe here?'

'They're not interested in your grandmother,' the police officer said.

'Fine,' Anna said with a sigh. 'Any idea how they knew I was here?' she asked the police officer.

'No, 'fraid not.'

After he left, Florence helped her pack. 'Do you think Ben Miller said something? He could have easily seen you walk to the house from the newsagents.'

Anna shook her head. 'He wouldn't, he's a good kid.'

Her gran shrugged. 'Maybe.'

Anna sighed. 'Maybe you're right, maybe Ben did tell people. And if so, it's all my fault everyone found me here. I shouldn't have talked to him. I put myself in danger, I put Joni in danger. Jesus.' Anna slumped down on the bed. 'Is this what it's going to be like from now on, baying crowds on my doorstep?'

Florence sat next to her, placing her plump arm around her shoulders. 'The police won't let it get to that.'

'I hope not. I really do.'

They both sat quietly for a few moments then Florence clapped her hands. 'Right, let's get this finished then get you to your mother's. Who knows, maybe it will be good for you both to live together for a few days?'

Anna raised an eyebrow. 'Really?'

Florence sighed. 'I can but dream.'

When Anna got to the bungalow half an hour later, her mother disappeared into the kitchen mumbling something about the washing up. So Anna took her bags to her old room. The light from the hallway streamed into the gloom, picking out the shiny red radio taking pride of place on a shelf filled with books and collected shells; the tape recorder still home to the mock news reports she used to make; the photo of her dad taken at the beach, caught by surprise, a smile on his face, his dark hair lifting in the wind. All those smiles disappeared when he was investigating the Ophelia Killer. He'd been so caught up in it all, he hadn't seen the depression sneaking up on him. It was like Anna earlier, questioning Ben Miller, putting everything at risk to get a few pointless answers. All she'd done was put her and Joni in danger. Her gran too.

'I made you tea.'

She turned to see her mother standing in the hallway, a flowery cracked mug in her hand.

She walked over and took it. 'Thanks, Mum. And thanks for letting me stay.'

'Why wouldn't I? You're my daughter.' Beatrice peered towards the window. 'There's a woman hanging around outside, that little blonde friend you used to have at school.'

Anna frowned. 'You mean Yvonne Fry?' Her mother nodded. 'Great, the press are already on to me. Don't answer if she knocks.'

'I won't.'

Anna looked around her. 'I thought you would have cleared all this out by now.'

'I keep meaning to.'

Anna passed her fingers over the tape recorder. 'I used to love this thing.'

'Your father made me buy it for your birthday. I didn't like it.'

'Why not?'

'I knew what it would start.'

'Start what?'

'You following him into journalism.'

Her mother had never been keen about Anna following in her father's footsteps considering what it had done to his stress levels.

'I've been proved right,' her mother continued.

'What do you mean?'

'Your name all over the papers, people targeting you, like earlier.'

'That has nothing to do with what I do. Even if I wasn't a radio presenter, I'd still be targeted for what I did.'

'To this extent? I think not, Anna. It gives you a sense of godliness, doesn't it?'

Anna shook her head in confusion. 'Excuse me?'

71

Her mother clenched and unclenched her fists. 'I'm not sure you would have killed the boy if it weren't for the confidence your job and status gives you. The knowledge that every decision you make is the right one.'

'I had no choice! I didn't *decide* to kill him. The only decision I made was to protect my child.'

'Do you really believe that, Anna? I can see the doubt in your eyes, the guilt. Was it really a natural instinct to protect?'

Anna grabbed her bags. 'It was a mistake coming here.'

Beatrice strode towards her, putting her hand on her arm, her eyes pleading with hers. 'I'm sorry. Don't go.'

Anna looked into her mother's eyes. Why couldn't they just have a normal relationship?

'Please, Anna.' Beatrice's hand slipped away from Anna's and she twisted her fingers around each other, biting her lip as she looked outside. 'You know how I get, the stress, it makes me – me—' She shook her head. 'It's very difficult for me, Anna, very difficult.'

Then she left the room.

Anna sank down onto her bed. How long would she be able to stand staying here with her mother?

Anna peered down at Joni as she strode along one of Ridgmont Waters' cobbled back streets. Joni was sitting in her new pushchair, the seat now angled so she was facing Anna. Joni smiled up at her and Anna felt herself relax. People she knew greeted her, some stopping her to praise her for how she'd protected herself. It was over two weeks since her name had got out, and the reaction from the public and the press had been overwhelmingly positive.

Newspaper columnists were talking about Anna's 'bravery and compassion', the *Daily Mail* even calling her 'lioness mother protecting her cub'. Her old school friend Yvonne had tried to grab her for an interview one day when she walked out of her mother's house to put some rubbish out. But she'd made it clear she wouldn't be giving interviews. Yvonne had surprised her by being quite aggressive about it, following her up the path. In the end, she'd written a positive story too, if a little more lukewarm than the others.

Twitter notifications had been filled with messages of support as well, mainly people praising her for 'taking a stand against the scum'. And all her friends and colleagues had emailed or texted with praise and admiration.

Anna sighed. Was Elliot Nunn really 'scum'? Even if he had tried to kill Joni, he was still a kid himself. What exactly *had* driven him to that point, what sort of life must he have led? The more Anna found out about his family, the more she despaired. His father clearly had anger issues, and his mother seemed very fragile.

She'd been too scared to leave the bungalow until now, remembering the look of rage on Elliot's father's face. But it wasn't fair on Joni to stay cooped up inside. More importantly, she had to get away from her mother. Two weeks inside the bungalow brought back too many memories, memories now turned into her day-to-day reality as she struggled to cope with her mother's up and down moods, one minute distant and brooding, the next non-stop chatter about pointless things like the birds in the trees and the colour of the sky, anything but what Anna was going through.

And anyway, people from The Docks didn't tend to venture into the village due to the huge shopping centre on their doorstep catering to their needs. This more upmarket part of Ridgmont Waters was quiet, people letting others get on with their lives. They were used to seeing the occasional famous face here, the large holiday homes overlooking the beach nearby attracting the rich and famous over the summer holidays.

Anna walked into a small seaside cafe. It had recently attracted new owners, the once dry sandwiches and warm lemonades replaced by sharing platters and unusually flavoured ice creams.

She walked through towards the small veranda at the back which overlooked the beach. Nathan was already out there on one of the white iron tables, signing a woman's napkin. Anna frowned. So much for villagers not intruding.

Nathan noticed Anna walk outside and jumped up, manoeuvring a chair so Anna could get the pushchair in. People glanced up as she passed, recognition flickering in their eyes. But they quickly returned to their Sunday papers and Anna took a breath of relief.

'Look at you,' Nathan said, taking his sunglasses off and smiling at Joni. She giggled and grabbed his hand. 'Isn't she gorgeous?'

'She is,' Anna said, finding a highchair in the corner and lifting Joni into it, safe and snug. 'My gorgeous perfect little girl, aren't you?'

'Mama!' Joni exclaimed.

Nathan laughed. 'She seems well. How did the visit from social services go last week?'

'Short and sweet. It was clear they were just there to tick some boxes.'

'Good,' he said. 'And how are *you*? You look tired.'

Anna thought of the restless nights, dreams filled with blood and Elliot's dying blue eyes.

'Not sleeping great, as you'd expect,' she said as she sat down. 'But things are starting to feel a bit more normal.'

'Good. We're still getting lots of emails in to the show.'

'I've been listening. Georgia's doing a great job,' Anna said, referring to the news anchor who'd temporarily taken over from her.

'Yes, she's great, I've always liked Georgia.' Nathan raised an eyebrow. 'But she's not you, Anna.'

'You're too kind.' The waitress came up and Anna ordered an iced coffee and lemon drizzle cake as she pulled some snacks out for Joni. In the distance, the sea was calm, the skies bright blue. The heatwave hadn't really let up, but it was more bearable than previous days. People sat in the village's distinctive fuchsia pink deckchairs that dotted the seafront. A child ran along it with a red flag in the air, his father laughing as he followed him. A golden retriever jumped in and out of the waves, yapping at them. Beyond, the lighthouse watched over them all, its windows twinkling in the sun.

It almost felt like a normal day.

'There's an article about Elliot Nunn's brother in the *Sun* today,' Nathan said, quirking an eyebrow as he jutted his chin towards a newspaper being read by an elderly couple on the beach. 'Bit of a local criminal, apparently.'

Anna followed his gaze to see the newspaper he was referring to, a large photo of a man staring out from it. Anna let out a gasp. It was the same man who'd helped her when Elliot's parents had confronted her a couple of weeks before.

'What's wrong?' Nathan asked.

'That's not Elliot Nunn's brother, is it?' Nathan nodded. Anna frowned. Elliot's *brother* had helped her? But why?

'What's wrong, Anna?' Nathan asked.

Anna shook her head. 'Nothing. Let's change the subject, shall we?'

Nathan smiled. 'Of course. So what are your thoughts about coming back to work?'

Anna looked at him, alarmed. 'Now?'

'Maybe in a month or so, whenever suits you.'

'It's not ideal, is it, the person reading the news *being* the news?'

'Exactly what we discussed yesterday. But we have a solution! You could work behind the scenes, you've done it before when you had laryngitis and couldn't talk, remember?'

Anna gave Joni her sippy cup and fanned her hot cheeks with the menu. 'Aren't there rules about employees who've been involved in an incident like this?'

He shrugged. 'You were released with no charge. It'll be good for you, Anna. You can get some semblance of a normal life back. You'll miss Joni, I'm sure, but I'm only suggesting part-time to start with, maybe a couple of days a week. Plus there's the money too.'

Anna sighed. He was right. Guy paid maintenance for Joni but it was now up to her to cover the mortgage on a house she wasn't even able to live in and everything else.

Joni threw a handful of mashed banana onto the floor. Anna thought about Nathan's offer as she leaned down to wipe the banana up. Regardless of the money, could she really leave Joni to go to work, even if it was for a few hours and even if she'd be left with family, either Florence or the nursery her mother-in-law owned? It was already so difficult when Guy had her. But Nathan was right, she needed the money…and she needed a semblance of normality.

'There's a lot to think about. Can I let you know in a few days?' she asked.

'Of course.' Nathan took a sip of his latte and leaned back in his chair. 'Did I tell you about what Heather said to me the other day?'

As they gossiped about work, Anna felt herself relax. Maybe life could begin to feel normal?

In fact, Anna felt so relaxed after her coffee with Nathan that she decided to stay out a little longer, strolling down the beach front under the sun, popping into the boutique shops to browse. It almost felt like she was back to her old life, before the terrible day Elliot Nunn had died. Anna batted that thought away and headed to her favourite second-hand bookshop, flicking through the books that were laid out on the long tables outside, the sea breeze providing some respite from the growing heat.

'Anna!' She turned to see her friend Maxine striding towards her, her little girl, Lissie, singing away in her pram as her son, Will, clutched onto her hand, both of their faces shiny with suncream. Anna gave Maxine a hug. She'd decided to go to dinner at Maxine's the week before to discuss the November fireworks. It gave all her close friends from the village the chance to hear what happened and ask the questions they needed to. She'd come away realising she wouldn't be ostracised for what she'd done, that her friends were as supportive as she'd hoped they'd be.

'I'm so pleased you took my advice and got out in the fresh air,' Maxine said, leaning town to tickle Joni. 'Look at her, she seems to grow more every week, we must do that play date with Suzanne this weekend.'

'Definitely.'

People walked past, smiling at Anna.

Maxine quirked an eyebrow. 'I told you, people respect you for what you did.'

Anna frowned. 'It feels weird.'

Maxine squeezed her arm. 'You did what any mother would.'

Anna's phone buzzed. She looked down, seeing it was her solicitor Jeremy. 'Sorry, I better get this, it's my solicitor.'

Maxine pulled a face. 'Oh, hon, is everything going okay?'

'It's fine. I'll text you about the play date, we can catch up then?'

'Perfect. I'll leave you to it.' She blew Anna a kiss then strolled off.

Anna put her phone to her ear.

'Elliot Nunn's autopsy results are back,' Jeremy said when she answered.

'Everything okay?'

'Cause of his death is as expected, severe blood loss from the comb penetrating a carotid artery.' Anna's head swam with images from Elliot's death. 'But there was something else.' He took a deep breath. 'He'd been poisoned before he died with digitalis, the poison found in foxgloves.'

Anna's blood turned to ice. Traces of foxglove had been found in all of the Ophelia Killer's victims. Though it wasn't what had killed the boys in the end, it was what would have made them weak enough to be drowned in their ponds.

'The Ophelia Killer,' Anna whispered.

'Quite. The police are rather perplexed.'

'I got an email from someone claiming to be the Ophelia Killer.'

Jeremy sighed. 'I know, Detective Morgan mentioned it. Makes it all even more alarming.'

'I don't understand, those murders were years ago. What does Detective Morgan say? Do they think Elliot was poisoned before I saw him? He *was* acting really out of it, I just thought it was drugs.'

'Try not to dwell on it too much, Anna, I just thought you'd appreciate the update. The results won't be released to the public for a couple of days, his family don't even know yet so please keep it quiet.'

'Of course.'

Anna walked to her mother's in a daze, trying to wrap her head around what she'd learnt. When she got back to the bungalow, Beatrice was sitting in the dark. Anna tiptoed past her, taking Joni upstairs for her nap. She knew when to leave her mother alone.

As she lay Joni in her cot, Anna's phone pinged. She went to turn it off; she couldn't cope with any more confusing, scary news. But before she had a chance, she saw it was another email from the so-called Ophelia Killer.

She found herself opening it, holding her breath.

From: Ophelia Killer
To: Anna Graves
Subject: Autopsy

I saw you in the village earlier, you looked rather
distressed, a little confused too. I wonder if they've told you

I poisoned young Elliot? I so wish I'd had the chance to cut him too, like I did the others. The holes would have been perfectly round. I use a special leather shape cutter, wonderful thing.

But alas, you took that opportunity away from me, Anna. My first chance in twenty years to experience that intoxicating wonder again at seeing their white lily bodies lain prone.

I have to confess, I am a little angry at you for taking that from me. But it also intrigues me, the idea it was you who took his life, the daughter of Simon Fountain, a man who grew so obsessed with finding me that it drove him mad enough to jump from his beloved lighthouse.

Don't pretend you didn't find it exciting, to stumble upon your father's body. There's a morbid curiosity, isn't there? I think it ties in to our desire to get to the root of the one thing we can't possibly know while alive: what it means to die. So we look and we look and we look because maybe if we do it long enough, we will grasp what death truly is.

Did you look, Anna? Did you look and look and look?

Take care now. TOK

Anna sat on her bed, putting her head in her hands. Images of her father's dead body tumbled through her mind. She tried to battle them away by getting up again and walking around the room. But there he was, limbs at odd angles, blood blossoming around the bottom of his untucked shirt, eyes staring up into the clouds, mouth wide.

And yes, she had looked and looked and looked because she

couldn't quite believe it was him, her wonderful vivacious father, lying broken on the rocks.

It had been the same when she watched the spark disappear from Elliot's eyes as he'd died. It had been something she'd grappled with since, the way she just couldn't drag her eyes away from his, the morbid, horrific fascination with it all.

Anna felt her mind spin out of control. She clutched her head. Was she going to lose her mind like her mother?

The door swung open and her mother appeared. 'Anna?'

Anna looked at Beatrice, tears falling down her cheeks.

'What's wrong?' Beatrice asked.

Anna shook her head, unable to say anything. Beatrice surprised her by pulling her into her arms. Anna froze for a moment, unused to the contact. Then she sank into her mother's arms.

They stayed like that for a few moments then Beatrice abruptly pulled away and walked from the room without saying anything. Anna stood in the middle of the room, not sure what to think. Then she heard the front door open.

'Mother?' Leo's clipped tones rang out from downstairs. Anna's heart sank. She'd been spared her brother the past two weeks thanks to his annual holiday to Devon with his wife and the twins.

She took a deep breath then walked downstairs to find Leo taking his jacket off in the hallway. Despite the stifling heat, he still felt the need to wear one. He paused when she appeared on the stairs, a frown on his face. 'What are you doing here?'

She hid her irritation. 'Joni and I are staying here,' she said.

He raised an eyebrow. 'I wondered how long it would be before you defaulted on your new mortgage payments.'

She shook her head incredulously. 'The mortgage payments are fine, Leo. I'm staying here on the advice of the police.'

'Why on earth would the police tell you to stay here?' She explained about the confrontation on the beach. Her brother shook his head in disgust. 'So you thought you'd expose Mother to danger by coming here?'

'For God's sake, Leo!'

He marched through to the living room. 'Mother, did you have any say in this or did Gran force your hand?'

'Have a say in what?' Beatrice asked.

'Anna staying here. You do understand how violent the boy's family is, don't you? Especially the brother. They'll be wanting revenge.'

Beatrice frowned slightly.

'There's no threat to Mum,' Anna said. 'The bungalow is out of the way and the police do drive-bys most nights.'

'You're being selfish as always, Anna.'

Anna pinched the bridge of her nose briefly. 'I know it's a strange concept to you, but this is what family do, shelter each other when in need. It's temporary and I'm incredibly grateful to Mum.' She turned to her mother, her face softening. 'I really am.'

Beatrice walked to the curtains, staring out. 'Could I be in danger, Leo?'

Anna's shoulders slumped. She grabbed her brother's arm and pulled him into the kitchen out of earshot of their mother. 'That's it now, you've sent her off on one.'

'By speaking the truth? She's naïve, Anna. She doesn't under-stand the danger you've put her in, it's my duty to tell her.'

'Your duty to terrify her, more like. She's safe, I would never put her in danger.'

'Like you didn't put your daughter in danger?'

Anna stared at her brother. 'Excuse me?'

'Those ridiculous walks of yours.'

'Walking my child along the beach is dangerous now?'

'Clearly. She nearly got killed, didn't she?'

Anger bristled. 'I see. So staying indoors all day every day like Trudy does is healthy for young children?'

'We've just come back from Devon!'

'Where you would have sat inside that cottage you hire and stare at the walls like you do every year. I can see Trudy getting more and more like Mum every day, you know.'

Leo laughed. '*Trudy*, like Mother? Look in the mirror, Anna. Trudy isn't the one scratching at her arms right now just like Mother does when she gets herself into a state.'

Anna looked down at her forearms which were red raw from scratching.

She pulled her sleeves down and peered into the living room at her mother, who was scratching at her arms too as she stared out at the road.

No, she wouldn't be like her mother, or like Trudy. She refused to sit in and feel sorry for herself.

She thought about Nathan's offer to go back to work. Maybe that's what she needed? It would only be two days a week to start.

'I need to make a call,' she said, pulling her phone from her pocket and finding Nathan's number. 'Go talk to Mum and make her feel even more paranoid, we all know how good you are at that, Leo.'

As Leo stormed out, Anna dialled Nathan's number. 'Is that offer still on the table about me coming back part-time?' she asked when he picked up.

'A hundred per cent!'

'Great. How's Thursday and Friday each week sound, I can start in August?'

'Perfect.'

Chapter Five

6 August 2015

***Your Say Question of the Day: Are there too many
immigrants in the UK?***

*Caller A: 'Of course! They're ruining this country. I'm a
midwife and we're filled to capacity because of all the
Eastern Europeans coming in.' (Sharon, 56)*

*Caller B: 'No, I say let's invite more in! They've contributed
almost £5 billion to the UK economy since 2004. How can
that be "too much"?' (Matthew, 38)*

*Caller C: 'Yes, we moved from our old town because our
neighbourhood was overrun by them. They hang around on
street corners, drinking and being aggressive.' (Albert, 47)*

Anna caught Nathan's eye through the window dividing
them. Typical that the day she returned to work, just over

a month after the incident, there was a question about immigration.

'Nice selection,' Nathan said, rubbing his hands together. 'Looking forward to this one.' It was strange being on the other side of the screen from him. But it was best she stayed off air for now.

Anna leaned back in her chair, aware of her producer Heather's eyes on her. She hadn't kept her eyes *off* her since Anna returned that morning, barely saying a word to her. But she was in the minority. Mainly, the response to Anna's return had been warm. People who knew her hugged her, sharing their support. Those who didn't know her but recognised her smiled, some even gave her a thumbs-up.

With all the horribleness of the past few weeks, it was good to be reminded just how supportive people were. Nathan had even shown her the logs of all the positive calls they'd received since the incident, many declaring Anna a modern-day saint. It made her uncomfortable, she *had* killed a boy, after all. But it could be worse, the public could hate her and she'd seen in her job what that could do to a person.

You'd think it would make her sleep better at night. But the nightmares were getting worse, more blood, more pain. She was losing weight too, unable to face eating most of the time, the scar even more pronounced against her stark cheekbones. Whenever she washed her hands, she got a quick flash of Elliot's blood spurting between her fingers. So she'd quickly turn the tap on and scrub and scrub and scrub her hands until they were red raw.

She looked at her hands now as the familiar sound of the radio show's theme tune tinkled in her ear. She quickly tucked them under her thighs and got to work. Over the next few hours, she disappeared into the show, manning the phone lines as Nathan and her stand-in, Georgia, presented the show itself. It felt good to be on the phones, just like she'd started out doing after she got her journalism degree. Her voice was distinctive, and some people calling in even asked if she was *the* Anna Graves. But she just laughed it off, saying there was more than one gravelly voiced person working in radio.

'Joni at nursery?' Nathan asked her as they had lunch together later in the small canteen overlooking the sea.

'Not this week. Guy's taken time off work so he can look after her while I start back. He's dropping her over tomorrow evening.'

'That's good of him.'

Anna nodded. 'Yeah, he's been quite supportive actually. Since all the positive publicity, he seems to have calmed down. He even agrees with me returning back to work.' She sipped her coffee, raising an eyebrow. 'Though half of me wonders if it's because his mother can keep an eye on Joni at her nursery when she goes back next week. In more good news, I'm returning home this weekend.'

Nathan smiled. 'That *is* good news. Sure it's safe though?'

'I think so. Detective Morgan threatened the Nunns with a restraining order.'

Nathan raised an eyebrow. 'You're going to take out a restraining order?'

Anna shook her head. 'The detective just used it to warn them off. He wanted me to, but how could I do that to the Nunns after all they've been through? Anyway, Detective Morgan seems sure the Nunns won't target me again.' What she didn't say to Nathan was that the detective suspected the emails penned from the person claiming to be the Ophelia Killer might actually have been from one of the Nunn family. They were the only other people to know about the autopsy results after all, so it made sense to suspect one of them – in particular Elliot's father, Neil Nunn – considering the results were referred to in one of the emails despite them not being public. 'It seems to be calming down then,' Nathan said.

'I hope so. I really do.' Anna peered out towards the sea. Could her life really return to normal after what she'd done? 'I'm just going to pop outside to call Guy and check on Joni. Be back in a mo.'

Anna strode outside, blinking up into the sunlight. Tomorrow she'd be with Joni. She wasn't ready to do their regular walk yet, but they could play in her mother's garden after Guy dropped her off, enjoy the sunshine together while it lasted before autumn came along. She picked up her phone then paused when she noticed a man leaning against the wall, smoking.

It was Elliot's brother, Jamie.

He straightened up when he saw Anna, flicking his cigarette away. He was wearing baggy jeans with oil on them, but his white t-shirt was clean. The sunlight exposed the exhaustion on his face, the fine lines of grief and dark circles of sadness.

He had eyes just like Elliot's, bright blue and fringed with dark lashes.

An instant image of Elliot staring up towards the sky flashed through Anna's mind, blood shining on the pebbles around him.

Jamie stepped closer to her, eyes hard. 'Anna Graves?'

'What are you doing here?' Anna asked, peering over her shoulder. If she cried out, someone would come, wouldn't they?

'Did you hear about my brother's autopsy results?' he asked her, his voice strangely calm.

'We can't talk about that,' Anna said, trying to keep her voice steady. 'It's a police investigation.'

'The police don't give a shit about Elliot.'

'Detective Morgan's doing all he—'

'I don't give a fuck what Detective Morgan says,' he snapped, making Anna jump. 'No way Elliot would poison himself.'

'That's what they're saying?' Anna asked, her curiosity getting the better of her despite how fearful she was.

'Yeah.' Jamie raked his fingers through his fair hair, his eyes filling with sadness. 'My brother was a good kid. *None* of it makes sense. That's why I came,' he said, his voice growing cold again. 'You're going to help me make sense of this.' He said it like he was giving her an order and he was used to his orders being followed.

'I can't help you,' Anna said firmly.

'You don't *want* to help, more like.' The sadness returned to his eyes and he turned away.

Anna sighed. 'I'm so sorry for what happened, truly.' Her fingers flickered up to her scar. She'd removed the gauze since having the stitches out. But it was unsightly to look at, her skin still red raw, a constant reminder of what had happened whenever she looked in the mirror. Jamie looked at her scar, face softening slightly. 'But I can't turn back time,' she said quickly, 'and I can't help you. I'm sorry.' She went to walk away but Jamie grabbed her wrist, hurting her.

'Did you see Elliot die?' he said. 'Did he say anything? Was he in pain?'

She stood still, thinking of the email the supposed Ophelia Killer had sent her.

Did you look, Anna? Did you look and look and look?

'I didn't see your brother die,' she lied. Then she yanked her hand away from Jamie and ran inside, leaning against the wall and taking deep breaths as she tried to battle away images from the moment Elliot died.

The next morning as Nathan and Anna had coffee in the canteen, Nathan seemed to sense something was wrong with Anna. 'Everything okay?' he asked her.

She couldn't tell him she'd laid awake thinking of her encounter with Elliot's brother the night before. She ought to be scared considering all she'd read about him, and the way he'd hurt her when he'd grabbed her. But she'd been filled with guilt. Should she have dismissed him like that? He'd only been trying to find out what had happened to his brother, wouldn't she want to know the same if Leo was killed? He hadn't threatened her, had he?

Nathan put his hand on Anna's arm, squeezing it. 'I'm always here if you need to talk, Anna.'

A couple of the girls from the admin team walked past, whispering and giggling as they looked at the two presenters.

'God, it's like being at school again with all the whispering schoolgirls and their crushes on the school jock,' Anna said, rolling her eyes, desperate to change the subject so she didn't have to think of the grief in Jamie Nunn's eyes.

Nathan pinched a roll of fat around his waist. 'Me, a jock? Yeah right.'

They both laughed.

A man sitting at a nearby table peered up sternly and stared at them, brow creased.

'I really do feel like I'm at school,' Anna whispered, 'annoying the headmaster with our laughter.'

As she said that, she noticed more people looking up at them from their phones. Nathan frowned. 'Strange atmosphere in here today.'

'It's so good to be proved right,' a voice said from behind them. They turned to see Heather watching them, her head cocked in a patronising manner.

Anna sighed. 'What are you talking about, Heather?'

'You two,' she said, looking them both up and down. 'I've been saying it for ages.'

Anna went very still. She looked around her, saw people peering at their phones, more accusing looks, more whispers.

'They know,' Anna whispered to Nathan.

Chapter Six

As they headed out of the canteen, Anna quickly pulled her phone out, checking her Twitter feed. And there it was:

> *So disappointed in @AGraves_Coast if DM story is true about her having affair with @NWheelerRadio #NotSoInnocentAfterall*

> *Woah, just read about @AGraves_Coast and @NWheelerRadio. So much for 'poor neglected single mum' angle. No wonder her hubby upped sticks!*

Nathan's face went white. 'Oh God.'
They looked at each other in horror. Anna never really dreamed the kisses they'd shared would get out.
'You need to call Valerie,' she said.
'How did they find out?'
'It doesn't matter, they did.'
'Oh, Anna.'
She searched his eyes, then shoved him away. 'Go call her, Nathan!'

He backed away, his eyes filling with tears. Then he jogged down the corridor. Anna wrapped her arms around herself as people walked out of the offices past her, many of them smiling slyly.

She ran into the toilets and locked herself in a cubicle, taking deep breaths. Could things get any worse?

Anna wrapped the old blanket around herself, peering out into the darkness. She was sitting in the lighthouse's watch room near the very top of the building. It was once used by the men who worked at the lighthouse to watch out for boats in trouble. Anna's father had converted it into a large circular study, his old typewriter sitting on an antique desk, the cracked leather sofa Anna was now sat on slung with blankets. In the middle of the room was the steel staircase, which wound down to a tiny room below with two locked doors either side leading to storage rooms. Then below that, the room where Anna's mother would draw from, her old easel, scrapbooks and pencils now long forgotten since her husband had died.

Anna's phone rang and rang, lighting up the steel bars of the lighthouse's staircase as it did so. She'd come here straight from work, needing to be alone to think. She thought back to that one drunken night with Nathan three years ago. It had been so foolish. But she'd found out Guy had kissed his secretary at a work Halloween party a couple of months before. It had been a quick kiss, a one-off according to Guy. But enough people had seen it for the news to filter back to Anna. She'd been so humili-ated! Things had been so tense between them after she found out, and then Guy had to go away for two weeks right before

Christmas. By the time her work Christmas party arrived, the wounds hadn't yet healed. One too many drinks later, Anna found herself stumbling as she walked along the path outside the restaurant with Nathan. The feel of his fingers on her bare arm when she hadn't had any human contact for weeks from Guy had sent a spark through her. His handsome face, those familiar smiling eyes. The world had gone still for a moment, and before she knew it, they were seeking each other out with their lips, stumbling into a dark alleyway. It had been so horribly sordid, her skirt hitched up, his fingers inside her as he breathed into her ear. They'd both instantly regretted it after and promised to wipe it from their memories.

But how could you explain that to people? All they saw was the infidelity, the drama and the scandal, two radio presenters who worked with one another day in day out, who seemed so fun and jovial, who'd also shared seedy kisses.

And that's all Guy saw when he found out his wife had cheated on him three years after it happened. To him, it was the nail in the coffin of a marriage that had been on the slip and slide for a number of years now. He found an email from Nathan referring to what had happened while he was fixing her computer. It wasn't a sordid email, Nathan was just talking about how guilty he felt. Anna thought she'd deleted it. But it was enough of an excuse to make Guy leave four months ago.

'Why keep pretending this is working, Anna?' he'd said to her after confronting her with the email. 'First I cheat, then you do.'

'Just kisses.'

He'd shaken his head. 'More than that. Symbols of the fact we've both fallen out of love.'

'No!' she'd said, grabbing his hand. 'I love you.'

'But it's not working. We just fight and fight and—'

'Fight? You're not fighting for our marriage!' Anna had said. 'You're just giving up.'

'I've been fighting for our marriage the past three years, Anna,' he said, voice weary. 'It's time to accept it's over. I'm sorry.'

Deep down, she had known Guy was right. But she'd been overwhelmed with fear, at the top of her mind the fact her mum hadn't been able to cope as a single mother: could Anna? And what would people say?

She knew what they'd be saying now. 'Ah, so *that's* why they split up.' She could tell people about Guy's kiss, about the fact the marriage had been troubled for a while. But she couldn't do that to Guy. And anyway, all people would see was the scandal of two radio presenters kissing.

She sighed and looked around the lighthouse. She rarely came in here, the memories of what her dad had done were too painful. Her great great grandfather had bought the lighthouse when he'd retired from his naval officer duties after the Second World War. Many of the men in Anna's mother's side of the family had been navy men. A lighthouse was an ideal way for her great grandfather to spend his retirement years, looking out over the rocky waves he'd spent his life battling. The lighthouse hadn't been used since its heyday in the eighteenth century when it would guide in the ships that would come to the dockyards for repairs, and see over the busy channel beyond.

Since then it had become dilapidated, its once shining white walls cracked and dirty. Its ownership had been passed from generation to generation and Anna's gran had insisted it become a 'family' lighthouse when Anna and Leo had been born, a place to escape to and play. And that's what they used to do especially in the top gallery, a white steel latticed structure with a circular outdoor walkway which offered stunning views of the sea and village.

Her father had wanted to renovate the lighthouse, using the money they raised from renting it out to holiday makers to turn it into a family home. He'd even drawn up plans of it. Anna had found them when she'd cleared out her mother's loft a couple of months before, her heart aching as she saw the notes he'd scribbled. If he hadn't died, who knows, she might be visiting her parents right now in their converted lighthouse?

But she wasn't. That was the reality and she had to accept it.

She stood up. 'Game face, Anna, game face.' Then she headed back down the steel staircase, ready to face the real world.

The next day, Anna sat anxiously in her mother's bungalow waiting for Guy to drop Joni off. She was desperate to see her daughter but was dreading seeing Guy after the revelations. Florence hadn't exactly been delighted, asking Anna why she hadn't told her and lecturing her on how you don't respond to infidelity by being unfaithful yourself. Luckily Beatrice had kept herself in her room most of the day, only appearing to eat, not once referring to Anna's dalliance with Nathan.

Maybe she didn't know?

The doorbell went and Anna took a deep painful breath. If it weren't for Joni, she'd stay inside with the curtains closed like she had all day, ignoring her phone, not reading any papers.

She opened the front door to find Guy standing there, face set.

'How the hell did the papers find out?' he asked as he handed Joni and her bag over.

Anna cuddled her daughter and kissed her face. 'I don't know, Guy. I'm sorry.'

'I thought only you, me and Nathan knew,' he said, spitting Nathan's name out.

'I haven't told anyone else, I swear,' Anna said.

'Then it must be Nathan.'

'He wouldn't,' Anna said, shaking her head. 'He's as sick and regretful about it all as I am. I'm under more scrutiny since what happened, every part of my life examined. Anyone looking hard enough might find something.'

'Have you seen the papers?' Guy said.

She shook her head.

'It's not great,' Guy said. 'To them, you were the poor single mum whose bastard of a husband walked out on her.'

'Guy, I never—'

He put his hand up, interrupting her. 'I know you didn't pitch it like that, Anna. It's just the way they spun it, it suits their "hero mother" story. Now they think I left because I learnt about Nathan, their story is skewed. They don't like it.'

Anna shuddered as she imagined the headlines. *From Hero Mother to Zero Adulterer.*

Guy looked down at his daughter. 'It's not just us I'm worried for, it's Joni too.'

Anna didn't say anything.

'What a mess,' Guy said, shaking his head. 'What a bloody mess you've made. First killing that kid, then this.'

Anna glared at him. 'What happened with Nathan is nothing like what I did to protect Joni.'

'Really?' Guy asked, examining her face. 'I never dreamed you'd kiss someone else.'

'And I never dreamed you would!'

He closed his eyes, pinching the bridge of his nose. 'You need to understand how it feels for me. First, I learn you kissed Nathan Wheeler, then a few weeks later, you kill a boy. Two things I honestly didn't think you'd be capable of regardless of what I did.' He opened his eyes, looking right into hers. 'I barely know you any more.'

Anna caught sight of her reflection, of the ragged scar across her cheek. She saw her dark eyes staring back at her. She imagined the red comb that killed Elliot in her hand and she saw herself raising it…

She quickly looked away. 'You must have to get back, Guy,' she said coldly. 'I don't want to keep you.' She looked down at her daughter. 'Say goodbye to Daddy then, darling.'

But Joni sucked her thumb resolutely, clutching onto Anna, her little blue teddy against her cheek.

'Come on, darling,' Anna said to her. 'Say goodbye.'

Guy took Joni and Joni burst into tears. He frowned. 'She's not done this before with me.'

'It's confusing for her. She's used to being with us when we're together.'

Guy looked at Anna, his eyes hard. 'Whose fault is that?'

Anna turned away, her own eyes filling with tears. What had she done to her little family?

What had she done to Elliot Nunn?

*　*　*

99

It took Joni two hours to go to sleep that night. Each time Anna left her room, she cried out. In the end, Anna had to lie on the floor, her fingers touching Joni's through the cot's slats until they both finally fell asleep.

Anna woke near midnight with an aching back, blinking in the darkness. Before she knew what she was doing, she reached for her phone, finding the news articles Guy had hinted at. She was shocked when she discovered they even had a photo of her and Nathan embracing in a dark alleyway. It was grainy but clear who they were.

Who had taken that photo…and why leak it now? Maybe they'd just been waiting for the right time and the perfect time was now, with Anna high on the news agenda.

She forced herself to read some of the articles. They weren't quite *From Hero Mother to Zero Adulterer*. They were more restrained than that, her old school-friend journalist from the local newspaper even quoting a 'source' who said her and Guy's marriage had been on the rocks for a while. But there was an implication underlining most of the articles: our hero of the moment isn't quite as perfect as we'd hoped.

She dreaded to think what sort of calls would be coming in to the station the next morning. Luckily she wasn't due back for another few days.

And that wasn't to mention how her colleagues would react once the dust settled, and her friends too. She'd only had a couple of texts from her circle of friends, including one from Maxine saying she was around if Anna needed to talk.

The last thing she wanted to do was talk about it.

She walked to the bathroom and stared in the mirror at herself. Her scar was puckered and jagged in the moonlight. She smoothed her fingers over it and remembered the sting of pain as Elliot's knife had sliced into her skin. She closed her eyes, saw the desperation in his eyes, the *fear*.

She took a deep breath then splashed some cold water on her face, drying it and stepping out into the hallway to find her mother standing in her nightie, rubbing her eyes.

'Is Joni okay?' Beatrice asked.

'She's had some problems getting to sleep. Sorry if she kept you awake.'

'It's fine. I was just about to make a hot chocolate. Do you want one?'

Anna looked at her in surprise. 'All right.'

She followed Beatrice downstairs and watched as she heated up milk, her nightdress aglow in the moonlight. It reminded her of when her mother would do this for Anna as a child, making her hot chocolate before going to bed. She dwelled too much on the bad memories sometimes. But before her father died, they'd had a good family life doing things like this.

'I know about the affair,' Beatrice said curtly.

Anna sighed. So much for a nice restful hot chocolate with her mother. 'It wasn't an affair. It was just a kiss, a kiss I—'

'No need to explain,' Beatrice said, stirring chocolate into simmering milk. 'I know more than anyone how people can do the most unexpected of things.'

Anna frowned. 'What do you mean?'

Beatrice went quiet as she carefully poured the frothing hot chocolate into two mugs and placed Anna's on the table in front of her.

'Mum, what you just said, what do you mean?' Anna asked again.

'It doesn't matter.'

'It does.'

'I said it doesn't!' Beatrice shouted. She flinched and put her fingers to her head. 'Now I have a headache.' Then she left the kitchen, her hot chocolate forgotten.

The next day, Anna and Joni moved back to their house. It felt strange, they'd only been in the house a few weeks when Anna had returned to work from maternity leave. It felt they were moving in again, starting over again. Anna liked the fact the house was less than a year old, its clean white walls and sparkling light fittings feeling safe and clean and new.

After Anna put Joni down for her nap, she reluctantly looked at her phone, trying to ignore all the notifications. The tweets and emails she'd been getting had taken on an accusatory tone. People were disappointed in her for having an affair, like she owed it to them to be the perfect mother protector they'd built her up to be.

But one stuck out, an email from a familiar name: the so-called Ophelia Killer again. She considered deleting it without reading it but she couldn't help herself, she quickly opened it.

From: Ophelia Killer
To: Anna Graves
Subject: Nathan and Anna sitting in a tree…

Don't tell me you don't feel a sense of relief, Anna, to finally have your big secret out there? It's like when I finally gave in to my desire to kill again, a twenty-year itch that needed scratching. This is much the same, a secret that has burdened you finally takes flight.

That's why you shouldn't feel bad about the stories circulating about you and Nathan. The truth purifies like water does, just like the water purified my boys. After the poison, they need cleaning. I did them a favour, Anna, like you did Elliot Nunn a favour.

Yours, TOK

PS. About that itch that needs scratching. I still haven't scratched it properly. Elliot didn't die at my hands after all. Not long though, not long…

Anna stared at the email in horror. Then she turned all notifications off her phone and shoved it in her pocket.

That night, she woke from a horrific nightmare. She'd been leaning over Elliot, her fingers itching at his wound, blood pooling around her nails, into the creases of her knuckles. She was trying to get to something. Finally, as she sank her fingers into the gaping wound in his neck, she found it.

One solitary foxglove, its purple bell-shaped petals shuddering in the breeze.

She got up and found her phone, staring at the email from the so-called Ophelia Killer. She thought of what Jamie had said about his brother being poisoned. She tapped into her phone's browser and found the Wikipedia page about the Ophelia Killer, scrolling down the footnotes until she found the link she was looking for: a link to her dad's old news reports. She clicked on it then found her earphones, slipping them in.

'It's Simon Fountain,' her father said, his deep voice filling her ears. Anna felt her heart clench as she listened to her father's familiar voice. 'I'm reporting from the scene of the latest killing to rock the Ridgmont Waters community.' There was a squawk of seagulls in the background, the sound of a passing car. 'This is a community waking up to the reality that a serial killer may be operating on their very doorstep. Today, a second boy, fourteen-year-old Sam Twiselton, was found drowned in his garden pond in the heart of the town's docklands estate. Sam's teachers report him leaving school at the usual time of three p.m. in good spirits. An hour later, he was found lying in his garden pond, just as Alex McDonald was discovered the week before, surrounded by flowers. With Alex's autopsy results revealing he had taken – or been administered with – a dose of digitalis, the chemical derived from foxgloves, will pathologists discover the same in Sam Twiselton's body? The community awaits the results with fear in their hearts.'

Anna sighed. Her father had been so talented, so wonderful with words. It was such a waste. She reluctantly clicked out of the report on her phone and looked up the symptoms of ingesting foxgloves. *Confusion. Hallucinations.*

That might explain why Elliot tried to hurt Anna, the hallucinatory effect of the poison making him imagine all sorts of things. He did seem out of his head.

But who administered the poison? The Ophelia Killer?

Or Elliot himself? But Anna tended to agree with his brother, it didn't *feel* right that he'd kill himself.

The next morning, she called Detective Morgan's number.

'Anna, how are you?' he asked when he picked it up.

'Good. Look, I was doing some research into foxglove poisoning, I don't know whether you guys have done the same? The symptoms can include confusion, even hallucinations.'

'It's a strong drug.'

'Maybe that's why Elliot targeted me and Joni, he was confused?'

'Yes, it's something we're looking into.'

'Okay, great.' She paused. 'I got another email claiming to be from the Ophelia Killer, I'll send it on.'

'Please do.'

'The last line implies they want to start killing again.'

'Just trying to scare you, Anna, ignore it.'

'But what if the Ophelia Killer really is back?' As she said that, her body shuddered. But it was a possibility, wasn't it? It was something that had been playing on her mind ever since getting the emails.

She heard the detective sigh down the other end of the phone. 'I appreciate your *concern*, Mrs Graves, but this is a police investigation. I'd rather you leave this to us, especially considering your involvement with it.'

'I know, I just—'

'Think about it, what's more likely? A kid with a troubled background and violent father tries to extract himself from his miserable life by killing himself. Or a serial murderer who hasn't committed a crime in twenty years returns? My money's on the former.'

'Really? The Ophelia Killer did stalk this very town, target boys who looked just like Elliot. What if the killer has been in prison for something else the past twenty years? What if—'

'That's enough, Mrs Graves,' Detective Morgan said, voice

sharp. 'I think you have more pressing matters to deal with, don't you?'

'What do you mean?'

He coughed slightly. 'All the stuff in the papers. Just focus on your family and let us focus on *our* investigation.'

Anna felt anger build inside. 'This *is* about my family. I've been getting threatening emails and—'

'Emails which we've been looking into. I really must go, Mrs Graves. But please trust us to do a thorough job. Goodbye.'

Then the line went dead.

Anna looked at her phone in disbelief. Jamie was right, the police weren't taking this seriously enough.

She impulsively did a search on her phone then called the number she found.

'Dockside Mechanics,' a bored-sounding woman said on the other end.

'Can I speak to Jamie Nunn, please?' Anna asked.

'Who's calling?'

'Just a customer. He said I could call to ask a question if I had any problems.'

'Jamie!' the woman screeched out. 'Some customer for you.'

Anna tapped her foot, trying to contain her nerves. Was this a mistake?

'Jamie speaking,' Jamie said when he came onto the line.

'Jamie, it's Anna Graves.'

There was a long pause on the other end of the line. She felt foolish. She shouldn't have called him. She was about to hang up the receiver when he spoke.

'What do you want?' he asked coolly.

'I looked up the symptoms of ingesting foxgloves,' Anna said. 'It might explain why your brother did something so out of character.' She told him what she'd told the detective a moment ago. 'I thought it might help knowing Elliot wasn't in his right mind when he attacked me and Joni.'

'My brother was *poisoned*. My mind is far from rested.' He sounded angry.

'I shouldn't have called, I don't know why I did. I'll let you go, sorry.'

'He knew you, didn't he?' Jamie asked quickly.

Anna frowned. 'Sorry?'

'I spoke to one of the kids who saw it go down. He told me Elliot seemed to know you before it happened.'

'He probably recognised me, I've done some work at the community centre.'

'The kid told me Elliot looked scared of you too,' Jamie said, voice stony. 'That was even before he got the knife out.'

Anna thought back to that day, the fear in Elliot's eyes. 'I don't know. It must have been the drugs.'

'Did he seem like he was out of it?'

'Yes, he did to be honest.'

'Did he actually aim for your face when he cut you?'

She got a flashback to his arm raised in the air, the feel of the blade on her skin. 'Jamie, I can't—'

'Was he in pain? Did he call out when he—'

'Jamie!' she shouted out. 'We shouldn't be talking like this, I shouldn't have called.'

'But there are lots of questions to be answered, aren't there? You're a journalist, surely you see none of this makes sense.'

She hung up the phone before he could respond.

What had she been thinking?

She tried to focus on playing with Joni after she put the phone down. But she kept thinking about what Jamie had said. He was right, none of it made sense to her.

Then something occurred to her. What if the person sending the emails had poisoned Elliot? As she got Joni a snack, she quickly found the so-called Ophelia Killer's last email and hit reply.

Did you poison Elliot Nunn? Was he running from you when he ran into me?

The next week rolled by too quickly and before Anna knew it, it was time to go to work. Nathan wasn't in, and Anna had thought about not going in too after spending a few quiet days in with Joni – well, as quiet as they could be with a nine-month-old. But she couldn't keep hiding away like she had the past week, she had to face up to it all. It didn't start well though, hammering rain meaning she couldn't walk to the studio like she did on dry days. Then her car refused to start. So she quickly jumped on a train at the station right near her estate. It wasn't too bad as it was so early in the morning, but the handful of passengers on the train clearly recognised her, one even trying to take a sly selfie with her in the background. Anna sighed. No doubt that would be on Twitter soon.

She walked into the studio a few minutes later, shaking her umbrella to let the raindrops loose.

'Hey, Jim,' she said, smiling at the security man.

'Mrs Graves,' he said, nodding curtly at her, no smile this time.

Anna's heart sank. She walked through to her studio, the wide smiles and 'how are yous' she'd grown so used to over the years now gone, replaced by tight nods and even disgusted looks from some colleagues. Anna took a deep breath, trying to mentally prepare for Heather's reaction. But all she got was a smirk from Heather as she stepped into the studio. It was the production assistant's reaction that was worse: he could barely look Anna in the eye.

Anna had to bite her lip to stop herself from crying. She deserved this, she knew that. But that didn't stop her from hating every moment.

As they gathered around the large table in the studio to go through their daily task of reading the morning's papers, the first thing Anna saw was her and Nathan's faces staring up at her.

'Maybe you should sit this one out, Anna,' Georgia said as Nathan's replacement, the man who usually did the sports, squirmed beside her.

Anna shook her head resolutely. 'Thanks, but it's fine,' she said, turning the page to look at another story inside. 'I thought this piece on the UK's infant death rate being the highest in Europe might be worth looking at? Would be of interest to our listeners who are parents?'

As they discussed the story, Anna's eyes strayed over to the other newspapers scattered over the large table.

Support for Anna Graves drops by 10% among our readers after affair reveal, one headline claimed.

They were running *polls* on her?

Nathan Wheeler's wife leaves, a headline from the local newspaper declared beside a grainy photo of Valerie packing up her car.

Oh God, poor Valerie, Anna thought. She'd always liked her. How could Anna have done this to her?

Heather peered at Anna and Anna turned away, trying to compose her face. But not before she caught sight of another headline: *Graves' case in danger after fling revealed.*

Her breath quickened. Her case was in danger? But there *was* no case. She'd been released. As soon as Anna got the chance, she made an excuse and went outside, calling her solicitor Jeremy and telling him about the article.

'Don't worry, Anna,' he said, 'your affair has nothing to do with Elliot's death. Even if the police were doing secondary checks on you, this isn't something they would really consider.'

'Secondary checks? What are they?'

'After what happened, the police would have done some cursory checks into your background, just to cover all bases. But they wouldn't have gone into huge detail, it was a pretty clear-cut case of self-defence on your part plus you have no previous. But if they begin to suspect you're not quite the person they thought you were, then they might begin to delve more into your character, question more people you know, do some more detailed investigations. But they won't, Anna,' he added quickly. 'Not based on a few kisses with a work colleague.' He paused. 'Unless you have anything to tell me?'

'Of course not.'

'Then you don't need to worry. You know more than anyone these articles will be paper for fish and chips tomorrow.'

Anna scratched at her arm with her free hand. No, she knew more than most how important public perception could be with things like this. If her image continued to deteriorate, it might influence the direction of the police investigation. Detective Morgan was already cooling towards her, she could tell during their phone conversation the other day.

By the time the workday was over, she was so relieved she virtually ran out of the door despite the heavy rain outside. She just wanted to go home and hide herself away from the world. But she needed to get a birthday gift for Florence. It was her seventieth birthday party that evening, a 'small gathering', as she'd described it, at her house. It was the last thing Anna needed but her gran had arranged it months ago and Anna couldn't let her down, despite what was going on in her life. As she walked to the shops from the radio studio, people scurried by under the rain, umbrellas vying for space. Anna was relieved. She could disappear head down into the clatter too. No one would see her, recognise her, *glare* at her as they had been doing all day at work. Then she'd get a taxi home and avoid getting the train during rush hour. Or maybe it would stop raining and she could walk home?

She spent the next half an hour browsing the shops and eventually found a small topaz locket for Florence. If she could find a photo of her and Joni when she got home, she could fit it inside. She would've liked to have Joni give it to her great gran but Guy had texted Anna that morning to say Joni had the beginnings of a cold so they'd both agreed it was best Joni didn't go to the party.

When Anna finished, she opened up her umbrella and stepped out into the throng, water splashing onto the bottom of her jeans as she jostled through the crowds to get to the train station. Someone bumped into her and she peered over her shoulder to see a man in a suit striding down the high street, shouting into his mobile phone. She quickened her step, rivulets of rain running down the back of her neck. Beside her, the sea lashed about in a frenzy, seagulls squawking away from the violent waves, the beaches empty and sodden as people ran across the promenade to get home.

When it rained by the coast, it *really* rained.

As Anna neared the taxi rank outside the train station, she passed a newsstand, her and Nathan's smiling faces staring out from the local evening newspaper. It was a group photo taken from the restaurant the night they first kissed, probably grabbed off someone's Facebook page.

A woman picked the newspaper up, shaking her head in disapproval.

'Oh don't be so judgemental,' the man with her said. 'It was just one mistake. We've always liked listening to Anna Graves on the radio.'

'I said it at the time and I'll say it again, Reg,' the woman said. 'After what happened with that poor boy – and yes, I know I'm in the minority when I say this – but after what happened, something hasn't felt right about Anna Graves. Everyone's quick to say they'd do the same but when you really think about it, would you? That takes something dark inside. And now with all this coming out about the affair, that just proves it to me. Mark my words, this won't be the last we hear.'

Anna ducked her head and continued walking, eyes on the soaking ground so she didn't have to see more newspapers, more disapproving looks and judgemental remarks.

But she couldn't help but dwell on the woman's remarks.

That takes something dark inside.

Was she right, did Anna have something dark inside her? Guy

had said the same, that he couldn't imagine killing someone when it came to the crunch. Leo too. Was there something within her, a *darkness,* that gave her the extra impetus to kill?

Someone smashed into her, sending her spinning.

She dropped to the wet ground on her knees, felt something heavy in her coat pocket. She reached inside, fingers brushing something metallic. She pulled it out then let out a gasp.

It was a round sharp metal leather cutter, dried blood on it. Attached to it was a note: *Good questions, Anna. Yes and yes. Enjoy my gift... TOK*

Chapter Seven

The Third One

'My friends call me Coolio,' the boy says.

I laugh.

'Not for the reasons you think though,' he adds. 'It's 'cos I once got my fingers stuck in a freezer door.'

I laugh again. This one's funny.

'I like it here,' the boy says. We're sitting in his garden, looking out towards the sea through the broken panels of his fence. It's boiling hot and we're both trying to huddle under a small tree, the one piece of shade out here. He's new here, only been living in The Docks for three weeks.

I can't help but look towards his pond. It shimmers under the bright exhausting sun and I have a flashback to the week before and the pale body that had lain prone in filthy water.

Guilt swirls with excitement. You said that will change, the guilt will eventually fade. I think you're right, I'm starting to feel braver, fingers tingling with excitement.

I think of you now, standing in the alleyway nearby and that tingle of excitement doubles. I know you'll be so proud of me.

'Where did you live before?' I ask the boy, looking at him. He's got dark hair like the one last week, but his face is a bit freckled.

Not ideal, but close.

'Some town you won't know,' the boy says. 'Hated it there, was too far away from the sea. It's a shithole here but at least I can smell the salt and sea, I like it.'

'You sound like you want to be a fisherman,' I say, jutting my chin towards a man who's casting his net out to sea in the distance.

'And? Maybe I do wanna be a fisherman. I'll run away, sleep on the beach.'

'It's bloody freezing at night.'

He shrugs, taking another sip of lemonade. 'So? I'll build a hut.'

'Won't your mum miss you?'

He looks down at his trainers, face all serious. 'Maybe. But she's got my sister, she'll be all right.'

'And she's at work now?' I ask, peering towards the empty house.

'Yeah.'

I knew she'd be at work but it's always worth double-checking. This isn't easy. It's not just a case of getting them alone and doing the deed. We need to be sure we're alone long enough to administer the poison before, then take the cuttings after. One looks out, the other does the deed. This is a team effort, you see.

The boy rubs his eyes as he examines my face. He looks like he's trying to focus. It's working, just like it did last week. Just a few drops of crushed Foxglove petals in his lemonade.

He retches.

It's starting. I imagine you behind the fence, body coiled in anticipation.

The boy gets sick on his trainers. 'Gross,' he slurs.

'I think I've got a tissue,' I say, rooting around in my denim pocket.

A shadow moves across the parched lawn. I look up, smile.

You're here just in time.

I pull out the shape cutter.

Chapter Eight

The shape cutter dropped from Anna's hands with the note, clattering to the ground, rain bouncing off it, cleaning the blood away.

She backed away, chest struggling to take in her terrified breaths.

She looked in the direction the person had run off in, but couldn't see them.

As people strode past her, she stood stock still, tears falling down her cheeks.

Was it the Ophelia Killer?

She quickened her step towards the taxi rank by the train station, heartbeat aflutter. She had to get the hell out as fast as she could.

But when she got there, there was a huge queue. She looked at her watch. Three minutes until the next train. What if whoever put the shape cutter in her pocket returned? She pulled her hood over her head and ran through the ticket gates as the train came sweeping up.

The train doors slid open and she jumped in. Just as the doors started to close, she suddenly thought of her father. He'd never leave a key piece of evidence behind, no matter how scared he was. If it was the Ophelia Killer who was sending her those emails, that blood could be from one of his old victims.

She swallowed her fear and went to run out again to retrieve the shape cutter but the doors slammed shut. She stood looking out of the window as the train drew away from the station, leaving behind a potentially crucial piece of evidence. She sighed, putting her head down as she shuffled down the train, managing to find a seat by a window. She stared out at the busy platform, fear making her numb as she searched the crowds for anyone looking suspicious.

The train filled up with men in suits and harassed-looking mothers with prams, rain shaking off them.

The train jolted, and Anna breathed a sigh of relief as it started chugging along.

She turned to the window, watching her reflection melt with the falling rain outside as the train trundled along over the next few minutes. She felt eyes on her, heard whispers. But she kept her eyes on her reflection, willing herself to keep it together whenever she saw her eyes grow glassy.

The train juddered to a halt, just one stop from hers. The people in the seats across from her got off and a crowd of suited men stumbled on, laughing, swearing, faces red from the beer they'd drunk during a long lunch. As the train continued its journey, the men swayed down the middle, trying to find seats.

One man – tall with black hair and a bulging waistline – stopped next to Anna's seat. She kept her eyes on her reflection, saw him looming above her.

'Oi,' the man said to the others. 'Look, it's her.'

Anna's stomach dropped. She hunched her shoulders, moved closer to the window.

The man slid into the seat next to her, the smell of beer and curry invading her nostrils. He waved a newspaper at her face. 'That's you, isn't it? That radio presenter, the one who killed that kid?'

'And shagged Nathan Wheeler,' another man said, squeezing into the tight space to sit across from her.

She clenched her jaw, kept her eyes on her reflection, her chest starting to feel tight.

Breathe, Anna, breathe.

'Was he a good shag, then?' the man next to her said, getting closer, overwhelming the space with his presence.

She didn't say anything.

'Never mind that,' the other man said. 'How'd it feel to kill a kid?'

She closed her eyes, took deep breaths as other passengers looked up from their newspapers and books.

The man next to her put his face close to hers. 'Don't worry, we're all friends here. I'd have done the same if anyone touched my little boy.'

'You say that, mate,' the other man said, 'but would you seriously? In the moment, could you actually stab a kid in a school uniform?' He did a jabbing motion with his hand. 'That takes something else, you know.'

Something dark.

Anna thought of the leather cutter she'd found in her pocket clanging onto the floor, saw the small traces of dried blood. Nausea swept over her.

Anna stood up. 'Excuse me,' she said, trying to get past them.

The man who'd been sitting next to her grabbed her wrist. 'Don't go. We're just having a little chat, that's all, fan to presenter. You don't want to ignore your fans, do you?'

Anna looked him in the eye. 'Let go of me,' she hissed.

The man across from her laughed. 'Yeah, mate, you don't wanna mess with a child killer.'

'Or Nathan Bell's mistress,' a woman whispered loudly to her friend nearby. Anna tried to yank her hand away but the man wouldn't let go. The train jolted and she stumbled, nearly falling into the man's lap. She scrambled up, trying to step over their knees as her face grew hotter, redder, her chest struggling to contain its breaths.

'Move your legs,' she said to them. 'Seriously, move, I need to get out.'

'Fucking move your legs,' a voice boomed. She looked up to see Elliot's brother Jamie standing over them all. He looked imposing in a black t-shirt, arms bulging, handsome face twisted in anger. 'I mean it, let her out.'

The two men exchanged a look. Then the man across from Anna moved his legs sideways so she could get out.

'We were only having a laugh,' the man said as she passed. 'Uptight bitch.'

Jamie leaned down and gripped the man's throat with his fingers, glaring at him as the man struggled to breathe.

'Stop!' Anna said, pulling at Jamie's arm.

He loosened his grip. Anna stumbled down the train trying to keep her face a mask as other passengers looked at her.

In the distance, she saw Ridgmont Waters' station come into view, relief sweeping over her. She jabbed at the open buttons as the train came to a stop, the doors sliding open. Then she exploded onto the platform, sobs welling up in her chest. Her bag slipped from her shoulder, the contents tumbling out. She knelt down, picking them up as people marched past her.

'Let me help.' She looked up to see Jamie crouching down to help her, his hair was wet, his long eyelashes sodden.

'Thanks,' she whispered as she stood on shaky legs. She went to walk but found she couldn't.

Jamie gripped her arm. She looked at him, alarmed. He loosened his grip then steered her away from the crowds to a bench beneath the stairs to the exit. She sat on it and put her head in her hands, trying to block out the world as Jamie sat next to her.

'This isn't easy for you either, is it?' he said.

She peered up at him. 'Maybe I deserve it? I k-k-killed your brother.'

His jaw tensed as he stared into the distance. 'Nothing's black and white, is it? I thought it was black and white when my mum first told me Elliot was dead. I presumed another kid killed him, a really fucked-up kid. And that I was going to go right out and fuck *that* kid up even more.' He looked at Anna. 'But then I discover it was a woman, a mum...a mum who had her kid with her at the time. And while the rest of my family were kicking off, saying they were going to find you, make you pay, all I wanted to know was what happened to the kid, to *your* kid.'

Anna looked into his eyes, saw they were shining with tears. 'Is that why you helped me on the beach that day?'

He shook his head, looking at his callused hands. 'I didn't mean to. I went wanting answers. Maybe I even wanted to hurt you too. All these rumours were swirling about you maybe knowing Elliot and I started to get angry again, started wondering if it really did play out like the papers said.' He looked at the scar on her cheek. 'But seeing what Elliot did to you right in front of my face.' He shook his head. 'I couldn't see you all bloody and beaten up at my feet.'

'Beaten up?'

'My dad,' he said, sighing. 'He's a bit over-enthusiastic with his fists.'

'Does he like sending threatening emails too?' Anna asked, thinking of the emails she'd been getting…and the leather cutter she'd found in her pocket.

'What do you mean?'

She looked into Jamie's blue eyes. Should she tell him? Could she trust him? It was madness, sitting here talking to the brother of the boy she'd killed. But it was like he said, nothing was black and white, was it? 'I've been getting emails from someone claiming to be the Ophelia Killer,' she said quickly.

'Threatening emails?'

'Sort of. Could it be your dad?'

'I don't know, my dad's more into physical retribution.' He frowned. 'The Ophelia Killer used foxglove poison too.'

'I know. In the emails, he implies he saw Elliot before he died. That Elliot *escaped* him.'

Jamie curled his hands into fists.

'Would your dad want to harm his own son?' Anna asked carefully.

'He already has, a bunch of times.' Jamie looked at Anna's shocked face and laughed bitterly. 'I know it's hard for you to wrap your middle-class head around, but yeah, my dad liked to give my brother a slap every now and again, me too, before l left.'

'Middle-class kids have their problems too, you know.' She looked towards the lighthouse.

He followed her gaze. 'I read about your dad. You found him on the rocks, right?'

Anna thought back to when she'd gone to the lighthouse to find her father. He often went there to prepare his news reports, especially when he needed some space. And he'd seemed particularly pensive that day. When she got there, she thought it was a pile of clothes on the rocks. Maybe he'd gone for a swim? She'd scrambled up then there he was.

She composed her face and looked at Jamie. 'So is your dad capable of poisoning Elliot?'

Jamie shook his head. 'I just can't see it.'

'Well, I think I just had an encounter with whoever's been sending the emails.'

Jamie frowned. 'What do you mean?'

'Someone bumped into me and left a leather cutter in my pocket.'

Jamie's eyes widened. 'Leather *cutter*?'

'The person sending me emails said they used it to cut holes from the victims' skin.'

Jamie looked at the pocket of her coat and put his hand out. 'Show me it.'

'I dropped it.' She swallowed. 'There was dried blood on it. I tried to go back for it but the train doors shut before I had a chance.'

Jamie jumped up. 'It might still be there. Where did you drop it?'

'Near the newsstand.'

'I'll go look.'

'Then what?'

'I'll take it to the police.'

'Wouldn't it be better if I did?'

He sighed. 'Fine, I'll call you. What's your number?'

Anna hesitated. Should she really be giving her number to him?

Jamie's blue eyes sank into hers. 'I know this is fucked up, us talking like this. You killed my brother. Every time I look at you, I see him.' His face softened. 'But I know you didn't mean to kill him, you were protecting your daughter. I'd do the same for Elliot. I *am* doing the same for him by talking to you right now because I have a feeling you're the only person who can help me get to the bottom of this. So will you just give me your number?' She looked into his eyes. 'Please?' he said.

She reached into her bag with trembling hands and scribbled down her number on a receipt. 'Text or call me.'

'Thanks,' he said, taking it.

A couple walked past, staring at Anna and Jamie, eyes flickering with recognition. Anna stood up. 'I should go.'

Jamie grabbed Anna's hand. She jolted, stepping away. 'Chill! I just want to give you my number too,' he said, taking her hand again. 'Just in case you need me.' He quickly wrote his number on her hand with her pen then looked her in the eye. 'Any problems with this sick fuck emailing you and the fuzz won't help, call me.'

Then he walked away.

Anna smoothed the skirt of her black dress down that evening, tucking her hair behind her ear. She'd spent longer than usual getting ready, applying make-up like it was war paint. She'd had a long hot shower too, desperate to wipe the day's events away before Florence's birthday gathering. When she closed her eyes, face up to the steaming stream of water, she saw flashes of the leather cutter that had been placed in her pocket again. She'd been stupid to drop it. Hopefully Jamie had found it but she'd heard nothing from him.

She thought back to their encounter earlier. He'd stepped in twice to help her now and yet she'd killed his brother. But as he'd said, getting to the bottom of the truth took priority now. This strange camaraderie they'd built up might be the key to doing just that.

When she was finally ready, she drove to her mother's bungalow to pick her up.

'Didn't you wear that dress to Betty's funeral?' Beatrice asked as she slipped into the passenger seat, eyeing Anna's dress.

Anna looked down at herself. She'd forgotten she'd worn it to their old neighbour's funeral.

'Well, it's too late to change now,' Beatrice said, wrapping her arms around herself as she looked outside. 'We're already late, thanks to you.'

Anna suppressed her irritation.

'You look nice anyway, Mum,' she said instead, taking in her mother's black trousers and green silk blouse. She'd even put in a bejewelled hair clip. But her trousers were crumpled and her eyeliner was already smudged.

Beatrice didn't say anything, just stared out of the window. She was no doubt anxious about being at a party full of people. Anna was surprised she was even going, she thought she'd pull out at the last minute. But then this was Beatrice's mother's seventieth birthday.

'Dad's old friend Ian will be there,' Anna said, trying to make her feel better. 'He's been helping out with the community centre so Gran invited him.'

Beatrice's jaw tightened just as it did each time her husband was mentioned.

'I bet the food will be good, you know what Gran's like,' Anna continued. 'She'll have spent all week making stuff.'

'Hmmm.'

'What did you get her?' Anna asked, gesturing to the present her mother clutched to her chest, a flat square object.

'I drew something for her, just a small sketch.'

Anna smiled. 'You're drawing again?'

She shrugged. 'A little.'

Anna smiled to herself. She loved of the idea of her mother drawing again. 'How thoughtful. What's it of?'

'Flowers from our old garden. I found a photo of our old house.'

'I think that's lovely, so personal.'

'What did you get?'

'Tickets to a show in London and a little locket with a photo of me and Joni.'

Beatrice looked at her sideways. 'Sounds expensive.'

'She deserves it.'

'Yes, only the best for your gran,' she said bitterly.

Anna frowned. 'That's not fair, Mum, you know how much she's helped me.'

'Yes, she's like a mother to you really, isn't she?'

'*You're* my mother.'

'Hmmm.'

'Why do you hate her so much?'

Beatrice flinched. 'I don't hate her.'

'You seem to.'

'She's too much.'

'What do you mean?'

'Sticks her nose in everything.'

'She cares.'

Beatrice shook her head. 'Overbearing.'

'Better overbearing than not caring at all,' Anna snapped back before she knew what she was saying.

Beatrice stared back out of the window, face closed. Anna sighed. What was the point?

They spent the rest of the journey in silence until they got to Florence's house. Beautiful exotic flowers adorned the door-frame, fairy lights delicately interlinked with them. Music and laughter tinkled out from an open window. In the background, the sea ebbed and flowed. After the downpour earlier, it had grown sunny again, the evening air very warm.

When they got out of the car, Anna's mother peered up at

the house, face fearful. Anna put her hand gently on her plump back. 'We'll find you a seat in the corner somewhere, get you a glass of wine, it'll be nice. I saw Leo and Trudy's car, they're already here.'

Beatrice nodded, eyes wide, present clutched close to her.

Anna took a deep breath. She knew how her mother felt. This was the first gathering she'd been to since what had happened. She knew everyone would be polite, charming, do what the British do best: pretend like nothing was wrong. But really they'd be watching her like a hawk, the sordid headlines percolating in their minds.

Game face, Anna.

She planted a smile on her face then pressed the buzzer. There was the sound of footsteps then the door swung open.

'Oh perfect, you're here!' Florence said, grabbing her into a hug. She was wearing a stunning silk dress over her plump body, swirling with bright colours, her lips painted pink.

'Happy birthday! You look so pretty, Gran,' Anna said. She peered behind her to see the garden outside and the beach beyond was crammed with people. Florence was popular because of the charity work she did in the town. So much for a small gathering. 'Wow, there's a lot of people here.'

'Yes, I think I got a bit too enthusiastic with the invites!' She frowned as she looked at Anna. 'How are you, poppet?'

She made herself smile, but she could tell Florence saw through the smile. 'I'm fine.'

'And you, Beatrice?' Florence asked her daughter.

'Okay,' Beatrice replied.

'Good. Well, thankfully the rain disappeared so most of us

are outside.' She led them out into the large garden. Fairy lights were hanging from the trees, and flames flickered in colourful lanterns dotted all over. A large table was set up on the veranda with enough food to feed triple the number of guests Florence had invited. People sat in garden chairs, or on colourful scatter cushions on the lawn, some out on the beach. Anna knew most of the people there, including Maxine, Suzanne and some other friends who were gathered by one of the trees lining the garden. She waved at them and they waved back, faint smiles on their lips. 'It looks beautiful,' Anna said to her gran.

'Thank you, darling.' Florence turned to her daughter. 'You have a reserved seat, Beatrice, that big comfy chair you like on the veranda. Leo and Trudy are here, they'll be sitting right next to you. You go chat to the girls,' Florence said to Anna, handing her a glass of wine. 'I'll take your mother to Leo and Trudy. You need a night off from everything. And don't worry a jot what people think,' she added in a low voice, 'they all have their fair share of skeletons in the closet. At least yours are out.'

Anna tried to smile. Didn't her gran realise this wasn't a night off, that she'd never get a night off now from the non-stop feeling of guilt and terror?

Anna took a gulp of wine and walked towards her friends. They went quiet as she approached. 'My gran's done a great job, hasn't she?' Anna said, peering around her.

One of her friends, a tall blonde called Chloe, narrowed her eyes at Anna. Anna frowned. She couldn't blame her. Her first husband had cheated on her, leaving her alone with her young girls while he went off with his mistress. Anna wanted to tell her what she had done was different. But was it so different?

'I've been meaning to get in touch with you all,' Anna said. 'I wanted to invite you over for dinner, maybe next week? It'd be good to catch up.' She looked at each of them meaningfully, hoping they understood she wanted to talk about what had happened with Guy.

'Catch up?' Chloe said. 'That's an interesting way of putting it.'

Anna went quiet, felt her face flushing.

'That'll be lovely,' Suzanne said quickly, touching Anna's arm lightly. 'I've been meaning to call you, Anna, but you know how it is with the kids...' She let her voice trail off, biting her lip.

'So how's Tuesday?' Anna said. 'Say, seven?'

'I'm busy,' Chloe said, folding her arms.

'Okay,' Anna said, not even bothering to suggest another night. It was clear Chloe wanted nothing to do with her now. 'What about the rest of you?'

'Sorry, Anna,' another friend said, nervously playing with the stem of her wine glass. 'We're all off to Italy the week after next and it's manic. Maybe when we get back?'

'Sure, totally understand,' Anna said, trying to battle away tears.

'Work's manic,' another friend said, standing close to Chloe. 'Probably best I give it a miss.'

'Maxine?' Anna asked her friend.

Maxine looked at each of their friends then smiled. 'Sure, I'll be there.'

'Me too!' Suzanne said, laughing nervously.

Anna let out a sigh of relief. At least she could rely on Maxine and Suzanne. She'd invite some of the other village girls too. She needed to start telling her side of the story. Sure, it didn't make her blameless but at least she could show them there was more to it than the papers were letting on.

'We'll see you Saturday at the party of course?' Suzanne asked.

Anna frowned. 'What party?'

'Little Timmy, Paula's son. He's in Joni's class at nursery, right? They're having a party at the outdoor swimming pool.'

Disappointment and guilt surged through Anna. So now her daughter was missing out on seeing her little friends because of what Anna had done. It was bad enough when it affected just Anna, but Joni too?

'Hello, Anna!' a voice exclaimed. She looked up to see Ian Roddis, her father's old producer and best friend smiling down at her. She'd always liked him. She smiled, and gave him a hug.

Over the next couple of hours, Anna tried to pretend everything was normal as she mingled with the other guests. But she could see it in their eyes and on the tip of their tongues: You *killed* a boy. You *slept* with Nathan Wheeler.

Eventually, Anna found herself in the corner of the veranda with Beatrice, Leo and his wife, Trudy. It seemed like that part of the garden was shrouded by some invisible force field that stopped all the fun and colour of the rest of the place from entering. The three of them sat quietly and rigidly, Beatrice and Trudy sipping from the same glasses of wine they'd started the night with. Leo was dressed in an ill-fitting suit, his dark hair slicked back, his cheeks pink from the heat and the wine he'd drunk. Trudy was wearing a grey cotton dress and black pumps, her thick dark hair pulled back severely in a neat bun. Anna's heart went out to her. She looked so unhappy.

'Trudy,' Anna said, leaning down to kiss her sister-in-law's pinched cheek, feeling slightly nervous. They hadn't seen one another since what had happened. They'd never exactly bonded anyway and this just made things even more uncomfortable. 'How are you?'

'Fine, thank you,' Trudy replied tightly, avoiding Anna's gaze as she stared ahead of her.

So that was the way it was going to be.

'Leo,' Anna said, nodding at her brother.

'Hello, Anna,' he replied in clipped tones. 'I see you've been enjoying yourself,' he added, flinging his hands towards the party guests she'd just been talking to.

'It's nice to catch up with people,' she said, ignoring the bitter tone to his voice. 'Did you see Ian's here?'

Leo peered towards their father's old best friend. 'I did.'

'You should say hello, I'm sure he'd love to see you.'

'Maybe later.' He looked Anna up and down, frowning. 'Didn't you wear that dress to Betty's funeral?'

Trudy raised an eyebrow as Anna's mother peered over.

Anna sighed. 'Yes, I forgot.'

'Bit inappropriate, isn't it?' Leo said.

Anna took a deep breath. 'It was too late to change, Leo. No one else cares here anyway, it was just us who went to Betty's funeral.'

He laughed bitterly. 'Yes, because that's all that matters, isn't it? What all these people think.'

Anna peered at his half-empty glass of wine. He got worse when he drank. 'Leo, please don't. Not here.'

'No, of course, silly me,' he said, flicking an invisible fleck from the collar of his jacket. 'We mustn't embarrass you in front of your important friends.'

Anna peered towards her mother who was staring straight ahead now, jaw twitching slightly.

'It's our gran's birthday,' Anna said, forcing a smile onto her face and taking a sip of wine. 'Let's just focus on that.'

'Smoke and mirrors,' Leo said in a loud voice, shaking his said. 'You are such a master of hiding the obvious. Let me guess, not one person has mentioned Elliot Nunn to you. Or Nathan Wheeler,' he added, looking her up and down in disgust.

Anna took a deep breath to calm herself.

'Wouldn't surprise me if Gran put a notice in the local newsletter,' Leo continued, 'enforcing a "don't mention the unmentionable at my party" rule so her precious granddaughter can spend the night pretending she's the angel everyone used to think she was.'

'Stop it, Leo,' Anna hissed. 'Just stop it.'

'Why? Somebody needs to pull you up. You haven't just ruined a marriage, Anna. You've taken a child's life too, all in the space of a month! There's something not right with you, Anna.'

Trudy nodded in agreement. Anna looked at her mother, pleading with her eyes for her to defend her. But Beatrice's face remained expressionless.

A darkness inside.

Maybe they were all right? Maybe there *was* no excuse for

killing Elliot Nunn? Now everyone knew Anna wasn't the Mrs Perfect they all took her to be, they saw what had happened to Elliot Nunn under the harsh gaze of reality: she'd killed a schoolboy. She didn't *have* to do it.

People turned and looked over. She ought to fight back, she usually would. But she was starting to think she deserved this.

'The problem with you, Anna,' her brother said, 'is that people have told you so many times how right and good and perfect you are, you truly believe it, even when the evidence is right there that you're not.'

'I do *not* think I'm perfect,' Anna said, voice rising, 'very far from it actually. I hate myself for what I've done, can't you see? So throw every stone you have at me, Leo. They won't hurt any more than the stones I throw at myself.' Anna leaned close to her brother. 'But for Gran's sake, please can we save the rest of your stone-throwing for another night?'

Brother and sister looked into each other's eyes. Then Leo turned away, folding his arms. 'Fine. But as long as you know you're as fake and as deluded as our father was.'

Beatrice clutched her bag so tight at the mention of her husband, her knuckles went white.

'Leave Dad out of this,' Anna said.

'Oh come on, we all know where your obsession with image comes from. He was shallow. That's why he jumped, he—'

'How dare you!' Anna screamed. The garden went silent but Anna barely noticed, anger mounting and mounting inside. 'How dare you say that about our father, *your* father, the man who held you when you cried and cuddled you when you needed affection? He was always there for us!'

Trudy looked alarmed. Beatrice simply shrunk further back into herself, closing her eyes.

'Was he always there for us?' Leo spat back. 'Are you really that deluded to overlook all those days and weeks he was away, all that time he was on his Dictaphone or computer? Or are you so alike, you barely notice? Poor Joni.'

'Leave Joni out of this!'

Anna looked at her mother beseechingly. Why couldn't she defend Anna, comfort her, like any normal mother would?

'What's going on?' They all looked up to see Florence glaring at Leo.

'Just telling Anna a few home truths, that's all,' Leo said, avoiding his gran's gaze as he drank more wine.

Florence put her hand on her granddaughter's shoulder, eyes exploring her face. Then she turned to her grandson. 'You're still that spiteful little boy who threw away Anna's tape recordings before her English assignment, aren't you, Leo? Just get out, right now.'

'Fine then,' Leo said, jumping up and grabbing his wife's hand. 'Come on, Trudy, we're clearly not welcome here.'

As he marched out, Anna felt everyone's eyes on her. She closed her eyes, head buzzing.

Florence took Anna's face in her hands, making her look at her. 'Don't let Leo get to you, poppet, he's just a jealous, bitter man.'

'But he's right,' Anna whispered.

Florence shook her head fiercely. 'Leo is shallow, you mustn't let him get to you. You see the layers, Anna, you see them and that's what makes you so very special,' she said with a strange intensity. She peered at her daughter then back at Anna again. 'Remember my friend from bridge, Gloria?' Anna nodded. 'She has a gorgeous house in Exmoor. We could just disappear there for a few days. Joni would love it, they have ponies practically in the front garden.'

'But I have to work.'

'Tomorrow you do, but then you have another five days until you have to go back. We can do Saturday to Wednesday. Imagine it: fresh air, long walks, books and scones. I think it'll do you good.'

Anna looked at her mother who was staring down at her knees now, brow creased. Then Anna looked at the party guests, who were trying to return to normal but couldn't help glancing at her every now and again, scandal in their eyes. She saw her friends huddled by the trees, heads bent as they whispered.

She nodded her head. Florence was right. She needed to get away before she lost her mind like her mother. 'Okay.'

After the party, Anna drove home in silence, Beatrice mute beside her. Streetlights swept past the windows, casting their glow over the pebbles and making them look like they were on fire. After a while, Anna couldn't keep quiet any longer.

'Why didn't you say anything to Leo?' she asked her mother. 'Even if you agreed with him, why couldn't you tell him to shut up, to leave me alone? Isn't that what mothers do, protect their children? You could see he was hurting me.'

Beatrice just continued staring ahead, her lips pursed.

'You know what?' Anna said after she pulled up outside the

bungalow. 'I think I'd rather you rant and rave at me like Leo did, *anything* but this silence.' She laughed bitterly. 'Who am I kidding? I need to stop hoping I'll ever get that from you.'

Beatrice flinched. 'I can't. It's just too much.'

'Everything's too much for you. Your mother's own love, *my* love.'

Beatrice looked at Anna briefly then looked away again.

'Oh for God's sake, say something, Mum! Please say something!'

Beatrice closed her eyes. 'I find it very hard to…to get a grasp on all the emotions. I worry they will take over and I – I will *break*.'

'What emotions?' Anna asked. 'What are you feeling?'

Beatrice flinched. 'Everything, every emotion, I'm filled to the brim with them.'

Anna frowned. She suddenly recalled a similar conversation she'd overheard her mother having with her father once.

'Is it because of what happened with Dad?' she asked softly. 'Or did you have problems with this before then?'

Beatrice avoided her gaze.

'Whenever it started, you're ill,' Anna said softly. 'Anxiety, depression, grief over Dad, God knows I understand, I think about him every day. But I talk about it too, to Guy when he was around, to Gran, to friends. Maybe it's best to get it all out.'

Beatrice shook her head vehemently. 'No.'

Anna took in a deep breath. It was so clear her mother was keeping things bottled up inside. She couldn't force this from her. 'You know you can always talk to me, don't you, Mum? It doesn't matter what I'm going through, I'm always here for you. I love you.'

Her mother turned to her, her face softening. She placed her hand gently on Anna's cheek, her eyes full of love. 'My baby girl,' she whispered.

'I'm so sorry you have to go through what you do, Mum, I really am.'

'And I'm sorry you're going through what you are, my darling Anna.'

Anna let out a sob and leaned her head against Beatrice's shoulder, her tears soaking her top. 'I'm so scared, Mum.'

'There, there,' Beatrice said, stroking her hair. 'It's okay, darling, it's okay.'

They stayed like that for a few moments. But then Anna felt her mother stiffen. 'I better get inside,' she said.

Disappointment flooded through Anna. She wiped her tears away. 'Right. I'll walk you inside, make sure—'

'No, I'm fine,' Beatrice said curtly, opening the door. 'You get home.'

'Goodnight, Mum.'

'Goodnight, Anna.'

Beatrice got out of the car and walked down the path, the moonlight streaming over her, making her look like a ghost.

When Anna got home to her empty house, she stood in the centre of her living room, loneliness swelling inside her. She saw the anger and disappointment in her friends' eyes, the scandal in others. She heard her brother's self-righteous voice. All of it intermingled with flashbacks to the afternoon Elliot died, the spurting blood, the gurgling noises.

Her scar throbbed, her whole being seeming to ache with the effort of keeping all the memories inside.

She strode out of the house and grabbed her rake, walking to the dark beach. When she got there, she stared up at the full moon. Then she started dragging the rake through the sand, not even looking for cockles, just focusing on the rhythm of her rake going back and forth as the waves crashed nearby.

Chapter Nine

The house in Exmoor was the perfect getaway, a long sprawling brick-built cabin overlooking Exmoor's valleys. Joni was fascinated by the three ponies grazing in the fields nearby and true to Florence's word, the long walks and reading *did* do Anna the world of good. She was able to separate her time there from what was going on back at home, keeping the emails and nasty gift from the so-called Ophelia Killer and accusing articles a hazy distance away.

'See, I told you this would be good for you,' Florence said, pouring some wine into Anna's glass the first evening there.

'What can I say, you were right as always,' Anna said, peering out at the darkening valleys as she smiled to herself. 'It's lovely.'

'Good. I aim to please.' Florence frowned. 'I hope you've forgotten those horrible words your brother said?'

Anna sighed. 'Not really. And you know what? I can't blame him.'

'He's a vindictive little brat, Anna.'

'Is he? Maybe he's talking the truth. I did kill a schoolboy. Maybe you have to have a certain *darkness* to do something like that,' Anna said, recalling what the woman reading the newspaper had said about her.

Florence tilted her head. 'Darkness?'

'Something bad inside.'

'Why do you think that?'

'It takes someone to kill a schoolboy, doesn't it?' Her gran was quiet. 'I think that's why Leo hates me so much, he can see that darkness. It disgusts him.'

Her gran's face clouded over. 'That boy knows nothing.'

Anna looked down at her drink. 'Really? I think part of him blames me for Dad's death.'

Florence looked shocked. 'Why on earth would you think that?'

'I had an argument with Dad before he died.' Anna swallowed nervously. She'd never told anyone this. 'He came back in a hurry from somewhere. I wanted to talk to him, I hadn't seen him properly in days because of his work. I followed him around the apartment as he grabbed some bits. He snapped at me, told me to give him some space, that he needed to be somewhere. I guess I lost it.' She bit her lip, tears flooding her eyes. 'I told him he was a crap dad, that all he cared about was his work. All the things I knew would really hurt him and – and I *enjoyed* it. I liked seeing him hurt. He stormed out of the house and I noticed Leo had been listening to it all. I realised I couldn't leave it like that so I ran after him. That's when I found him.'

'Oh, Anna.'

'All those things I said—' She shook her head, tears falling down her cheeks. 'I tell myself the work he did on the Ophelia Killings drove him to do it but the truth was, it was those words

I said.' She took in a deep shuddery breath, the grief and guilt still so pure despite the passing of time.

'No,' Florence said, clutching her hand. 'You must *not* blame yourself. You know what this is, don't you? Fabricated guilt. You feel guilty about what happened to Elliot Nunn, and about the affair. The guilt is becoming a monster and seeping into everything else. You have nothing to feel guilty about, banish that emotion from your life!'

'Easier said than done. It's not just Leo, anyway, I see it in Mum's eyes too, she blames me. At least Leo says it outright.'

'Your mother struggles with emotions.'

Anna took a sip of wine. 'I think Mum and I had a bit of a breakthrough the night of your party actually. But then Mum did her usual and got all tense.'

'What happened?'

Anna told Florence about the conversation. Her gran's face softened. 'Oh my darling Beatrice. She does love you very much.'

'I wonder sometimes.'

'I've told you before, your father's death broke her.'

'But was it just Dad's death?' Anna asked, recalling the memory of Beatrice telling Anna's father how she felt too much. 'Has she always had a tendency for depression?'

Florence examined Anna's face then sighed. 'Yes, not as much but yes.'

Anna thought of how she sometimes felt herself spiralling. Was it something she'd inherited off her mother?

Florence seemed to sense her concerns and squeezed her hand. 'I don't think it's something that's inherent in your mother. I believe it was triggered by something.'

145

'What?'

Florence leaned back and frowned, as though mulling something over. 'When your mother was a teenager, there was a boy she liked. Peter.'

'She's never mentioned a Peter. I thought Dad was her first boyfriend?'

Florence shook her head. 'Peter was her first love.'

'Love? Wow, it must have been serious.'

'Your mother thought so. Her father and I weren't aware. Peter lived near the dockyards, his father worked there.'

'So he was from the other side of the tracks,' Anna said, making quotation marks with her fingers.

'Quite,' Florence said, raising an eyebrow. 'Your grandfather was an old naval man, very strict. He wouldn't have approved.'

'So what happened?'

'Peter died,' Florence said sadly.

'Oh no, how?'

'An accident on the dockyard. He'd started working there with his father. I can't quite recall, it was such a long time ago, but I do know he'd been running late meeting Beatrice and in the rush, hurt himself. Your mother was devastated. It seemed to trigger this anxiety in her, she hasn't been the same since.'

Anna took another sip of wine, absorbing what Florence had told her. No wonder her mother sank into such a depression after her husband died. She'd lost the two great loves of her life.

Florence's eyes filled with tears.

'Oh, Gran,' Anna said, 'it must have been hard for you too.'

'I think that's why she struggles so much with me. After Peter died, and we found out about their little relationship, her father was very angry. In the argument, Beatrice blamed us for his death, said if we weren't such "snobs" they wouldn't have had to meet in hiding and he may not have been in such a hurry to get away from work to meet her. It was irrational, of course. But this is the way teenagers' minds work.' Florence shook her head. 'I tried to reach out for her, comfort her, but she just pushed me away, said I was overbearing. She's not like you and I, Anna. She doesn't welcome love and affection like we do.'

They smiled at each other, clutching each other's hands.

'You've kept me sane the past few weeks, you know,' Anna said. 'I really don't know what I would do without you. Sometimes I wish—' She stopped.

'What do you wish?'

'I wish *you* were my mum. Is that a bad thing to say?'

Florence smiled sadly. 'Not at all. But you're not, you're my beautiful talented wonderful *granddaughter* and that's just as good.' She held up the empty bottle of wine. 'Looks like you need a refill.'

Anna strolled down the cobbled streets of Lynmouth, Joni pointing at the seagulls from her pushchair. Anna looked out at the craggy cliffs and peaceful sea. They'd be heading back the next day. She felt a rush of anxiety. But then she shook her head. She needed to be stronger. Her gran was right. She'd been allowing herself to wallow in guilt for too long. She had to go back home and face what she had done, for Joni's sake. She needed to stop running away from it. And part of that was getting to the bottom of these emails from the so-called Ophelia Killer.

'I'll be sad to go back tomorrow,' Florence said.

'Me too,' Anna replied. 'But you know what, I feel ready to go back. I feel stronger.'

Florence smiled. 'Good, that was my intention. You just needed to gather yourself. I'm not saying it will be easy when you go home but your mind will be in a better place to deal with it.' They paused by a small clothes shop. 'This looks nice.'

'Not much space for a pushchair,' Anna said. 'You go inside, I might go up to the little pier, we can meet there?'

'Good idea.'

Anna strolled down the street towards the pier, smiling up at the sun. When she arrived there, she stared out at the sea, pointing out the fish swimming below to Joni.

Laughter rang out next to her. She turned, saw a young couple sitting down on the bench nearby. They huddled over an iPad, the girl swiping its screen as the man drank an iced coffee.

Something caught Anna's eye on the screen, a photo of Elliot's parents, hands conjoined, sombre expression on their faces. Above them was a headline: *World exclusive: Elliot Nunn's parents tell their story!* Then beneath it: *Anna Graves Ophelia Killer Copycat?* It was an article from her local newspaper, the *Ridgmont Waters Chronicle,* written by her old friend Yvonne.

Anna put her hand to her mouth, stifling a gasp. The woman reading it looked up. Anna quickly lowered her face and strode back away from the pier, her heart thumping. She pulled her phone from her bag, finding the article.

Paula and Neil Nunn have exclusively revealed the autopsy on their son Elliot showed he'd been poisoned by foxglove before he was stabbed by Anna Graves, the exact same poison used by the notorious Ophelia Killer who terrorised Ridgmont Waters twenty years ago.

'We think Anna Graves did it,' Elliot's father told us. 'She got obsessed with the case, like her dad did back in the day with all those news reports he did. She poisoned Elliot, he ran off so she stabbed him.'

'Jesus,' Anna whispered.

'What's wrong?' She looked up to see Florence watching with worried eyes.

'Read this,' she said, handing over her phone.

Florence took the phone, her eyes widening as she read the article. 'What utter rubbish,' she said, handing Anna's phone back in anger. 'Don't let this worry you, honestly. The *Chronicle* has turned into a trash rag, the website is even worse. It'll probably be taken down soon anyway, they can't report on an ongoing inquiry.'

'People will still read it though, especially if it gets into the print edition.'

'People with an IQ the same as my shoe size. Ignore it.'

But as they walked back to the car, all Anna could see was the headline: *Anna Graves Ophelia Killer Copycat?*

As Anna drove back from Exmoor the next day, she was quiet, thinking of the article Jamie's parents had sold. She was due to be making dinner for her friends that night. She hoped they hadn't read it.

After Guy picked Joni up, Anna spent the afternoon collecting mussels from the rock face near the lighthouse. She hadn't done this since she was a child, her father's death there turning what was once a fun family pastime into something tragic. But she needed to be close to her father and she felt closest to him there, at the lighthouse. She chose a spot well away from where his body had fallen. It faced right out to the sea and was thick with mussel colonies, their shiny black bodies stuck fast to the rocks, the sun gleaming down on them. She remembered when just her and her father had come here when she was very young, maybe six or seven. He'd taught her how to choose the right-sized mussels, not too small as they would be too bland, nor too big in case they were chewy. Just right in the middle. He also taught her to only take a few from each colony.

'We don't want to be too mean,' he'd say as he plucked a mussel from the rock, placing it in the green bag he'd brought along with the seaweed he'd put in there to keep them fresh. 'Just a few then move on a metre or so.'

'Isn't it mean taking them from their families though?'

He shrugged. 'You could say that about any animal we eat. But at least here we're leaving some space for others to flourish. They're hardy creatures,' he said, plucking another off and smiling at it. 'They survive harsh conditions by sealing themselves tight shut, closing their valves and sucking water within,' he said, tapping the inky shell. 'That's what you need in life, a tough shell to get you through the harsh spots.'

Anna peered towards the area of rock where her father died. 'What happened to your tough shell, Dad?'

And what was happening to hers? No, she wouldn't let all this ruin her. She'd hunker down, take comfort within her own shell, her community, the place she'd grown up in and loved. If she could just do her best tonight, make sure the girls understood she was still their Anna, then hopefully the rest of Ridgmont Waters would see that too.

'Anna?' She peered up to see a small blonde woman looking down at her.

Yvonne Fry from the local paper.

'I remember you used to do this when we were kids.' Yvonne crouched down, stroking her finger over a mussel. The shell cracked slightly. She glanced up at Anna. 'Oops, always been a clumsy oaf.'

Anna sighed. 'What do you want, Yvonne?'

'I think it's time you told your side of the story.'

Anna shook her head. 'I don't know how many times I've told you, but no. It's not going to happen.'

Yvonne's face went hard. 'I think that's a mistake, Anna. Public opinion is really turning against you. You need to do something to address it.'

Anna laughed. 'What are you, my PR manager?'

'I'm a friend,' Yvonne said softly, putting her hand on Anna's arm. 'I'm just looking out for you.'

'We haven't been friends for years. I didn't hear anything from you after you left school, despite trying to call you. So don't try to pull that card on me.'

'You're making a mistake,' Yvonne said, standing up and brushing the sand from her skinny grey jeans. 'You know what this community is like, one minute you're their shining starfish, the next just a mussel being pulled from its home, ready to be devoured.'

'You were never one for metaphors,' Anna said, trying to keep calm.

Yvonne smiled then she strode off.

That night, Anna checked her face in the mirror hoping the pink lipstick she'd dug out and thick black mascara would hide how tired she was. She smoothed down her cream dress, and took a quick sip of wine, peering out at the table she'd carefully set in the garden outside. It was on a raised wooden platform that allowed glimpses of the sea and the lighthouse. Not enough for Anna, but at least the sea was close by. It was silly, she'd known the girls for many years but tonight she felt nervous, like she was meeting them for the first time, and that thin glimpse of the sea wasn't enough to help calm her.

That encounter with Yvonne hadn't helped. She'd tried to wipe it from her mind as she prepared the mussels earlier, tugging the 'beard' out – the hairy-looking fibres attached to the shell – carefully scrubbing barnacles and grains off the shells. It usually cleared her mind, focusing on the task at hand, not letting any other thoughts intrude, her own personal form of meditation. But it didn't work this time. All she could think of were Yvonne's words.

You know what this community is like, one minute you're their shining starfish, the next just a mussel being pulled from its home, ready to be devoured.

She peered at the clock. Ten past seven. Her friends were due at seven but she knew what it was like when you had kids, you could never predict when you'd get out of the house.

She checked the mussels which she'd left simmering in onion, garlic and herbs. They didn't need long to simmer, most of the work came in preparing them. She'd made some crusty bread too which was in the oven, as well as spicy wedges.

She wandered outside, sitting down with her glass of wine and peering out towards the ribbon of sea. It was still so hot, so close. Strange how it had been like this twenty years before too, when the Ophelia Killer had been terrorising The Docks.

About that itch that needs scratching. I still haven't scratched it properly. Elliot didn't die at my hands, after all. Not long though, not long...

Anna shuddered, pulling her blue shawl around her shoulders. No, she refused to think about all that tonight.

She looked at the clock again. Five more minutes had passed. She frowned, checking her phone. Nothing. She quickly sent a text message to all her friends then went back into the kitchen, lowering the temperature on her hob. The mussels would spoil if they overcooked. The girls had all agreed they hated the dilly-dallying when people went to others for dinner. So it had become a habit to have dinner ready right on time. She wished she'd waited now.

Her phone lit up. She quickly picked it up to see it was a text from Suzanne. *Sorry, Anna. I've been deliberating over this all afternoon and I've decided not to come over. Gertie got picked on at school today because of the fact I'm friends with you. Having talked to Jez tonight, I think it best we have some distance for a bit, for the kids' sake. xx*

Anna sank into her chair, staring at the text for what seemed like an eternity. At least Suzanne had been honest, not made up some excuse. But it still stung. Her phone buzzed again. It was Maxine.

So sorry, Lissie just puked everywhere. I'm going to have to give it a miss. x

Then two more text messages from her other friends with

excuses. Anna thought of what Yvonne had said to her. So that was it, she was being ostracised? Maybe it was what she deserved. You kill a local schoolboy, what do you expect? Why had she *ever* expected her life could return to normal? That was it now, all normality out of the window.

She gulped down her wine, then poured herself some more, the waves a melancholy orchestra in the distance. She picked up her phone, googling her name. She knew she shouldn't but wine and disappointment made her want to punish herself. The internet was full of speculation about her, rumours, lies, truths. One post on a well-known website for mums – the same website Anna had turned to for advice after having Joni – had received over one thousand responses already. The title was *'Am I being unreasonable to think there's something amiss with Anna Graves?'*

Some people jumped in defending Anna, but many echoed the original poster's comments.

I never quite warmed to her when I listened to her on radio, one wrote. *I enjoyed listening to her, her sarky comments and the way she obliterated that racist idiot who called in once. But I've always found her a bit* cold, *if that makes sense?*

Others brought up the kiss she'd shared with Nathan – or the affair, as many people were referring to it.

Anyone who can go to dinner with the wife of the man they're shagging must have a cold heart, one person said, referring to a photo that had been published of Anna and Valerie enjoying dinner while Anna was pregnant.

Is the child even her husband's? another asked.

But worst of all were the carefully worded barbs they directed at her in relation to what she had done to Elliot.

When I first heard, I thought I'd do the same. But the more I think about it, the more I have to wonder. He didn't actually try to hurt her kid, did he? Couldn't she have just run away?

Bit convenient she had a comb like that in her bag, wasn't it? another asked.

Anna couldn't stop reading, her eyes running down the comments, more appearing as she did so, her index finger swiping down and down and down, the jet black words piercing her pupils.

Her phone beeped, Jamie Nunn's number popping up. She quickly opened the message.

Just heard about the story my mum and dad sold, nothing to do with me. Went back to street but couldn't find shape cutter.

She hesitated a moment then wrote back. *Thanks for trying. And no worries about the article, I'm used to the bad press now. Even my friends hate me.*

It was a few minutes before she got another text. *You okay?*

She slugged more wine back. *Just cooked dinner for four friends, none of which turned up. Best to keep some distance, apparently. My fault.*

They're not real friends then.

I thought they were, that's the problem. Known them since school. Everyone seems to hate me, just made the mistake of looking online and you should see some of the comments. Anna looked out towards the lighthouse in the distance. Maybe she should hide herself away there until everything calmed down? Wouldn't that be better for Joni? She turned back to her phone. *I just hope this doesn't have an impact on Joni. Maybe she'd be better off without me around?*

There was no answer.

'Probably best,' Anna slurred to herself, putting her phone aside and staring up at the stars. 'At least you all have each other,' she said to the stars. 'It's just me here tonight, lonely old me.' She sat there for the next twenty minutes, drinking more wine, feeling more sorry for herself.

Then she heard her doorbell go. Maybe one of the girls had changed their mind? She jumped up and looked up at the bubbling pan. 'Shit,' she hissed, quickly pulling it off the hob, boiling water splashing onto her carefully applied make-up, making her scar sting. 'Shit, shit, shit,' she said again, wiping the water with a cloth and running to the door.

But instead of finding one of her friends there, Jamie was standing at the door in dark blue jeans and a short-sleeved, checked shirt, his fair hair combed back.

Anna looked at him in shock. 'How'd you know where I live?'

'My friend Charlie reckons herself a bit of a hacker. She tracked you down after your name came out, thought she was doing me a favour.'

Anna stepped back, fear rushing through her.

'I didn't do anything with the information, did I?' He raised an eyebrow. 'Other than turn up and try to save you from what looks like a non-existent suicide attempt.'

'*Suicide* attempt?'

'"Maybe she'd be better off without me around?"' he quoted.

'I meant I'd just run away for a few days! I wouldn't kill myself.'

'I can see that now,' he said. 'I'll leave you to it.' He went to walk away.

'Wait!' He turned back. 'Why don't you come in?' she said,

holding the door wider. Maybe it was the drink, or maybe it was the way he'd looked so worried about her. But she couldn't just let him go.

He frowned slightly, peering around him. Then he shrugged. 'Sure.' He strolled inside, looking around him. 'Nice digs. Never been in one of these new builds.'

Anna led him into the kitchen. 'I would offer you something to eat,' she said, gesturing towards the steam coming from the hob. 'But I've just overcooked the mussels.'

'Mussels? Nice.'

'I collected them myself.'

Jamie looked surprised. 'Didn't take you for the type.'

'I'm a Ridgmont Waters girl through and through, I'll have you know. No buying seafood from supermarkets for me. Not that all the hard work was worth it,' she said with a sigh. 'Not considering none of my friends turned up.'

'They probably have kids like you,' Jamie said. 'Must be hard getting out at night.'

'No, you're being polite,' Anna said, shaking her head. 'They just don't want to be associated with a child killer any more.'

Jamie stood awkwardly in the middle of the kitchen, his hands shoved in his jeans.

'Shit, sorry,' Anna said, raking her hands through her long hair. 'That was insensitive. I blame the drink.'

Jamie eyed the empty bottle of wine outside. 'A whole bottle to yourself?'

'Yeah, I'm pretty hammered,' Anna said, going to the fridge and getting another bottle of wine out. 'Want some?'

He laughed. 'Got any beer?'

She shook her head. 'Nope. No need ever since my husband left me.'

Jamie raised an eyebrow.

Anna laughed. 'Welcome to my pity party.'

'Well, considering it's a party,' Jamie said with a smile. 'I could probably stomach one glass of wine.'

'You don't have to, I'll be fine on my own,' Anna said, suddenly becoming conscious of how she must appear to him. 'You don't have to feel sorry for me.'

'I don't. I feel sorrier for myself, I'm thirsty as hell.'

She laughed, pouring him some wine. 'Come outside,' she said.

He followed her out onto the decking and they sat down. He took a sip of wine and peered towards the lighthouse. 'Heard your family own the lighthouse.'

'My great great grandfather was a naval officer and decided to buy it.'

Jamie raised an eyebrow. 'Naval officer, hey?'

'Most of the men in my family are navy men, including my grandfather.'

'I've seen your gran at the community centre a few times, not your granddad though?'

Anna shook her head. 'He ran off with a ballerina, we never see him.'

'You're joking?'

'No joke. My gran met someone else though.'

'Another naval officer?'

Anna laughed. 'No, doctor this time.' The smile disappeared from her face. 'But then he died too, cancer.'

'Sorry,' Jamie said. 'My nan died of cancer, I wish that disease

158

would do one.' They were quiet for a few moments as they looked at the lighthouse.

'Elliot liked the lighthouse,' Jamie said after a while. 'He used to joke that as long as you stood up there on the rocks with your back to The Docks, the view was good.'

'The Docks aren't so bad,' Anna said. 'My dad would come up and look at the cranes and the concrete, said it reminded him of the town's history.'

'History? I thought the dockyards had been wiped from Ridgmont Waters' history, too ugly.'

'They shouldn't be wiped out,' Anna said. 'We should be proud of them.'

Jamie laughed. 'Honestly, the way you village lot romanticise about the place. It's a cesspit of poverty.'

Anna felt her face flush. 'But the dockyards had their heyday, I just feel it's important we don't lose sight of that.'

'Really? Don't lose sight of how they worked people to the bone?' he said, blue eyes sparking with anger. 'Or how as soon as Thatcher felt like it, they pulled the plug on the place and left people jobless, people like my dad?'

Anna looked at him in surprise. She hadn't expected a political outburst like that from him. She wasn't sure why, maybe it was his age. But then he must only be a few years younger than her. The age gap felt larger than it was though, she had her daughter, her house, her high-profile job. And him…she inwardly kicked herself. What a snob! Just because he was a mechanic who lived in The Docks didn't mean he was immature.

He shook his head. 'Sorry, I sound like my dad. It's just there's so much bullshit in Ridgmont Waters, so much glossing over. I just wish people saw the reality. It's like all the nuclear waste buried here,' he said, looking out over the lawn. 'Dig deep enough and you'll get a nasty little surprise.'

'That's an urban myth!'

'Trust me, it isn't.'

'We better get some masks on then.' She picked a napkin up and placed it over her mouth.

He shook his head, laughing. 'I've been listening to one of your shows on iPlayer. You're actually quite funny.'

Anna smiled to herself. 'Why are you surprised I'm funny?!'

'Dunno. Just expected something a bit more serious.'

Anna raised an eyebrow. 'It isn't a comedy show. We do serious stuff too, you know.'

'Like that dog who could do cartwheels?'

Anna laughed out loud, taking a sip of wine. 'High jumps actually.'

They both smiled, holding each other's gaze.

Jamie's phone rang. He looked down at it. 'My mum,' he said with a sigh.

'You should get it.'

'I should. But I just need a break from it all tonight, you know?'

'I know. What's she like, your mum?'

Jamie took in a low breath. 'Battered by life. Battered by my dad too.'

The taste of wine in Anna's mouth turned bitter. 'Sorry to hear that.'

Jamie's jaw tensed. 'Doesn't happen much now, she knows how to keep in line. She used to talk back, used to be clever too. She liked writing, even talked about writing a novel one day. Then she met my dad and turned into a baby-making, dinner-creating, kitchen-cleaning machine which was fair enough when we were young. But nothing should be stopping her now.'

'Happens a lot.'

'Yeah. She was a good mum, still is sometimes. I just think when you get beat up enough and downtrodden enough, you go numb and dumb.'

Anna thought of her own mother. 'Interesting you use the word numb,' Anna said. 'That's how I describe my mum sometimes.'

'Did your dad knock her about too?'

Anna shook her head vehemently. 'Not at all! She's ill. Severe anxiety. Been like it since he died. She'll sink into these bouts of depression, just sit in the dark and not say anything. Or she'll freak out, start crying, shout.'

'Must've been hard for you after your dad died?'

Anna nodded. 'Must've been hard for you too,' she said softly, the alcohol making her brave. 'To lose your brother.'

He looked down into his wine glass. 'Yeah.'

'Why don't you hate me?'

He peered up at her under his dark eyelashes. 'You know what I asked the police officer assigned to us when I found out what happened to Elliot? I asked about your kid. I wish you hadn't killed Elliot, Anna.' His eyes glanced over her scar. 'But I understand why you had to.'

Relief flooded through her, making her eyes fill with tears. 'Thank you, Jamie. Thank you for saying that. The guilt is just—' She swallowed a sob down. 'It's so hard. I know it's more difficult for you, losing your little brother. But still, the guilt I feel just tears me apart sometimes.'

His face filled with emotion. He leaned forward, his fingertips nearly touching hers. 'Anna, you shouldn't—'

His phone rang again, interrupting him. Anna pulled her hand away. 'You really should answer it. Anyway,' she said, turning away, 'I'm pretty tired.'

Jamie nodded, standing up. She led him back inside towards the front door. As she opened the door, her phone buzzed. She looked at it, seeing it was an email from the Ophelia Killer. Jamie followed her gaze.

'Another email?' he asked.

Anna nodded, feeling herself start to tremble. She opened the email, saw the subject line: *'So apparently you're copying me...'*

Jamie grabbed the phone off her and quickly deleted it. 'Don't let whoever it is get to you,' he said. 'Delete all of them. Block the address.'

She nodded. 'You're right.'

'You okay?' Jamie asked.

She looked into his blue eyes which were full of concern. 'I'm fine.' She opened the front door wider. 'Thank you for coming.' He took one last look at her then walked into the darkness. Anna looked down at her phone again. Was deleting the emails enough to make her feel safer?

She sighed and walked up to bed, exhausted. That night, she dreamed of leather cutters sliding into soft young skin, blood dripping down her fingers. When she woke the next morning, there was a text from Jamie on her phone.

I've been thinking about those emails you've been getting. So I contacted the friend I mentioned, Charlie. She thinks she can trace them, if you still have any. Want to meet her?

Anna sat up in bed, her head throbbing from all the wine she'd had the night before. *Yes. How about the lighthouse?* she wrote back. *It's quiet there, especially around the back, on the rocks. Neutral territory. 7?*

She didn't get a text back for a few minutes. Then her phone lit up. *Fine. See you there.*

That day at seven, she headed to the lighthouse, walking around the back and sitting on the rocks there, just as she'd done as a teenager many years before. The spot where her father had died was behind her, hidden by the curve of the lighthouse.

The sun was starting to set above the sea, turning the sky pink. Anna wrapped her cardigan around herself, exhaustion sweeping over her.

She heard movement behind her and turned to see Jamie walking towards her, wind making his fair hair blow about. He sat on the rock next to her, staring out to sea.

'You mind?' he asked, gesturing to a packet of cigarettes he'd pulled from his pocket. 'Gave up a couple of years ago but taken it up again recently.'

'I guess not.'

He popped a cigarette in his mouth, striking a match and protecting it with cupped hands as he lit it up. 'My friend Charlie will be late, she's always late,' he said, blowing a circle of smoke out.

'How do you know her?'

'School. I wasn't there much but when I was, she kept me sane.'

Anna wondered if she might be his girlfriend.

'How's your head?' Jamie asked with half a smile.

Anna grimaced. 'Not great. Sorry about last night, I was a bit of a mess.'

He laughed. 'No worries, you were funny.'

A tall blonde girl approached then, a satchel with skulls all over it slung across her thin frame. She had a pierced nose, a crown tattooed into her cheek.

'Charlie,' Jamie said, standing up.

'The famous Mrs Graves,' Charlie said when she got to them, looking Anna up and down. She turned to Jamie. 'You know how fucked up this is, don't you, Nunn? You meeting up with the bird who killed your brother?'

'Ignore Charlie,' Jamie said, 'she's always like this, toxic like the nuclear waste under our feet,' he added, winking at Anna. 'You just have to roll with it.'

'So, your phone,' Charlie said, putting her hand out to Anna. She was wearing a ripped lace glove, her nails painted different colours.

Anna dug her phone from her bag and handed it over. Charlie sat cross-legged on the rocks, pulling a small laptop from her bag. She connected the phone to it with a USB lead then started tapping.

'You just talk amongst yourselves, this could take a while,' she said, waving her hand at Jamie and Anna. Anna walked over to the lighthouse, placing her hand against the grainy white wall. It was warm, the day's heat having seeped into it.

'I was thinking when I walked back last night,' Jamie said. 'That article my folks did was out of order but what if some of their theory is right? What if whoever poisoned Elliot and is emailing you *is* a copycat Ophelia Killer?'

Anna thought about it. 'It's a possibility.'

'Shit,' Charlie whispered as she stared at her laptop.

They both looked at her. 'What?' Jamie asked, strolling over.

'The tower block,' Charlie said, looking up at him. 'The email was sent from the tower block. It's your fucking dad, isn't it?'

Anna shouldn't have been surprised. The police thought it might be him and didn't he have motive? But it still felt strange to hear it confirmed.

Jamie's face filled with rage. 'I'll go talk to him.'

He went to march away but Charlie grabbed his arm. 'Jamie, be careful.'

He shrugged her away. 'I can handle my dad.'

Charlie looked into his eyes, her own concerned. 'Can you?'

'Yeah,' Jamie said, 'yeah, I can.' Then he scrambled down the rocks.

Anna wrapped her arms around herself as she watched him. 'Will he be okay?'

Charlie nodded. 'He can handle himself. Though last time he fought with his dad, he ended up in hospital.'

'God, what happened?'

'It was when Jamie decided to move out. He was sixteen. His dad stopped trying to slap him around when it was clear Jamie was big enough to fight back. But I guess they had a pretty bad argument. His dad knew he wouldn't have a chance with just his fists, you seen the size of Jamie's arms? So he grabbed an old cricket bat.' Anna flinched. 'Yeah, you can imagine the damage. Jamie moved out after that.'

'I can't let him get hurt,' Anna said, thinking of how terrible it would be, first Elliot dead then Jamie badly beaten up. 'I should stop him.'

She went to follow Jamie but Charlie grabbed her wrist, stopping her. 'No, you need to let him deal with this himself. You won't be able to stop him anyway. Once Jamie gets an idea in his head, that's it.'

'His dad sounds awful.'

'He is. The whole estate knows what a cock he is.' Charlie frowned. 'Wasn't always that way, apparently. My mum reckons he was quite the catch back in the day, just like Jamie. A real smooth talker, intelligent too. But then his kid brother died, sent him a bit loopy loo. That said, most of us are loopy loo in The Docks.'

They were both quiet for a few moments, peering over at The Docks.

'Well, better go,' Charlie said eventually. 'Take care, yeah? And look, for the record, Elliot was a good kid. Something must've seriously gone wrong for him to hurt you and try to hurt your baby. *Seriously* wrong. But you did the right thing stabbing him up.' Then she strode down the hill, her satchel bouncing against her slim back.

Anna looked towards The Docks again. Could Jamie's father really be the person sending the emails? If so, that led to another possibility: what if Jamie's dad really *was* the Ophelia Killer? He'd lived in the area all his life. Anna placed him at about fifty now. That meant he'd have been in his thirties when the murders took place. He could have even poisoned his own son. Sounded like he'd subjected Elliot to physical abuse most of his life after all.

What would he do to Jamie now?

She took a deep breath. She couldn't just stay here and wait to find out. She'd go home and hope Jamie texted her. But two hours later, Jamie still hadn't been in touch, not even replying to her texts. Anna paced her living room. She could call him, but what if his dad answered? Maybe she should call the police?

Just as she was thinking that, there was a knock on her door.

She peeked through the glass to see Jamie standing there, his eye swollen, his nose bloody. 'My dad busted my phone,' he said through chattering teeth. 'I didn't know how else to talk to you.'

She pulled him inside, grabbing some tissues and pressing them against the cut above his eye. He didn't flinch, just stared at her, blue eyes unblinking.

'What happened?' she asked.

'He denied it,' he said. 'But then he would, wouldn't he? He went mental at me daring to even ask if he'd sent you emails. Then he saw your name flash up on my phone. That's why I wanted to come over, give you the heads up.'

Anna peered out of the window. 'You think he'll come here?'

'Hopefully not. I lied, said you have a police patrol outside your house. But I wanted you to know, just so you can be extra vigilant.'

'Thanks.' She looked at the cut above his eye. 'Shouldn't you go to hospital?'

He shook his head. 'I've been through worse, I'll be fine.'

Her heart went out to him. 'Oh Jamie, I'm so sorry.'

'For what?'

'For the fact you've had to put up with a dad like that.'

'I guess Charlie told you about him then.'

Anna nodded.

He shrugged. 'You get used to it in the end. It's like that hard skin on the bottom of people's feet. The more you walk on rough ground, the tougher it gets.' He walked to the front door. 'I better go. I just wanted to let you know.'

'Thanks.' She looked out at the street. What if someone saw him leaving her house?

He followed her gaze. 'Don't worry, no one saw me come in.' He put his hand on the doorknob then paused. 'Dad said something when we were arguing.'

'What's that?'

'He said our families go way back, yours and mine.'

Anna frowned. 'Do they?'

'I asked the same but he changed the subject. Well, you know, punched me in the face if you count that as changing the subject.'

Anna flinched.

He laughed softly. 'You village girls.'

Anna crossed her arms. 'You keep saying that. I'm not some helpless rich girl, you know.'

His face hardened. 'I know you're not helpless, Anna. You stuck up pretty well for yourself against my brother, didn't you?'

Her eyes flooded with tears. She turned away.

'Shit, sorry. That came out all wrong.'

'You shouldn't apologise. You're right. I deserve it.'

'You're not the only one full of guilt.' He took a deep breath. 'You know the knife he hurt you with? That was mine.'

'I had no idea,' Anna said, surprised.

'I gave it to him before I moved out. I had to get out of there, get away from my dad, even if it meant leaving Elliot alone. Before I left, I gave Elliot a knife. He was just a kid but I couldn't leave him with nothing.' His nostrils flared as he looked

168

down at the floor, blue eyes growing glassy. 'Maybe if I didn't give it to him, he'd be alive right now.' He looked up at Anna again, eyes glancing over her scar. 'And maybe you wouldn't have that scar on your face.'

'Oh, Jamie,' Anna said, putting her hand on his arm. 'This isn't your fault.'

He looked at her hand, face softening. Then he moved away from her, eyes going hard again. 'Better go. Take care, yeah?' Then he strode down the path.

Anna returned to work the next day to discover Nathan was leaving the station. Valerie had insisted he leave, according to one of the few admin staff who still confided in Anna. They'd upped sticks to move closer to his in-laws, apparently. Anna had mixed feelings. Half of her was sad to have lost a friend. The other half was relieved. It would have been so awkward to have to work together again given the circumstances. But then she berated herself for thinking like that. Her mistake had led to him having to leave.

No, *their* mistake. Still, she couldn't help feeling guilty.

But there was one bonus, which Anna noticed while the team looked through the newspapers: coverage had died down about the affair.

'Why the smile?' Georgia asked Anna.

'Oh, just good not to see my face in any of these papers,' Anna said.

Georgia nodded. 'I bet it's a relief.'

'It is.'

Heather raised an eyebrow. 'Really? I think you secretly enjoy it.'

Anna stared at her. 'Pardon?'

'The attention,' Heather said without looking at her, flicking through the papers as she took a sip of herbal tea. 'I think you enjoy it, Anna.'

'I've had threats to my life on Twitter, Heather. My child's life.'

'All brought on yourself,' Heather said.

Anna peered down at the newspaper she'd been looking at. Heather was a class-A bitch but she was right, wasn't she?

Heather shook her head. 'Your poor kid.'

Anna quickly looked up. 'Sorry?'

'Your little girl. Imagine what she's going to find when she googles you when she's older.'

Georgia's eyes widened. 'Heather...'

Heather folded her arms. 'It's true!'

Anna took deep careful breaths, trying to suppress her anger. 'I never thought you and I had much in common, Heather. But there is one thing.'

Heather narrowed her eyes at Anna. 'What's that?'

'Most of the people here hate us.'

Heather's mouth dropped open.

'But at least before the mistake I made with Nathan,' Anna continued, 'people seemed to like me. Not you though, Heather. They've always hated you, right from the start. I hear it every day.'

She could see Heather's face starting to go red, her eyes even growing glassy with tears. But Anna didn't care, her jibe about Joni the last straw.

'And it's not just because of one horrible mistake you've made,'

Anna said, leaning towards her and glaring at her. 'No, it's because *every* thing you say is poison. *You're* poisonous.'

Heather jumped up, banging her knee against the table and making her coffee spill. 'How dare you!'

'It's true,' Anna said.

'Right, that's it,' Heather said. 'I'm going to HR, bullying in the workplace!' She looked at Georgia. 'You heard that, Georgia! You're my witness.'

'I heard nothing,' Georgia said, looking at the assistant producer. 'Did you hear anything?'

The assistant producer shook his head. 'Nada.'

Heather scraped her chair back and ran outside.

As Anna watched her run away, she ought to have felt vindicated. But all she felt was terrible.

That night, Anna struggled to sleep, going over and over what she'd said to Heather. She shouldn't have stooped to her level. She'd just been so sick of the constant digs! She thought about what she'd said about Joni too. It was true. Anna's actions would have an effect on her. It was inevitable. Take the birthday party Maxine had mentioned. Joni hadn't even got an invite when the invites had poured in after Elliot died.

Anna woke the next morning determined. She wouldn't let her actions affect Joni. So she packed Joni's little swimsuit and sun cream and headed to Ridgmont Waters' outdoor pool. She was going to that child's party whether his parents liked it or not. She had to make a point, show people they might be able to shut her out, but they wouldn't shut her child out.

But as she walked to the swimming pool, she received a call that took the wind from her sails. It was from her solicitor, Jeremy. 'I just wanted to let you know your colleague Heather Budd has given a statement to the police, Anna.'

'What?!'

'She informed them about an argument you had yesterday *and* an incident before you went on maternity leave last year.'

'She's exaggerating,' Anna replied carefully, the incident from the year before coming back to her. 'She's sore after our argument yesterday.'

'I'm not too bothered about the argument yesterday,' Jeremy said, voice stern. 'But I am about this official complaint from a while back. What happened, Anna?'

'I was pregnant,' she said, wiping the sweat from her brow as she pushed Joni's buggy along the coastal path. 'My hormones were all over the place. She'd just started in the job and was already pushing her weight around, making everyone feel like crap. I – I lost my temper with her, told her to piss off.'

'And?' Jeremy asked.

'It wasn't pretty,' Anna said, recoiling at the memory. 'I grabbed her wrist, probably a bit too hard. But – but she was driving me crazy, and I was so exhausted and hormonal.'

'You should've mentioned it to me,' Jeremy said, a hint of irritation in his voice.

'It seemed irrelevant.'

'A complaint to HR about you being aggressive is very relevant. I need to know everything. What with the affair with Nathan Wheeler...' Anna cringed. 'Detective Morgan won't be looking too kindly upon all this.'

172

Anna stopped pushing Joni, heart hammering. 'You're saying it could affect the inquiry?'

'Yes, he could approach your HR department and get access to your records then use the incident as bad character evidence in his investigation into Elliot's death.'

'But I wasn't *charged* with Elliot's death.'

'No, you weren't. But you still might be if Detective Morgan begins to suspect it was more than a simple case of self-defence.'

Anna's heart went into a panicked flutter. 'But I had no motive, how can they possibly put this on me?'

'I said the same to Detective Morgan when I spoke to him.'

'You spoke to him? What did he say?'

'Not much, he was very cagey. But he did imply they're looking into a motive.'

Anna felt sick. 'What motive?'

'I have no idea, Anna. Is there anything else you want to tell me?'

'No, nothing.'

'Okay. I'll keep you posted.'

Anna put her phone down and stared out to the sea, shocked. What possible motive could the police be looking into?

She peered behind her. Maybe she should head back home? She suddenly didn't feel so ready for this. But then she saw Joni pointing into the distance towards the swimming pool, letting out a yelp of excitement.

She took a deep breath. She had to be strong for Joni. She planted a smile on her face and headed towards the pool. It was on the edge of the village, overlooking the sea, a square expanse of clean shallow water for children to play in. There was a small blue slide that swept into the water, and a large green dinosaur in the middle of the pool. Lining the pool was an old-fashioned ice-cream parlour selling delicious ice creams and milkshakes with views out to the sea. It was *the* venue for summer birthday parties in the village. Anna and Guy had talked about hiring it for Joni's first birthday too.

There were already parents and children gathered there, mums and dads frantically rubbing sun cream into their toddlers' plump red arms as the sun beat down on them, a table already a metre high with presents.

Anna wheeled Joni's pushchair towards the table, placing the present she'd got on there, ignoring the frowns directed at her. Out of the corner of her eye, she noticed Timmy's mother, a tall blonde woman called Paula, whispering to her husband as she stared at Anna. Anna could imagine what she was saying: 'We didn't invite her, did we?' Anna wondered if Paula would confront her. But knowing the people here, it would all be said in whispers, not to Anna's face. That was fine. Anna just needed to be seen here, show people the world wouldn't implode if her daughter attended one of their children's birthday parties.

Anna pulled Joni from her pram and laid her on her changing mat, gently wrestling her summer dress off and changing her into a swimsuit before slathering on more sun cream. She kept a smile on her face, nodding at people she recognised. When Joni was ready, Anna walked up to Timmy's parents with her.

'You look amazing, Paula,' Anna gushed. 'Thank you so much for inviting us.'

Paula smiled but her eyes told a different story. 'I didn't expect you here, Anna,' she said diplomatically.

'We wouldn't miss it,' Anna said, looking at Timmy who was in his father's arms. 'Timmy is such a lovely little boy, Joni adores him, don't you, darling?' she said to Joni, who was trying to reach for her little friend's hand. 'Guy's mother said he's one of the cleverest little boys in class.'

Overpower them with niceness, that's what her gran often said.

Timmy's father beamed. 'He's certainly a clever little thing.'

Paula looked at Anna, clearly trying to figure her out.

'Anna!' Anna turned to see Maxine jogging towards her, Lissie in her arms as her son trailed behind them. 'You came! Isn't it wonderful she came, Paula?'

Paula smiled tightly. 'Wonderful,' she said unconvincingly.

'Come on,' Maxine said, hooking her arm through Anna's. 'Let's get a chocolate milkshake and I can tell you all about Lissie's pukefest. Presents over there?' she asked Paula.

Paula nodded. 'And the milkshakes are on us, of course.'

'Thanks again,' Anna said, looking into Paula's eyes.

Paula's face softened and she nodded. 'No problem.'

Anna felt relief rush through her. It had worked.

Over the next hour, Anna and Maxine played with the children in the pool. It was clear Lissie really had been sick, it hadn't just been a fabricated excuse from Maxine to avoid Anna's dinner. That made Anna feel better.

'How was work?' Maxine asked, stretching out on her lounger as they watched the children play with some toys on a large towel.

Anna rolled her eyes.

'Let me guess,' Maxine said. 'Heather?'

'Yep.' Anna told her about their confrontation, missing out

what had happened the year before. Maxine didn't need to know about that, nobody did.

'Ha!' Maxine said after, laughing. 'Good on you, talking back. She deserved it.'

'Maybe. I felt a bit mean after.'

'No, you shouldn't. She's a nasty piece of work. Oh well, let's forget about her.' She looked around her. 'This is the life, hey?'

'It's nice,' Anna said, blinking up at the sun as she sipped another milkshake. 'I need this.'

'You do, hon.'

They both went quiet, lying back on their loungers as they watched the children. Anna looked at the couple next to her, both glued to their phones as they lay on their loungers. She shouldn't judge, hadn't her and Guy been like that once?

'Oh no,' she heard the woman exclaim.

'What's wrong?' the husband asked.

'Ben Miller, that boy from the newsagent? He's gone missing.'

People around the pool peered over.

Anna sat up, blood turning to ice. 'Ben Miller?'

The woman turned to Anna, frowning. 'Yes. He went missing after school yesterday, his father's frantic apparently. I wouldn't be surprised usually, it's a boy from The Docks after all, I imagine they go missing a lot then turn up, safe, sound and stoned.' She raised an eyebrow at another woman sitting nearby. Anna ignored the woman's snobbery and thought of Elliot's friend, the sweet boy who worked at the newsagents. She saw his dark hair, his long eyelashes. Then she thought of an email she'd received from the so-called Ophelia Killer: *About that itch that needs scratching. I still haven't scratched it properly. Elliot didn't die at my hands after all. Not long though, not long…*

'You okay, Anna?' Maxine asked.

She nodded, hiding her terror. 'Fine. I think it's time we headed back actually,' she said, looking at Joni who was yawning.

'Okay. Dinner next week, maybe?' Maxine asked.

'Yeah, sure, I'll text you,' Anna said, throwing stuff into Joni's changing bag before placing her sleepy daughter in her pushchair. She gave Maxine a quick hug, waved at Timmy's parents then headed back home, Ben Miller's disappearance scratching at her mind.

The next morning, Guy came to pick Joni up.

'I heard about Ben Miller. How's Kevin?' she asked, referring to Ben's father who worked in Guy's building.

'Very worried,' Guy replied. He clenched his jaw, taking Joni's bag. 'You didn't mention Heather Budd complained about you to HR.'

'How do you know about that?'

'My old school friend Duncan's a police officer, remember?'

Anna sighed. That was the problem with living in such a close-knit community. 'He shouldn't be telling you stuff,' she said.

'Well he did.' He leaned down to pick Joni up, giving her a kiss. 'Heather said you were violent in her statement, apparently.'

'She's exaggerating! I just held her wrist for a moment to stop her walking away, I needed her to hear what I was saying.'

'Why didn't you tell me about it?'

'You were so preoccupied at work, I didn't want to bother you.'

'It's a pretty major deal, someone making an official complaint at work about you being violent with them.' He peered down at Joni. 'I'm concerned.'

Panic fluttered in Anna's chest. 'What do you mean?'

'I have to question whether you have an anger management issue. And if you do, what does that mean for my daughter?'

My daughter.

She tried to compose herself. If Guy wanted to, he could try to get full custody of Joni considering what had happened lately.

'Guy,' she said softly, stepping towards him and looking into his eyes. 'You know me. You *know* I would never hurt our daughter.'

'*Know* you? I'm really not sure I do.' His phone buzzed in his pocket but he ignored it.

'You believe I'd hurt Joni?' Anna said, tears flooding her eyes.

His face softened. 'Of course not,' he said with a sigh. 'But you can't blame me for not exactly being thrilled with how things have been lately.'

Anna looked at him, unsure what to say. Half of her thought he was being unfair but the other half understood. Wouldn't she feel the same if they swapped positions and he'd been the one to kill a schoolboy *and* had complaints of violence against him at work? 'I promise Joni's safety and happiness is at the forefront of my mind,' Anna said. 'Like it's always been.'

He nodded, jaw still tense. 'Fine. I better go.'

She watched him walk away with Joni, trying not to imagine what it would feel like to watch him taking Joni from her for ever.

That evening, Anna pulled out some old photo albums, yearning for some positive happy thoughts. The first photo she looked at was of when Joni was born, sleeping against Anna's chest in hospital. Anna looked at her own face in the photo. She was clearly exhausted and already there was the hint of worry in her eyes that had never seemed to go away. Beside her, Guy beamed down at Joni, his hand on Anna's shoulder, a look of pride on his face. He had been proud, watching in awe as she'd screamed during labour. Her stomach sank with regret. Now what? He seemed so disappointed in her.

And wasn't she disappointed in herself too? There was only so long she could continue justifying her actions as more and more people turned against her, doubted her. Elliot needn't have died. And now Ben Miller was missing. Was that a coincidence?

Her phone buzzed. She looked down to see it was her gran.

'Hello, poppet, how are you?' Florence said when Anna picked up.

'Not bad.'

'I suppose you've heard about Ben Miller going missing?'

Anna nodded. 'It's worrying, isn't it?'

'Very. Have you had any more emails from that strange person pretending to be the Ophelia Killer?'

Anna thought about sharing her suspicions about Jamie's dad with her but decided against it. It would only lead to more questions about why she had those suspicions which in turn would lead to Anna having to tell Florence about the fact she'd been talking to Jamie. She wasn't ready for that. 'No,' she said instead.

Florence sighed. 'All sorts of rumours are flying around The Docks about Ben Miller's disappearance.'

'Like what?'

'People are saying the Ophelia Killer's back.' Anna's spine tingled with fear. 'A search has been set up for Ben tomorrow,' Florence continued. 'That's why I'm calling. I think you should come.'

'I'm not sure me turning up at The Docks is a good idea.'

'Kiara suggested you come along actually,' Florence said, referring to the woman who ran the community centre.

'Kiara?' Anna said, surprised. She was a real figurehead in The Docks, the residents there having a huge amount of respect for her.

'Yes,' Florence said. 'She thinks it's important people see you trying to help, might be a way to get you back in their good books.'

Anna laughed bitterly. 'I don't think I'll ever get back into their good books.'

'Don't be so harsh on yourself, poppet! Not everyone thinks like the Nunn family. Some people have told Kiara they'd have done the same themselves to protect their children. It's starting at ten, we're all meeting at the community centre. Maybe I'll see you there? I really do think Kiara's right, I think it'll be good for you, for the community. And we'll need all the hands we can get to find this boy. This is what we do, Anna, we help people.'

'Maybe. Actually,' Anna said, twisting the phone cord around her fingers, 'while I have you. Have the Nunns ever been connected with our family before the incident with Elliot?' Anna asked, remembering what Jamie's father had said to him.

'Not from what I know. Why are you asking about that?'

'Oh, it's just something Detective Morgan said,' Anna lied.

'He didn't say what the connection is?'

'No, he was being quite elusive about it.' Anna peered in at the kitchen as her pasta started bubbling over. 'I better go. I might see you tomorrow.'

She put the phone down and jogged into the kitchen, turning the hob down. As she drained her pasta, steam rising up and misting her vision, she thought about Florence's suggestion that she join the search. Wouldn't the community at The Docks frown upon her presence there? Or maybe Florence was right, maybe it was only Elliot's parents who hated her for what had happened?

But then after the revelations about Nathan, Anna just couldn't predict how people would react to her.

Her phone buzzed, interrupting her thoughts. She looked down to see it was an email from the 'Ophelia Killer'.

She went to delete it then noticed there was an attachment.

She quickly clicked on it then let out a gasp. It was a school photo of Elliot Nunn side-by-side with a school photo of Ben Miller. Both had dark hair, both had vivid blue eyes, long eyelashes and pale skin – just like the Ophelia Killer's other victims.

Anna's eyes flicked down to what was written in the email.

This one's a fighter.

Chapter Ten

The Fourth One

'That one was a fighter, wasn't he?' you mumble to yourself as you stare out towards the dockyard. You're drunk. It's been two weeks since the last boy. You wanted me to try another one last week but I feigned illness.

'I think I'll go outside,' I say. I don't like it when you're drunk. You've been pacing up and down the past fortnight, wanting more, needing more. You tell me I do too.

I think you're right.

'Wait.' You reach over, grabbing my wrist. 'Come here.' You're holding my wrist too tight. I wince. 'Come on,' you say, loosening your grip. 'I won't bite.'

I go to you.

'See that?' you slur, pointing towards the rusting crane outside. The skies are bright blue, making the rust even more noticeable. I don't like looking at the dockyards. It lies ugly across this part of town, the two cranes making me think of a photo I once saw of two soldiers tangled in barbed wire, caught dead mid-fire, arms still in the air like they might start shooting at any minute. Weeds twist out of the concrete ground below and the abandoned buildings are heavy with graffiti.

'That crane used to be a marvellous thing,' you say. 'Would lift submarine parts like they weighed nothing. Might look ugly now but they were majestic beasts in their day.'

I tentatively sit in the chair next to you. Your mood could change at any moment.

'And there,' you say, pointing to the larger building. 'That's where they kept the subs once they were done. My God,' you say, shaking your head, 'the first time I saw them, I was astounded.'

You throw back your head, emptying the contents of your glass down your throat. You hold the now-empty glass up to me and I reach for the bottle, pouring you more. 'I'd watch the train puff along the coast until it got here,' you say, 'letting all the workers out. I imagined being one of them.' Your face hardens. 'Young and naïve then, of course. The dockyards were starting to die even then, less and less work to be done. Death certificate pretty much signed.'

'Why did they close?' I ask, even though I know why. If I feign interest, you won't get into one of your moods.

'No more demand, simple. Thatcher didn't help either.'

You lean towards me, breath smelling of brandy and cigarettes.

'I'll tell you one day that sticks in the memory,' you say, eyes sparkling. 'I was watching for the train from this very spot then I see something out at sea.'

I lean towards you. Now this is interesting. 'What did you see?'

'White. Lots of frothing white creeping across the sea.'

'What was it?'

'Sea foam. It got everywhere, including the dockyards.'

'Foam? Like in the bath?'

You nod. 'Lots of it, muffled the whole town. You'd walk down the streets and it'd be there. I had to wear my wellies and snow coat. Great fun.'

You take another slug of drink and go quiet, peering out towards the sea.

I imagine walking through the foam, feeling it on my fingertips. I see the boys there, their bodies prone, pale, almost merging into the foam too.

'Will it happen again?' I ask.

'Not likely,' you mumble. You get a faraway look in your eyes. 'I made a friend that day with the foam. Just bumped into him at The Docks. We had a foam fight.' You lean forward, peering out of the window. 'Look at those two.'

I follow your gaze to see a boy and girl walking along the beach, the setting sun behind them.

'That kid looks a bit like the one I met that day, you know,' you say. 'Recognise him?'

I nod. 'I talked to him the other day.'

'Good. He'll be the next one.'

I hesitate. 'He's the sole carer for his mum, his little sister too. He's all they've got.'

'Then we'll be doing him a favour,' you say, impatient with me now, eyes hard. 'What sort of life is that for a boy? How would you feel, having to look after an ill person all day and night?'

I wouldn't mind, I really wouldn't. That's why I like it after they die, their bodies vulnerable, quiet. But I don't say that.

'Shouldn't we slow down?' I say instead.

'It's been two weeks!'

'But the police…' I let my voice trail off.

You laugh. 'They don't care about the kids in The Docks!' You clutch my hand, looking into my eyes. 'But we care, don't we? We give them more care and attention than they ever dare to dream of. We'll give that boy more care and attention than he's ever had too. Think about it. If he died, the first thought will be that his mother won't have someone to care for her. It'll all be about her, his little sister, not him. He'll be given a cheap funeral, a rush job. But we can take care over him, show him our love.'

I think of that an hour later as I lay the last flower by the boy's ear, smoothing down his wet hair. I imagine the water cleansing the poison from his system, making him clean and pure.

I imagine climbing into the pond next to him, laying down, cleansing the dark thoughts that are starting to dominate my nights.

'There,' I whisper, feeling like I'm saying goodbye to an old friend. 'It'll all be fine now.'

Chapter Eleven

Detective Morgan peered at Anna over his reading glasses, his phone in his hand. They were sitting in his messy office, police officers on their phones or computers outside.

'This photo doesn't prove anything,' he said.

She tried to hide her frustration. She'd called the station as soon as she'd got the email from the supposed Ophelia Killer with the photo of Ben Miller attached. But nobody took her seriously. So as soon as she woke, she went there in person. But clearly it was making no difference. 'It says this one's a fighter,' she said, pointing to the line in the email. 'That suggests if this *is* the Ophelia Killer and he has the boy, then he may still be alive?'

As she said that, she thought of Jamie's father. Maybe she ought to tell the detective about where Jamie's friend Charlie had traced the email to? Jamie had asked her not to. But what if his father was sending the emails?

And what if he really had Ben Miller?

'The boy's photo is on the news,' the detective said. 'He's local to you so it's the ideal way to wind you up. We simply can't justify wasting resources on this.'

'But a boy's life is in danger!' Officers outside peered up.

The detective raised an eyebrow. 'There's no need to shout.'

'Sorry, I didn't mean to shout,' Anna said, face flushing. 'Look,' she said, lowering her voice, 'surely just an hour of someone's time—'

'You did shout, Mrs Graves.' He tilted his head. 'Do you have a problem with your temper?'

'I don't have a problem with my temper,' she said carefully. 'I'm just worried about this boy.'

'We had an interesting chat with your colleague Heather Budd the other day.'

She felt herself tense. 'So I heard.'

'I'm beginning to wonder whether we had you all wrong initially.'

They held each other's gaze and she felt her stomach turn as she remembered what Jeremy had said about the police trying to build a case against her.

'I didn't realise I was being questioned all over again,' Anna said calmly. 'Should I call my solicitor?'

He broke her gaze, looking down at some paperwork. 'No need for that.'

She stood up. 'If you don't want to investigate this further, then fine,' she said, shoving her phone back into her bag. 'At least I can say I tried.'

He peered up at her. 'If you really want to help, there's a search taking place today.'

'My gran said.'

'Then feel free to join it.'

'I might just do that.'

She felt the detective's eyes on her as she walked out, police officers looking up with raised eyebrows as she walked through the investigation room. In the corner, she caught a glimpse of Ben Miller's photo, so young, so vulnerable...just like Elliot Nunn. Her stomach churned with guilt and regret and she quickened her step to leave the station.

As she walked out, she looked towards The Docks in the distance. She peered at her watch. Nine-thirty. Maybe she *should* go join the search? Kiara was such a respected member of the community, really had her finger on the pulse when it came to how they were feeling. If *she* felt Anna ought to go, then maybe she should? And it would show Detective Morgan she was serious about her concerns for Ben.

Yes, she'd go.

She headed in the direction of The Docks, sun already searing down on her, taking a route down the town's dark alleyways until they opened up onto the vast abandoned dockyards. She'd only been here once or twice as a kid with some friends. Most of the time, the kids from her village kept clear of this area. It hadn't changed, the cranes still looking as imposing as they had before, but somehow fragile too, like they might collapse over her at any minute. She pulled the hood of her thin cardigan up and walked across the concrete platform past abandoned buildings. A whiff of something – pot, probably – trickled its way towards her from a broken window, mingling with the low beats of some music.

She stepped out of the old dockyard into the sprawling estate: The Docks. Anna tried to steady her nerves as she walked through it. It was only a ten-minute walk from the village and yet it felt so different. She remembered the first time she visited The Docks, driven there by her dad for some community event he was involved with. As she left the comforts of her village, the scenery completely changed: pretty cottages and quaint pubs replaced by plain council houses and garish off-licences; Mercedes and Jaguars making way for wheel-less Peugeots and knackered-looking mopeds. She'd been shocked.

She felt the same now as she walked into the heart of the estate, past overgrown lawns and cars with bricks for wheels, trolleys littered here and there like art homages to an abandoned world. When she got to a line of shops, she paused, peering out at the sorry-looking green and the community centre nearby. There were about sixty people on the green sitting under the blazing sun. Some had even pulled old sofas out and were sitting on them drinking cans of lager; a group of children sat on a tatty picnic blanket, giggling in excitement. Anna recognised Ben's dad, Kevin, handing out photocopied photos of his son and her heart went out to him. And nearby was Yvonne Fry, notepad in hand, a photographer with her taking photos.

'Ridiculous, isn't it?' a voice slurred next to her. 'It's like a friggin' party.'

A man was standing nearby, russet hair a mess.

Jamie's dad.

He looked drunk, eyes out of focus as he swayed.

She went very still, heart thumping. Could he really be sending her those emails?

'And those kids.' He jutted his chin towards the children gathered on a picnic blanket. 'See them? S'like it's a fucking picnic, can you believe it? They did this when my boy died, even bought some candles. No disrespect but that annoys the fuck out of me.

It's like when Princess Di died, remember that? All those people lining the streets to watch her procession. I remember thinking then, "Jesus, look at these people, weeping and grieving for someone they don't even know." Same here, isn't it? It's ridiculous, half these people have never even met the kid. Just like half of 'em didn't know my Elliot. They all know this family is fucking cursed though,' he said clenching his fists. 'First Peter, now my boy.' He shook his head and stumbled away.

She felt a hand on her elbow and was roughly pulled back. She looked up to see Jamie glaring down at her. 'What are you doing here?' he hissed, pulling her behind a tree. He looked around him, eyes filled with concern. 'Are you mad? I just saw you talking to my dad.'

'He was upset,' Anna said, trying to match the drunk sad man she'd just been talking to with the person sending her those calculating emails. 'He was talking about someone called Peter.'

'Peter's my uncle,' Jamie said, raking his fingers through his hair. 'Dad's always going on about him.'

'What happened to him?'

'Some accident at The Docks.'

Anna frowned. Hadn't the boy her mother loved died at The Docks...and wasn't he called Peter? 'I think my mum was dating him.'

Jamie raised his eyebrows. 'Really?'

Anna nodded. 'Your dad said our families had history, maybe that's what he was referring to?' They both looked towards Jamie's father who was now mumbling to himself as he swigged from a bottle of cheap cider.

'Why are you here, Anna?' Jamie asked.

'I'm joining the search for Ben Miller.'

'Sure that's such a good idea?'

'I don't know. I got another email last night.' She told Jamie about the email. He looked at his father, his jaw flexing and unflexing. 'Is your dad capable of hurting a boy like Ben?' she asked him. 'He hurt Elliot, didn't he?'

'No,' Jamie said, shaking his head. 'No way, Anna. He treated Elliot like shit, me too. And yeah, people are intimidated by him. But he's never hurt anyone else and he's good friends with Ben's dad, known Ben since he was born. He wouldn't hurt the kid.'

'Are you sure?' she asked, looking Jamie in the eye.

He avoided her gaze. 'I'm not his shadow, am I? I can't say for sure.'

He looked over her shoulder and Anna followed his gaze to see her gran walking over, her flowery skirt blowing in the summer breeze.

'There you are!' Florence said, smiling at Anna. Then she noticed Jamie next to her, her brow puckering.

'This is Elliot Nunn's brother,' Anna said.

'Yes, I know. Hello, Jamie,' Florence said, giving him a tight smile. She looked at Anna. 'Everything all right?'

'Everything's fine. Jamie and I were just talking.'

'Are you joining us for the search too, Jamie?' Florence asked him.

He shrugged. 'Sure.'

'See you in a moment then,' Florence said, steering Anna away. 'What on earth are you doing talking to him?' she whispered to Anna as they walked towards the crowds, leaving Jamie behind.

'He's fine, Gran. He's been helping me, actually.'

Florence stopped walking, staring at Anna in shock. 'Excuse me?'

'We're been trying to figure out why Elliot tried to hurt me and Joni.'

'But that's up to the police!'

Anna sighed. 'I know. But he's been a real help, he even traced the emails from the Ophelia Killer to The Docks. We think they might be sent by his dad.'

Florence eyed Jamie's father who was swaying as he jabbed his finger at Jamie. 'I'm not sure that man could string two words together,' she said.

'Maybe. But he has a motive.'

'But the emails aren't threatening to you, are they? From the ones you've shown me, anyway.'

Anna sighed. 'Not overtly.'

'Just be careful, darling. You say Jamie's a good man but he has a motive too, just like his father. You *did* kill his brother. Are you sure he's just trying to help and there's not an ulterior motive?'

'Like what?' Anna followed her gaze towards Jamie who was now shaking his head and walking away from his father. 'I trust him.'

Florence sighed. 'Fine. I don't like to pry but I'd prefer it if you told me things like this, in case anything ever happened.'

'What do you mean?'

'Like you get hurt, Anna. Jamie has been in trouble with the police. Kiara tells me people are terrified of him on the estate.'

Anna looked towards Jamie. 'I find that hard to believe.'

'Well, people can surprise you.'

'Speaking of surprises,' Anna said. 'Was Peter, the boy Mum was in love with, related to the Nunns?'

'I don't think so.'

'Jamie's uncle was called Peter. He died in an accident at The Docks. It can't be a coincidence.'

Florence quirked an eyebrow. 'I had no idea. I only ever knew his first name.' She looked towards the crowds. 'Come on. Let's try and find Ben. Hopefully, he's in an allotment somewhere reading comic books.'

They strolled towards the crowds at the community centre, a small tired-looking building squatting in the middle of the green, the tower block Jamie and his family lived in right behind it. People stared at Anna as she passed but her gran didn't give them a chance to say anything, greeting people, thanking them for coming, introducing Anna like she hadn't killed one of their own. People seemed so taken aback at the fact Anna had shown her face in The Docks, they didn't seem to know how to react. Apart from Yvonne Fry, who watched with a raised eyebrow.

In the background, Jamie talked to two men. They looked scared of him, nodding at him, almost bowing down to him. Anna thought of what Florence had said, that he was feared on the estate. She just couldn't see it, he'd helped her so much.

Kiara, a large black woman with cropped hair and red-painted lips, clapped her hands together. 'Right then, everyone,' she shouted. 'We're here to find our boy Ben. You all have his photo, not that you need it anyway as we all know him, don't we? Can't miss him with that big smile of his.' She looked at Ben's father who smiled sadly. 'The lovely Florence here is going to get you into groups,' she said, gesturing towards Anna's gran. 'And her granddaughter Anna has been kind enough to join her, so make her feel welcome, all right?' She shot the crowd a hard no-nonsense look, clear she wouldn't take any harassment directed at Anna.

Yvonne started frantically scribbling away in her notepad, smiling to herself.

Anna gave Kiara a grateful look but she also felt embarrassed. If people didn't know who she was before, they would now.

'I want each group searching a particular area,' Kiara continued, 'so we don't get no duplication. Sound good?' People nodded. 'The police are here,' she said, gesturing to a police car by the shops. Anna looked over to see Detective Morgan standing by the car, his hands in his pockets as he appraised the crowds. His eyes caught hers and he gave her a curt nod. She nodded back. 'If you see any sign, bring him back here,' Kiara continued. 'And see anything that might be his? One person stays with it, another come get a copper. All clear?' People nodded. They seemed alert and intent on finding Ben Miller. It made Anna realise this is what a real community was, just like her dad always used to say about The Docks. 'Right, let's go, see you back here in an hour for some of Florence's delicious cake. Over to Florence.'

Anna watched her gran get people into groups. When she approached Jamie, he shook his head, stepping back and popping a cigarette in his mouth as he surveyed the crowds with narrowed eyes.

Florence led Anna to a small group of people. 'This is my granddaughter,' she said, turning to the group. Two of the teenage girls appraised Anna, sneering as they looked her up and down. 'Right then, let's go.'

They all trudged off across the green, the teenage girls giggling. One of the men in the group was taking it more seriously though, stopping every now and again to appraise rubbish on the ground. As they searched all the nooks and crannies of the estate, the sun seemed to beat down even harder on them, seagulls sweeping over them, the distant sound of a ship horn carried like a scream on the summer breeze.

Soon, the girls grew bored, trailing off, and it was just four of them left: Anna, Florence and two men. Anna talked to them as they searched the area. Both of them were unemployed, one had three children. He went to the seafront most days to scavenge for treasures washed ashore, copper piping and old tyres that could be resold for barely anything, but 'barely was better than nothing' as he said. He told Anna he admired her for what she'd done. The other man wasn't so supportive, just stared at her through narrowed eyes.

When they got to the back of the estate, they stopped at a row of abandoned houses backing onto a small hill.

'Hard work in this heat,' Florence said, puffing as she sat down on a broken wall to take a break.

'Why don't you head back?' Anna said, handing her some water. 'I can take it from here.'

'No,' Florence said, shaking her head as she took a sip of water. 'It's just the heat. Let's get this lot out of the way then we can head back.'

'We'll go look at those two,' one of the men said, pointing to the house to the left.

'Okay,' Anna said. 'We'll check these then. We'll make it quick, I'm sure the police have searched here anyway.' Anna put her arm through her gran's.

'They only searched half-heartedly,' Florence said as the two men walked off. 'I'm really not sure the police are taking Ben's disappearance seriously enough.'

'I am.'

Florence patted Anna's arm. 'You're a good girl for doing this.'

'I liked Ben.'

'Me too. Come on.'

They walked down the path of the first house. The windows were boarded over, the grass overgrown.

'Why aren't these places occupied?' Anna asked.

'Nuclear waste,' Florence said. 'Council said too much of it was buried in this part, could pose a risk.'

'I thought that was an urban myth?'

'Oh, all the rumours about your estate are, no chance I'd have let my girls move in there if that was true. But this bit.' She sighed. 'It's true, I'm afraid.'

Anna raised an eyebrow. So Jamie had been right.

'Should we even be here?' Anna asked.

'We're not planning to plant some flowers, are we? It's only the soil that's slightly toxic. But let's do this quickly, this heat is ridiculous.'

Anna looked at her gran in concern. She was so robust, the gardening making her fit. But that didn't stop Anna being aware of not over-exerting her, she was seventy now after all. 'You should have stayed back at the community centre and made sure no one nicked your cakes.'

Florence gave her a disapproving glance. 'They're not all thieves and layabouts in The Docks, Anna. Some are, granted. But there's a lot who are doing their best to get by.'

'Like Jamie Nunn,' Anna said, moving an old dustbin aside to reveal a squirming home for worms and lice.

'Really?' Florence said, raising an eyebrow.

'He's a mechanic.'

'A mechanic who likes to rough people up for his gangster boss, from what I've heard.'

Anna looked at her in surprise.

'You seem to like him though,' Florence said, peering at Anna sideways as she fiddled with the gate at the side of the house.

'He's all right. He could have hated me, but he wants to help.'

'Are you sure he wants to help?'

Anna tried the gate too and it sprung open. 'We've already discussed this, Gran. I know he's not doing this for me, it's more about figuring out what happened to make his brother do what he did.'

Florence sighed. 'Well, you know my views.'

They walked down a narrow alleyway. 'Smells musty,' Anna said, wrinkling her nose.

'All that nuclear waste,' Florence said, winking.

They stepped out into a small overgrown garden, the foot of the hill fenced off with spiky metal.

'Can't see Ben Miller coming here,' Florence said, looking around her.

'I don't know, kids like to get away from it sometimes. A place like this might make a good hideaway for a kid who misses his mum.'

'Like the lighthouse for you when you were a kid missing your dad?' Florence asked.

Anna smiled sadly.

'My poor darling, all you've been through, then and the past few weeks. It's not fair.'

'I'm a tough cookie,' Anna said, echoing Nathan's words to her.

'But cookies can crumble.'

Anna smiled. 'Exactly what I—' She paused. She could see something through the overgrown grass, a hint of red.

'What's wrong?' Florence asked, following her gaze.

'Isn't the uniform Ben wears at the newsagents red?' Anna asked.

Her gran nodded.

'There's something red over there,' Anna said. She trod through the long grass, the musty smell she'd first detected when walking into the garden getting stronger and stronger.

A red shirt came into view, crumpled and lying on the ground.

Anna paused, head swimming slightly.

Florence put her hand to her mouth.

'It could be anyone's,' Anna said quickly. 'We should let the police know though.'

'There's a pond there,' Florence said in a voice filled with doom, peering towards a sludgy-looking pond to the right of the garden.

They both walked towards it, treading down the long grass, breath coming out all ragged, the musty smell now rotting, making Anna retch, making her heartbeat pound so hard and fast in her ears she could barely hear her gran talking behind her.

And then Ben Miller came into view, lying open-eyed in the middle of the pond, his head surrounded by wilting flowers.

Anna heard a scream then Florence collapsed to the ground.

Chapter Twelve

Police sirens swirled around Anna as she sat in an ambulance with her gran outside the house they'd found Ben's body behind. Anna closed her eyes, hoping it would block out the images of Ben Miller, pale and naked, lying in the pond, five cruel circles cut from his skin, lifeless blue eyes staring up into the sky.

'Your gran will be fine,' the paramedic said. 'Just dehydrated.'

'Good,' Anna said, squeezing Florence's hand as people with white forensic suits walked into the garden. Florence was lying on a stretcher in the ambulance, her face very pale, blue eyes sad.

Detective Morgan approached from the garden, face ashen. He noticed Anna and walked up to her. 'So Mrs Graves, you found the body?' he asked.

'I found Ben, yes,' Anna said, feeling like every word she said now had to be carefully considered.

'Funny that.'

'I don't think it's funny,' Anna said.

'Weird then. Weird *you* would be the one to find him.'

'What are you saying, Detective?' Florence asked, struggling to sit up. 'My granddaughter was good enough to join the search. It could have been any one of these people,' she said, gesturing to the gathering crowds. Anna caught sight of Jamie amongst them, his eyes unreadable. Yvonne Fry was also watching, notepad in hand, her photographer click click clicking away.

'Let's get rid of this lot,' Detective Morgan said to one of his officers. He turned back to Anna and her gran. 'I'd like to ask you both some questions,' he said, taking his notepad out.

'We already told your officer everything,' Florence said.

'It's okay,' Anna said gently, knowing how important it was to appear compliant now. 'Of course we'll answer your questions, Detective Morgan.'

For the next five minutes, Anna and Florence explained once again how they found the body.

'And you only know Ben Miller through his work at the newsagents?' Detective Morgan asked Anna after.

'His father is a caretaker at my husband's office,' she explained. 'Ben came to our house a couple of times with his dad for work BBQs.'

The detective looked into her eyes. 'So he's been to your house?'

'Yes, like all the children of Guy's employees did.'

'I see.' He scribbled something down. 'So did you talk much to Ben Miller at these BBQs?'

'Very briefly,' Anna said, fear making her feel faint. He can't possibly be thinking *she* had killed Ben, could he?

'Why is this relevant?' Florence asked, the same fear etched on her face.

'Anyone who knew the boy is of relevance now,' Detective Morgan said.

'I hardly knew him,' Anna said.

'But you did question him after Elliot died?' the detective said. 'He told his father.'

Anna's face flushed.

'My boy!' She heard a man shout out behind her. Kevin Miller ran through the crowds, Jamie's father with him. A police officer went up to him, putting his hand on Kevin's shoulder. 'Sorry, you can't go through.'

'But he's my boy!' the man screamed. 'My dead boy.'

Anna and her gran exchanged pained looks.

Kevin looked towards Anna. 'Why are you questioning her?' he asked.

Anna felt like coiling up in a ball, blocking it all out.

'She found his body,' someone shouted from the crowds.

Rage filled Jamie's father's face and he went to storm towards Anna. But Jamie pulled him back.

'Always seem to be around dead boys, don't ya?' his father shouted out to Anna over Jamie's head. 'Make sure you ask that bitch about her whereabouts the past two days.'

Anna looked at the baying crowds as the police tried to push them away. She wrapped her arms around herself as Florence put her hand on her shoulder.

'I had nothing to do with this,' she whispered.

But as she said that, her gut told her something different. Deep down she felt she had something to do with Ben Miller's disappearance, even if she didn't quite know what.

After making sure her gran was settled at her house, Anna headed back to her estate. As she drew closer to her house, she saw Yvonne

Fry waiting for her, along with several other people Anna presumed were journalists.

Anna took a deep shuddery breath. She better brace herself. She parked on her drive then jumped out. The journalists ran to her, Yvonne at the front.

'Tell us how it felt to find Ben Miller's body, Anna,' Yvonne shouted, shoving a Dictaphone in Anna's face.

Anna batted it away, pushing her keys into the lock.

'Do you think the Ophelia Killer's back?' another one asked.

'No comment,' Anna said, opening her door.

Yvonne put her foot in the doorway. 'Anna,' she said, face very serious. 'It's time to talk.'

'No, it isn't, it's the very worst time to talk. Now get your foot out of my door or—'

'Or what?' Yvonne said, green eyes sparkling. 'I was chatting to your colleague Heather Budd yesterday. Seems you have some anger issues.' She cocked her head, examining Anna's face. 'Interesting *you* found Ben Miller.'

Anna felt tears spring to her eyes. 'Leave me alone,' she whispered.

'I'll leave you alone when you stop cropping up next to dead bodies.'

Anna used her foot to push Yvonne's foot away then slammed the door, leaning against it and sobbing.

Ophelia Killer Returns! Anna shoved the papers away the next morning, the breakfast she'd just eaten threatening to work its way up from her stomach. She put a shaking hand to her temple to massage away the headache that had been mounting all night.

She was sitting in the dark, blinds shut, even more journalists prowling outside. She'd heard a car screech past in the night, 'child killer' screamed out of the window, a bottle thrown out and smashed on the ground as the car sped away.

She'd barely slept, mind on Ben, on his body. Turned out he'd lain in the pond for forty-eight hours, meaning he had died not long after he went missing. Toxicology reports were still to be released but rumours were swirling he'd been poisoned…and the cause of death was drowning, just like the Ophelia Killer's victims. Everything was pointing to the same modus operandi as the Ophelia Killings, especially with the five circles of skin removed. The press was even drawing parallels with the fact there had been a heatwave during the previous Ophelia Killings too.

And of course, journalists were salivating at the fact Anna was the one who'd found his body. The interview Elliot's parents gave suggesting she was copying the Ophelia Killer came back to haunt her again, editorials that day hinting at some kind of connection.

But what, they couldn't say.

Anna picked the newspapers up and shoved them in the bin. She'd go to the newsagents and stop her order.

The newsagents.

She let out a sob as she thought of poor Ben Miller, the sight of his pale body making her head throb even more.

Her phone buzzed. She quickly went to it, hoping it was a message from a friend. She'd not heard from any of them after news got out about her finding Ben's body, not even Maxine or Suzanne. You'd think someone would be in touch to offer support, she had found a dead boy after all. But nothing. Instead, it was a text from Jamie. She hesitated before opening it. If her own so-called friends couldn't bring themselves to message her support, why would Jamie? Especially as people in The Docks were no doubt asking the same questions the press were.

She opened it quickly and read it.

Best keep your head down and keep inside. Lots of people angry around here.

Anna sank down onto her chair. She looked towards the front door. Would they come here, as they had to her gran's?

She wrote back with trembling fingers. *You have to know I have nothing to do with Ben's murder.*

There wasn't a reply for a while. Then her phone lit up. *I know. Look after yourself, Anna.*

She let out a breath of relief. It was silly, she barely knew him. But it meant so much to know he wasn't judging her like everyone else. With her friends, and even some of her own family, turning against her, that simple text felt like the world.

God, what had her life become that she was seeking validation from the brother of the boy she'd killed? And possibly the son of the man behind Ben's death. Wasn't that the theory they'd had, whoever was sending the emails took Ben? But it just didn't tally up in Anna's mind; the drunk, depressed man she'd met the day before sending such cold, calculated emails.

Her phone pinged again. She looked at it then felt her blood turn to ice. It was another email from the Ophelia Killer, the subject line: *A memento.*

She stared at it without opening it for a few moments. *Memento.* What did that mean? Only one way to find out.

She quickly opened it. There were no words, just an attachment.

Her finger trembled as she hovered over the download button. Then she pressed it, the photo slowly revealing itself.

She let out a gasp.

It was a long pale body; wet black hair; long eyelashes; vivid blue eyes staring up from a deathly pale face.

Ben Miller, dead in the pond.

Anna ran to the toilet and threw up.

She slumped to the floor and leaned back against the wall, staring up at the ceiling. Then she took a deep breath and looked back down at her phone, at the photo.

There was something about the lighting. She peered at the yellow sun which was low in the sky.

The photo had been taken in the early morning. And yet Ben's body had been found just before eleven. So it must have been taken *before* his body was found.

Should she call Detective Morgan? Or was that too risky when he seemed to have suspicions already about her? The fact was, she was in possession of a photo which had been taken before Ben was officially found. How would that look?

She found herself calling Jamie instead. 'I got another email,' she said when he picked up. 'There was a photo attached of Ben—' She paused. 'Of Ben dead.' She swallowed, feeling sick again. 'It was taken before I found him.'

'How do you know?' She explained about the sun. 'Jesus,' Jamie whispered. 'So that's it, whoever's sending the emails definitely killed him.'

'Or they found his body before I did.'

'Unlikely. It's not my dad, if that's what you're thinking. He's in bits, and he's not faking it. He's known Ben since he was a baby.'

Anna walked to her French doors, looking out at the garden, seeing the hint of blue sea in the distance. To the right, the light-house stood proud in the mid-morning sunlight, the dockyard's cranes stretched out beyond. 'I want to come to The Docks, ask some questions.' As the words came out, they surprised her. But she had to do this. She couldn't hide away. If she let this all unravel, it would come back at her, she knew it.

'No chance,' Jamie said. 'People hate you here. The police held a meeting at the community centre yesterday, people are fucking scared, Anna. Scared and angry. It kicked off, people even saying they want you questioned.'

'God,' Anna whispered. She wasn't feeling so brave now.

'Kiara was the only person who seemed to calm them down,' Jamie said. 'Said all the things I wanted to say, like you were just in the wrong place at the wrong time.'

'Maybe I should talk to Kiara?' Anna said.

'What's she going to know?'

'She knows the community.'

'And?'

'And maybe I can beat the police to finding out what's going on before they pin it on me.' Anna peered at the photo she had in the living room of her and her dad sitting on a towel on the beach, hair blowing in the wind as they smiled at the camera. 'My dad always said it's best to talk to the ones right in the heart of the community, that's where you get the real meat on the bone. I have to talk to Kiara.'

'You an investigative reporter like your dad now, then?'

'Maybe I always have been,' Anna murmured. 'Can you help me talk to Kiara?'

'You're asking a lot of me, Anna.'

'I have no one else.'

'So you turn to the brother of the kid you killed?'

Anna felt tears fill her eyes. 'You're right. This was a mistake, I'll—'

'Wait!' He sighed. 'I'll help. I'll let you know when it's quiet. You don't want to go when some youth group is going on. Then I'll meet you there.'

'I'm not expecting that of you, Jamie.'

'Tough. Just wait for my text, yeah?' Then he hung up.

An hour later, she got a text from Jamie. *Nothing on at 2.30, sound good? I can meet you by the lighthouse, walk you there?*

At two-thirty, Anna headed towards the lighthouse. Jamie was already there in black cargo shorts and flip-flops, his black t-shirt highlighting his tattoos, a baseball cap shadowing his eyes. He was peering up at the window Anna's father had jumped from, brow creased. When Anna turned up, he quickly looked away.

'Hot, isn't it?' she said.

He looked at her like she was mad, talking about the weather at a time like this. 'Yeah, boiling. Have this,' he said, taking his baseball cap off and putting it on her head. 'It'll protect your head from the sun. Good disguise too.'

She looked into his blue eyes. 'Thank you, Jamie. I know what a risk this is.'

He quirked an eyebrow. 'Risk? No one'll touch me, Anna. They know what'll come to them if they do.'

Anna examined his face. Was he really such a hard man? He

was helping her, wasn't he? Maybe he was like the mussels she picked, all hard on the surface but soft inside.

They started heading towards The Docks.

'How you doing?' Jamie asked, looking at her sideways.

'I keep thinking about Ben.'

'Me too. I was listening to your dad's old reports.'

She looked at him, surprised. 'Really?'

'Yeah, I have working ears, you know. He was good.'

She smiled. 'He was.'

'He got the atmosphere across well back then. It feels the same now, the mounting tension, you know? People are really scared, even covering over their ponds. You know all the gardens in The Docks were built with ponds in them?'

'Really?'

Jamie nodded. 'The guy who designed the estate thought it would add to its "ambience",' he said, using his fingers to make quotation marks. 'After the Ophelia Killings, people covered them all over. Was only a few years ago they started using them again.'

They were quiet as they walked through the dockyard, the cranes creaking above them, the slosh of dirty waves nearby. Anna turned to look at Jamie, taking in his pensive face, the stubble around his jaw line. His long lashes cast shadows over his tanned cheeks, his blue eyes were sad as they contemplated the sea.

He caught her watching him and held her gaze a moment. Then he quickly looked away. 'I feel sorry for Elliot,' he said, jaw tensing. 'It's like his death never happened. Does that sound stupid?'

Anna got a flashback to that day, felt Elliot's blood on her hands, felt the comb jutting into his skin. 'I'll never forget.'

'Me neither.'

'What was he like?' Anna asked. 'The little things. What was he into?'

'Computers,' Jamie said, smiling to himself. 'I reckon he would've ended up an IT geek. He thought Charlie was pretty cool.'

'She is.'

'He was quiet, some people thought he was a bit moody too. It wasn't that though, he just thought a lot, you know? He liked eating Oreos, was obsessed with them, should've been a fat bastard.' He laughed. 'And he liked watching *Fawlty Towers*, weird for a kid his age but he thought it was hilarious. That laugh of his, fucking mental.' Jamie shook his head, the smile disappearing. 'God I miss him.'

Anna wrapped her arms around herself, pursing her lips to stop crying. 'I'm so sorry.'

Jamie stopped, putting his hand on her arm. 'No more sorrys, yeah?'

'Okay,' she said, nodding

When they got to the fringes of the estate, Jamie stopped Anna, his callused hands on her shoulders. He pulled the baseball cap further down her brow. 'You got something to tie your hair up?' he asked.

She nodded, reaching into her bag and finding one of Joni's little hair bands. Jamie smiled. 'Peppa Pig. Nice.'

She tied her hair up and slipped her sunglasses on. Jamie looked her up and down. 'It'll do.'

They headed into the estate, Jamie nodding at people as he passed them, Anna lowering her gaze. When they got to the community centre, it was quiet, only a couple of people sitting on the grass outside with their children.

Kiara was tidying up when they got in, face shiny with sweat.

She greeted Jamie with a raised eyebrow. 'Long time since I've seen you here, Jamie. Come help me with these chairs, won't you?' He strolled over and helped her lift some chairs onto tables. She peered at Anna. 'New girlfriend?' she asked him.

Anna took the baseball cap and glasses off. 'It's Anna.'

Kiara raised an eyebrow. 'What you doing walking around looking like that, girl?'

'Jamie insisted.'

Kiara's face darkened. 'Probably for the best. What brings you here, sweetheart?'

'Just wanted to ask a few questions.'

'Ask away. You'll have to earn your keep though,' Kiara said, handing Anna a cloth and pointing to a particularly mucky table.

Anna took it. 'No problem, I'm an expert when it comes to food stains now.'

'I bet you are with that little girl of yours. How is she?'

'She's fine.'

'Florence loves that kid. Doesn't stop talking about her, or you.'

'We love her too,' Anna said as she started wiping the table down, Jamie placing more chairs on tables behind her. 'So how are things since Ben was found?' Anna asked Kiara.

'Not good,' Kiara said. 'People are scared. Even covering up their ponds, you know? It's like nineteen ninety-five all over again.'

'You remember all that?'

212

Kiara whistled. 'Do I remember all that? Oh yes I do. That rot is hard to scrub from the brain, darlin'. The first kid, poor Alex. We just thought it was an accident. Bad enough like that, drownings are never pleasant. But then when the other kid was found a couple of weeks later.' She shook her head. 'Was like a lightning bolt passed through the community. Everyone's nerves on edge, air electric and I don't mean in a good way. Same now. You have to remember, the Ophelia Killer claimed a victim every couple of weeks back then. People remember that so they're all looking over their shoulders like any day another child will turn up dead in a pond.' She paused, looking at Anna, her brown eyes filling with tears. 'It's like déjà vu, sweetheart, and I just think of your poor father, rolling in his grave.'

Anna focused on a particularly stubborn spot on the table. 'Gran said you knew Dad. What do you think he'd have made of all this?'

'He'd have a gut feeling about it, like he had that gut feeling about your uncle, Jamie.'

Jamie frowned. 'Uncle?'

'Peter. Anna's father always thought his death was suspicious.'

Anna paused. 'But that was an accident at the dockyard, right?'

'Yep, that's what everyone thought. But a few years later, your dad started asking a lot of questions about it, even implied Jamie's father was involved.'

Jamie shook his head. 'It was Dad's brother. Why would he hurt his own brother?'

Why would he hurt his own sons, Anna wanted to ask.

'Yeah, well, your dad got real angry,' Kiara said. 'Even sent Simon threatening letters.'

Jamie glanced at Anna.

'Letters?' Anna asked.

Kiara paused and poured them both some lemonade, handing the cups over. 'Yep, a couple of weeks before your dad died. Sorry, I thought you'd know all this. It's the reason for your dad's first stint in prison, Jamie. Just a few weeks, for sending death threats to Simon.'

'*Death* threats?' Anna asked. Kiara nodded. Anna thought back to the way her father had been before he took his life, pacing back and forth, anxious. 'Maybe that's what drove him to do what he did,' she whispered.

Jamie clenched his jaw and turned away.

Kiara nodded. 'I did always wonder. The straw that broke the camel's back. Poor Simon.'

'Interesting, isn't it?' a voice asked from the door. They all looked up to see Detective Morgan watching them. He strolled inside, looking at Anna. 'How a bunch of threatening letters could change the course of someone's life…a lot of people's lives.'

'What are you saying?' Anna asked as Kiara shot the detective a hard look.

'Revenge,' the detective said. 'It's quite a motive, isn't it?' He looked between Anna and Jamie. 'Everything okay here?'

'It's fine,' Anna said quickly.

'So these threatening letters Neil Nunn sent to your father,' Detective Morgan said to Anna. 'Why didn't you mention them to me?'

'I knew nothing about them until just now, when Kiara mentioned it.'

'You sure about that?'

Anna shook her head, confused. 'A hundred per cent.'

He looked at Kiara. 'Okay if we borrow your office?'

She nodded, pointing to a door at the back of the hall. Anna followed the detective into the small neat office while Jamie watched with hooded eyes.

'What's this about?' Anna asked, sitting on the chair the detective gestured towards.

'I just learnt about the threatening letters too,' the detective said. 'From your brother, in fact.'

Anna looked at the detective, incredulous. 'My brother? What's he got to do with this?'

The detective looked at her curled fists. 'He told me he found the letters when you all cleared out your mother's loft in June. He was pretty sure you saw them too.'

Anna thought of the big clearout they'd had at the bungalow back in June. Her mother had had one of her terrible episodes, the anniversary of Anna's father's death looming the next month. She'd disappeared into her own world, refusing to eat, having trouble sleeping. It culminated in her calling Anna and Leo over, insisting they clear the loft of all her husband's possessions. They'd spent the whole weekend clearing his stuff out, some of it going to Anna's, some to Leo's, the rest to the dump.

'I would've remembered seeing letters like that,' Anna said.

The detective quirked an eyebrow, writing something in his notepad. 'I spoke to one of your father's old colleagues too, Ian Roddis?'

Anna nodded. 'I know Ian. What did he say?'

'Your father was very worried by the threats, he couldn't sleep.'

'That's what we were just chatting about.'

He nodded. 'I heard. And you're sure you didn't read the letters?'

'I keep telling you,' Anna said, trying to banish the frustration from her voice. 'I didn't read them. I knew nothing about them until now. What are you trying to get at, Detective Morgan?'

'Well, if they caused your father's death then you'd have every right to feel sore towards the Nunn family.'

Anna went very still. He was trying to find a motive for her killing Elliot. She stood up. 'If you want to continue questioning me like this, I need to call my solicitor.'

The detective smiled, pushing away from the desk. 'I don't think that's necessary yet.' He peered out of the window at a few teenagers kicking a ball against the hall's wall. 'I'd be careful coming here alone though, Anna. There's a bit of bad feeling right now. People seem to think you killed Ben Miller. But then I suppose you have Jamie Nunn to look after you, one of my officers saw you enjoying a nice walk through the estate.' He tilted his head. 'I have to say, I'm surprised he's not torn you to pieces yet. Watch yourself with that one, I knew him well when he was a kid. Let's just say the violence and anger that runs through the Nunn family line doesn't stop with his father.'

He looked into her eyes then left the room.

Anna leaned against the wall, her eyes flooding with tears. There was a knock on the door and Jamie walked into the room. He watched her for a few moments then he walked over, crouching in front of her and putting his hands over hers. 'You okay?' he asked softly.

She turned away, trying to hide her tears. 'We shouldn't talk any more,' she said.

'Why?'

'We just shouldn't. You know how bad it looks.' She stood up, Jamie's hands slipping from hers.

'I'll walk you back,' Jamie said as he followed her from the office. 'You shouldn't be alone out there.'

Kiara raised an eyebrow as she cleaned a table.

'No, seriously, Jamie. We just have to cut off contact from now on. I'm serious. No more.'

Then she walked from the hall.

'Leo Fountain, Senior Accountant. How may I help?'

Anna twisted the cord of her phone around her fingers, cutting the blood off and turning them white. As soon as she'd got in, she'd phoned her brother. 'Hello, Leo. It's Anna.'

'I'm at work, Anna,' he said in clipped tones. 'I only gave you this for emergencies.'

'This is an emergency. Detective Morgan tells me you've been talking to him.'

'That's right. He came to talk to me yesterday.'

'Why?'

'He was just going over some notes from Elliot Nunn's case. Not sure why he spoke to me but then I suppose we've all been drawn into your mess.'

Anna rolled her eyes. 'What's this about Neil Nunn writing Dad threatening letters?'

'Exactly how it sounds.'

'Why didn't you tell me?'

'I thought you'd read them while we were clearing the loft out.'

'I would've said, you should've told me the moment you read them.'

'What's wrong, Anna? You sound incredibly uptight.'

'You know Gran and I found Ben Miller's body, don't you?'

Leo didn't say anything at first then he sighed. 'I do.'

'Yeah, well, thanks for the support on that one. Might've been nice to have some family around.'

'You're not the one who lost a child, Anna! Don't be so selfish.'

She closed her eyes. He was right. 'I mean, a phone call would've been nice. Gran fainted, you know.'

'I didn't know.'

'Back to the letters.' Anna sat on her armchair, exhausted already from the phone call. 'Detective Morgan thinks the letters might have contributed to Dad wanting to kill himself. He's trying to suggest that gives me a motive to hurt Elliot Nunn.'

'I see,' Leo said in a measured voice. 'That's why he asked for them.'

'So he has them now?'

'Of course. I very much doubt he'll use them as evidence against you, Anna. It's all a bit tenuous.'

'He might. He seems to really have it in for me at the moment.'

'Oh well,' Leo said casually.

Anna shook her head. 'I know you detest me, but surely you care for your niece?' She realised her voice was shaking. 'If I get done for murder, she loses her mother.'

'Murder?'

'Yes, Leo, murder. If Detective Morgan thinks I purposely

218

targeted Elliot Nunn as a form of twisted revenge, then they can do me for his murder.'

'I see. Anna, I do *not* wish that upon you. And I do not *detest* you.'

'It seems that way.'

'If you're referring to Gran's ridiculous party, we both said things we regret.'

'You regret them?'

He didn't say anything.

She sighed. 'Look, I just need you to be careful when you talk to that detective from now on. And tell me anything you know to do with the Nunns, all right? I don't want anything to come as a surprise. I know we're not the best of friends but we're still brother and sister.'

He sighed. 'Fine. I have copies of the letters, by the way. I've been scanning all Father's stuff into my computer at work for that archive project the library is doing. Thought I'd scan these while I was doing it. I can email them to you?'

'Yes, please do.'

'Give me two minutes.'

True to his word, exactly two minutes later, scans of the letters dropped into Anna's inbox. Maybe he did care after all? There were nearly thirty of them, dated one a day from the month her father died. In each, Jamie's father went on and on about why Anna's father's investigations into Peter's death were barking up the wrong tree and he needed to stop. As they went on, they became more and more erratic with the final one saying Neil would find Anna's father and 'lynch you up on one of the dockyard cranes'.

It made Anna sick to think her father had read these in the days before he died.

What also became clear to Anna as she read them was that Neil Nunn's writing style was completely different from the emails she'd received from the person proclaiming to be the Ophelia Killer, littered with spelling and grammatical errors; holding none of the chilling calm style of the emails she'd received. Unless Neil Nunn had taken writing lessons since he'd written them, or had been hiding his true writing style in the letters to her father, she doubted even more than ever that he'd sent the emails.

But if he hadn't, who had?

She leaned her head back against her chair, staring up at the ceiling. It was all unravelling and she just couldn't pick the pieces up fast enough.

There was a knock on the door, Guy dropping Joni off.

At least she had that, her daughter safe in her arms. But for how long?

That night, Anna dreamed of her father, his body broken and bleeding on the rocks. She saw her bare feet as she walked across the rocks, her flip-flops discarded below so she could run to him quicker. She still felt the jagged points dig into her soles, even smelt the seaweed and heard the roar of the waves like she was right there again.

'Daddy?' she whispered as she neared him, knowing he was gone but unable to bear it, to comprehend it.

His arm was at an odd angle, flung above his head, bone jutting out at his elbow, blood pooling on the rocks below. She wanted to move it back into place, make it better, but she knew she couldn't, wouldn't ever be able to.

'Daddy,' she said, kneeling beside him, rocks sinking painfully into the skin of her knees.

His eyes were closed, his thick greying hair smeared with blood and sand. She heard movement above and looked up just as a dark figure disappeared from the open window of the lighthouse, long pale-blue curtains billowing out in the wind.

Her father's eyes opened, his fingers circling her wrist. 'Look,' he said. 'Look, for God's sake, Anna!'

Anna woke with a start, heart an erratic beat against her chest. She wrapped her arms around herself and bent over, whispering her father's name. Would she ever stop seeing him like that in her nightmares?

She took a deep breath, pulling herself together. Then she slipped out of bed and looked out of the window towards the lighthouse.

'Oh Daddy,' she whispered. 'What a mess.'

She sighed and padded to the bathroom to get some water. As she passed Joni's nursery, she felt a breeze on her shoulders.

She frowned. She wouldn't have left a window open in there. She darted into the nursery, reeling when she saw the window was half open. Then she ran to the cot, relief flooding through her when she saw Joni was fine. She gently picked her up, holding her sleepy form against the thunder of her heart.

The window must have been opened by someone.

Oh God, what if whoever did it was still there?

Anna quickly walked into her room with Joni, turning on the bedside lamp as she gently laid Joni on her bed. Joni yawned then turned around, clutching her little blue teddy to her chest.

Anna frowned, staring at the teddy. Under the lamp's yellow light, it looked like the teddy had marks on it. She leaned closer then clamped her hand over her mouth to stifle the scream that was about to abrupt.

Five small circles had been cut out of the teddy's tummy. Attached to its furry ear with a safety pin was a handwritten note:

Don't forget me. TOK

Chapter Thirteen

'Oh God,' Anna whispered. She snatched the teddy away from Joni and Joni instantly opened her eyes, reaching out for it.

'Sorry, darling, Mummy will get you a new one.' She grabbed the phone by her bed and dialled 999, stroking Joni's head.

'Someone just broke into my house,' she said in a trembling voice as soon as the operator answered. 'They were in my daughter's nursery. It's Anna Graves.'

A few minutes later, sirens punctured the silence outside. Anna jogged downstairs, holding Joni close to her, trying to shush her as she cried for her teddy. Anna opened the door to two police officers.

'Is everything okay?' the female officer asked.

'No,' she said through chattering teeth, staring out into the darkness. 'No, everything is *not* okay.'

She explained what had happened as she led them back up to Joni's room. The two police officers exchanged a look when they saw the teddy. The woman officer carefully picked it up and slipped it into a plastic evidence bag.

'It's the Ophelia Killer's signature,' Anna said, feeling frantic, terrified. 'Five holes cut into the skin, see?'

'We see, Mrs Graves,' the policewoman said.

'He – he was in here,' Anna said, looking around her.

'Can you stay anywhere else tonight?'

She thought of her gran. She couldn't wake her in the middle of the night like this, worry her. And she couldn't bear going back to her mother's place. Staying at Leo's was out of the question and none of her friends seemed a possibility any more, either. 'Can I get some protection over the next few nights?'

'I'll find out if we can set up a patrol.'

They managed to find two police officers to sit outside in their car. But Anna didn't sleep a wink the rest of the night. She just sat up in bed, watching Joni sleep, jumping at any sound.

When daylight came, she got a text from Jamie.

Charlie noticed the fuzz outside your house when she drove past. Everything okay?

Anna wrote back. *House broken into last night, message from so-called Ophelia Killer left in Joni's nursery. We're unharmed though.*

Anything I can do? I'll go see my dad, torture the truth out of him if I have to.

Your dad didn't send the emails.

How'd you know?

Writing style. I saw the letters he sent my dad.

Bad?

Yeah but not as bad as receiving emails from the Ophelia Killer. If you need anything, call, yeah?

Okay. Thank you.

Anna looked down at Joni who was still sleeping, the restless night taking its toll. She gently stood up then walked into the en-suite, watching Joni through the open door as she quickly showered. After she got changed, Joni started stirring so she took her downstairs, peeking out to see a police car still sitting outside. She took tea out to the officers.

'Thanks for staying,' she said.

''Fraid we'll be heading back soon,' one of them said, taking the tea.

'But you'll be back tonight?'

The two officers exchanged a look. 'Been told we haven't got enough people on duty.'

'You saw the note!' Anna said, pulling Joni close.

The officer shrugged. 'Sorry, they're our orders, love.'

'Who gave the order, Detective Morgan?'

They avoided her gaze.

She sighed. 'Fine, it's not your fault.'

She marched back inside then grabbed her phone, calling the detective.

'It's Anna Graves,' she said when he answered. 'Why can't you assign a couple of police officers to me?'

He sighed. 'Resources. Have four officers off ill. We can't spare them.'

'But I've been threatened.'

'Not specifically.'

'Jesus! Can't you see whoever's sending those emails means me and Joni harm?'

'Not really, Mrs Graves. Like I've said before, it's just someone trying to get a bit of attention. Why don't you stay somewhere else if you're so concerned, what about your mother's?'

'I can't, she's ill. Plus I don't want to put any more of my family in harm's way.'

'Ill?'

'She suffers from anxiety.'

'I see,' he said, a knowing tone in his voice. 'Your grandmother's? A hotel?'

'I don't want to put my gran in harm's way either. Looks like I'm going to have to fork out for a hotel.'

'I thought money wouldn't be a problem for you,' he said, sounding surprised.

Anna laughed, incredulous. 'I don't *own* the radio station. Plus I'm a single mother now.'

'And we don't have money pouring from our veins either. Look,' he said, voice softer. 'The threat just isn't big enough to justify dedicating two officers to you, I'm sorry.'

'So am I.'

Anna slammed the phone down in frustration. Her phone buzzed. She looked at it, saw it was another text from Jamie.

Just checking in. Everything okay? Fuzz looking after you?

No, she typed back. *Not enough resources so they've all going home. Going to have to stay in a hotel I can't afford tonight.*

I'll come over after work.

Anna looked at the text in surprise. *No, honestly, it's fine. Thank you anyway,* she typed back.

I'll just sit outside in the van, keep an eye.

She looked at Joni who was babbling to herself as she played on the floor. All her friends seemed to be ditching her one by one with each new revelation. She couldn't possibly let Guy know what had happened, he'd definitely try to get custody of Joni then.

Who else did she have?

She quickly sent a text saying yes before she thought better of it.

That evening, a white van parked outside her house and Jamie stepped out, peering around him before walking to her door. He was wearing grey tracksuit bottoms, a white t-shirt half tucked into the waistband. His arms looked more tanned, face more stubbled.

Anna opened her door. 'Thanks for coming.'

'Your kid all right?' he asked as he stepped inside.

'She's sleeping upstairs. She was upset not to have her teddy.'

Jamie frowned. 'Teddy?' She explained what happened and his face filled with anger. 'That's sick.'

'I know.'

They walked into the kitchen. 'I'll make you a flask of coffee, I've made some sandwiches too.'

'Thanks. So how'd this sick fuck get in?'

'The police think they got in through the back door, they reckon I left the door open. Thing is, there's no chance I left the back door open, I'm so bloody paranoid nowadays.'

Jamie walked over to the door and tried the handle. 'Weird. Maybe they got a key from somewhere.'

'There's only one and I have it. I haven't had the chance to get new ones cut since moving in.' She watched him check the locks, brow creased. He was doing this for her, despite what she'd done to his brother. Her heart went out to him. 'All looks secure to me.' He peered out into the garden, raising an eyebrow. 'I don't need a mask to protect me from the nuclear stuff, do I?'

Anna rolled her eyes, going to her coffeemaker. 'I told you, urban myth. So, do you have your own place?'

He nodded. 'A small flat in the same block my folks live in, right near the top though. I'm saving up to move out of The Docks, won't be long.'

'You've done well to get your own place.'

'Have I?' he said, looking around him at the high ceilings and expensive furniture in Anna's home. 'I'm a mechanic living in a shitty flat with a banged-up old van that keeps breaking down. You're a radio presenter with a Mercedes living in a three-bed semi with a gadget that has constant coffee on the go,' he added, gesturing to her coffeemaker.

'You can't compare us. We've had different lives.'

'You've still worked to get where you are,' Jamie said as Anna handed him his flask.

'I did, bloody hard too. But I sometimes wonder if I would've been taken on at Coast to Coast if I weren't Simon Fountain's daughter. He *was* their flagship reporter.'

'And I sometimes wonder what would have happened if I hadn't got done for hitting a kid at school,' Jamie said wryly. 'But the kid was bullying Elliot, I had to stick up for my little bro.'

Anna thought of what Detective Morgan had said to her the day before about Jamie. 'Was that the first time you were in trouble with the police?'

'Na, not the first or the last.'

'People respect you in The Docks, right?'

He smiled to himself. 'Respect. I guess that's what you call it.'

'What's your boss like?'

He looked up at her, eyes hard. 'You've been reading too many articles about me. I'm not Reggie Kray, Anna.'

'I know. So,' she said, wanting to change the subject. 'If you could do anything, what would you do?'

He smiled to himself, the hardness in his handsome face disappearing. It gave him a vulnerability that made Anna smile too. 'I was always good at art and design,' he said. 'Hated everything else at school. But I really enjoyed my art classes, especially the ones that involved messing about with Photoshop and stuff.' He jutted his chin at her. 'What about you, you always wanted to be a radio presenter?'

Anna leaned against the kitchen unit. 'Yes, for as long as I can remember. I used to record my dad's shows on tape.'

'You never thought about TV presenting?'

'No, it's always been radio. Plus I haven't really got the look for TV.'

Jamie laughed. 'You're kidding, right? You ever looked in the mirror?'

Anna's face flushed as he looked into her eyes.

Then Jamie's phone started ringing. He looked down at it, frowning. 'My mum keeps calling. Them finding Ben's body is making her think of Elliot.' He shook his head. 'I can't face talking to her when she's like this.'

'You should, Jamie. She needs you.'

'I've already spoken to her a million times.' He tucked his phone in his pocket.

Anna poured some coffee into a flask.

'So you said you have the letters my dad sent your dad?' Jamie asked.

'You can see them if you want,' she said, opening her laptop and pointing at them.

He sat down at the table and read them, shaking his head. 'Mental. Mum says Dad really went downhill after Peter died, especially when he went to prison the first time, she reckons that first stint in prison sent him down the wrong path.' He looked up at Anna. 'I've been thinking about what Kiara said. What do you think about your dad's theory that my uncle was the Ophelia Killer's first victim?'

'The time gap seems strange.'

'There's been a twenty-year time gap this time.'

'*If* the Ophelia Killer murdered Ben.'

'Who else could've done it? Other than you, of course,' he said, raising an eyebrow.

She rolled her eyes. 'A copycat?'

Jamie's face shadowed over.

Joni cried down the monitor.

'I better go to her,' Anna said.

'I'll be outside. I'll probably be gone by the time you wake. So text me about what you decide to do. If you're still here tomorrow night, I'll come over again.'

'That's sweet of you, thanks.'

As he reached down for his bag, Anna found herself looking at the tanned nape of his neck; his long eyelashes and plump lips. Her eyes travelled over his fingers as he flicked through his belongings, the flex of his biceps and she felt her breath quicken.

She turned away, surprised.

'Try to sleep, yeah?' he said, looking at her.

'Fat chance of that.'

His gaze lingered on hers a moment. Then he walked outside.

The next morning, Anna woke early. After checking on Joni, she went straight to the window and saw Jamie sleeping in his van. She got ready then fed Joni before taking her outside with her, knocking on the van window. Jamie woke with a start, rubbing his eyes. Then he noticed Joni, a frown appearing on his face. He wound his window down and hesitated a moment before taking Joni's chubby hand. 'Good to meet you, kid.' He shook his head. 'Can't believe my brother tried to hurt her with the knife I gave him.'

'But she's fine, look at her.'

'Yeah, I know.'

'And you're here, protecting her, me. It more than makes up for it. Here's some more coffee,' Anna said, handing him the mug. 'I really appreciate you doing this for us, Jamie. You're the only person I can rely on at the moment, you and my gran, anyway.'

He shrugged, taking a sip of coffee. 'Someone has to look after you. I can come again tonight?'

'I think we'll be fine, Jamie. You said yourself the house is secure. I feel better today. I'll let you know though, I appreciate the offer.'

Jamie peered in the car mirror, smoothing down his hair. 'Better head to work.'

He looked at Anna then his eyes dropped to Joni again. 'But do call if you need me, yeah? I don't like the idea of you both being alone.'

'I will.'

He rolled his window back up and Anna walked back inside, smiling to herself. It was good to have someone looking out for her. She'd felt so alone lately, so isolated. But Jamie made her feel safe. And that was good, right? Even if he was the brother of the boy she'd killed.

The next morning, Anna woke to her doorbell ringing. She groaned, pulling herself up and going to the window. When she opened her curtains, she was shocked to see people milling around outside.

Not just people, journalists. Dozens of them.

She pulled the curtains shut again and stood in the middle of the room. Why were they here? Sure, a few had been hanging around but not this many.

She walked downstairs to find a pile of national newspapers on her mat, including some tabloids that weren't in her usual daily delivery. She picked the first paper up, frowning as she took in the photo on the front cover of her and Jamie talking intimately outside her house, heads bent together.

Shocking exclusive: Anna Graves caught with Elliot Nunn's brother.

It had been taken the evening before last, when Jamie had driven to her house to protect her and Joni.

'For God's sake!' Anna hissed, gathering all the papers up in her arms.

She ran to the kitchen and shoved them into the recycling bin with all the other papers. But as one newspaper slipped into the recycling bin – the *Ridgmont Waters Chronicle* – one headline caught her eye: *Elliot Nunn's brother vows to get revenge.*

Anna took in a sharp breath. She quickly picked the newspaper back out of the bin and read it. It was written by her old friend, Yvonne.

In an exclusive interview, Elliot Nunn's aunt Dawn Williams shared the grief and anguish the Nunn family are still contending with after the death of the young schoolboy at the hands of local radio presenter, Anna Graves. She revealed her nephew and Elliot's older brother, Jamie Nunn, is particularly devastated, even threatening revenge on the radio presenter.

'Remember when we all rocked up to Anna Graves's grandmother's house that evening? Jamie arranged that,' Dawn divulged. 'We were all surprised when he helped Anna though. But he's a clever kid. He told me after that he'd come up with a new tactic: grow close to her to mess with her mind. Never seen him hate someone so much.'

Anna slumped down onto the chair, the newspaper falling from her hands. She'd let Jamie into her house. He'd held Joni's little hand. But all the time, he'd been trying to get close so he could get revenge.

All this time, he'd hated her.

Chapter Fourteen

The Fifth One

The sun's shining bright and bold above and it invigorates me. I ought to be exhausted; you kept me up talking all night about the last boy. But I'm starting to feel what you told me I would: that strange energy. I'm buzzing with it.

'There, that one,' you say.

I follow your gaze to see a boy and girl sitting in a back garden. The girl is all long legs and red lips. The boy thinks he's the one, combed back hair, sunglasses, even a leather jacket, despite the heat.

'His girlfriend's with him,' I say.

'Wait until she's gone. Here,' you say, gesturing towards a small gated area where bins are kept. It stinks. I wrinkle my nose. 'Only a bit of rubbish,' you say, 'you take ours out enough to be used to it. Go on. Let's listen to them.'

'Okay,' I say, feeling a strange determination.

We slip into the rubbish area and I put my hand over my nose.

'God, Cheryl, seriously,' I hear the boy say. He's got thick black hair, a tanned neck. He's what my mum would call a 'looker'. 'You're doing my head in now. Kimberley was just helping me with my homework.'

'She's thick as shit,' the slut says. 'What are you talking about? I can't believe you, Matt, you're so full of crap.'

She pulls away from him and I see the boy roll his eyes behind her back.

'Whatever,' he says, shrugging. 'Go home then if you don't believe me.'

She crosses her arms. 'I will.'

'Go on.'

She jumps up and looks at him, hands on her hips. He turns away. She huffs then strides from the garden and down the alleyway.

You give me a gentle nudge. I take a deep breath then walk towards the gate, letting myself into the garden.

'Hello, Matt.'

Matt sits up, frowning as he looks at me. Then his eyes flicker with recognition. 'Oh, it's you.'

'Want a drink?' I say, lifting the bottle I have. 'Real lemonade just out of the cooler.'

'Na.'

'Sure? It's hot out here.'

'Sure I'm sure,' he says, sneering at me.

'So who's Kimberley?' I ask.

He raises an eyebrow. 'You hear that?'

'Bit hard not to.'

'Nosy parker. She's no one. Cheryl's just paranoid.'

I take in his open shirt, the gel in his hair, the blueness of his eyes. I doubt Cheryl's just paranoid, girls must throw themselves at him.

'So what you up to now, then?' I ask.

He shrugs, blowing out some smoke. 'Was planning on a picnic on the beach,' he says, gesturing to a ropey-looking plastic bag of sandwiches in his hand. 'Guess I'll be staying here now.'

'Oh come on, it's not that bad,' I say.

He eyes the dog muck on the lawn, the filthy plastic chairs, the pond. 'Yeah, right,' he says, laughing bitterly.

I stare at the pond, feel something stirring inside.

'Here, have a lemonade,' I say, going to pour him some and handing it to him.

'I said no!' He bats me away, his hand catching on the glass I'm holding, making it spill all over my new top.

'Oh for fuck's sake,' I hiss.

'All right, chill your boots!' He laughs at me and rage fills me all of a sudden. I go to slap him but stop myself. You said I need to be careful.

'No disrespect but can you go, please?' he says. 'You can't just go walking into someone's garden anyway, yeah? So, you know, fuck off.'

That's it, I can't stop the rage this time. I lean down, grab his chin. 'Don't fucking talk to me like that.'

He shoves me away. 'Get off me.'

I knee him in the groin then squeeze his nose. He opens his mouth to breathe and I quickly pour some of the lemonade down his throat. He pushes me away, spluttering. I fall against the fence.

He jumps up, blue eyes filled with anger. 'What the hell are you doing, you stupid—' He curls his fist and starts striding towards me. But then he sways slightly, eyes blinking. I can't help but smile to myself. Just as well I doubled the dose this time.

He stumbles. 'What's going on?' he slurs.

I walk over to him and shove him. He falls backwards, feet splashing into the filthy pond. 'Chill your boots,' I say, mimicking his voice. 'It's just some poison, chill!'

He swallows, eyes blinking, trying to gain focus. 'Poison?'

'Not such a big man now, are we?' I say, shoving him again. He falls down, bottom splashing in the water. He looks vulnerable, scared, several years younger than his fifteen years.

Now he knows who's boss, anyway.

'Well done.' I turn to see you behind us. You have your plastic gloves on. 'Be careful not to lose your temper like that again though,' you say. 'Lack of control leads to errors. It's fine though, it's all fine, I'm here now.'

I think of the times you lose your temper with me. But I suppose this is different.

'Who the fuck's that?' the boys asks as he looks at you before leaning over and retching.

'We haven't got long,' I say, realising it's not fear I'm feeling right now but excitement.

'You do it,' you say, beaming with pride. 'You're ready.'

I go to Matt, sweep his fringe from his face as he gets sick into the pond.

'It's okay,' I say, shrugging his leather coat off. He tries to fight me off but he can't, the boy's losing control of his limbs.

I peer up at you and you smile. 'I've never been prouder of you than I am right now,' you say.

As I hold the boy's head under water a few moments later, I make sure to savour it, just like you told me to.

And I realise for the first time in my life, I'm proud of myself too.

Chapter Fifteen

'I can't say I'm surprised,' Anna's gran said as they had tea and cakes later. She placed the article to the side. 'I mean, I *am* surprised you let Jamie Nunn into your house. But this,' she said, gesturing to the interview with Jamie's aunt. 'This doesn't surprise me at all.'

'I feel stupid,' Anna said. 'All this time, I've been wondering how someone whose brother I killed could be so nice to me and now I know. He wanted to get close to me, mess with my mind.'

Her gran examined her face. 'Not too close, I hope?'

'God no! Those articles are wrong, there's nothing going on between Jamie and I.'

'He's a handsome man, if you like that rough and ready look.'

Anna pushed away the memory of the spark she'd felt between them the night before. '*No*, Gran. No way.' Anna peered at her phone. 'What if *he's* the one sending the emails?'

'Definitely a possibility. Have you also wondered if Jamie convinced Elliot to target you and Joni?'

'No, how would he have known where I'd be that day? It seems a bit much.'

'Really? Maybe Jamie has been watching you all this time, waiting. That's how he knew you'd be at the beach that day. He then convinced his little brother to target you and Joni in a twisted form of family-on-family revenge? He would have known all about the Ophelia Killer from his father who surely must have told him about his uncle and the investigation your father was doing.'

Anna thought about it. Jamie said himself, Neil Nunn's life had fallen apart after that first stint in prison. It had ruined the Nunn family. Jamie may have blamed Anna's family for that.

And what about Ben Miller's death? Could Jamie really have had something to do with that?

Anna put her head in her hands. Was the Jamie she knew really capable of *killing* someone? But then what *did* she know of Jamie? She'd been taken in by the support he'd offered when everyone else but her gran was turning against her.

How naïve she'd been!

Florence put her hand on Anna's arm. 'Look, at least you now know. You can steer well clear of him.'

Anna nodded, trying to hide her disappointment. She'd *enjoyed* spending time with Jamie. But that was over. He'd been using her. Now all she had was her gran. She felt helpless, like everything was spinning out of control around her and she was unable to do anything about it.

The doorbell went. Anna got up and peeked out of the curtains to see Guy battling his way through the throng of journalists. He was taking Joni out for the morning so they could go to his niece's birthday party. She let him in and he could barely look at Anna, the disgust clear in his eyes. Joni crawled down the hallway towards him and he picked her up, kissing her cheek. 'Before you say anything, it's not true,' Anna said. 'Jamie Nunn has just been helping me out.'

'Helping you out?' he said, shaking his head. 'I feel like I'm living in a parallel world. Have you lost your mind?'

Florence looked in from the kitchen.

'If those papers print a photo of my daughter, I'm going to sue their arses off,' Guy said, pulling the hood of Joni's cardigan over her head and pressing her cheek against his chest. He glared at Anna over her head. 'This just isn't fair on Joni, Anna.'

Anna thought of Joni's butchered teddy. 'I know,' she whispered. She put her hand to her scar, felt it raised and angry under her fingertips. This was all her fault. One moment of rash violence on her part – because that was what it had been with Elliot, she'd felt the surge of anger before she'd raised her arm – one moment and this was the consequence.

'If things don't calm down over the next few days,' Guy said, 'I'm going to have to take some advice.'

'Advice? From who? I don't understand.'

'I'm sorry, Anna, but I just don't feel you can provide a safe environment for our daughter at the moment.'

Anna's blood turned to ice. 'Guy, you can't do this.'

'I can and I will.' He picked his car keys up. Anna looked down at Joni's head, panic swirling inside her.

She gave her daughter a fierce kiss on the cheek, looking into her eyes. 'I love her more than anything,' she said, tears falling down her cheeks. 'You know that, Guy, her safety is everything to me.'

'Me too. That's why I'm going to do all I can to guarantee her safety. I'll drop Joni back off by three.' Then he walked out of the door.

She watched Guy run down the path with Joni as the journalists called out to him, cameras flashing.

'What do you think about your ex-wife being caught with Jamie Nunn?' one of them shouted out.

'Do you think Anna is connected in some way to Ben Miller's death?' another said – Yvonne, Anna's old school friend. She caught sight of Anna watching and smiled slightly.

Anna yanked the blinds shut and leaned against the wall, tears falling down her cheeks as Guy's words echoed in her mind.

'He won't take her.' She turned to see her gran standing in the kitchen doorway, eyes sparking with tears.

'Oh Gran!' Anna said.

Florence walked over and pulled Anna into a hug. 'We'll fight him, Anna, we'll bloody fight him. He doesn't have a hope.'

'Hasn't he?' Anna said, pulling away. 'In his position, I'd be worried too. This can't be good for Joni.'

'Nonsense! She doesn't have a clue what's going on, as long as she's with her mummy and great granny, she's happy.'

'She's been restless.'

Florence put her hand on Anna's shoulder, looking her in the eye. 'She can sense it off you. I'll stay again tonight, you won't have to lift a finger. I can cook, clean, give you a chance to relax.'

'No, it's fine,' Anna said with a sigh. 'I need to get back into a normal routine, I have work tomorrow.'

Florence frowned. 'Is that really a good idea, going into work?'

'I can't afford not to, Gran. Me not being able to provide for Joni will just be another stick Guy can beat me with.'

As Anna sat at her desk on Thursday morning, half of her wanted to head right back home again. But she needed to present as normal a picture as possible of a hard-working mother who could provide for her child even if it meant having to deal with the whispers and raised eyebrows when she walked into work, the story about her and Jamie still strong in people's minds.

She'd had missed calls from Jamie, but she chose to ignore them. She wanted him out of her life now and she'd sent a text message saying just that. She hadn't got a reply and there were no more calls.

It only strengthened Anna's resolve. She wouldn't let the men in her life, and the press, take the one thing she had left: her strength as a mother. So she knuckled down and got on with work, focusing on Joni and gathering strength from the photo of her on her desk, even sneaking to the loo and watching videos of Joni playing when she felt like hiding under her chair after Heather walked in and glared at her.

As she walked back from the toilets, she saw the station's controller walking down the corridor, his white hair bouncing with every step.

'Anna!' he called out to her.

'Hi, Lucian.'

'I've been trying to find you. Can you pop into my office for a few moments?'

'Of course.'

She followed him to his office and sat down across from him.

'I know you're aware of everything that's been going on. It's great to be at work, to be honest. It gives me—'

'Let me interrupt you there,' he said, face serious. 'I'm sorry, Anna. You know how much we adore you, how much our listeners do too. But we've all been talking and we think it might be worth you taking some time off.'

Anna opened her mouth and closed it again.

'Just with all the attention lately, we don't think it's good for you or the station if you stay. Heather suggested you take a month off then take it from there. Full pay, of course.'

'Heather,' Anna said, shaking her head. 'You know this is a dream come true for her, don't you? She hates me.'

'I wouldn't say that, Anna. I thought you'd welcome the opportunity, it must be a very stressful time for you.'

'Even more stressful twiddling my thumbs all day.'

He let out a nervous laugh. 'Oh, I can't imagine you're the type to sit around. You could take a hobby up, see more of your little girl.'

'So your decision is final?'

'This is a *collaborative* decision, Anna.'

'But if I say no…?'

He cleared his throat. 'Well…'

'Fine,' Anna snapped. 'If that's what you want, I suppose I get it. So when does the month start from?'

He avoided her eyes.

'Today?' she asked, incredulous.

He nodded. 'This isn't ideal, Anna, you're such an asset to the station. But you have to understand our position.'

'I'm not sure I do, really. I've dedicated the past seven years to this station, played a key role in turning it into what it is today.'

His face hardened. 'We had no problem with you coming back after you killed that boy, Anna, in fact we suggested it. But I'm afraid things are out of control now. All the rumours about Ben Miller then the articles about you and Jamie Nunn. You have *become* the news, Anna. It's impossible.'

Anna stood up. 'Thanks for the support, Lucian.'

Then she strode out of the office, eyes stinging with tears. She quickened her step and ran outside, gasping in the fresh salty air. She carried on walking until she reached the beach then walked some more, the sea wind tearing into her hair, tears streaming down her face.

She was losing everything.

When she got to the lighthouse, she peered up at the window her father had jumped from.

Is this how he'd felt before he jumped?

She imagined climbing the metal stairs, then walking to the window, opening it, stepping onto the windowsill. She saw herself looking down at the rocks, contemplating them.

Then she saw Joni.

'No,' she hissed at herself. 'Pull yourself together.'

She wiped her tears away, raking her hands through her messy hair. She'd get through this, she wouldn't let it defeat her. She'd go back to Lucian and tell him she'd take two weeks off. Then she'd be back.

She headed back to the studio, strength gathering with every step.

But when she got back, one of the admin team ran up to her,

face full of worry. 'Anna, your mother-in-law's been trying to contact you. It's about Joni.'

Anna's heart skipped a beat. She pulled her phone from her pocket to see there were several missed calls from the nursery. She quickly called them.

'Anna!' her mother-in-law said as soon as she was put through. 'Joni's gone missing.'

Chapter Sixteen

The Sixth One

The baby is crying upstairs. I can hear it through the windows, whining, high-pitched. It makes it hard to focus.

The boy doesn't bat an eyelid though, despite the fact he's supposed to be looking after her while his parents are out. I imagine them down the pub, getting pissed, not giving a damn.

You're right. These boys aren't loved enough. But we can care for them.

Doesn't stop the guilt though. You said the guilt would dissipate, then the thrill would truly take over. The thrill's there but I'm still feeling the guilt, waking in the night with the boys' wretched eyes on my mind. It's the moment before they die, the helplessness and desperate fear. I know you like that moment, you say it's the best part, the moving from one plane to the next. Life to death in just a bright succulent moment. But I hate that part. I see my actions through their eyes, I see the role I've played as my own reflection bounces back at me from their pupils and the water beneath them.

But then it all redeems itself when they're lying there, prone, dead, *all life gone.* That *is when the thrill begins. No thrashing about, no fighting, no retching and pitiful moans.*

Just silence. Stillness. Life gives in and I can begin my garland, pulling the flowers from my bag, laying them around their heads, stroking their hair, whispering it'll all be okay as you watch. I sometimes think you aren't breathing yourself, you're so still. You tell me you're just in awe, enraptured and so proud, so very proud.

'My mate Todd said the dead boys were found with their hearts removed,' the boy says now, interrupting my thoughts.

I resist the desire to roll my eyes. Instead I feign surprise. 'Really?'

'Yeah! Just cut right out of their chests. His second cousin saw the second kid dead, said he had a hole in his chest.'

The rumours going around are astounding. Eyes removed. Frogspawn sewn into the tongue. Even a cat's carcass lying beneath each victim. As for who did it, a teacher was seen running from the scene apparently. An off-duty police officer too. Even a vicar!

I tried to tell you about the rumours the other week but you stopped me. You said you don't want to mar our memories with unnecessary tactless gossip.

The baby's whines go up a dial. I think briefly about marching up there and smothering it with a pillow.

The thought shocks me. Is this what I am becoming, someone who fantasises about killing babies in their sleep?

I pull the lemonade out instead. 'Want a drink?' I say to the boy.

Chapter Seventeen

'Gone?' Anna shouted down the phone. People around the studio peered up. 'What the hell do you mean, gone?'

'She was having a nap with the other children on their daybeds,' her mother-in-law said. 'Lacey popped into the kitchen for just a few seconds. When she came back, Joni was gone. We've had the whole team out checking all over.'

'I'm coming.' Anna slammed her phone down and grabbed her coat, running from the studio. She didn't remember the car journey, only the sheer blind white panic. It was similar to the moment she saw Elliot holding the knife except it was worse. Anna couldn't see Joni, she was nowhere near her, she couldn't do *anything* to protect her.

When she got to the nursery, the police were everywhere, blue lights flashing. Other parents were picking their children up from the nursery, casting disapproving glances at Anna. In the distance, the sea sparkled under a bright sun, a red kite dancing in the coastal breeze, children's laughter as they played on the beach tinkling in Anna's ears.

The scene made Anna feel sick, more stricken with terror.

Her mother-in-law ran out when she saw her, face white, tears in her eyes. 'I'm so sorry. You know how good the security is, all the doors were locked, it was just me and the other girls. I have no idea how she disappeared. Guy's on his way.'

'You've searched everywhere?' Anna said. 'Absolutely everywhere?'

'Every little nook and cranny. She's just gone. I don't know – I can't—'

Anna shoved past her, going to the nearest police officer. 'What's happening? What are you doing to find my daughter?'

'We have officers searching the area,' the officer said.

'Is Detective Morgan here? I want Detective Morgan.'

'He's on his way, Mrs Graves.'

'What about Jamie Nunn? Has anyone tried to track him down?'

The office frowned. 'Elliot Nunn's brother?'

She marched away, digging her phone out and calling Jamie. He answered straight away. 'Anna, I—'

'Where is she?'

He paused. 'Where's who?'

'Joni. Where have you taken her?'

'Joni's missing?'

Anna laughed. Her laugh sounded hysterical. 'You know what I'm talking about. You can do whatever the hell you want to me, but do not touch my daughter. I swear, do not touch her.' Her voice broke and she started sobbing. 'Please, Jamie, please, whatever my father did to yours—'

'Anna, calm down! I did not take Joni. I would never hurt her.'

'Mrs Graves!'

252

She looked over to see Detective Morgan jogging towards her. His face was red, forehead shiny with sweat. She'd never seen him look so dishevelled. It made her feel even more terrified.

'I've got Jamie Nunn on the phone,' she said. 'You need to go to his place.'

'Jamie Nunn?' the detective said.

'It's obviously him who took Joni. Who else would it be?'

'If this is to do with that article in the *Ridgmont Waters Chronicle*, I had a word with him about that. Turns out his aunt exaggerated things, she discovered he'd gone to your house to protect you so she sold the story in the hope it would drive the two of you apart. He seemed sincere, Anna.'

Anna hesitated. Could it be true? She shook her head. 'Why do you believe him? He could be a killer. He could have my daughter right now!'

The detective shook his head. 'I don't think he has Joni.'

'So who does?'

A police officer ran over, a police radio in his hand. 'They found her,' he said. 'She's fine.'

Relief flooded through Anna and her arms ached to have her daughter in them. 'Where?'

'Just a street down,' the officer said.

Anna exchanged a look with the detective. How could Joni have got a whole street away?

They all ran down the street, a nice street with rows of Victorian houses like the one Anna used to live in with Guy and Joni. She knew which house it was as several police officers were outside, an elderly woman talking to one of them. A female officer approached from the back, Joni wrapped in a blanket as she sucked her thumb. Anna let out a cry and ran over, pulling her daughter into her arms and sobbing.

'Are you okay, baby?'

Joni burst into tears and Anna held her close, heart thumping against her little chest.

'How the hell did she get here?' Anna asked the police officer. 'And why's she so wet?' she said, noticing her blue leggings were soaked through.

'We found her sitting in a pond,' the policewoman said, looking at Detective Morgan with worried eyes.

'In a pond?' Anna said, blood turning to ice. 'My God, she could have drowned.' She checked Joni's face, running her fingers over her cold wet skin. The wail of ambulance sirens sounded in the distance. 'Did – did she *crawl* there?'

'Unlikely,' Detective Morgan said, peering at the house with hooded eyes.

Anna followed his gaze. 'So you think she was brought here?'

'Maybe.'

Anna closed her eyes, tears squeezing out between her eyelashes. It was all too much.

'It's not just that,' the policewoman said.

'What else?' Detective Morgan said.

Anna opened her eyes as the officer jutted her chin towards the open gate. It led through to a large well-kept garden, in the middle of which was a small pond. Floating on its surface was an array of beautiful flowers.

'The owner said the flowers weren't there before,' the policewoman said. 'We've checked. They're the same flowers found with Ben Miller. Pansies, daisies and—'

'"Rosemary for remembrance,"' Anna quoted quietly as the detective nodded. 'Fennel, columbines, daisies and violets.'

'All from Ophelia's garland in *Hamlet*,' the detective explained to the bemused-looking policewoman. 'I think it's time we talked to some local florists, these flowers can't be that easy to source. Right,' he said, turning back to Anna with a big sigh as an ambulance turned in to the street. 'Let's get Joni checked over then let's talk.'

'Did the Ophelia Killer do this?' Anna asked the detective as a paramedic gently checked Joni all over, helping Anna to change her into the spare set of clothes she always had in her handbag.

'Twenty years on?' Detective Morgan said. 'I don't know.'

'So a copycat?'

'Maybe.' He tilted his head. 'What do you think?'

'I think whoever it is wants to send me a message. I don't know why, maybe it's to do with the reports my dad did. I just know I'm a target, Joni is.' She looked around her. 'We're not safe here any more.'

Her phone rang. She looked down at it, saw it was Guy. 'I need to take this, it's Joni's father.' She put the phone to her ear.

'Mum said Joni's safe. I'm trying to find a flight back. How is she?'

'Fine, she's been checked over and she's fine,' Anna said quickly. 'I have her in my arms right now.'

'What happened?'

Anna took a deep breath, looking at Detective Morgan. 'They found her sitting in a pond a street down from the nursery.'

'What the fuck?'

'Calm down, Guy. She's okay.'

255

'How the hell did she end up in a pond?'

'They're trying to figure that out.'

'What the hell is going on, Anna?'

'Detective Morgan is right here, he's going to—'

'Put him on the phone.'

Anna held the phone out to the detective. 'He wants to speak to you.'

The detective took it. 'Mr Graves, it's Detective Morgan. Your daughter is safe.' He paused, nodding his head. 'That's right, in a pond.' He paused again, looking at Anna with hooded eyes. 'You're right, we don't believe she would've crawled there. We're going to do all we can to get to the bottom of this…Ben Miller? I don't know, Mr Graves. That will be a line we'll investigate. Yes, yes, of course.'

The detective handed the phone back to Anna.

'Guy, I promise I will keep her safe,' Anna said to Guy. 'We'll leave Ridgmont Waters tonight and—'

'No, my mum will have her tonight then I'll pick her up when I'm back tomorrow.'

'But it's my turn to have Joni!'

'I don't care. I'm taking my daughter somewhere safe.'

My daughter.

'She's safe with me,' Anna said, trying to keep her panic at bay. 'We'll leave Ridgmont Waters, I'll text you the address of the hotel we find. You can then come to see her and—'

'Listen to me, Anna,' Guy hissed. 'She is *not* safe with you. I don't care what it takes, I'm not letting her stay another night with you.'

Anger mounted inside Anna. 'I won't let you take her from me. If you try to I'll—'

'Stab me?'

She froze. How could he say that to her?

'Guy—'

'My mother's taking her. Goodbye, Anna.' Then he slammed the phone down.

'Interesting conversation,' the detective said.

'It's been a difficult time for all of us,' Anna said.

The detective looked at Joni, who was still crying, tears rolling down her chubby cheeks. 'Mrs Graves, I—'

She interrupted him. 'Please, can I just take my daughter home?'

'Will you listen, Mrs Graves?' the detective shouted 'Where were you before Joni disappeared?'

Anna went very still as he shouted. Everyone on the street went quiet, eyes directed at her: police, paramedics, nursery nurses, neighbours. All accusing, suspicious.

'What did you say?' Anna asked in a trembling voice.

'You heard me. Where were you between twelve-thirty and one today, Mrs Graves?'

'You can't be suggesting I kidnapped my own daughter and put her in a *pond*?'

'Just answer the question, Mrs Graves,' the detective said.

'It was my lunchbreak, I went for a walk along the beach outside the studio.'

'Did anyone see you?'

'I'm sure lots of people did.' She blinked away tears. 'I need to get my daughter home so I can pack. The sooner we get out of this town, the better.'

'I wouldn't recommend leaving town, Mrs Graves. We will assign a police team to you.'

'No. I need to get away, that's the only way to keep me and Joni safe.'

'Mrs Graves, I insist on—'

'Insist on what? She's my daughter, I know how to keep her safe when nobody else seems to be able to. You can't take her from me, Detective Morgan.'

'Not now, no.' He shot her a look that implied he might be able to, soon.

Anna's whole body shook with terror. She marched away through the throng of police officers and gathering neighbours until she got to her car outside the nursery.

Guy's mother strode up to her. 'Guy said I—'

'You're not taking her, Pam,' Anna said, opening the back door and strapping Joni in.

'But Guy said it would be best if—'

'Joni's best with me.'

Her mother-in-law took a deep breath. 'It's clear someone's trying to target you. You know it's for the best that Joni come with me.'

'For the best?' Anna asked. 'You're saying it's for the best Joni stay with someone who let her disappear under her nose?' Anna laughed bitterly, shaking her head in disbelief. 'I don't think so, Pam.' Then she got into her car, feeling everyone's eyes on her as she drove off.

It was only when she was out of sight that she burst into tears.

Anna battled her way through the ever-growing throng of journalists to get to her house. After double locking the front door and checking the back door, she jogged upstairs with Joni, placing her on her bed with some toys as she started packing items.

'We're getting out of here, darling,' she said, forcing herself to smile. 'We're getting away and we're going to be safe, I promise.'

Her phone buzzed in her back pocket. She reluctantly paused and took it out, seeing she'd missed calls from Guy, her gran, Jeremy…and Jamie. There was a voicemail too. She quickly called it, tucking her phone under her chin as she flung Joni's bodysuits into a suitcase.

'Hello, Anna. My name's Linda Cain, I'm calling from the local authority's Child Protection Services.' Anna's stomach sank. 'Can you call me back about us visiting you tomorrow?'

As the social worker reeled off her number, Anna sat on the bed, blinking into the distance. So Guy had called them. A second visit from the social services in the space of two months.

But this one felt different.

She took a deep breath then called the number back. 'Hi, Linda, it's Anna Graves. You called a moment ago?'

'Ah, yes, Anna. So is tomorrow okay?'

'I'm planning to leave Ridgmont Waters tonight. But maybe we can meet once I know where I'll be?'

'I'm afraid I'd advise against leaving, Mrs Graves.'

'But my child's life is in danger. I presume you heard what happened at the nursery?'

'I did. I also know Detective Morgan asked that you stay in town. It's important you stay, Anna.' Her voice was gentle but Anna could hear the threat in her tone.

'I presume my husband called you?' Anna said.

'I'm afraid I can't divulge. How's midday tomorrow?'

Anna hesitated. What choice did she have? 'Midday's fine.'

She put the phone down and gently lifted Joni up, drawing comfort from the warmth of her little body.

Joni stared into her mother's eyes, putting her hand on her cheek. 'Mama,' she said.

'I love you so so much, darling,' Anna said, tears falling from her eyes and wetting Joni's fingers. 'I'm so sorry you're going through all this with me, my darling girl. It's all Mummy's fault.' She let out another sob. 'It's my fault,' she whispered again. 'But I'll make it right, I promise I'll make it right.'

She curled up next to Joni in the semi-darkness, the sound of the clock in the hallway tick-tocking loudly, counting down to what Anna knew might be the most challenging few days of her life.

Chapter Eighteen

Just after midday the next day, the doorbell went. Anna took a deep breath, picking Joni up from her play mat and opening the front door. A tall woman with brown hair and green eyes was on her doorstep. She wasn't how Anna imagined a social worker to look.

'Linda?' Anna asked. The woman nodded, smiling at Joni. 'Come in,' Anna said, opening the door wider for her.

The woman walked in, looking around her.

'Come through,' Anna said, leading her to the living room, wondering if the woman could smell the newly sprayed cleaning products, see the fresh hoover marks in the carpet. It was a wonder Anna had got any cleaning done considering how clingy Joni had been that morning. 'Cup of tea?' she asked the social worker as she sat down, placing her folder on her lap.

'Lovely, thanks.'

After Anna made tea, she sat across from the social worker, jogging Joni up and down on her knee. Joni whimpered, reaching for Anna and wrapping her arm around her neck as she stared at the social worker under her little furrowed brow while sucking her thumb.

'I'm going to ask a few questions, it's just standard procedure, Anna,' the social worker said. 'I'd then like to look around the house.'

'Of course.'

Linda smiled and looked down at the form she'd brought with her. Over the next twenty minutes, she reeled off a series of questions about Joni's health, wellbeing, development, similar to the questions the other social worker had asked Anna a couple of months before. Joni squirmed against Anna halfway through so Anna placed her gently on her play mat, aware of the social worker's eyes on her, feeling like every move was being judged. She felt a moment of deep dark sadness. How had it come to this, yet another visit from social services?

When Linda finished asking questions, she asked to look around. Anna led her upstairs, Joni in her arms.

'Here's where Joni sleeps most of the time,' Anna said, opening the door to the nursery.

'Most of the time?' the social worker asked.

'I sometimes have her in with me.'

'I see,' the social worker said, scribbling down some notes.

'Co-sleeping's fine, right?' Anna said. 'I don't drink much nor smoke.'

'Of course, as long as you take all the precautions. This room is lovely,' Linda said, smiling as she took in the tree mural on the wall with its big-eyed owls perching on the branches, the cream cot and wardrobe, the stuffed toys. The social worker peered into the wicker basket of nappies, nodding, then opened the wardrobe.

She let out a gasp.

Anna followed her gaze to see a long-toothed red comb sitting on the middle shelf…just like the comb she'd used to kill Elliot Nunn.

Anna's legs suddenly felt weak, terror rushing through her.

'I have no idea how that got there,' Anna said with a trembling voice. She quickly picked it up, her heart hammered uncontrollably against her chest as she examined it. Joni went to grab it then yelped when it scratched her chubby wrist. She started crying and the social worker quickly took the comb from Anna, placing it out of Joni's reach on the windowsill.

'Is this your comb, Anna?' the social worker asked, all smiles gone now.

'Of course not! The police have the one I—' She swallowed. 'I don't own a comb like that any more,' she said instead.

The social worker took down some notes, face very serious. 'I think I've seen enough now.'

Anna felt like collapsing on the floor but instead, she followed the social worker downstairs and let her out, all the time her mind on the comb, the red comb, the same sort of comb that had pierced Elliot's neck, killing him.

She ran upstairs when the social worker left, placing Joni in her cot before staring at the comb which was lying on the windowsill.

She shook her head. How had it got here? She looked at the window, the locks on there. She wrapped her arms around herself.

That was it, she was definitely leaving, she didn't care what anyone said.

She ran into her room, flinging clothes into a suitcase.

Then the doorbell went.

She paused then walked to the window, peering out. It was Guy. He looked up at her, catching her eye.

She felt her heart gallop. Had it happened that quickly, had the social worker called the police, told them about the comb and now Guy was here to take Joni from her?

She thought about not answering the door. But how would that look?

She picked Joni up and went downstairs, opening the door with trembling hands. Guy went to hold Joni but Anna stepped away. 'You're not taking her.'

His face hardened. 'Anna, we have to think about what's best for Joni.'

'What's best? Is having a social worker scrutinise her every move best for her?'

Guy frowned. 'Social worker?'

Anna shook her head in disbelief. 'I know you called them.'

'I didn't call social services.'

'Don't lie, Guy. I just had a visit from one.'

He shook his head. 'I'm serious, Anna. I didn't call them.'

She looked into his eyes. She'd known him for nearly fifteen years. She could tell when he was lying and he wasn't now.

'Then who did?' she asked. 'Would your mum?'

'No, of course not.' He sighed. 'Can I come in? I've been travelling all night, I'm desperate to see this little one. I expected to see her at Mum and Dad's.' He shot Anna a look. 'You shouldn't have been so hard on my mum, Anna.'

'I couldn't let her take her.'

Guy walked in and took Joni from Anna, kissing her cheek. 'She okay?'

'She's fine.' Anna peered at the ceiling towards Joni's room, thinking of the comb.

'What's wrong?' Guy asked.

She examined his face. Should she tell him? He'd no doubt hear about it anyway. She closed her eyes, taking a deep breath. 'The social worker visit didn't go great.'

He frowned. 'Why?'

'There was a comb in Joni's wardrobe.'

'Comb? So what?'

'A red long-tooth comb.'

She opened her eyes to see Guy's face go pale. '*The* comb?'

'I don't think so,' Anna said quickly. 'That's in evidence. But it was exactly the same and I don't own another like it.'

He rubbed her hands over his beard. 'Jesus. Maybe the same person who took Joni yesterday left it?'

'I don't know. Maybe.'

'The Ophelia Killer?' Guy said, voice hoarse.

'We don't know *who* it is, Guy.'

'But it could be. That's what Mum said the police were saying.'

'It could be a copycat.'

He paced the hallway with Joni in his arms, kissing her head.

'Whoever it was didn't hurt Joni,' Anna said quickly.

'No, just left her in a pond.' He stopped walking, looking at Anna, face deadly serious. 'What's the most important thing in our lives?'

Anna stood close to him, stroking their daughter's head. 'Joni.'

He nodded. 'The fact is, Anna, and you can't deny it: Joni isn't safe at the moment.'

Anna swallowed, eyes filling with tears.

'I *know* you would never harm her,' he said, his own brown eyes filling with tears too. 'I was wrong to be so hard on you yesterday. The truth is, you saved our daughter's life, risked your own doing it. I know you'd never hurt her, not in a million years and whichever idiot reported you to social services needs their head examined. But,' he said, 'she is not safe here with you. Not at the moment, anyway.'

'That's why I want to leave Ridgmont Waters.'

'No,' he said, shaking his head. 'Whoever it is will follow you, they seem fascinated with you. All those emails...'

Anna frowned. 'You know about those?'

'Detective Morgan told me. After I calmed down, I called him again. You should've told me about them.'

'I didn't want to worry you.'

'Look, Anna,' he said, clutching her hand and squeezing it. 'Whatever's passed between us, Joni is the thing that binds us. And Joni's safety is paramount. Honestly, right now, who do you think she'll be safer with? You or me?'

Anna looked at her beautiful beloved daughter and felt her face collapse. She put her hand to her mouth. She knew Guy was right.

'I can take her away until it all dies down,' Guy said. 'Social services will look kindly upon that, it'll show you're taking steps to keep your daughter safe.'

Anna shook her head, her heart aching.

'It wouldn't be long,' Guy said. 'Just until they catch this madman.'

'That could take months, years even!'

'We'll take it week by week.'

'I'm not sure I can bear being without her that long.'

'This isn't about you, Anna,' Guy said gently.

She paused. He was right. This was about Joni.

'Remember when your show started getting more popular and we were having dinner with James and Liz?' he said, referring to his brother and sister-in-law. 'Liz asked you why you thought you were connecting with listeners and you said you stripped away all the drama and the nonsense and got down to the blunt facts, said what everyone else was thinking deep down inside. Look deep inside, strip away the drama. The simple fact is, Joni will be safe with me until this settles down. Whoever is targeting her is targeting you...and you need to figure out why.'

Anna did remember that dinner. It was a year after she'd joined the station and she'd just heard listening figures were going up and up. She'd been so happy, feeling like she was on the cusp of something truly exciting. How different things were now. She looked into Guy's eyes. She'd thrown it all away. He was a good man, a wonderful father. And he was right, she *was* being selfish.

She clenched her jaw. 'How shall we do this, then?'

He let out a breath of relief. 'Thank you, Anna.'

'You're right. I have to think of Joni.' She wiped away a tear. 'Where will you take her?'

'That place we stayed at that Christmas, the one Dave at work owns?'

Anna nodded. It was a lovely log cabin only fifteen minutes from the village in a small wooded area away from the coast.

'My mum and dad'll get time off work and come too,' Guy

said. 'Let's say a week and take it from there. You can come visit after that week and we'll figure out what to do next.'

Anna put her hands out to her daughter. Joni smiled and reached for her mother. Anna held her, breathing her in like she might be able to somehow bring her back inside of her, safe, out of harm's way.

'I want to Skype every night,' Anna said, her tears wetting Joni's hair. 'The cabin has wireless, from what I remember?'

Guy nodded, face solemn.

'And you can't start getting all bolshie like you did yesterday, Guy. I'll want to see her after a week, I know I will. It'll kill me if not. We need to be in this together, no threats you'll take her away for good and—'

Guy squeezed her arm. 'I promise, Anna. Look, why don't I stay for an hour or so? We can chat, get some lunch, you can say goodbye. Not feel rushed.'

'Okay,' she whispered, trying to stamp down the rising feeling of panic.

'You need to do what you do best, Anna. You need to figure out what's going on, just like your dad used to.'

'I know,' Anna said, nodding. She looked into Guy's eyes. 'You know me so well. We were good once, weren't we?'

He smiled sadly. 'We were, for a few years.'

'What went wrong?'

He shrugged. 'I think we just fell out of love. You didn't want to accept that.'

'Because I love you,' Anna whispered.

'Yes, but you're not *in* love with me. But that was unacceptable for you, divorce is unacceptable, what will people say? It's always been about perception, Anna. For once, bloody dig inside, stop caring what people think, get to the truth. I know you can do it. For Joni's sake.'

'I've tried, it's no use. I'm not my father, I don't have his skills.'

'Don't you? Even if you don't, you have an incentive he didn't.'

They both looked down at their daughter who flung her arms around both their necks and giggled.

A couple of hours later, Anna finally found it in herself to say goodbye to Joni. She stroked Joni's soft cheek, remembering how paper thin the skin had seemed when she was first born. She loved kissing that chubby cheek now, stroking it, pressing her own cheek against it.

Joni reached up for her and Anna felt tears spring to her eyes. She looked away, it was too painful.

'It's only a few days,' Guy said.

'I know,' Anna said. She kissed her daughter's forehead, her cheek, her bare shoulder. 'Mummy loves you,' she whispered in her ear.

Joni popped her thumb into her mouth, leaning her cheek against Anna's chest. It took all of Anna's will not to crumble onto the floor right then and there with her.

Guy stepped forward, his arms out. Anna kissed Joni's head again, waited a moment, then handed her over to Guy, her whole body trembling.

'You'll be with her soon,' Guy said, shrugging the bag Anna had packed for Joni over his shoulder.

'Mama!' Joni declared, putting her arms out to Anna.

'Sorry, baby,' she said through her tears. 'I'm so sorry.'

'We'll Skype tomorrow,' Guy said. 'Take care of yourself, Anna.'

Then he let himself out. The door slammed shut behind him, the walls shuddering, and Anna fell against the wall, everything inside her seeming to collapse as though every sinew, every fibre had left that house with Joni.

Chapter Nineteen

Anna blinked into the darkness, head throbbing. She sat up, limbs aching. There was a knocking on the bedroom door. It opened, the light slicing through the room making her wince.

'Hello, sweetheart,' her gran said, a tray of tea and toast in her hand. She placed it on the bedside table then swept the curtains open, revealing the shimmering sea outside. Anna had been staying with Florence the past few days on the advice of the police after she'd reported the comb to them.

'I'm not hungry,' Anna croaked, her hair lifted up by the fan in the corner.

'Nonsense. You didn't eat your dinner, you must be starving.'

'I'm fine. I just need to sleep.'

'Sleep!' Florence said, laughing. 'More sleep? That's all you've done since Guy took Joni, sleeping or reading one of those depressing books.'

Anna moaned and sank back into bed, burying her head under the duvet. She didn't want to think about not having Joni with her. She didn't want to think about anything. She just wanted to be enveloped in nothingness.

Florence didn't say anything. She heard the floorboards creak. *Good, she's going,* Anna thought. Then she felt the bed sink. Her heart sank with it. Why couldn't she just be left alone?

'Don't do this, Anna,' she heard Florence say through the layers of duvet. She squeezed her eyes shut. She didn't want a lecture. What was the point of doing anything? She'd tried and it just seemed to make things worse. Best thing she could do was keep her head down and count the days until she could see Joni again.

The duvet was pulled back. She tried to keep it over her.

'It's too hot to be under there. You're behaving like your mother did when your father died,' Florence said.

Anna paused.

'Disappearing into her bed for days on end,' Florence continued, leaning close to Anna. 'Blocking the world out, not confronting anything.'

Maybe she was? And if so, so what? Wasn't it inevitable, Anna turning into her mother? She ought to just let it happen. And in fact, it made sense. Yes, finally, after all these years of thinking her mother weak, she realised her mother was just being *clever* blocking everything out: Anna's father's death, the death of Peter Nunn, her childhood sweetheart. Just don't think about it and it won't hurt.

Anna yanked the duvet away from her gran. 'I'm not hungry,' she said again.

Florence sighed and stayed where she was a few moments then she left the room.

*   *   *

272

Anna looked up from her book that afternoon. She could hear raised voices from downstairs. She slowly got up and went to the door, pressing her ear against it.

'I'm sorry,' she heard Florence say, 'but I just can't let you in.'

Fear threaded through Anna. What if it was Detective Morgan, finally coming to charge her with murder?

'Please, it's important.'

The voice made her still. It was Jamie. She clutched her book to her chest, heart thumping.

'Anna,' he shouted up the stairs. 'Anna, come down, I need to talk to you about something.'

'Please leave,' Anna heard Florence say. 'Leave or I'll call the police.'

Anna heard Jamie laugh. 'That's the last thing Anna needs right now, the fuzz bowling up. Anna,' he shouted again. 'Charlie found something.'

Anna held her breath.

'That's enough,' Florence said. 'I'm—'

'Wait!' Anna said, appearing from her room and looking downstairs. Jamie was standing on the doorstep, hands sunk into his pockets. He peered up at Anna and his face softened.

'It's okay,' Anna said to Florence. 'Let him up.'

She wasn't sure why she was doing this, letting Jamie inside. If that article had been true, it might be another way to get close to her and get revenge. But her desire to get to the truth was taking over.

Florence hesitated. 'I'm not happy about this, Anna.'

'Please,' Anna said.

Florence sighed then opened the door wider. Jamie strolled

in, walking up the stairs as Florence watched him through narrowed eyes.

'I know, I look terrible,' Anna said as his eyes ran over her. She tried to cover her stained top with her long black cardigan.

'You look like my mum did after Elliot died,' he said.

Anna felt tears start to come. She clenched her jaw. 'You mentioned Charlie?'

Jamie looked down at Florence who was still watching them. He steered Anna into the bedroom, shutting the door behind him. 'She said some druggie told her brother he stole Elliot's bag.'

Anna frowned. 'So?'

'So he stole it when Elliot was running away from The Docks the day he died. Elliot dropped it and the kid grabbed it. There's stuff in it.'

'He didn't sell it?'

'Too scared it'd be traced back to him by my dad. So he's just kept it all this time. He was off his head when he told Charlie's little brother.'

Anna's shoulders slumped. 'It's nothing.'

'It's more than nothing, Anna! We have to assume whoever killed Ben Miller tried to kill Elliot too, right? That they're the ones who took Joni too the other day. Whether it's the Ophelia Killer or some copycat. There might be clues in that bag.'

Anna turned away. 'Then call the police.'

He grabbed her elbow, making her spin back around. 'Jesus Christ, Anna, snap out of it. If we can figure out who the Ophelia Killer is—'

She started sobbing and Jamie's face softened. He pulled her into his arms. 'Oh Anna.'

She pushed him away. 'Get off. I don't trust you.'

''Cos of that fucking article? My aunt said all that to keep us apart, Anna. Yeah, sure, I might have hated you at the start but not now, nowhere near it.'

'I don't know,' Anna said. 'I don't know anything any more.'

'Yeah you do. You know you have two choices: fight or give up. Stop lying in this room feeling sorry for yourself like your mum does. Don't give up like your dad did.'

'But that's what my family does. We just give up.'

'Na, not you,' Jamie said, shaking his head. 'You're Anna Graves, you *killed* for your child. You fight, like I'm fighting to find out why my brother did what he did.' He stepped away and opened the door again. 'So now you have a choice, don't you? Stay here and do nothing. Or do what you did that day and fight for your daughter, for yourself. Come to The Docks with me, figure this out like you know your dad would've. Don't you want to prove your innocence, make sure Joni stays with you?'

She thought of Elliot's knife arching in the air towards her and Joni again; that fierce desire to protect her daughter. She felt it well up inside her, energising every part of her and she saw that fierceness in Jamie's eyes.

He was right. She had to fight.

Anna walked through the estate. The heat was oppressive, cloying around her, making it hard to breathe. Jamie had lent Anna one of his tops, the hood drawn over her head covered most of her face, making her feel even more claustrophobic in the unbearable heat. She could smell Jamie on it, the oil and his aftershave. She glanced over at him. Could she really trust him? But what did she have against him, some story in the local paper? That proved nothing. And she needed him if she wanted to get to the bottom of what happened with Elliot, with Ben Miller.

She *needed* him if she wanted to prove her innocence.

'The kid lives in the same block of flats I live in,' Jamie said, pointing towards the huge tower block in the middle of the estate. It loomed above them, elbowing for position against the shipyard cranes behind it. She'd heard about this place, once pitched as 'affordable housing with stunning sea views'.

Not so stunning now.

Jamie laughed. 'Yeah, it's not exactly Buckingham Palace. Come on.'

She hesitated. 'You've not been so keen about me coming to The Docks in the past. Why now?'

He examined her face then shrugged. 'I plan to kidnap you.' Anna stepped away from him and he laughed. 'Jesus, Anna, when will you figure out we're on the same side? I know you haven't been at work, I tried calling you there. Plus I overheard Ben Miller's dad saying your ex had taken Joni away. I figured you were hibernating and needed a kick up the jacksie.'

'Jacksie?'

He shook his head, smiling. 'You posh birds. It means arse.'

She raised an eyebrow. 'Nice.'

The smile disappeared from Jamie's face. 'Must've been hard seeing your ex take Joni away.'

'It won't be for long. We both decided it's for the best.'

'Still tough though?'

He looked into her eyes and she turned away. 'Look, Anna, it'll—'

'Don't tell me it'll work itself out. My gran keeps telling me that but it really might not.'

'I wasn't going to say that. I was gonna say next time you see Joni, even if things don't work out, make it happy, yeah? Go away thinking about the next time you'll see her, then the next time after that. 'Cos at least you know you will, even if it's for a bit.'

Anna looked into Jamie's eyes. 'You're right.'

'See, that's the thing with you. Grit. That's why I wanted you to come today too. I figured you can handle yourself, you managed to protect your daughter pretty good, didn't you? And you're the one with the brains,' he said, tapping his head. 'Brains and investigative skills. I need you if I want to figure out what happened to my brother before he died.'

A local newspaper tumbled down the road, both their faces staring out from it.

'I can't believe all the press about us,' she said. 'How's it been for you?'

'Why do you think I'm wearing this?' he said, gesturing to his cap and sunglasses. 'I'm a bit of an outcast.'

'I'm sorry.'

He shrugged. 'Not your fault everyone thinks we're shagging.'

Anna felt her face flush. 'Awful how the papers can twist things.'

Jamie didn't say anything but she could feel his eyes on her.

They entered the innards of the tower, stepping into a dirty, concrete entranceway about the size of a hotel foyer. People were hidden in the shadows – some leaned against the tower's graffitied walls, smoking; others slowly walked from group to group, discreetly exchanging items. Anna could see needles were being passed around in gloomy corners, glimmering like silver threads in the dark. As Jamie passed, their eyes widened and they moved further into the shadows. She thought of what the detective had said about Jamie, then she thought of what Guy had said.

Perception.

Anna would give it another word. *Survival.* She kept up appearances so she could survive and thrive in her community; feel part of something so she didn't feel alone and abandoned as she had when her father died. For Jamie, it was about surviving in his estate, keeping people at arm's length, being safe. She saw that now.

She followed him up two flights of narrow steps until they entered a brightly lit corridor.

'It's the end one,' he said, pointing towards a scuffed door at the end.

'What's he like? Will he get violent?'

Jamie laughed. 'Not with me, he won't.' He reached into his pocket, pulling out a small penknife.

Anna stepped back in shock. 'I can't be connected to anything like this. Detective Morgan is already on my case as it is.'

'Nothing'll happen. It's just a precaution.'

Like my comb was? Anna wanted to say.

They walked down to the end of the corridor and Jamie knocked on the door. 'Special delivery,' he shouted, making his voice a pitch higher. 'It's what the local dealer says when he's delivering,' he explained to Anna, lowering his voice.

The door opened and a boy with red hair peered out, face shiny with sweat. He looked so young, just seventeen or eighteen. When he saw Jamie, his eyes widened in fear. 'Shit.'

He went to shut the door but Jamie grabbed him, slamming him against the wall. 'Don't even try it.'

Anna stood back, watching. The kid looked terrified.

'I know you nicked my brother's bag,' Jamie said, right in the kid's face.

'I did nothing with it, I swear! When I found out he was your brother, I knew I was in trouble.'

Jamie glared at the boy and the boy visibly trembled. Then Jamie loosened his grip, smiling. 'Luckily for you, I don't shed blood in front of ladies. So where's the bag?'

'I haven't got it no more,' the kid said, eyes shifting to the right of him. Anna followed his gaze towards a cube coffee table in the middle of the living room.

'Mind if I come in?' she said. He looked at her, frowning. Then recognition flooded his face. She walked past him into the living room, twitching her nose at the stench of gone-off food and old cigarettes mingling with the boy's sweat. It was even hotter in the flat than it was outside. Anna shrugged Jamie's top off.

Jamie pulled the kid in and shut the front door, watching as Anna knelt by the coffee table. It was a small wooden table with grids, a filthy throw slung over some of it. She swept the rubbish off its lid then opened it, peering inside.

There was something under there.

She reached in, her fingers latching onto a rough drawstring. She pulled it out to reveal a blue bag with an alien on the front.

'My brother's,' Jamie said, voice full of emotion. He looked at the kid. 'Tell me what happened.'

The kid's eyes darted away.

Jamie shook him. 'I don't give a shit about you nicking it off my brother. I just need to know what happened to him before he died. You tell me everything you saw, then I take this bag away and it's over, all right? You don't need to spend your pathetic life shitting yourself about what I'll do to you.'

Anna stood up, the bag in her hands. 'Jamie's right,' she said softly. 'We just need to find the truth about Elliot. What did you see before you took the bag?'

'Answer the lady's questions,' Jamie said.

The kid licked his lips nervously. 'I saw Elliot running from just out there,' he said, jutting his chin towards a street outside. 'He looked *out* of it. Stumbling all over. Scared too. Fucking scared, kept looking behind him.'

Jamie took in a deep breath.

'He dropped the bag,' the kid continued, wiping his nose. 'He tried to pick it up but was all confused. And, well, that's when I took it.' He shrugged. 'Man gotta eat.'

'Get stoned more like,' Jamie said, looking at him in disgust.

'Did you see anyone else?' Anna asked him.

'Just school kids taking their time coming back from school. No one else.'

'You sure?' Jamie asked.

'Yeah. Next I hear, the kid's dead.' His eyes darted towards Anna then away again. 'Knew you'd be after me if it got out I nicked your brother's bag,' he said to Jamie. 'So I kept it here well-hid so no one would ever find it and connect it to me.'

Anna handed the bag to Jamie. Jamie shoved the kid towards his tatty-looking sofa and they all sat down. Jamie reached in, eyes soft as he pulled out a school notepad and some pencils, a pair of trainers and PE kit. He put it to his face, breathing it in. 'Elliot,' he said. Jamie put it to the side then reached in again, frowning as he pulled out a chunky silver watch. 'I don't recognise this.'

'Can I have a look?'

Jamie nodded, handing it to her. One of its links was broken, the face shattered. She turned it over to see an engraving.

To Simon, forever and a day. x

'Isn't Simon your dad's name?' Jamie asked.

'Yes,' Anna replied with a trembling voice. 'And this is his watch, I'm sure of it. He was wearing it when he died.'

Chapter Twenty

'How could it have got into Elliot's bag?' Anna asked as she looked at the watch.

Jamie's face hardened. 'Maybe he took it from the person who poisoned him? Who got the watch after your dad died?'

'My mum got all my dad's possessions. We cleared out the loft but I don't remember seeing this, I would have remembered.'

'Then you need to talk to your mum, don't you?'

Anna ran her thumb over the engraving. 'I don't understand all this.'

'We all done?' the kid asked.

'Yeah,' Jamie said, putting all the items back apart from the watch. 'We're done. Tell no one about this or that promise I made about not being after you? I'll take it back.'

'Yeah, sure,' the kid said. 'This over, then?'

Jamie walked up to him and looked him in the eye. 'Yes. But if I hear you've nicked anything off a school kid again, you're done for.'

'I won't, I promise.'

'You better not,' Jamie said, shoving him.

The kid looked at Anna again. 'You really tapping her like the papers are saying?' he asked Jamie.

'Of course not!' Anna said. Jamie smiled to himself, shaking his head.

'Thought not,' the kid said. 'Birds like you don't end up with nothings like us.'

Jamie's face filled with rage. 'Nothings? Speak for your fucking self! Come on,' Jamie said to Anna. 'Let's get out of this shithole.'

As they left the tower, Jamie seemed quiet.

'We're going to figure this out,' Anna said to him. 'I feel like we're getting closer to the truth.' As she said that, Anna realised she wasn't sure she wanted to get closer to the truth. What if she didn't like what she discovered?

It took Anna a few moments before she felt able to ring her mother's doorbell twenty minutes later. She held the watch in her hand, turning it over and over, questions tearing through her mind.

Her mother took a while to answer the door. When she did, she looked tired, dark circles under her eyes.

'Come in, then,' Beatrice said, holding the door open for Anna as she fanned her face with a leaflet. 'Too hot out there. I bet it breaks tonight, I can sense a storm coming. Sure I won't sleep.' Anna followed her mother into the living room. 'I heard Guy's taken Joni away,' Beatrice said.

'Only for a few days.'

'Where have you been? You smell of smoke.'

Anna ignored her question, holding the watch up. 'Is this Dad's watch?'

Beatrice took the watch, running her fingers over the engraving. A range of emotions ran over her face.

'It is Dad's, isn't it?' Anna said. 'He was wearing it when he died, I remember.'

'Why does it matter?' Beatrice said, shoving it back into Anna's hand. Anna suppressed her anger. This was her father's watch, how could her mother treat it so roughly?

'He was wearing it when he died,' Anna said. 'I'm sure of it. I need to know where it's been all this time.'

Beatrice turned away. 'You and Leo cleared the loft out, didn't you? How am I supposed to know?'

Anna shook her head. 'I didn't see it. Elliot Nunn had it in his bag before he died.'

Beatrice turned back sharply, her brow furrowing. 'Why would he have it?'

'That's what I'm trying to figure out.'

Beatrice crossed her arms, staring at the watch. 'I don't like it in here. Can you remove it please?'

'But you *gave* it to Dad.'

'Exactly.'

'Why do you hate him so much? I don't get you,' Anna said, shaking her head. 'I know you probably feel let down by Dad doing what he did, I do too. But the fact was, he was a good husband, a good dad.'

'He wasn't the Mr Perfect you all think he was, you know,' her mother spat.

'What's that supposed to mean?'

Beatrice put her hand to her temple, massaging it. 'I'm tired. I'd like to go to sleep now.'

Anna grabbed her mother's shoulder. 'You're hiding something, Mum. Tell me!'

Beatrice pulled her shoulder away. 'I'm not. It's like you said, he let us down, didn't he?' She couldn't look Anna in the eye.

'Mum,' Anna said, making her voice gentle. 'If there's something you need to say about Dad, please please tell me. There's some sort of connection between the Nunns and us. Not just Peter Nunn.' Her mother squeezed her eyes shut. 'I know this is hard for you,' Anna said. 'But I could be in a lot of trouble. I think Detective Morgan is building a case against me, I really think he believes I meant to kill Elliot. And social services visited me the other day.'

Beatrice's eyes darted open. 'Why?'

'Someone made a complaint about me. It's all unravelling and the only way I can try to stop it is figuring out what happened to Elliot Nunn and proving my innocence.'

'Innocence? You didn't mean to kill that boy, anyone with half a brain would know that.'

'Not just Elliot.' Anna sighed. 'The police are trying to connect me to Ben Miller's death, I'm sure of it.'

'That's ridiculous!'

'I know! But they don't have anyone else, they're desperate. So I need to figure out who hurt Ben Miller myself, don't I?'

'Well, it's not the Ophelia Killer.'

'How do you know that?'

Her mother scratched at her arms. 'I just do. Why start again after twenty years?'

'There are loads of reasons. A stint in prison. Moved away and is back now. Or it could be a copycat.'

Her mother frowned. 'Copycat?'

'Yes, someone trying to copy the Ophelia Killer for a bit of fame.'

'Who would do that?'

'I don't know, that's what I'm trying to figure out!'

Beatrice's face hardened. 'Leave it alone, Anna. You don't want to go digging all that up.'

'I have no choice, Mum.'

Beatrice sank into her armchair, closing her eyes as her fan cooled her face. 'I'd like to sleep now.'

Anna looked at her mother's drawn face, her pale eyelids. She thought of the days she'd lain in bed the past week. She couldn't be like her mother. She *refused* to be like her mother. She had to get to the bottom of this.

She jumped up. 'Fine. I'll let myself out.'

Anna walked outside into the cloying heat then headed to her house. She could go back to her gran's, where she was staying, but she needed to be alone to think. Her mother was hiding something. She just knew it. But what?

As she was getting some ice from the freezer to press against her neck, her doorbell went. She opened the door to find Jamie standing on her doorstep. 'I tried to call you back but you didn't answer,' he said.

'Come in,' she said, peering behind him to check no neighbours were watching.

He stepped in and she shut the door.

'So, what did your mum say?' he asked, following her to the kitchen.

She sighed as she gestured for him to sit down, pouring him

some lemonade and dropping some ice into it. 'The watch is definitely my dad's.' He clenched his jaw. 'Mum doesn't know where it was last though.'

'That's not much help.'

'Can we delay telling the police? I want to do some more digging. It's just yet another thing to connect me with Elliot before he died. It would reflect badly on me.'

Jamie paused a moment. 'Yeah, it will.'

Anna frowned. Was he starting to doubt her again? 'You know I knew nothing of Elliot before he died, don't you? Elliot or your family.'

'I want to believe that, Anna. But all the evidence is starting to suggest otherwise.'

'I understand how it must look but—'

'But you stabbing my brother in a random attack isn't looking so random any more?'

She looked at him in surprise. 'Jamie, please, you have to believe me.'

'Like you believe me when I say my aunt was talking trash to that reporter about me hating you?'

They stared at each other.

'I still don't think you believe me,' Jamie said. 'I can see it in your eyes.'

'And maybe you don't believe me. But we need each other.'

'Yep, just using each other 'cos God forbid, a radio presenter like you would hang out with a *nothing* like me for anything other than a means to an end.'

She sat at the table with him, handing him his lemonade. 'Jamie, I didn't mean it like that.'

He peered at the recycling bin which was bulging with unread newspapers. 'I doubt you've read the articles about us, have you?'

She shook her head.

'What was it that journalist at the local rag wrote?' he said. '"Anyone who truly believes a woman such as Anna Graves would hook up with a mechanic from a rundown estate is deluded."'

Anna didn't say anything, unsure what he was getting at.

'It's true, isn't it?' he said. 'I'm just a means to an end.'

'Like I am to you,' Anna said carefully.

'Ah,' Jamie replied, nodding. 'So I really am.' He shrugged. 'That's cool.'

He went to stand up but she grabbed his hand, making him stay. It felt warm, callused in hers. His eyes lifted to meet hers, his face pained.

'What's this about, Jamie? Is it what that kid said about you being nothing? Because you're not, you know.'

His jaw clenched. 'That's nice of you, Anna, but you and I know the truth. I'm nothing and I'll amount to nothing. You though.' He looked at her, shaking his head. 'You're as far away from nothing that you can get.' He looked into her eyes. 'I've never met anyone like you, Anna. You fucking fascinate me.'

Anna almost stopped breathing for a moment. 'Jamie…'

His eyes searched hers. 'You said I'm using you. Yeah, maybe it started like that. But now it's more than that.'

Anna struggled to catch her breath. The way he was looking at her, the low intimate tone of his voice…

She quickly closed her eyes. If she kept looking at his eyes, his lips, she might say and do something she regretted. 'Don't say anything else, Jamie.'

She heard the scrape of his chair, felt his knees against the outside of her thigh. She held her breath as he put his hand on her knee, his other on the back of her neck, under her hair. She felt his warm breath on her cheek, that warmth seeming to radiate through her, make her grow hot.

'Anna,' he whispered in her ear.

She let out a breath.

'Look at me, Anna,' he said.

She shook her head. If she just kept her eyes closed and didn't look at him, it would be a dream. Nothing more.

'Please,' he said, running his thumb gently over her eyelid.

She opened her eyes, saw his beautiful eyes on hers.

He leaned forward and her heart raced. She ought to stop him but she found she was powerless. He pressed his lips against hers and she sighed. Her lips moved softly against his and her fingers danced over his thigh. He slipped his hand into the opening of her cardigan, fingers cold against the flimsy material of her top as he slid his hand across her waist.

Feelings clashed and rolled inside her, the sound of the distant waves rising and falling with them, growing more violent. She matched their franticness, wanted more of Jamie, all of him, pulling him closer, fingers sinking into the skin of his thigh, his neck, lips clashing against his as he moaned.

Then the doorbell rang.

They both paused.

Someone hammered at the door.

'Fuck,' Jamie said under his breath.

They both pulled apart and reality hit Anna like a sledge-hammer. What had she been thinking?

Anna got up to answer it but Jamie grabbed her wrist, stopping her. 'Let me answer it. With all the threatening emails and what happened with Joni...'

She shrugged her hand off. 'It's my door, I'll answer it,' she said.

He frowned.

She went down the hallway while Jamie watched from the kitchen. She opened the front door to find her brother Leo standing there, his forehead shiny from the heat, sweat patches under the arms of his shirt. He peered behind her, eyes widening when he saw Jamie.

'Hi, Leo,' she said, choosing to ignore the look of shock on her brother's face.

'Mother is in a state,' he said. 'What did you say to her, she said you visited?'

'Come in,' she said, opening the door wider for Leo.

'I'd rather not,' he said, looking at Jamie.

'Oh for God's sake, Leo. Just come in, won't you?'

He let out an exaggerated sigh and walked inside.

'Leo, this is Jamie,' Anna said, walking down the hallway. 'Jamie, this is my brother, Leo.'

'All right,' Jamie said, putting his hand out to Leo. Leo looked at it in disgust then grabbed Anna's wrist, pulling her into the living room.

'What on earth is he doing here?' he hissed.

'We're trying to figure out what happened to his brother before he died.'

'I've seen the articles about you two, Anna. I hope they were wrong.'

'They are,' Anna said, trying not to think about the fact that what she and Jamie had just done had made them a reality.

'I hate the way my family has been dragged into all this scandal,' Leo said. 'There have been journalists outside my house too, you know.'

Anna's stomach sank. She didn't get on with her brother but she wouldn't wish that on him. 'I'm sorry about that, Leo, really I am.'

He looked her up and down. 'My sister, cavorting with a mechanic and brother of the boy she killed.'

All her pity dissipated. She crossed her arms. 'I've heard it all already. Let's talk about Mum, shall we? Did she tell you what we talked about?'

'She wouldn't.'

Anna pulled their father's watch out. 'Recognise this?'

He frowned. 'Dad's watch.'

'Yes. It was in Elliot Nunn's bag before he died.'

'Probably stole it. You know what the children in The Docks are like.'

Jamie appeared in the doorway and his face sparked with anger. 'My brother wasn't a thief,' he said, striding into the room. Anna stood between him and her brother.

'How do you know that?' Leo said, crossing his arms and glaring at Jamie.

'Leo, don't be an arsehole,' Anna said.

Leo looked at them both. 'This is a disgrace. I won't stand

292

here and be shouted at by the two of you. I'm leaving.' He strode down the hallway, opening the front door.

Anna ran after him and grabbed his arm. 'Don't go! We need to figure out where the watch has been. Did you see it when we cleared out the loft?'

'I'm going,' he said, shrugging her hand away.

'Leo, I just—'

'What are you going to do to make me stay?' Leo shouted. 'Stab me with a comb?'

In the distance, a couple walking their dogs stopped and looked over.

Leo shook Anna's hand off his arm and marched down the path.

'Did you notice your brother's wrist?' Jamie said.

Anna peered up at him. 'What about it?'

'He had a tan line, like he usually wears a watch. Does he usually wear a watch?'

Anna thought about it. 'I have no idea.' She pulled her phone out, scrolling through to the photos from her gran's party. There was no watch on his wrist, just the tan line. She scrolled farther back to the twins' third birthday party in June.

And there it was, their father's watch on Leo's wrist.

Anna ran outside, calling out her brother's name. He stopped, took a deep annoyed breath then turned around.

'*You* had Dad's watch!' she said, showing him the photo on her phone.

He looked at the phone, his face flushing. 'So what?'

'You lied.'

'I lost it. I went to put it on one morning and it was gone, simple as that. I didn't want to have you moaning at me about losing our precious father's watch.'

'You're lying,' Jamie said.

Leo glared at him. 'This has nothing to do with you.'

'It has everything to do with me,' Jamie said, stepping towards him, grabbing the watch from Anna. 'My brother was *poisoned* before he died. And what do we find in his bag? *Your* fucking watch.'

Anna's mind reeled from the possibility.

Leo looked them both up and down in disgust. 'You two have lost your mind. But then why does that surprise me? Look what you've become, Anna, a killer cavorting with filth like this,' he said. He shoved her away and strode to his car, getting in and screeching off.

Jamie turned to Anna, eyes sparking with anger. 'You know him, he's your brother. Do you really think he's capable of killing?'

'No,' Anna said, shaking her head. 'No way.'

'What if he's been copying the Ophelia Killer all this time? He'd have seen the work your dad did on the murders, maybe got all obsessed too, like your dad did. Did your dad have photos of the murders?'

'Yes.'

'If he saw them, that can twist a kid's mind.'

She'd seen them. Had it twisted her mind? She thought of the comb plunging into Elliot's neck again, the rage she'd felt before.

'My brother is not capable of murder, for God's sake,' Anna said. 'He's a spiteful little shit but murder? No, no way.'

They glared at each other then Anna stepped into her house. 'I need to be alone. I'll let you know if I find out anything else,' she added, avoiding his gaze.

'Anna, about what happened between us earlier…'

'That's not important,' she snapped.

His face hardened. 'Fine. But we'll need to go to the police about this eventually. I need to get to the bottom of what happened to my brother.'

Anna watched him walk to his van through the glass, her heart thumping. Had they really just kissed? She shook her head. She didn't have time for that. She needed to figure out how Elliot got her dad's watch – the same watch her brother had been wearing.

She walked into her living room and paced up and down it. She refused to believe her brother was a killer, there *must* be another explanation.

She caught sight of some of the boxes she'd got down from the loft the other day with the intent of looking at her dad's things. She went over to one, opening it, finding what she was looking for: the photo her dad used to carry about in his wallet of her and Leo. It had been taken a few weeks before he died on the very rocks where he'd met his death. Leo was standing over the sea, a fishing net in hand, while Anna watched him. They were both smiling. It was an unguarded moment, brother and sister having fun.

She looked at her brother's face. Was he really capable of murder?

She sighed and went to put the photo back then noticed an envelope in the box, The Docks Community Foundation's familiar logo along the top of it. She opened it, finding a compliment slip inside with a message scrawled on it. *Simon, I thought you'd appreciate these letters from some of the boys you met. Thanks so much for coming along to the event. Kiara.*

She remembered reading these back in June when she'd got the boxes down. She pulled the letters out again. Some were very short, Kiara had clearly 'encouraged' the boys to write them. They were all thanking her father for doing a radio workshop at the community centre. Dates were on some: May 1995, four months before her father died…and the same month the Ophelia Killings started.

Anna frowned as she read one from an Alex McDonald. Where did she know that name?

It was one of the Ophelia Killer's victims.

She ignored the erratic thump of her heart. That wouldn't be so unusual, all the victims were from The Docks after all. She flicked through the other letters. Another name stood out: Sam Twiselton. Another of the Ophelia Killer's victims.

She noticed a photo at the bottom of them all. She pulled it out, saw her father standing in front of two rows of boys, a microphone in his hand as he held it up to one of them. Anna looked more closely at the boy he was holding the microphone to. Dark hair. Blue eyes. Alex McDonald again, the Ophelia Killer's first victim. Her eyes scanned the other boys' faces. She quickly got her phone out, finding the Wikipedia page about the Ophelia Killer with photos of all his victims. She held it up against the photo, matching some of the boys: Luke Culnane, Matthew Beaman…

Anna put the letters down, a sudden thought occurring to

her. Her father had met some of the victims through his volun-
teering work, maybe all of them. The police said the victims
must have trusted the killer as they let him into their gardens,
accepted drinks from him.

Is that what her mother had been keeping from Anna? Had
she guessed?

'No,' Anna said to herself, shaking her head. Her dad was
trying to track the killer down, why on earth would he do that
if *he* was the killer?

'He thought it would make a good cover,' she said to herself.
'Give him the chance to get close to the case, get a head start
if the police started suspecting him.'

She looked at the photo again, at her father's smiling face.
Maybe Leo even knew? He might have even *helped* her dad
and—

'No!' Anna shouted to herself, shoving the photo back in the
box.

She would not consider the possibility.

Anna played around with her food that evening, her gran
watching her with concerned eyes. She simply couldn't
comprehend the possibility her father *and* her brother had
been hurting boys.

But the thought just wouldn't stop whirring around her mind.

Anna looked at Florence. She'd known Anna's father and
she knew Leo as well as Anna did. She took her father's watch
from her pocket and put it on the table between them. 'Elliot
Nunn had this in his bag when he was running from whoever
poisoned him.'

Florence took the watch, staring at it. 'Your father's,' she said, looking up.

'Yes. Leo has been wearing it until recently.'

Florence nodded. 'I did notice at the twins' birthday. Why would Elliot Nunn have this?'

Anna pushed her plate aside. 'What if Leo's the one sending me those threatening messages?' Anna swallowed. 'God, this sounds even crazier saying it out loud. But what if Leo's been copying the Ophelia Killer?'

'You're saying your brother killed Ben Miller?' Florence shook her head in disbelief. 'I'm sorry, but that's just ludicrous.'

'Want to hear something even more ludicrous? What if Leo's a copycat and Dad was the actual Ophelia Killer?'

'Anna! Are you being serious?'

Anna shook her head. 'I *know* it's crazy, I know it. But the investigative part of my mind can't ignore the evidence right in front of me. You knew Dad, do you think he could be capable of killing?'

Florence looked down at her plate, brow creasing.

Anna leaned towards her. 'Gran?'

Her gran peered up at her. 'Of *course* I don't think he was capable of killing. But—' She paused. 'After he died, the killings stopped. Just like that,' Florence said, clicking her fingers together. 'The police were suspicious.'

'So the police thought Dad may have been the Ophelia Killer?' Anna asked, the horror of it making her feel sick.

Florence sighed. 'They questioned your mother about your father's whereabouts before each killing. She was in no fit state really. They could see that. Whatever she said seemed to satisfy the police though, no more questions were asked afterwards.'

Anna raked her fingers through her hair. 'Jesus.'

Florence put her hand over Anna's. 'You look exhausted, poppet.'

Anna examined her gran's tired eyes, her pale skin. 'So do you. How are you feeling?'

'Oh I'm fine,' she said, waving her hand. 'Doctor Sekheran said I'm as strong as an ox, the tests showed nothing.'

'Of course, your check-up.' Anna inwardly kicked herself. How could she have forgotten? Her gran had been sent for a series of blood tests after she'd fainted. Today was when she was getting the results. Anna had been so wrapped up in herself, it had slipped her mind. She squeezed Florence's hand. She shouldn't be bothering her with all this. 'Look, let's stop talking about it, it's not good for either of us. Let's just enjoy our dinner.'

As Anna forced the rest of her dinner down, she tried not to think of the day's events. But as darkness fell and she went to bed, they whirred around her mind, combining with the oppressive heat to make it impossible for her to sleep. When her phone buzzed at three in the morning, she was still awake.

She picked it up then froze. It was an email from the Ophelia Killer with the subject line: *History repeats itself.*

Had her brother sent it?

She opened the email with trembling fingers. There was one

line in it: *Better hurry before it's too late. TOK.* There was an attachment too. She downloaded it then frowned. It was a gif of someone falling from a lighthouse. Not her family's lighthouse, but very similar. It must have been a random image pulled from the web. But the implication wasn't so random: Anna had a horrible feeling the Ophelia Killer was trying to convey a message that someone was about to get hurt.

She instantly thought of Jamie. If her worst fears were true and Leo was sending the emails, killing too, maybe he'd target Jamie after their confrontation? She quickly dialled Jamie's number, relieved when he picked it up.

'Thank God,' she whispered.

'Everything okay?'

She told him about the email. 'I'm worried whoever sent it is implying someone is about to fall from the lighthouse. I thought it might be you.'

'Jesus,' he whispered.

'I think I need to call the police.'

'No,' Jamie said quickly. 'I'll go there first, check it out.'

'I'm coming too,' Anna said, getting up and pulling her jeans on. 'It's just a few minutes' walk from me.'

'Anna…'

'You said yourself I'm made of grit. I'll meet you there.' She quietly finished getting changed then sneaked out of the house through the back, not wanting to wake her gran. The moon above made the pebbles shine like blades as they ran along the beach, the waves eerily calm in the oppressive heat.

When she got to the lighthouse a few minutes later, Jamie was waiting just outside, face filled with concern.

She couldn't help it, her tummy tilted at the sight of him, the kiss they'd shared earlier searing through her mind.

'Did you see anything?' she asked him, pushing the memory away.

'Just got here,' he said. 'Show me the gif.' She showed it to him and he peered towards the window. 'It could be a trap.'

She looked at his pocket. 'Still have that penknife?'

He nodded. 'I doubt I'll need it, I'll easily be able to overpower your brother.'

'You really think Leo sent the email?'

He nodded. 'Looks like you're starting to believe it too.'

Her eyes filled with tears. 'Maybe.'

'Let's go.'

Anna turned her phone torch on and they both walked around the back of the lighthouse.

As they drew closer, something came into view.

Beneath the moonlight, limbs at awkward angles on the rocks, blood pooling beneath their head, was a body.

Anna stopped walking, unable to put one leg in front of the other, flashbacks to her father's death clashing with fear inside.

'I think it's time to call the police,' Jamie said, his voice trembling slightly. 'You go home, Anna. You don't want to be mixed up with this.'

'No, I need to see.' She forced one foot in front of the other.

Dark hair came into view, a pale hand.

She exchanged a look with Jamie. Was this another young boy, like Ben Miller? How would it look, her being the one to find the body again?

But despite wanting to stop walking towards the body, she found her legs were taking her closer.

As the face came into view, she let out a scream.

It was her brother.

Anna broke into a run, sinking to her knees beside her brother's broken body. 'Oh Leo, oh God, no.'

Jamie sank down beside her, putting his arm around her shoulders. She leant her cheek on his shoulder.

'We need to call the police,' he said, digging his phone out. 'We have no choice.'

After a while, blue lights flashed in the distance, three police cars and an ambulance appearing. They came to a screeching halt and officers ran out, reminding Anna of the day Elliot had died.

Paramedics jogged up to Leo, crouching down over him as Detective Morgan strode towards Anna and Jamie. They both rose.

'We'll need to take a statement from you both,' the detective said.

'Of course,' Anna said, wiping her tears away as she looked at her brother. She thought of his children and Trudy.

He was gone, really gone.

As Anna and Jamie gave their statements, police and forensic officers walked up the lighthouse like an army of ants in the moonlight.

After a while, one officer came out and beckoned Detective Morgan over. They whispered, and both glanced at Anna.

Then the detective walked over with the officer. 'Your brother was pushed,' he said. 'There were signs of a struggle up there.'

'Oh God.'

'Anna Graves,' he said, face very serious. 'I'm arresting you on suspicion of murdering Elliot Nunn, Ben Miller and Leo Fountain.'

Chapter Twenty-One

The Seventh One

I take the first circle of skin, stretching it out and placing tiny pins around its edges. I've already scraped the blood and tissue off the back, the flannel I used now in the bin next to me. I carefully do the same with the other circles, gently caressing the skin with my fingers as I think of the boy. He was particularly beautiful, eyes so blue they didn't look real. I overheard his mother talking about the killings a few days ago in the newsagents, discussing the theory it was a local teacher.

'Yeah, I know, can you believe it?' she said to the woman working behind the counter, shaking her head as she chewed some gum.

That's when I first saw the boy, that day at the newsagents. He looked bored, ignored. I knew he had to be our next one. When I tracked him down, he was stretched out on the plastic sun lounger, naked from the waist up, sweat pooling into the curves around his taut belly button. He said yes to lemonade straight away and didn't struggle when he realised something was wrong a few moments later. He seemed to almost welcome it. I think he even smiled at me just before he died. Oh I know, I'm probably imagining it. But it's nice to think that.

I place the pin board upright, admiring my handiwork. After the circles dry, I will colour them and then tomorrow, my masterpiece will be finished.

'I love watching you work.' I look up, see you watching me. 'You're so artistic, so gentle.'

'It calms me.'

'That's good, you need something to distract you afterwards. It can get overwhelming.'

'What about you? What distracts you?'

You smile. 'I have my work, don't I?' You gesture towards a bag by your feet. It's from one of the fancy shops in town. 'I got you a present.'

'You didn't have to.'

'I did. You've been so wonderful the past few weeks. So clever and patient and—' You laugh. 'I'm a sentimental old fool, aren't I? But you don't know what it means to have someone to share this side of my life with. Not just share it but turn it into something I can keep for ever too,' you say, gesturing to the circles. 'Come on then, open it.'

I jump up, walking to the bag. I love it when you're like this, full of light and laughter. To make things even better, we're going out for dinner tonight, a proper dinner.

I open the bag and peek inside. 'Oh, it's gorgeous,' I say.

I pull the dress out, putting it against me and twirling around as you laugh, the pieces of skin I've shaved away from the circles fluttering in the air like confetti.

Chapter Twenty-Two

Anna sat across from Detective Morgan, her arms wrapped around herself as she stared at the concrete wall ahead.

'Anna?'

She forced herself to look back down at the table. Nine photos were laid out before her, the same photos she'd been confronted with again and again over the past few hours of questioning. All the same – black hair, blue eyes, pale skin. All dead and lying naked in a pond except two: Elliot, his throat punctured, blood bleaching the pebbles below. Then her brother, his head smashed on the concrete ground, the lighthouse looming above.

She let out a sob, putting her hand to her mouth. Her brother was really dead. Her brother who she'd run around the beach with as a child. Her brother who she'd played hide and seek with.

And now he was gone. Really gone, leaving his twins behind, leaving poor Trudy behind.

'All these males are connected by one thing,' Detective Morgan said. He leaned forward, looking into her eyes. She felt the room close in, the unbearable heat making her feel faint. 'You, Anna.'

Anna shook her head. 'We've gone over this again and again.

I had nothing to do with their deaths, apart from Elliot and that was an accident.'

'Your brother,' he said, tapping his finger on the photo of Leo's crushed head. Anna looked away, unable to bear it. 'Pushed after an argument. Was he getting too close to the truth, Anna?'

'I have no idea what you're talking about,' Anna said through chattering teeth. 'I was at my gran's when he fell.'

'No proof of that. Your grandmother was sleeping.'

'It was three in the morning! You have to believe me, I wouldn't kill my brother.'

'But your neighbours reported the two of you had a fight on the street.'

'Hardly a *fight*. We were just arguing.'

'Over what?'

She swallowed, looking at the photo of her brother again.

'Anna?' Detective Morgan pushed. 'Why did you argue with your brother?'

She took a deep breath. 'I told you. He had my dad's watch, the same watch Jamie and I found in Elliot's bag.'

'And you thought this proved he poisoned Elliot, killed Ben Miller? Bit of an outlandish theory, Anna,' the detective said.

'I see that now.'

'But your father on the other hand…while you had a break just now, I was told the team have found some other interesting items in the lighthouse, Anna.'

What now? Anna thought.

The detective looked towards the officer standing by the door, who walked over with a plastic bag. Detective Morgan took it, placing it on the table. In it were several shape cutters.

Anna shivered. 'Where did you find these?'

'In an art box in a small room at the back of the lighthouse. We found some hair too, and blood. We're getting it tested, of course. Your father liked to work in the lighthouse, didn't he? He knew the boys who were killed, there was even a photo of him with some of them in the local paper. You were very close to your father, weren't you?'

'I was.'

'You admired his work.'

She nodded. 'Yes.'

'If our theory is correct, and your father was the Ophelia Killer—' Anna flinched '—*if* our theory is correct, then maybe you knew about it.'

She shook her head in disbelief. 'I was eleven when those boys died.'

'An impressionable young mind. Maybe he told you about what he did?'

Anna closed her eyes.

'Or you saw the photos he had of the crime scenes,' he continued. 'That can have quite an effect on a young mind. Some negative, others positive. Maybe you grew obsessed with it all.'

There was a knock on the door. The officer opened it, air rushing in, a brief respite from the cloying heat in the small room. Another officer gestured for the detective to join him.

'Just be a moment,' he said, leaving the room.

Anna turned to her solicitor, Jeremy. 'How long will this go on?'

'He can't keep you much longer, Anna,' he said, wiping the sweat from his bald head with a hanky.

'This is all ludicrous.'

Jeremy sighed. 'I know.'

The detective came in and sat down. 'Well, our theory has just become fact. Your mother has given a statement confirming your father was the Ophelia Killer.'

Anna felt like the ground had collapsed beneath her. It had been a possibility in her mind, yes, but she hadn't truly believed it, *couldn't*. She thought of her wonderful father, saw him smiling at her, the sun winking behind his shoulder.

'Oh God,' Anna whispered.

'Your mother broke down when she was told about your brother's death,' Detective Morgan said. 'She said she discovered your father was the Ophelia Killer just before he died. That might even be why he committed suicide, knowing his wife knew.'

Images of her father's broken body came to her, interspersed with Leo's.

Anna felt herself grow faint. 'Can I have some more water, please?'

The detective nodded at the officer standing by the door who disappeared outside.

'Now let's go forward twenty years,' the detective said, pushing the photo of Elliot towards her. She turned away, unable to see another dead boy. 'Elliot Nunn. What triggered that, Anna?'

'What do you mean? You know what happened.'

The detective nodded. 'Seeing him must have been strange though. Black hair, blue eyes, pale skin. It must have brought back memories of the boys your father killed, ignited something inside you? Is that why you targeted him? Because he looked like them?'

Anna slumped against her chair, exhausted. She just couldn't keep saying it over and over.

'Detective Morgan,' Jeremy said. 'You've kept Anna for nearly ten hours now. You have two hours left to produce definitive evidence or you must release her.'

Detective Morgan shuffled the photos up and stood up. 'Take her back to her cell then,' he said to the officer standing behind him.

When Anna got to the cell, she lay on the lumpy bed staring up at the ceiling.

Her dad was the Ophelia Killer?

Tears ran down her face, pooling on the pillow below.

Maybe that's where she got her darkness from? She'd inherited it. How else was she able to kill a young boy?

An hour later, the door opened again.

'You're free to go,' Detective Morgan said.

She sat up, confused. 'Free?'

'For now.'

Officers led her outside with Jeremy towards her gran's familiar car. Anna felt a surge of relief. She ran towards it then paused when she realised her mother was in the passenger seat, her eyes red as she stared ahead.

'She can't be alone right now,' Florence said, leaning over to open the back door for Anna to get in.

Anna climbed in and Beatrice's eyes rose to meet hers in the wing mirror, unblinking. Then she looked away.

'You knew about Dad?' Anna asked, gripping her seat to lean forward and look at her mother. 'Why didn't you *tell* me?'

Florence looked between Anna and Beatrice. 'Tell you what?'

'Dad was the Ophelia Killer,' Anna said, tripping over the words as she tried to comprehend it. 'Mum knew.'

Florence gasped as she looked at her daughter. 'My God, Beatrice, why didn't you say?'

Beatrice shook her head. 'I can't talk about this now. My little boy has gone.' Her voice sounded robotic as she said that, her eyes staring into the distance.

They drove back in silence, Beatrice staring ahead, Florence's knuckles white as she gripped the steering wheel. Anna stared out at the sea, grappling with the idea that her father had killed all those boys. Dark clouds were gathering, the sea starting to twist and turn in a tumultuous dance.

When Anna got back to her gran's house, Beatrice said she needed to go to bed and disappeared into one of the guestrooms, slamming the door shut behind her.

Florence sank onto the sofa, putting her head in her hands. Anna went to her, slipping her arms around her.

'I'm sorry this is happening,' Anna said.

Florence peered up at her through tear-drenched eyelashes. 'I can't believe your mother has kept that secret in her heart all this time. No wonder she's the way she is.'

Anna stood up, pacing the room. 'Okay, so if Dad was the Ophelia Killer, then who pushed Leo? Who killed Ben Miller? And who's sending me those emails?'

'Darling,' Florence said, 'you're exhausted. Please let me make you something to eat.'

'I'm not hungry,' Anna said, continuing to pace the room, her mind running over everything she knew. If she could just figure it all out, she could prove her innocence.

Florence rose and gently took Anna's shoulders, stopping her. 'You haven't slept. Sit down, stop pacing, eat.'

Anna slumped down on the sofa, trying to make her tired brain go through everything. She felt something was there, spinning just out of grasp. But did she have the strength to reach for it?

She paused, noticing something peeking out of her mother's bag. A small edition of Shakespeare's *Hamlet*. She pulled it out. The front cover of the book featured the *Ophelia* painting by John Everett Millais, Ophelia lying half submerged in water, palms facing up to the skies, head back as though she were waiting for something, someone, to take her. Anna looked at the girl's face, her abandonment, the sadness too in the way the flowers scattered around her head.

She thought of Ben Miller when she found him dead, and the photos of all the Ophelia Killer's victims – her father's victims.

Anna looked out towards the angry sea, imagined going out there and submerging herself, wading in farther and farther, no turning back.

No, she wasn't her father or her mother. She'd fight this.

As she went to put the book back into her mother's bag, something fell out. She picked it up to see it was a small colour drawing of a boy submerged in water, a beautiful boy with dark hair, blue eyes staring up into nothingness surrounded by flowers.

Her eyes lowered to the title and signature at the bottom.

Peter by Beatrice Lowell

Anna walked into the kitchen, the painting fluttering like butterfly wings in her hands. 'Did Peter Nunn drown?' Anna asked her gran.

Florence looked at the painting. 'He was found in the sea by the lighthouse.'

'I thought he'd had an accident at The Docks?'

'Yes, he hit his head. They think he collapsed a few hours later and fell into the sea.'

'Did Mum see him dead?' Anna asked.

Florence shook her head. 'Not from what I know. She may have drawn that from her imagination.'

'Strange thing to do.'

Anna walked to the room her mother was sleeping in.

'Mum?' she whispered, knocking on the closed door. No answer. She knocked again then opened the door to find an empty bed, the French doors leading out to the beach open.

'She's gone,' Anna shouted out.

Her gran walked to the French doors, stepping outside, raindrops starting to fall on her head. 'Beatrice?' she called out. She shook her head, eyes filled with worry as she pulled the doors shut. 'No sign of her.'

Anna looked around the room. 'She's taken her mobile phone and cardigan.'

'She's probably heading back to the bungalow. Let me call her.'

As Florence called her and left a message, Anna looked back down at the drawing. 'It can't be a coincidence Mum drew Peter like this. Maybe he was discovered like this? *Maybe* he was the first victim?'

She thought of the shape cutter found in the lighthouse, and the hair the detective had mentioned.

Would the hair turn out to be Peter's?

'I don't know,' Florence said, her face dubious. 'Everyone said it was an accident at The Docks.'

'Was it witnessed?' Anna asked.

'No idea.'

'He was a love rival for Dad, wasn't he? I mean, Dad had a motive to kill him. Or maybe they argued, his death was an accident. But it triggered something in Dad...he *enjoyed* it.' She closed her eyes, not quite believing she was talking about her own father. 'But then why would Dad be digging his death up again all those years later?' she said, thinking of what Kiara had said about him delving into Peter's death. 'And why the time gap between Peter's death and the other killings if it triggered something?' She looked at her mother's drawing again. 'Peter looked like the other victims, didn't he? Dark hair, blue eyes.'

Florence nodded. 'I suppose he did.'

Anna tapped her finger on the painting. 'Why would Mum *draw* this?'

'She did obsess about the death a lot,' Florence said, brow furrowing. 'This isn't the first of the drawings she did like this, her father and I started to get concerned about it. She seemed strangely fixated with how Peter died.'

'In the sea, surrounded by flowers...' Anna looked towards the open French doors. 'Maybe she *was* there when Peter died?'

'No, Anna,' Florence said. 'She would have said.'

'Not if she didn't want people to know.' Anna went very still. 'What if Mum wanted Peter dead for some reason? What if she and Dad were working together and Mum's just been carrying on his work? There are serial killing couples: Myra Hindley and Ian Brady. The Wests.' Anna shuddered. 'Or Mum did it all herself, she's the only one to see Dad with the last victim, after all.'

'Anna, that's ridiculous! She wouldn't kill her own son!'

Anna realised Florence was right. 'I know, I know.' Anna put her hands up to her head. 'I feel like my brain's going to explode.'

Her gran came to her, pulling Anna into her arms. 'Stop, poppet, just stop and give yourself a break from all this torment. You've just lost your brother, give yourself time to grieve.'

'But there's no time! Detective Morgan is probably right this minute finding some kind of ludicrous reason to charge me again. He won't stop until he gets me behind bars and then I won't see Joni.'

Florence pulled away and looked into Anna's eyes. 'This is all about Joni, isn't it?'

'Of course it is.'

'Then for Joni's sake, rest, refresh yourself, then we'll come back to this tomorrow. We need this evening to grieve. I'll keep trying to call your mother.'

Anna felt herself relax against her gran. 'Okay,' she whispered.

That night, Anna tried her best to sleep. But the rain had grown heavier, lashing against the window, the sea a roar so loud it drove sleep away. Anna twisted and turned in her bed, the drawing her mother had done running through her mind. She still hadn't returned and she wasn't answering the phone at the bungalow either. Florence had called the police and they promised to keep an eye out for her. But until she was missing for a substantial amount of time, it was hard for them to dedicate extra resources to finding her.

Anna veered between being worried for her mother to being suspicious of her. After being told her father was the Ophelia Killer, nobody seemed beyond the realms of possibility now.

Eventually, Anna fell asleep but was woken by the sound of her phone ringing. Outside, the storm was in full force, thunder crashing across the skies, lightning turning the room white. Anna grabbed the phone, seeing it was Guy. Panic gripped her as she looked at the clock. Two in the morning. Why would he be calling that time of night?

'What's wrong, Guy?' she asked when she answered it, a terrible feeling of foreboding running through her.

'Your mother's taken Joni.'

Chapter Twenty-Three

'Your mother just turned up,' Guy said, the sound of thunder in the distance. 'Told me Joni was in danger and she couldn't stay with me. She was acting crazy, Anna. There was no way I was going to hand Joni over. I went to call you, leaving my mother with her, but then I heard something. I ran inside and – and Mum said your mother had shoved her, grabbed Joni. Last I saw was her driving off with Joni in the back.'

Anna put her hand to her mouth. 'My God. Have you called the police?'

'Of course.'

'Good, that's good,' Anna said, jumping off the bed.

'I'm in the car now, we're heading to your mum's bungalow,' Guy said.

'You think that's where she's gone?'

'That's all I can think. The police'll be there too. She'll be there in about five minutes or so if she puts her foot down.'

'I'll go there now.' Anna grabbed some jeans and pulled them on under her nightdress. 'Gran!' she shouted, running into Florence's room. She froze. Her gran's bed was empty.

'Gran?' she said, running downstairs.

But the house was deathly silent, horribly empty.

She ran into the living room for her car keys then paused. A vase was toppled over, cushions scattered across the floor as though there had been a struggle. She must've not heard whatever had happened above the noise of the storm. Laid out on the table was a large scrapbook, just like the ones she'd seen in the lighthouse once. Anna walked towards it. It was open on a page with a large pressed flower, lilac petals and a green stalk. Written beneath it was one word: *Alex.*

Anna frowned. She reached down, placing her finger on the petal. Then she snatched her hand back.

It was hard, rough.

She crouched down and peered closer.

The petals didn't look like normal petals. They were wrinkly in places.

The image of a bloody shape cutter came to her mind. She saw the photo of Ben Miller's body when she'd found him, five perfect circles removed from his torso.

She counted the petals on the flower.

Five.

She reeled back, feeling nauseated.

Skin. The petals were made from skin.

Anna went to the next page. Another flower, the name Sam at the bottom. A few more pages. *Ben.*

Every single hair on her body seemed to stand on end. Who did the sick scrapbook belong to: her mother? Maybe Florence found the scrapbook in her daughter's belongings and there had been a confrontation.

Anna grabbed her car keys, then flung her raincoat and shoes on, running outside into the storm, wind flattening her jeans against her legs and making her hair fly out behind her.

She jumped into her car and headed to the bungalow.

When she got there, there were blue lights illuminating the sky, several police cars lining the street. She stopped the car then noticed her mother's car was on the drive.

She jumped out into the rain and ran down the path.

'Anna!' a voice said. She turned to see Detective Morgan. 'We must stop meeting like this.'

'Is my daughter in there?' she asked, trying to peer around him into the dark windows.

'I'm afraid not, Anna.' He tilted his head, rain splashing onto his red cheeks. 'Maybe you know where she is? Maybe you and your mother are in this together?'

'Of course not! Where has she taken her?'

'We're getting the whole area searched, she would have gone on foot from here so can't have gone far.' An officer called the detective away. Anna paced up and down the path as the detective spoke to his colleague.

Where had her mother taken Joni?

'Think, think,' she hissed to herself, peering out towards the sea, the lighthouse shining tall and white under the moonlight.

She paused.

Hadn't Detective Morgan said they'd found items at the lighthouse? Her mother had all her art stuff there…maybe she created her scrapbooks there?

Her stomach turned.

She looked around her. All of Ridgmont Waters' police force was *here*, the lighthouse left quiet and empty.

As Detective Morgan was distracted, she took the chance to slip away into the night, running through the unlit streets of Ridgmont Waters until she finally got to the beach.

She ran across the pebbles to the lighthouse, memories of the day she'd discovered her father's body jagged as they pierced her mind. The moon stood in a crescent above, its spiky ends pinpoints in the dark as the sea worked itself into a frenzy beside her, screeching in her ears as rain hammered down.

When she got to the lighthouse, it loomed threateningly above her. Anna noticed one of its windows was open. She wouldn't have left it open!

A cry echoed out, carried on the wind from the open window. Joni's cry!

Anna ran to the lighthouse's door, yanking it open. It swung back against the wind. She scrambled up the metal stairs towards her daughter's cries, passing her mother's art room on the way. She glanced at the scrapbooks lining the wall.

Could it really have been her all this time?

Another cry from the lantern room.

Anna ran to the next room, the small hallway, then she paused, peering up the staircase leading to the lantern room. The door was ajar. Through the gap, Anna saw her mother walking back and forth with Joni in her arms, her hair erratic, her face drawn.

'Shush shush, darling,' Beatrice cooed to her granddaughter.

Fear twisted at Anna's gut. Every instinct told her to rush in there and grab her daughter, but she held back. It would be foolish

322

to just burst in there and she'd had her fill of making rash foolish decisions lately.

Anna heard movement below. She turned. Further down the stairwell was her gran, her pale face half cast in moonlight, revealing a purple bruise around her right eye.

'Anna?' she said.

Above, Anna's mother paused.

Anna held her breath, fear rushing through her. She pressed a finger to her lips, warning Florence to be quiet, then pointed up at the room. Florence nodded, understanding.

Beatrice began pacing back and forth again; she hadn't heard them. Anna beckoned Florence over into the darkness. They both hugged each other.

'What happened?' Anna whispered.

'I found something—'

'The scrapbooks?'

'Yes. When your mother returned, I confronted her. She went wild and attacked me.' She gestured towards her bruised face. 'I knew she'd bring Joni here; I had to stop her, I thought I could fix things before you woke up. I didn't want you to know what she'd done.' Her eyes filled with tears. 'I'm so sorry. It's stupid, after everything, I'm still trying to protect Beatrice.'

It didn't seem stupid to Anna. She understood the power of a mother wanting to protect her child, no matter what.

'We need to get Joni from her,' Anna said. 'I'll go in first, distract her, then you grab Joni.'

Florence nodded, taking a deep shuddery breath.

Anna squeezed her hand again then walked up the metal stairs, not attempting to disguise her footfalls. Beatrice stopped pacing and stared down at Anna. Wind and rain whistled through the open window behind her...the same window Anna's father had jumped from.

Joni let out a cry, reaching for her mother, her face red and wet from tears.

'It's okay, baby, Mummy's here,' Anna said, carefully stepping into the room. She looked at her mother. 'Mum, hand Joni over.'

Beatrice pulled Joni close to her, eyes wild. 'No,' she said, shaking her head. 'Go away.'

'She's my daughter, Mum, just like I'm your daughter.'

'Ma ma ma ma ma,' Joni cried, scrambling to get away from Beatrice.

Beatrice stepped back, precariously close to the open window. It took all of Anna's willpower not to run over and grab Joni. But she knew any wrong move might mean jeopardising her daughter's life.

'I know everything, Mum,' Anna said, putting her hand out as though placating a wild dog. 'And it's okay, it's fine, I understand.'

There was a sound behind her and suddenly, Florence darted towards Beatrice, pulling Joni from her arms.

'No,' Beatrice screamed, going to grab Joni back. But Anna sprinted across the room and circled her arms around her mother, holding her.

'Don't do this, Mum!' Anna said, struggling to keep hold of Beatrice who thrashed against her, a fox caught in a snare. Joni wailed and Florence shushed her, pressing her face against Joni's dark curls.

'Get off me! You don't understand!' Beatrice yelled. 'She killed Peter! Isn't that right, Mother?'

Florence looked up.

'You brought Peter here,' Beatrice said, looking around her. 'That's why they didn't find him for hours. You and Father needed time to *think* about what to do.'

Anna's grip on her mother loosened and she looked between them, confused. 'What are you saying?'

Florence shook her head as Joni squirmed against her. 'She doesn't know what she's saying, Anna.'

'You hated him,' Beatrice snapped at Florence. 'He was too *poor*, too *common*. What would your village friends say? What would Father's Admiral say? So you went to confront him at The Docks.'

'Mum, don't be ridiculous,' Anna said.

'Ask her! Look in her eyes and ask her,' Beatrice said. 'See if she's telling the truth, go on.'

'I won't ask her, you're talking nonsense. I just want to take Joni and get out of here.' Anna walked to her gran and put her arms out to Joni.

But Florence stepped back, a faint smile on her face. 'She's fine with me, poppet.'

'I just need to get her out of here.' She went to lift Joni out of Florence's arms but she shoved Anna away, stepping back towards the open window.

Anna paused, fear making her whole body tingle. 'What are you doing, Gran? Give Joni to me now.'

'No,' Florence said, shaking her head. 'I don't think so, poppet.'

Anna's blood turned to ice. She looked between her mother and gran, the reality dawning on her. 'No,' she said, shaking her head. 'It can't be true.'

Florence looked into Anna's eyes for a moment then she sighed. 'Oh, you'd have found out eventually, just like your father did.'

Anna looked at Joni then at Florence, suddenly struggling to breathe. 'You *did* kill Peter Nunn? And Dad knew it was you?'

'Let's get one thing clear first, darling,' Florence said, voice clear and strong. 'I did not mean to kill Peter. It was an accident.'

'Oh God,' Anna said, putting her hand to her mouth as she looked at Joni.

'We went to the dockyard to warn him off,' Florence continued. 'Your grandfather even had a cheque with him. Two hundred pounds, a lot back then. But he refused the money, refused to leave Beatrice alone. I confess, I got angry when he called me a jealous bitch. I've never been *jealous* of you, Beatrice,' she said, turning to her daughter. 'I just wanted the best for you.'

'Not for me, you wanted the best for you,' Beatrice said. 'But I loved Peter.'

'Yes, he was very beautiful. I often think of how attractive he was.' Anna felt nausea rise inside her. Were these words really coming from her *gran*? 'But what else was there to him other than his pretty face?'

Joni started wriggling in her great gran's arms.

'Joni needs me,' Anna said in a shaky voice as she put her hands out to her daughter, eyes on the open window.

Florence shook her head. 'She has her great granny, she'll be fine.'

'Mama!' Joni said, reaching for Anna.

Anna took a step towards them but Florence walked right to the open window. The wind howled and salty air gushed into the small room with the deafening sound of the waves crashing below.

'Not one more step, Anna,' Florence said, her eyes turning to steel. 'We don't want another member of our family falling to their deaths from here, do we?'

Anna froze as she imagined Joni tumbling down into those waves. Her head buzzed, terror making her weak. She saw her father's broken body again, imagined that body being Joni's. Her breath came in spurts, her mind unravelling.

'Mama!' Joni said again.

'Shush now, your great granny's here,' Florence said. She smiled down at Joni, the same smile Anna once took comfort from but which now filled her with horror.

Anna clenched her fists, digging her nails into her palms to stop herself from running to her daughter. She grappled with what to do. One wrong move and Joni may be gone for ever. One step backwards, and her gran could throw Joni from the window. Anna looked around the room, trying to find some sort of weapon. But there were just old books, a desk, her father's typewriter...

She focused on it, drawing strength from it. Her father once told her people were most preoccupied when talking about themselves. Their egos drew them into a strange little reverie, made them confess to things they wouldn't normally.

Distracted them.

She had to play this carefully, cleverly, she saw that now. She thought of the emails she'd been getting, emails she now realised had been sent by her gran. They revelled in sharing the details of the murders.

That's what she would do. Let Florence talk about the subject she must love the most.

'What happened with Peter Nunn, then?' Anna asked, trying to keep the tremble from her voice.

Florence sighed. 'I shoved him. Just a little shove, nothing really. But he tripped over on some concrete and fell backwards, hurting his head badly. There was lots of blood and he was very confused, the poor boy.'

Anna's mother let out a sob, turning away.

'Tell me more,' Anna said.

Florence cocked her head. 'You want to know?'

'Of course.'

She smiled. 'Your grandfather got into a panic. He was a hard man on the surface, like my father. But he didn't have my father's inner strength. I had to take charge, get him to put Peter in the car while people weren't looking. Luckily, we were in a quieter part of The Docks. Your grandfather headed here to the lighthouse with Peter while I went to my WI meeting. It wouldn't look right if I didn't turn up, I'd been to every single one since we'd married!' She laughed and Anna tried to hide her disgust. 'When I returned to the lighthouse, I'd never felt emotions like it. I knew the boy might die and I was scared, very scared. But there was something else too. *Excitement.*' Her smile deepened at the memory. 'I even hid in the little room below to watch him for a while. When he eventually died, your grandfather carried him down to the sea and we laid him out.'

'Oh Peter,' Beatrice whispered.

Florence looked at her daughter sternly. 'He wasn't just shoved there, Beatrice. I made sure to do a garland for him.

Your grandfather was racked with guilt after. I think that's what made him leave me for that dancer. Every time he looked at me, he saw Peter. Such a weak fool.'

'You're sick,' Beatrice hissed.

Anna put her hand on her mother's arm, trying to calm her, her eyes always on Joni. One false move…

'Thank you for finally telling us, Gran,' Anna said carefully. 'It must be a weight off your shoulders. It was an accident, we understand that. There's no need to ever tell anyone else now, is there, Mum?' Anna said, looking at her mother. Beatrice looked into her eyes then quickly nodded. Anna turned back to Florence, eyes flickering to the open window then back again. 'So let's just go home, shall we? Get Joni tucked up in bed and try to move on now you've got it all out of your system.'

Anna put her trembling hands out to her daughter.

But Florence held Joni even tighter. 'What's this, no more questions from the investigative reporter?' she asked. 'What about all the digging you've been doing the past few weeks, just like your father? Come on, ask me some more questions then.'

Anna looked into her gran's eyes. She was *enjoying* this.

'Let me help you,' Florence said. 'Why don't you ask me how I felt when Peter eventually died? Feelings, emotions, that's what your father used to say people wanted to know about.'

'Do you feel any guilt?' Anna asked.

'Did *you* feel guilty about Elliot?'

'Of course.'

Florence examined Anna's face. 'Really?'

'I'm not like you,' Anna said, finally letting the tremble into her voice.

'Really? I wouldn't be so sure.' She kissed Joni's cheek, giving her a smile that chilled Anna to the bone. 'Alistair always said the ability to see the beauty in the terrible was hereditary. My father was the same, as was Alistair's father.'

'Alistair?' Anna said, thinking of the step-grandfather she'd so loved.

'Yes, Alistair,' Florence replied with a happy sigh. 'He understood the thrill I got from seeing Peter die and helped me draw that out with the other boys a few months after we met.'

Anna shook her head in disbelief. Alistair was part of it? 'You killed the boys together that summer?'

Florence nodded. 'Of course, I didn't have the confidence to do it alone back then. And who else but a doctor could teach me how to remove the boys' skin for my scrapbook?'

As Florence talked, Anna noticed her mother had gone very quiet. Anna looked at her out of the corner of her eye, saw her mother take a small step towards Florence.

'So the year you met Alistair was the year the killings happened?' Anna asked quickly, wanting to keep her gran talking, her eyes on Anna.

Florence nodded. 'He saw how the boys in The Docks all trusted me, good old Florence from the community centre with her cakes and lemonade. He said it was the ideal way to repeat the thrill I'd felt at seeing Peter dead.' Anna felt her skin crawl with disgust but she kept her face neutral as she looked at her gran, aware of her mother moving closer and closer to her in the shadows.

'So you wanted to recreate Peter's death?' Anna asked her.

Florence smiled. 'Yes, spot on. The sight of his beautiful

330

prone body lying in water, surrounded by flowers, will never leave me.' Then the smile disappeared from her face. 'The deaths that summer never did match up to Peter's death though. But Alistair said that was always the way, the first was always the best.'

'Jesus Christ,' Anna whispered, unable to help herself.

Florence narrowed her eyes at Anna. 'Oh, don't play the innocent, Anna. You've killed too.'

'It's not the same.'

Florence shuffled back and sat on the window ledge as Joni clung onto her neck, her little body close to the edge.

Horror filled Anna. She had to get Joni away from her. Her gaze darted towards her mother. She was still too far away. Would she reach them in time? Florence's eyes narrowed and she started to turn her head towards Beatrice.

'Why did you stop killing if you enjoyed it so much?' Anna said in a rush.

Florence turned back to Anna, making Anna let out a breath of relief. 'Your father's death changed things. He'd got so close to the truth, even happened upon the last boy just after we killed him. Alistair and I realised we were getting a bit sloppy, needed to step back, reassess.' Her eyes filled with tears. 'Just as we were planning to start up again, Alistair started to get very ill. Well, you know the rest.'

'Your accomplice was gone,' Anna said.

'Quite.' Her gran's face hardened. 'I blame Simon for that. The fear of finally being caught made Alistair ill. I didn't feel so bad about pushing your father after that.'

'You *pushed* Dad?' Horror filled Anna as she imagined her

father falling, heard the crunch of his bones on the rocks below. She peered towards the open window.

'He was getting too close to the truth,' Florence said. 'I had to do it.'

'And then you started killing again,' Anna whispered. 'You tried to kill Elliot Nunn before he ran into me, didn't you?'

'I did,' Florence said, smiling again. 'I lost all my confidence after Alistair died, spent years wanting to resurrect it all. But I just couldn't imagine doing it alone. Then while clearing out my loft to sell items along with those you'd cleared from your mother's, I found some memories I'd written down for Alistair. He'd wanted to relive our great adventure when he was dying.' She got a faraway look in her eyes, lost in the memories.

As Florence reminisced, Beatrice moved closer to her.

'Reading those memories to Alistair as he lay dying reminded me of what we had achieved together and just how much I'd learnt,' Florence said, stroking Joni's hair as she looked out of the window. 'When I saw Elliot Nunn at that community event, I was struck by how much he looked like Peter. I only discovered recently that he was Peter's nephew. I knew it was a sign sent by Alistair. I *could* do it alone!'

'But you couldn't,' Anna said, taking a careful step forward with her mother while Florence continued to peer outside. 'He got away.'

Her gran's face clouded over. 'Yes, he had a knife on him. I didn't foresee that. I didn't foresee he'd take your father's watch too, silly me. Leo left it at my house by accident after delivering your father's junk for me to throw away. I was rather pleased. I never did get something of your father's.' She peered down the stairs towards the scrapbooks. 'And we know how I like to collect my trophies. I used it to lure Elliot in. He wouldn't have the lemonade at first. So I offered the watch for him to sell to go towards that silly computer he was going on about.'

Anna's heart clenched at the thought of Elliot walking so innocently into her gran's trap.

'But then he managed to get away. He must've recognised you as my granddaughter and in his addled mind, thought you were going to hurt him so attacked you. But you finished the job for me.' Her face lit up. 'Oh Anna, you can't know how *proud* I was of you.'

Anna felt sick to her stomach. 'Proud?'

'Of course! I even began to think we could start off what Alistair and I never got to finish. You and I, working together. That's why I sent the emails. When I heard that you killed Elliot, I saw potential in you, like Alistair saw it in me. It's so hard doing it alone. But with you, Anna—' She smiled a twisted smile. 'What a team we could have made. I sent those emails in the hope you might eventually confess how much you enjoyed killing Elliot.'

'Are you saying you thought I might want to *help* you kill boys, like Alistair did?'

She let out a dramatic sigh as Joni sucked her thumb, eyes wide as she looked out into the darkness, rain flecks on her chubby cheeks. 'That was the hope, Anna. I rather enjoyed confiding in you.'

'They terrified me! What about the comb you left in Joni's nursery? I presume that was you? And the holes in her teddy?'

She shrugged. 'I confess, I grew angry, disappointed. You were ignoring me. It became clear I'd overestimated you. I wanted to send you a message, make you wake up and see the darkness inside you.'

Anna put her hand to her mouth, shaking her head. 'And when Joni went missing? You did that?'

'I did.'

'But she could have drowned!'

'No, poppet! I was standing right there, watching. I wouldn't have let her drown.'

'But why did you do it?'

'I wanted you to think it was Jamie Nunn. I didn't like how close you two were getting, even with the argument you had and that silly interview his aunt gave. I can see you like him, that you *want* him. I knew you'd grow close again.' Her face clouded over. 'And I couldn't have that, not my Anna ending up with a mechanic from The Docks,' she spat. 'And yes, a part of me wanted to bring you to your knees, make you experience the absolute worst to find your inner darkness. I knew you could handle it, you're strong, like me. When I saw the look in your eyes when we found Ben Miller's body, how fascinated you were, I thought it might have worked.'

Anna shook her head, incredulous. 'I was horrified, distraught.'

'Oh Anna,' Florence said, peering down at Joni. 'You are so deluded.'

'*Me* deluded?'

'I chose Ben because I knew you liked him. I did it for *you*, Anna. I followed him, found him in that garden, offered him some lemonade. I'm not as strong as I once was. But it was easy, he was so weak.' She cocked her head. 'You know, it seems a strange thing to say but he reminded me of Leo. Or what Leo could have been if his father's death hadn't twisted him.'

Anna looked at the window her father had fallen from…and her brother. 'You pushed Leo too.' It was less a question, more a statement. Of *course* her gran had.

'Spiteful boy,' Florence hissed. 'I grew sick of him bringing you down.'

'Oh Jesus,' Anna said, putting her hand to her mouth.

'Oh, don't be so pathetic, Anna!' Florence shouted at her. 'I did that for you too!'

Joni started crying, looking up at her great granny in fear. Anger surged through every fibre and sinew of Anna's body. But she kept a lid on it, eyes focused on Joni.

'What was the point though?' Florence said, looking at Anna in disgust. 'I now see I got you all wrong. Alistair would be so disappointed. He truly thought you and I were alike, but clearly not.' She looked down at Joni. 'Maybe I'll have better luck with this one when I take her away.'

Anna's eyes widened. 'I won't let you!'

Florence laughed. 'Oh please! Don't play the mother lion. You're just as bad as Beatrice, I can see that now. I *told* you you shouldn't have gone back to work after you had Joni, but off you went anyway. Probably why you were distracted during the walk, thinking non-stop about work. At least Joni knows I'll be there every minute of every day,' she said, smiling down at her great granddaughter.

Beatrice drew closer to them. Joni saw her and tried to squirm away from Florence.

'What's wrong with her?' Florence said. 'She's never like this with me.'

'She's *scared*,' Anna said gently, trying to make Florence look at her, not at Beatrice. 'If I can just—'

The window swept open in the wind, rain lashing in and wetting Joni's face. Joni started crying uncontrollably, fat tears falling down her cheeks, her tiny face turning red.

'Oh shut up!' Florence screamed at her.

The shock of her voice made Joni go still.

Panic fluttered inside Anna.

Beatrice took the chance to run at Florence.

Anna screamed out.

Florence scrambled up onto the windowsill, balancing precariously with Joni in her arms, the wind from the wide-open window making her white hair swirl around her head. 'Not one more step, Beatrice!'

Anna and her mother froze.

Florence twisted around so she was facing the sea, one hand clutching onto the window frame, the other circling Joni's small body. 'Look,' she said, leaning Joni out slightly. 'That's where your grandfather and uncle both died.'

'Don't do it!' Anna screamed.

'Don't do what?' Florence asked, eyes dancing with mischief as she looked over her shoulder at Anna. 'Maybe Joni will disappoint me too? Maybe I should save myself the bitter disappointment.'

She held Joni out farther.

'No!' Beatrice screamed. She clambered onto the windowsill, grabbing Joni away from Florence.

Florence went to snatch her back but Beatrice quickly leaned down with Joni in her arms, handing her over to Anna. Anna ran into the corner of the room with her daughter, watching her mother and gran with wide eyes as they both balanced on the windowsill, lightning darting through the black sky behind them, rain wetting their hair.

'Give Joni back to me!' Florence screamed at Anna. She went to climb off the windowsill but Beatrice yanked her mother's arm back, making her stay.

'You're *hurting* me, Beatrice,' Florence said, struggling against her daughter.

'I don't care. You're not hurting my girls, you sick twisted woman.'

'Me? Twisted?' Florence shouted back, wincing as Beatrice's grip tightened. 'You're the twisted one, a woman who can't even mother properly, not like me.'

'Mother? You murdered young boys! You murdered your own grandson!'

'I loved every single one of those boys as if they were mine,' Florence said. 'Gave them more compassion at the end of their lives than any of their pathetic mothers did. They were all just like you, Beatrice, oblivious, distant, not caring one jot. You are such a bitter disappointment to me, to Anna...and to Leo.'

Beatrice blinked, her grip loosening. Florence took the chance to twist away from her. Beatrice went to grab her again and Florence stepped back, her foot finding just air.

But before she could fall, Beatrice grabbed her hands, steadying her.

They looked into each other's eyes. Then Florence frowned.

'No more, Mother,' Beatrice said. Then she released Florence's hands.

Florence's arms circled in the air, trying to find traction. Her

337

feet lifted beneath her, her elbow smashing against the glass of the window as it swung about in the wind.

Then she disappeared over the edge.

Anna covered her daughter's ears from the sound of Florence's screams, screams that grew more and more distant as they reached the rocks below.

Chapter Twenty-Four

The Eighth One

I woke up this morning feeling frantic, like time is running out. You say I'm being silly. But I don't want to go out today, I want to wait. We're pushing our luck.

But of course, you insist. And of course, I comply. Not because I'm weak. It's because I want to, need to.

I wonder if I'm anxious because of the news reports on the radio, Simon's reports. He's getting close, he's even digging into Peter's death. When I saw the children yesterday, he was watching you in this strange way. You say I'm being paranoid but something tells me it won't be long before he figures it out, looks into your past, learns about the missing stepson, the missing paperboy.

But we're here now and all paranoia is gone because this boy is beautiful, his hair longer than the others but somehow still neat, ink black, glossy. I remember the first time I met this boy, at the event Simon attended last week. I couldn't keep my eyes off him, he was so beautiful and you knew, you caught my eye and all it took was a smile, fate sealed.

I can't stop stroking his hair now, his wet hair, drenched with rosemary and violets. You grow impatient. The police are questioning each household again after Simon's report about their incompetency aired last week. They need to show they care. And right now, there are police officers just two streets away doing lots of caring.

The truth is, it thrills me. Who'd have thought it? A few weeks ago, it would have terrified me.

You're right. I've come on leaps and bounds.

'Florence,' you hiss. 'Come.'

'Wait,' I say, carefully putting the circles of skin in a Tupperware box to make my flower pressings later. I take one last look at the boy. 'Goodbye,' I whisper.

Then I stand and take your hand, walking from the garden and out of the side gate.

'We were pushing it a bit fine there,' you say, eyeing the police in the distance.

'It worked out, it's fine.'

'He was truly beautiful, wasn't he?'

I smile. 'He was.'

'And his mother is a drug addict, yes?'

I sigh. 'Afraid so. Beatrice actually mentioned her the last time I saw the children. She used to be a good friend of hers.'

'Now he's saved,' you say. 'Clean and pure.'

I smile. 'Yes.'

'Florence?' I look up, see Simon watching us from a distance, frowning.

He didn't hear us. He couldn't have. I smile, stride towards him. 'How are you, Simon?'

He peers over my shoulder towards the garden we've just been in.

'Looks like your report did wonders,' you say, joining me. 'Police are out in full force.'

But Simon is still staring at the garden. He can't see the boy, it's impossible. We closed the gate.

'Simon?' I say.

He blinks and looks at me. 'Yes, seems to have done the job. What are you both doing here?'

'The community needs us at a time like this,' you say.

'You heard about the buffet lunch we're putting on?' I ask.

Simon nods, distracted. 'Yes. I think Beatrice might be going.'

I look at him in surprise. 'Beatrice?' My daughter wouldn't usually appear at an event I've arranged, she wasn't exactly delighted when Simon accepted my invite to run a radio workshop for the kids earlier this summer.

'I told her how impressed I am with what you're doing here, Florence.' His eyes stray to the garden again then back to me. 'I think she thought it was time she supported you.'

You squeeze my hand and smile. I've wanted this so long, for Beatrice to stop this strange little battle she has with me. But I can't feel happy right now. All I can see is Simon's eyes straying to the garden.

Does he know somehow?

'Where have you come from?' he asks.

'The play park,' you say, smooth as ever. 'Lots of rubbish,' you add, gesturing to my bag where the Tupperware box is, the boy's top and the bloody shape cutter too. 'Thought we'd give it a clean for the kids, you know.'

'Right,' Simon says, narrowing his eyes at you.

'Well, better go set up,' I say.

'Will you join us, Simon?' you ask him. 'We could do with an extra pair of hands.'

'Not yet,' Simon says. 'I have a few more people to talk to for my report. I'll see you later?'

I feel his eyes on us as we walk away. Before we step onto the green, I turn and see him walking towards the garden.

My fingers are trembling as I put all the food out.

'It'll be fine,' you say, putting your hand on my arm.

'He knows, Alistair.'

'You're being paranoid.'

As you say that, I see Beatrice running across the green, her face streaked with tears.

'Finish putting these out,' I say to you, my heartbeat thumping. Something's wrong.

I walk out but it's too late, Beatrice is in her car and driving off. I go to head back to the hall to tell you something isn't right. But I bump straight into Simon who also looks like he's been running.

His face goes white when he sees me.

Yes, he knows.

'You saw the boy too,' I say quickly. I peer behind me, towards you, making my eyes fill with tears. 'Please, he can't know I know.'

'Alistair?' Simon asks.

I nod. 'I went to check on the boy's mother, you know she's an addict? I found the – the—' I put my hand to my mouth, stifling a sob. How easy it is to act. 'I found the boy in the pond. I ran out to tell the police and bumped into Alistair. I just knew he—' You approach from the community centre. I feign fear, moving closer to Simon, clutching his hand. 'Don't go to the police yet,' I whisper. 'I

342

beg you, Simon. I need to tell you everything first then we need to figure out what to do. Meet me at the lighthouse in an hour.'

He snatches his hand away. 'No, Florence. I'm going to the police, we can both go. Then I need to find Beatrice, she went to check on her friend and saw me looking at the boy. She thinks I did it, for God's sake!'

'Simon, I'm being very serious,' I say. 'Alistair will kill me. He will do everything he can to destroy you too, Beatrice, the children. You don't know what he's like.' Simon's eyes fill with fear. There, I've hooked him. I thought mentioning the children would work. 'I have so much to tell you,' I say, 'all I need is twenty minutes.' I grab his hand. 'One hour, the lighthouse. I beg you.'

He looks into my eyes and I try to conjure up memories of what my father did to me, the horror and the fear.

He sees it in my eyes and nods. 'Okay. One hour. But then we're going to the police.'

I watch Simon walk across the beach, his dark hair catching in the wind. He's a handsome man, serious and intelligent. I'm surprised my daughter attracted him with her flighty artsy ways and constant hand-wringing. But then opposites do attract. I suppose you and I seemed like opposites when we first met, a doctor and a housewife. But deep inside, there's something that binds us.

I hear the door open below, then the sound of Simon's shoes on the metal stairs. He pauses a moment then he steps into the room.

'His mother found him twenty minutes ago,' he says. 'If anyone discovers I saw him first...' He shakes his head. 'I'm risking a lot for you, Florence. I need to know everything.'

'Of course.' I take a deep breath. 'It started with Peter Nunn.'

I tell him about Peter's death and he shakes his head. 'I knew his death was connected in some way to all this.'

'It was an accident, I swear to you, Simon. It's been this horrific secret I've had to live with the past few years.'

His face is unreadable.

I turn away, going to the window. 'When I met Alistair, I finally felt I could tell someone.' I shake my head. 'But he seemed excited by the story. I knew then something was wrong with him and even though I haven't admitted it to myself, as soon as the first boy died a few weeks ago, I suspected Alistair.'

'Why didn't you go to the police?'

I turn back to Simon. 'I love him.'

He holds my gaze and I see he doesn't believe my story. I sigh. This is going to be difficult.

'I've seen the photo of Peter Nunn's body,' he says. 'He had flowers around his head, like they were placed there.'

'No,' I say. 'There's a tree that hangs just over the rock pool. They must have come from that. When I described the scene to Alistair, it added to the appeal. That's why he does what he does now with the flowers, he wants to recreate Peter's death.'

'A boy he didn't know?' Simon asks, unconvinced. 'And as for the flowers, there's no tree, Florence.'

He doesn't believe me. I sigh. If this is the way it needs to be, so be it.

'There is. Come see.' I beckon him over and open the window, peering out to check no one is about. 'There, see?' I say, pointing towards the rock pools nearby. 'You need to lean out a bit.'

It's so easy, it surprises me. He does as I ask, just like my beautiful boys do when they're slurring their words and stumbling.

344

So compliant. Except foxglove isn't Simon's poison, his thirst for answers is.

All I have to do is lean down and use all my strength to pull his legs out from under him. The top half of his body slams into the windowsill then he topples out, twisting around to look at me, eyes filled with horror.

I hear the crack of his bones below. I won't look. I've never liked blood and gore. Instead, I pick my bag up and walk out, no turning back.

Epilogue

1 July 2016

Your Say Question of the Day: Are working mothers taking on too much?

Caller A: 'Yes, back in my day we just made do with a tiny house and a clapped-out old car between us so my wife could be with the kids. Women don't need to work if they pull the belt in.' (Tony, 67)

Caller B: 'No, of course not! It's important mothers show their children the importance of hard graft.' (Jeanette, 47)

Caller C: 'Only mothers called Anna Graves.' (Jamie, 28)

Anna shook her head, smiling to herself.

'Coffee for the road?' Georgia asked, holding up a steaming mug, her bulging belly stretching the material of her dress.

Anna smiled. 'Is the Pope Catholic?'

Georgia laughed, giving her the coffee. 'Hard night?'

'Joni decided to hold a teddy bears' picnic in the middle of the night. I could hear her chattering away *and* singing.'

'Let me guess. "Let It Go" from *Frozen*?'

Anna raised a wry eyebrow. 'How did you guess?'

'I've got it all to come,' Georgia said, rubbing her belly. Anna smiled. She missed Nathan but it was good to work with someone like Georgia, their morning show was going from strength to strength. Anna had even started to do more investigative reports, launching a regular series exploring hard-hitting issues, something her father had talked about doing.

Anna looked at the photo she had of Joni with her mother on her desk. Joni was dressed in a full-on Disney Elsa dress, Anna's mother wearing a princess tiara on her head as they both smiled into the camera. Joni had grown so much the past year, she was nearly two now, talking and walking. It still astounded Anna each day how quickly she was growing.

It could have been so different.

She shuddered, recalling those moments after her gran went crashing to the rocks below the lighthouse. As they'd waited for the police, her mother had told her she'd dedicated the years since her husband had died protecting Anna and Leo from the despicable things she thought their father had done.

'Especially you, Anna,' she had said, stroking her daughter's cheek as police sirens drew closer and closer. 'You so looked up to him. It ruined me, I couldn't let it ruin you. I came so close to telling you, so close. But I knew I couldn't. I found that if I just closed myself to you, to everything, you would never need to endure the pain of thinking your father was a murderer.'

'Oh Mum,' Anna said, squeezing her hand. 'All this time, it's been about protecting me. I wish I'd known. I haven't supported you enough. I've been impatient, angry at you for shutting me out. If I—'

'Shush,' her mother said. 'It's not been easy for you. And with my mother taking so much of your time, your emotions, *isolating* you from me in her clever little ways. That's what she used to do with me, manipulate me so she was my whole world. She's always been so needy, so desperate to be the centre of my life. Then Peter came along and he showed me how to break away, how to gain some independence.' Her face lit up. 'He represented everything I was taught not to love: he was poor, and rough in his ways. He didn't really have many prospects. But he knew me for what I was and he wanted to be more than people *thought* he was.'

Anna thought of Jamie.

'But that's the past,' her mother said, looking down at Joni and smiling. 'Everything's different now. No more hiding, no more secrets.'

The sound of footsteps had clattered up the steel staircase then. Mother and daughter stood, holding hands.

Detective Morgan appeared at the doorway, face red, breath coming out in spurts. More officers appeared behind him.

Anna looked at him, holding her breath. She knew they would be after her now with her gran dead on the rocks below, there were just too many coincidences. And how would they believe her, a woman who killed a schoolboy? And why would they believe her mother, a woman with a history of depression and anxiety?

Anna stepped towards the detective, putting her hands out.

'Just take me in. I didn't have anything to do with my gran's death. But I know you won't believe me, just get it over with.'

Detective Morgan frowned. 'Anna, we're not taking you in. We found some notes your grandmother wrote to her late husband when we searched her house for you just now. We know what she did. You're free.'

The media onslaught had been intense after that, the whole family now the target this time, not just Anna. Strangely enough though, the journalist who'd been the most aggressive – Anna's old friend, Yvonne Fry – had been the most supportive since Florence's death, writing articles showing Anna in a good light. Those articles played a role in separating Anna and Beatrice from the Ophelia Killings, and with her mother by her side, Anna was able to ride the wave until things died down.

Part of that was trying to come to terms with what Florence had done. As they'd cleared out her house, they'd found a diary she'd written as a child and discovered the horrific abuse she'd endured at the hands of her strict naval father. Children who'd gone through worse didn't turn to murder, but it went some way to explaining how her mind had become so broken and twisted. Detective Morgan had also let Anna read the notes Florence had written for Alistair, charting how they'd murdered all those boys that summer. It had been the perfect storm, a teacher and a willing pupil drawing on each other's darkness. Florence had wanted to recreate that with Anna, using the emails she wrote to her and the little sick gifts – the shape cutter in her pocket, the damaged teddy, the comb left in Joni's nursery – a twisted way of making Anna find the innate darkness Florence thought they shared. And she'd succeeded for a while,

Anna had begun to wonder if there was something rotten inside her.

But now Florence was gone, Anna was finally able to see that what she'd done the day Elliot died was inevitable and not the result of some inherited darkness.

'Look who it is,' Georgia said now, nudging Anna.

Anna looked up to see Jamie at the studio door. Her heart quickened as he shot her one of his lazy smiles, his jeans covered in oil, his fair hair messy.

She lifted her headphones off her head and went up to him. He pulled her towards him, softly kissing her on the lips.

'Hey,' he said softly. 'Ready?'

She nodded, grabbing her bag and coffee and waving goodbye to Georgia.

Jamie took her hand as they strolled out of the studio. It had taken them a few months to get together, the wounds still raw from everything that had happened. But when they had, it had seemed completely natural, mechanic and radio presenter, the perfect match.

They stepped outside, the wind whipping their hair around their faces. Jamie pulled her close and she smiled. They followed the sea, feet crunching on pebbles.

When they got to the stretch of beach where Elliot had died a year ago, they both paused. Anna watched as Jamie laid some pebbles Joni had painted for Elliot on the beach, then Anna reached into her bag, kneeling down and burying her father's watch beneath them.

Then they both continued on their journey until they got to the lighthouse.

It had been newly painted, and stood even brighter and whiter against the calm sea. Jamie's van was outside packed full of his tools. He'd worked so hard on renovating the lighthouse over the past few months, spending weekends and evenings on it.

In the distance, people started strolling over from The Docks, children whizzing towards them on scooters, their shoulders burnt red from the sun. Their mothers shouting out for them to slow down, fathers lifting some onto their shoulders.

Jamie squeezed her hand and they both walked to the front of the lighthouse.

'Mummy!' a little voice shouted. Anna looked over to see Joni running towards her in her Elsa dress.

Anna's mother followed her, rolling her eyes. 'She refused to wear anything else after I got her from nursery.'

'You learn to pick your battles,' Anna said, laughing as she lifted her daughter up and swirled her around.

In the distance, she caught sight of rocks where her father, brother and gran had fallen to their deaths.

'What's wrong, Mummy?' Joni asked, following her gaze.

'Just remembering,' Anna said sadly, exchanging a look with Jamie.

'What you 'membering?' Joni asked.

'So many questions,' Anna said, stroking her daughter's cheek. 'One day I'll tell you.'

'One day,' her mother said, squeezing Anna's hand, her eyes filling with tears.

People started to gather around them and Jamie looked at his watch. 'It's three-thirty,' he said.

Anna felt a thrill of excitement go through her. She stood before the crowds, crowds who had once accused her, harassed her, hated her, but were now slowly starting to accept her. At the back, she noticed a familiar face: Guy. He'd brought his girlfriend Carly, a vivacious woman who had a little girl too. Anna smiled at them both. He'd been a wonderful support after discovering what had happened, and more than ever, Anna felt as though they were a team despite not being married any more, their joint love for Joni making what could be a difficult situation into a bearable one.

'They're waiting for you,' Jamie said.

Anna took a deep breath and turned to the crowds. 'Welcome everyone! I'm absolutely delighted to be able to welcome you all to the SEL After School Club. I could launch into a long speech but I don't think many words are needed, for once. All I want to say is this community has been through hell and back.'

She sought Kiara out in the crowds. She was going to run the club with Anna and Jamie. She'd been shocked to discover Florence's role in the deaths, especially when she learnt Florence had sent some emails to Anna as the 'Ophelia Killer' from Kiara's office, which piggy-backed on the tower block's wireless.

'Now it's time for healing,' Anna said as Kiara nodded. 'And I hope this goes some way to helping with that. I know the club's namesakes my father, Simon, Elliot Nunn and my brother, Leo, would have been proud to be part of this.'

She swept open the door behind her and watched as children filed inside. Jamie put his arm around her shoulders, tears in his eyes as he stared up at the sign above them. As they watched the children, Anna imagined Ben Miller and Elliot Nunn among them, even her gran as a child, wanting some peace and solace from home. She imagined herself too as she walked upstairs with Jamie,

353

Joni and her mother. She imagined herself as she was after her father died, desperate for solace, gripping onto the steel banister and twisting up the winding stairs until she found the room at the very top with its shelves and shelves of books. She imagined curling up in a corner and staring out towards the sea, finding a safe haven from her troubles.

She looked down towards the rocks now, and felt her eyes fill with tears as she thought of all that had happened.

'No more living in the past,' her mother said, standing beside her and following her gaze. 'This is all about the future now.'

Anna turned to watch Jamie lift Joni up to show her a book. 'No turning back,' Anna whispered.

Her mother smiled. 'No turning back.'

As they said that, a seagull swept past them, swooping up into the sky then out towards the horizon, content and free.

THE END

Acknowledgements

Bundles of thanks go to the wonderful team at Avon. This includes Oliver Malcolm and Helen Huthwaite who had such faith I could get this novel written in time when I didn't have faith myself. I'd also like to say particular thanks to my new editor, Kate Stephenson, who made some fantastic notes and has worked tirelessly to reach intense deadlines. And I want to thank everyone working on publicity including Jo Marino and Kayleigh Ross from Way To Blue and the brilliant Helena Sheffield and Louis Patel at Avon.

My previous editor Eli Dryden doesn't get away without a thanks too. Thank you, Eli, for giving this idea the green light and continuing to support me from afar.

Big hugs and gratitude as ever to my agent, Caroline Hardman, who reads at the speed of light and makes a great brainstorm buddy when trying to figure out difficult plot points. On the fact-checking front, thank you to Rhoda Nikolay who helped me get to grips with the legal side over a lovely phone chat, and Samantha Young and Amanda Dickson for their advice on the child protection side of things. And of course, my copy editor Jo Gledhill and proof reader.

What would my acknowledgements be without big thanks to my writing buddy Elizabeth Richards and my ever-patient supportive husband, Rob. And finally, thanks to the two most important girls in my life, my mum and my daughter, who motivate me as I strive to make them proud.

How far would you go for the one you love the most?

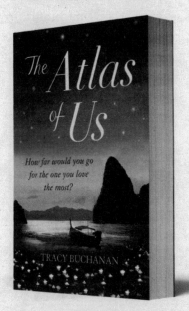

**A stormy love affair. A secret.
A discovery that changes everything…**

**Everything you've built
your life on is a lie.**

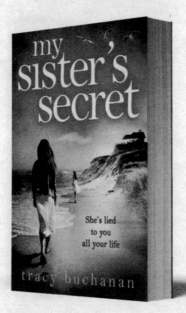

**Addictive, gripping and emotionally powerful,
this is the perfect summer read
from the No.1 bestselling author.**